"WHAT

Benjamin shrugged. "I know how much you want your own family. I presume that hasn't changed. More than anything, you desire a home filled with love and children—a place where you can feel as if you belong. Am I right?"

She nodded, unable to say a word. It sounded so simple, so tedious when he said it aloud. Yet, indeed, it was her dream, and he'd known it all along.

"I respect that dream, Bri," he said quietly. "In fact, in a way, I envy it. I'll not do anything to take that away from you."

Horrified, she felt the prick of tears at her eyes and blinked rapidly to force them back. "I . . . I thank you, then."

He held out a hand and Bridget looked slowly up into his face. She saw a curious mixture of tenderness and sadness.

"Come," he said. "I'll walk you home."

She hesitated to take his hand, to touch him. "It's not necessary. I know the way."

"I know. But just for a moment, I thought we could imagine ourselves as children again." He kept his hand outstretched. "Indulge me just this one time. I gave my word, Bri. I'll behave as the perfect gentleman."

Dear Romance Reader,

In July of 1999, we launched the Ballad line with four new series, and each month we present both new and continuing stories set everywhere from medieval England to the American West—the kind of passionate, romantic stories you love best, written by the most gifted authors. At the back of each book, we tell you when you can find subsequent books in the series that have captured your heart.

Premiering this month is **Light a Single Candle**, the first in the dramatic new trilogy *The MacInness Legacy*. Written by sisters Julie and Sandy Moffett, the series is about three long-separated sisters who discover their heritage includes witchcraft. Talented newcomer Pat Pritchard is next, with the first in a pair of books about two men whose lives are changed by a game of poker. Meet the first of the delectable *Gamblers* in **Luck of the Draw**.

Reader favorite Kathryn Fox returns with another of her *Men of Honor* in **The Seduction** in which an intrepid young reporter looking for scandal in gold-rush territory finds passion instead. Finally, beloved author Jo Ann Ferguson introduces a heartwarming new series called *Haven*. In **Twice Blessed**, when an orphan train stops in this small Indiana town, a shopkeeper becomes an instant "mother"—but when she meets a widowed father new to town, she dreams of becoming a wife.

There's romance, passion, adventure to spare. Why not read them all? Enjoy!

Kate Duffy
Editorial Director

The MacInness Legacy

LIGHT A SINGLE CANDLE

Julie Moffett

ZEBRA BOOKS
Kensington Publishing Corp.
http://www.kensingtonbooks.com

ZEBRA BOOKS are published by

Kensington Publishing Corp.
850 Third Avenue
New York, NY 10022

Copyright © 2002 by Julie Moffett

All rights reserved. No part of this book may be reproduced in any form or by any means without the prior written consent of the Publisher, excepting brief quotes used in reviews.

If you purchased this book without a cover you should be aware that this book is stolen property. It was reported as "unsold and destroyed" to the Publisher and neither the Author nor the Publisher has received any payment for this "stripped book."

All Kensington titles, imprints, and distributed lines are available at special quantity discounts for bulk purchases for sales promotion, premiums, fund-raising, educational or institutional use.

Special book excerpts or customized printings can also be created to fit specific needs. For details, write or phone the office of the Kensington Special Sales Manager: Kensington Publishing Corp., 850 Third Avenue, New York, NY 10022. Attn. Special Sales Department. Phone: 1-800-221-2647.

Zebra and the Z logo Reg. U.S. Pat. & TM Off.

First Printing: March 2002
10 9 8 7 6 5 4 3 2 1

Printed in the United States of America

*To my brother, Brad,
for the great idea of Salem witches,
and because you served as an inspiration for
the hero's mischievous streak.*

and

*To my sister, Sandy,
because not only are you my sister,
you're my best friend.
The book wouldn't have been
written without you.*

Prologue

Salem Village, Massachusetts
October 31, 1692

Priscilla Mary Gardener was about to hang.

After twenty-one years of life, it would end here on Gallows Hill, not far from her home, with a rope around her neck and a suffocating black wool hood draped over her face.

How ironic, she thought, that death would embrace her now. Blessed with health, youth, and vibrancy, she had never given herself leave to contemplate her own demise. But during these past two weeks she had been forced for the first time to ponder death and the fragility of life.

She did not want to die. Even as she stood precariously over a rickety trapdoor with a noose around her neck, she still dared to hope that there was a possibility she might be saved.

But it was not to be.

It saddened her deeply that not one of her neighbors or friends came forward to speak for her, to challenge the preposterous claims that had been made against her. Not one raised a voice in protest against her execution. She was alone and condemned.

The thick rope weighed heavily on her neck, chafing her skin. Her wrists were tied uncomfortably behind her back, rubbed raw. At first, her arms had ached fiercely, but now only a dull pain throbbed. Her legs were unbound, but she feared moving even a hairbreadth, lest the trapdoor open and hasten her demise.

Priscilla drew in a painful but steadying breath and reflected upon her life, one that had once been blessed and good. She'd had a husband who had loved her deeply, and a mother and father who had adored and sheltered her. As death neared, she saw that little else mattered.

Breathing became more difficult beneath the hood. Cold sweat trickled down her temples and neck, causing her to shudder uncontrollably. Perhaps, if God were truly merciful, she would suffocate beneath the black hood before they ever got on with the hanging. If not, she prayed her death would be quick and clean. She had no wish to suffer a long and agonizing death while the people she had known all her life looked on, wondering, whispering.

Priscilla supposed it was almost time now. A man on the scaffold said something, but she couldn't make out the words through the hood. She was no longer certain she was breathing. She felt lightheaded, weak, as if she had already taken leave of her body. A hand pressed into the small of her back and she heard more mumbling. Then the noose tightened around her neck just as the trapdoor opened. Priscilla felt herself fall and then yank to a stop as pain exploded in her head.

The pain passed and there was nothing but a suffocating stillness.

Was she dead?

Without warning, the chilling darkness turned to

light, shocking her senses. When her vision cleared, Priscilla could see a body swaying from the gallows a short distance away, the horrid black hood still in place. It seemed so insignificant, a tiny black dot against the enormous gray-tinged skyline.

Yet as she watched the body sway, she sensed something was not right. She knew not how she could be so certain, but the feeling grew stronger. Inexplicably, her sight became riveted on the black hood, as if beneath the coarse woolen fabric lay the answer to her death. Somehow, she willed her spirit forward until she almost touched the hood. Her hand trembled as her fingers brushed against the coarse fabric.

Does a dead person's hand still tremble? she wondered. Steeling herself, she yanked off the hood in one swift motion.

"John!"

Priscilla woke in terror, screaming her husband's name. Thrashing out, she reached blindly across the bed, seeking the warmth and comfort of his body. For a moment, poised precariously between dream and reality, she felt her husband beside her, solid and familiar. She could even smell the oatmeal soap that had stubbornly clung to the rough but steady hands of the master carpenter.

Fiercely, she squeezed her eyes shut and crushed a pillow to her chest, clinging to the memory and scent of him. But the tighter she clung, the looser her hold became, and his memory slipped from her grasp as did the last vestiges of her dream.

She opened her eyes, alone in the bed.

A profound sorrow clutched at her heart, twisting and turning until she could bear no more.

John was gone. Forever.

Trembling, Priscilla sat up in the bed. Although a

heavy chill hung in the air, her nightdress clung to her chest and arms in several sticky patches. Her thick, unbound hair tumbled about her shoulders in a long, fiery tangle; her temples were slick with sweat.

Even worse, she felt physically sick to her stomach. Pressing her hand hard to her midsection, she willed it to pass. When it finally did, she threw aside the heavy wool blanket and stood.

A quick glance at the one tiny window in the house showed dawn at hand. She would sleep no longer. Another day had arrived, utterly indifferent to her loss. Time had not stopped when John died. It marched on without pain or regrets, dragging her along with it.

Slipping into her shoes, she walked over to the hearth. She knelt on the dirt floor, adding a bit of kindling and blowing softly to fan the embers she had carefully banked the night before. After a minute, the embers sparked and the kindling caught fire. She added a few larger pieces of wood and then rose, rubbing her hands along her arms. She needed to draw water for the large black kettle that hung at the hearth before any of the other townsfolk awakened.

She walked to the window and leaned her forehead against the thick leaded glass. All Hallows' Eve had dawned majestically. Pink and orange slivers streaked across the sky, and the early-morning mist rose rapidly from the ground, whirling and rising into the sky until it faded from sight.

Barely two months had passed since John's death. It might have been two years—or a score, for that matter—for her soul had died with him. She lived each day now as a prisoner, ostracized and shunned, in the very house he had built with his own loving hands.

Life clung stubbornly to her body, though she rarely felt anything except sadness these days. She lived only because she knew John would want it and had died for it. Even had she felt the need for human comfort, she had no one. Her parents had been dead for some time, and those who had once been her friends were no longer. John's mother still lived in Salem, but she refused to speak to Priscilla anymore.

She glanced about the room. Once this cottage had known so much happiness. A giant hearth warmed its comfortably large room, casting merry shadows and light against the pinewood walls. They had filled their home with furniture built by John himself, and they had bartered with Simon Codhorn, the village weaver, for several thick rugs that they placed by their bed and near the square pine table where they ate their meals together. They had filled their home with love and joy—a life that was now shattered.

Feeling an acute sense of loss, Priscilla pulled out one of the chairs and sank unsteadily into it.

"I miss thee so much, my love," she whispered aloud, putting her elbows on the table and her chin in her hands. "What shall I do?"

As if in answer, a knock sounded on the door. Priscilla lurched to her feet, her heart pounding. No one had come to the house since John had died. No one dared. Certainly no person would come to her today on All Hallows' Eve.

The knock sounded again. For a moment, Priscilla could only stare in shock at the door, wondering at the identity of the visitor. Surely it must be John's mother. God willing, she had finally come to her senses and realized the cruel gossip she had heard about her daughter-in-law had been nothing but lies.

The knock sounded a third time, this time more

sharply. Priscilla snatched a shawl from the table beside her bed and pulled it tightly about her shoulders. Slowly she walked to the door. Trembling, she put a hand on the latch, pushed down and pulled the door open.

On the doorstep stood a young woman with long black hair that hung in a single thick braid down to her waist. A white cloth cap covered her head. She was pretty in a dark sort of way, tall with round shoulders and skin so white, it was nearly bloodless. Her face was narrow and the nose too thin, but they were offset by her most prominent feature—heavy, striking black eyebrows shadowing a pair of pale blue eyes as wicked and cruel as Priscilla had ever seen.

"Thee!" Priscilla gasped in horror. "How dare thee come to my home."

"I dare to do what is necessary," the visitor answered stiffly. "Thou knew I'd come eventually."

"I knew nothing of the kind," she retorted.

The visitor fixed her vicious blue eyes intently on Priscilla. "We have an unfinished matter between us. 'Twas not John I wished to kill. But thou knew that as well."

Priscilla let out a hiss so violent and angry that it surprised even herself. "Don't dare to speak his name," she warned in a low voice. "I'll not permit thee to soil his memory." She felt a small twinge of satisfaction when she saw the woman recoil slightly.

"Thy words do not frighten me," the woman replied in a threatening tone. "I know about thy powers. I've known all along and have no fear."

Priscilla stiffened. "Thine accusations have been made and dismissed. I was acquitted before all of Salem."

LIGHT A SINGLE CANDLE

Her lips pursed into what Priscilla thought a particularly loathsome smirk. "Fools," she hissed. "All of them. Thou wast saved only because thy husband issued a preposterous confession of witchcraft. Yet ye still live here on the edge of the village alone. No one dares to converse or visit thee. Why? Because, like me, they know the truth."

Priscilla clenched her hands into fists at her side. "I'll tell you what the truth is. Ye loved my husband enough to try to murder me. Know now that he would never have loved thee. He would have seen through to thine impure heart and cast thee aside. Now begone from here."

Priscilla tried to close the door. But with surprising strength and speed, the woman put her hand on the door, holding it open.

" 'Tis not so easy," she spat out. "Now is the time of reckoning for thine actions."

"My actions? Thy mind is truly full of madness."

" 'Twas thee who should have died," she insisted, her pale eyes narrowing. "Thy neck should have swung in that noose. I would never have harmed John. I loved him. But 'twas not I who let him die."

Priscilla felt a stab of guilt directly in her heart, so painful and strong that it momentarily took her breath away. But when she finally spoke, it was in a soft, controlled tone.

"Take thy vile tongue of wickedness and begone from my house. I feel only pity for thee. Pity that ye never knew his love no matter how many years ye longed for it. 'Twas me he chose for his wife. And now, thine evil accusations have caused the loss of a good man. My husband."

Two bright spots of anger appeared on the young

woman's cheeks. "Darest thou to lecture me? We are far too alike for that."

Priscilla recoiled in disgust. "We are nothing alike."

"But we are," she hissed back. "Bound by fate, tied by destiny, borne of an unholy womb. Thou knowest what today is."

"As does all of Salem. 'Tis All Hallows' Eve."

Her lips curled into a smile. "Nay, 'tis Samhain, the eighth Wiccan Sabbath, and the Night of the Blood Moon. Today is a time of celebration and curses, of communing with the spirits that have passed on to the other side. The veil between our worlds is thin, and my power courses through me now like at no other time of the year. I shall show thee." Glancing over Priscilla's shoulder, she stared directly at the hearth.

With a growing sense of dread, Priscilla followed her gaze and saw the fire in the hearth begin to swell and roar. Flames licked and danced wildly, casting frightening, grotesque shadows on the wall. She shuddered.

The woman looked back at Priscilla with triumph in her eyes. "I see no surprise in thine eyes," she gloated. " 'Twas as I suspected. The bond, the secret that binds us together, truly exists."

"No!" Priscilla whispered, feeling violently ill. She doubled over, clutching her abdomen. Gasping, she fought back the nausea, nearly sobbing when it subsided.

She felt the woman clutch her arm, pulling her upright. "Thou art with child?" she screeched, her voice horrified.

Priscilla wrenched her arm from the woman and

tried vainly to shut the door. But the woman was fully across the threshold now and refused to budge.

" 'Tis why he hanged for thee," she spat out, her pale face now red and blotched. " 'Tis why he confessed to thy sins. I should have known."

Furious, she shoved Priscilla back hard against the wall. Priscilla stumbled and tried to right herself when another wave of nausea swept through her.

"Treachery, this is," the woman shrieked. "Thou shalt pay for thine actions." Raising her arms, she began to chant softly. Her eyes closed and her braid began to sway behind her back. A breeze swept through the room, softly at first and then abruptly surging in fierce gusts.

Priscilla's unbound hair began to whip about her cheeks and sting her eyes. "Who are you?" she asked in a raised voice. "For generations we swore never to use our power. Why dare you? From whence have you come?"

The woman didn't answer, but her chanting grew louder and more sinister.

Priscilla grabbed on to the doorjamb as the wind grew stronger. "Thou art foreign and not of my house," she shouted. "I would have felt it."

The woman snapped her pale blue eyes open and Priscilla felt her blood chill. "I am your enemy."

Priscilla gasped. "Then thou must be . . . nay, 'tis not possible," she whispered in dread. "The last descendants of Clan MacGow died years ago in Scotland."

"So ye thought."

Priscilla felt icy fingers of fear creep up her spine. If it were true—if this woman were truly a descendant of the dark, malevolent clan, then she was very, very dangerous.

"Thy evil shall have no effect on me," Priscilla declared, but her voice was weak, and in her heart she did not know it to be so.

The woman smirked, her eyes glowing with an odd and unnatural light. The wind howled unmercifully in a strange, high-pitched whistle.

"I curse thee, Priscilla Mary Gardener, and all thy descendants. I curse thee with loneliness, for that is thy curse to me. If thou or thine offspring shall wed, thy mate will not live past the twenty-sixth year, just as John did not. Thou and all thy kind art cursed to grow old alone, nursing bitter, grievous, and broken hearts."

Priscilla clenched her jaw. Fury at what this woman had done to her husband rose in her like a white-hot, raging fire. Uttering a small cry, she broke the ancient and solemn vow taken by all her kin and thrust out her hands, abruptly calming the wind.

Priscilla saw a flash of fear in the other woman's eyes and felt a fleeting moment of triumph. "How dare ye come to my home and cast a curse upon me!" she growled in a low and dangerous voice. " 'Tis thy heart which is twisted. And 'tis thee who is bitter and grievous. Thy curse is no more than a foolish whisper on the wind. Ye dare to cross me? Do you know who I am? I am of Clan MacInness."

The woman laughed. "Aye, I know thou art the last of thy line, as I am the last of mine. But I can feel that thy magic is weak. 'Tis so among those who ignore their birthright. I am strong, for I have nurtured and fortified my power. Thou art not strong enough to break my curse. Nor will thy descendants have such ability."

Priscilla tightened her jaw, her eyes flashing angrily. "Thou knowest nothing of the kind. Nonetheless, I shall

LIGHT A SINGLE CANDLE

not let thy curse stand unchallenged. I counter thy curse. If my descendants are able to break the curse within one century, then 'tis thy children who will suffer another hundred years in grinding destitution, misery, and heartache. I have commanded it so."

Priscilla waved her hand and the fire in the hearth leaped to a roar and then died down.

The woman stared for a long moment at Priscilla and then nodded. " 'Tis thy right. Now, we shall see what our destinies hold for us. Know that I am not afraid. I have served my justice here."

With a cruel laugh, she turned and left the house, the fire spitting out hissing sparks before settling down in the hearth.

Priscilla inhaled a deep and steadying breath and stepped forward, firmly shutting and bolting the door.

For a moment, she simply leaned with her back against the door. John, her dear beloved John. She had begged him not to make a foolish confession to save her. She had pleaded with him to let her hang. It had been the truth when she said she'd rather die than be left behind to live without him.

But none of it had mattered. None of it mattered more than the child who lay deep within her womb. In the end, they had both known it.

She laid a hand on her stomach and began to cry.

The woman had been right. She was weak, and had not foreseen or stopped the curse. Nor would her child be likely to overcome it, either. The woman's magic had indeed been powerful. But it was not too late to save future generations if she began anew and kindled and nurtured what she knew was deep within her.

She had to learn and strengthen her magic, pass it on, and teach her children and grandchildren about their birthright. It would have to be done carefully, quietly and discreetly, but it could be done.

It must be done.

"Magica tua anima tua est." She whispered the witches' creed her mother had taught her years ago and that she had not repeated since. "Thy magic is thy will."

One

*Nearly one hundred years later
Salem, Massachusetts
May 1792*

Bridget Goodwell awoke with a start, her heart thundering with fear, her nightgown soaked with sweat. She sat up in bed and gripped her coverlet, reminding herself that she was safe in her room with her younger sister, Sarabeth, asleep in the bed beside her.

Shakily she pushed a hand through her tumbled red tresses, feeling the tension slowly leave her neck and shoulders.

"Magica tua anima tua est," she heard a voice echo from her dream, and she shuddered. Years ago, after she first had the nightmare, she'd discovered it was the Latin for *"Thy magic is thy will."* What it meant and why she dreamed such an odd phrase eluded her.

In the dream, a woman came to her beneath a full moon, dressed in a long, flowing white gown, with a wreath of birch stems wound around her neck. The woman seized her hands and began chanting the phrase over and over. Soon, they began spinning in a circle, and the chanting became louder until she could hear naught else. Then a bolt of lightning shot from the sky directly into her, turning her into a fiery, burning inferno. Screaming, Bridget tried to free herself from the woman's grip, but she could not. The fire ate away at them, piece by piece, until she woke up in a sweat, trembling and cowering in fear.

She took another breath and then cocked her head when she heard a door close, soft laughter, and the unmistakable noise of guests in the parsonage parlor.

She firmly pushed aside any remaining vestiges of the nightmare and threw off the coverlet.

"Sarabeth, rouse yourself from your bed," she urged her younger sister. " 'Tis morning."

Sarabeth grumbled and rolled over. "Go away. I've only just gone to sleep."

"Poppycock," Bridget countered. "We've already lain abed half the morn." She slid her feet into a pair of worn slippers that sat near the bedside, and padded over to the window, throwing open the shutters.

It was a beautiful morning and Bridget inhaled deeply of the fresh, cool air, feeling the unpleasant remnants of her nightmare disappear. She loved the unique smells of Salem: the rich, salty scent of the sea, the faint aroma of exotic spices brought from ports all over the world, and the distinct smell of filleted cod being dried on hundreds of racks along the wharves. For nearly all of her twenty years, she had started the day exactly like this—by opening the bedroom window and reveling in Salem's fascinating and diverse melange of scents. It was more than just a habit; it was a tradition that served to remind her daily of God's miraculous creation of the world, and especially the sea.

"Oh, 'tis a glorious morning, Sarabeth," Bridget said, leaning out of the window. The old oak tree with gnarled branches that touched the window was showing the first signs of new buds. " 'Tis but the end of May, but I do believe today will be the first real warm day of summer."

She lifted her face as a gust of wind stung her cheeks and blew through her hair. Today, with the strong gale, the water was surely choppy and crested with white foam. Bridget loved the sea with all her heart. At night, when all in Salem was still, she could open the window and hear the waves lapping against the wharves in a calming and peaceful rhythm. As a child, she had spent many hours both in and by the water, watching and marveling at the sea's many mysterious moods. For the past several years, her responsibilities as the elder daughter of the Congregationalist Reverend Ichabod Goodwell and his wife, Abigail, allowed her far less time there then she would have liked. But occasionally she still managed to set aside an hour by the sea for quiet reflection.

Sarabeth groaned and pulled the covers over her head. "Surely you jest. 'Tisn't day yet," she protested in a muffled voice.

"Four hours ago, I'd wager."

"Four hours?" Sarabeth exclaimed. "I promise, that's the last time I stay awake listening to one of your wicked tales."

"Need I remind you how you begged me to tell the tale?" Bridget replied dryly. "Twice I refused to tell it, but you insisted."

Sarabeth peeked out from under the covers. "Well, you do have a way with words. But I was positively frightened out of my wits when you came to the part where the witches were chasing the young girls through the forest. It's a wonder I fell asleep at all."

Bridget regarded her sister with a measure of exasperation. At fourteen years of age, Sarabeth was a near-woman of exceptional beauty. Blessed with thick, wheat gold hair, high cheekbones, and a slender nose, she was truly breathtaking. Her eyes were as lovely and sky blue as their mother's best china plates, and her skin translucent with just the right touches of pink. She had the kind of stunning loveliness that caused perfect strangers on the street to stop and stare dumbfounded. Yet as far as intelligence went, Sarabeth often had as much sense as that same china plate.

"Don't be such a silly goose," Bridget said. "I'm just telling you some of the stories old Widow Bayley told me. I sincerely doubt any of them are true."

"But they sound so real, and Father says there are truly such things as witches and hexes and beseechings. I'm terrified of witches."

Bridget absently fingered a loose tendril of hair on her cheek. "I don't recall witches being mentioned anywhere in the Bible. And even if there are witches, I don't think they would all be bad. At least that's what Widow Bayley says."

"That's because she's a witch herself."

Bridget laughed. "That's ridiculous. She's not a witch; she's a lonely, blind old woman."

"How can you be certain?"

"Because she's in assembly nice and proper every Sunday morning. How could a witch do that without being struck down?"

"Nonetheless, she frightens me."

"Well, it doesn't matter. You may no longer lie abed. We have a visitor."

"We do?" Sarabeth sat up in bed quickly, reaching up to touch her gorgeously tousled hair. "Why, whoever could it be at this hour?"

"I don't know. But I heard Mother and Father laughing and talking with him."

"Him? Do you think it is Peter? Mayhap he was thinking of you and couldn't wait another moment to see the woman he loves." She sighed dreamily. "I think it is so romantic that you'll get to wear a lovely dress and walk down the aisle on the arm of a man who will vow to love and cherish you forever. You will truly be a lovely bride, Bridget."

"I suppose I'll look adequate after Betty Corwin finishes my dress," Bridget commented.

"Oh, no," Sarabeth protested, hopping out of bed. "You'll be far more than adequate. You'll look magnificent. Why, Peter insisted on the finest silk, the most delicate lace, and real pearls. The gown will be beautiful."

"Mother had a perfectly suitable gown. I'm not certain why we had to go to the extravagant expense of an entirely new gown."

"Peter insists on only the best, as he should. You'll look lovely."

Sarabeth steered her in front of the chipped oval looking glass that hung above the small wooden chest of drawers they shared.

"We'll sweep your hair up like this," Sarabeth said, holding Bridget's hair on top of her head. "We'll make ringlets here, here, and here," she explained, pointing to each side of her face and the back of her neck. "And if Mother will permit, we'll apply just the faintest bit of powder to your cheeks and neck. Just imagine it."

For a moment, Bridget allowed herself to be swept along by Sarabeth's enthusiasm. Slowly she reached up to touch her hair. Unlike her sister's golden mane, she had a wild head of flyaway red hair. Witch's hair, she'd often heard whispered among the townsfolk.

Her face was ordinary—a straight, slim nose, green

eyes, and a heavy dusting of freckles across her cheeks and nose. She was tall and thin, and her shoulders were a bit too wide for her frame. Her hips were small, making her figure look slightly lopsided, and she had long, skinny legs and knobby knees. Not a lush curve in sight.

Bridget made a face at herself in the mirror. She'd never be beautiful, but perhaps Sarabeth was right. On her wedding day, she'd likely look the best she ever would.

At that moment, Sarabeth let out a horrified gasp and pointed to a hornet that had come through the window and perched on one corner of the mirror.

"Bridget!" she exclaimed in terror, pointing at the insect.

"Take a slow step back," Bridget said grimly, picking up a slipper from the floor. She smashed it against the hornet, killing it instantly. Delicately scraping it off the slipper with a handkerchief, she dropped what was left of the insect out the window.

Sarabeth gave a shaky laugh. "My champion."

Bridget summoned a smile on her sister's behalf, although her own hands were trembling. They'd almost lost Sarabeth years ago when she was stung and became deathly ill. Now the arrival of any such insect in their home became far more than just a nuisance for the family.

For a moment they simply stared at each other until the murmur of a deep male voice sounded downstairs, jolting them into action. "Oh, I do hope it's Peter," Sarabeth said, hurrying to the wooden wardrobe.

Bridget yanked her nightgown over her head. "I don't think it's him. Why would he come unannounced at such an early hour?"

"Because he has an insistent, yearning, burning desire to see you," she offered.

Bridget burst out laughing. "That's the silliest thing I've ever heard. Peter doesn't yearn."

"All men yearn."

Bridget's eyes narrowed. "And where did you hear that?"

Sarabeth blushed deeply. "Jane Molloy told me."

"Jane Molloy? Jane wouldn't know the first thing about men yearning. Why, she's a full year younger than you."

"So, men don't yearn?" she asked, her blue eyes wide and innocent.

"Perhaps there are some foolish young men who do. Certainly, Peter is far too sensible to yearn or to show up here at the house at this hour. What possibly couldn't wait until a more reasonable hour? The wedding is not for another three weeks after all."

"Mayhap there is some important detail that needs to be worked out," Sarabeth said, looking through her gowns and choosing a cheery blue-and-white one with a fitted bodice. She laid it carefully on the bed and pulled off her nightgown.

Bridget struggled into her chemise. "No, it couldn't be Peter. Mother would never keep him waiting. It must be someone else. I'm going down for a look."

Bridget joined her sister at the wooden wardrobe and hastily chose a gown. She pulled it over her head and sat down on the bed to pull on her shoes.

"Wait for me," Sarabeth pleaded, hurrying to ready herself. "I want to look nice for our guest. I know appearances don't matter to you, Bridget. But it's all I've got. I'm not as clever as you are. And I've heard people talk, saying I'm simple."

Bridget walked over to her sister and held her

squarely by the shoulders, shaking her gently. "People can be very unkind. You are a sweet, generous person with a good heart. Don't ever forget that."

"Oh, whatever will I do without you?" Sarabeth's eyes began to mist, and Bridget wagged her finger warningly.

"No tears. I simply won't stand for it. You'll do just fine, Sarabeth, and I sincerely doubt you'll be alone for long. Why, with all the men in Salem falling over themselves for an opportunity to court you, you'll find someone in no time. And I promise that you won't be nearly as old as I before you get married."

"It's just that you've had a three-year engagement. If Peter had married you sooner, you wouldn't be so old."

Bridget opened her mouth to say something and then decided it was safer not to comment. Instead, she picked up the comb and began running it through Sarabeth's thick tresses as her sister straightened and then smoothed down her gown. Once Bridget had finished, she stepped back to examine her sister.

Sarabeth smiled radiantly and Bridget marveled at the amazing transformation. Sarabeth looked as fresh and dewy as if she had spent two hours preparing herself. Her pretty gown of blue and white complimented her skin, and her cheeks still had a pink glow from sleep. A few wisps of golden hair curled softly about her ears and neck. Her eyes, which just minutes ago were sleepy and red-rimmed, were now breathtakingly blue and wide.

Bridget looked down at her own brown-and-yellow gown. It was functional and comfortable, but she probably should have paid more attention to her selection. Still, it wasn't as if she were going out anywhere. She was at home and could quickly change gowns later if she had to go out. Too late to worry about it now.

Bridget threw open the bedroom door and bounded down the stairs into the parlor. She skidded to a very unladylike stop when she saw who sat comfortably in an armchair, chatting companionably with her father.

Their handsome young visitor turned his head slowly toward her, a grin rising to his lips when he saw her.

"Hello, Bridget," he said, rising from the chair. "How nice to see you. I wondered when you'd decide to get out of bed and see who was here."

Bridget gaped in surprise. "You . . . you're here?" she stammered in shock.

The visitor's grin widened, showing a flash of dazzling white teeth. "Left you speechless, have I? Now, that's a first."

Bridget fought to control her expression, but her emotions were shooting darts and pins into her stomach. She could barely breathe.

It was *him*.

The first man she had ever loved.

The bane of her existence.

A trickster, a scoundrel, and a rogue.

And her best friend since she was six years of age. He'd first caught her attention by slipping a garden snake down the back of her gown during assembly, causing her to squeal and claw off her clothes in front of the entire congregation.

She hadn't seen him in almost a year. His father's shipping business had him regularly sailing to exotic ports. In fact, she had barely seen him at all since her engagement to Peter three years ago. That he would show up unexpectedly on her doorstep just weeks before her wedding was not only disconcerting, but worrisome as well.

Bridget opened her mouth to say something when Sarabeth suddenly pushed past her in a colorful flash of blue and white.

"Benjamin!" she squealed, launching herself into the visitor's arms. "Oh, you're back. We've missed you so. A year is such a long time. Bridget talks about you all the time."

Heat rose to Bridget's cheeks as she gasped, mortified by her sister's words. "I do not," she protested.

Benjamin gazed at her over Sarabeth's head, his lips curving into a smile. Bridget's blush deepened as her heart thumped hard within her chest. She hated that he could still do that to her a mere three weeks before her wedding to another man. She took a deep breath, determined to keep a calm expression on her face.

"It's a surprise to see you back in Salem so soon," she said, annoyed when her voice came out sharper than intended. "I thought you'd be in Lisbon at least through the end of the summer."

"I've come back for the impending nuptials, of course," he replied, politely disengaging from Sarabeth's embrace. "I wouldn't miss the wedding for the world."

"Of course not," Bridget murmured, but her stomach began to churn uneasily. Benjamin had an uncanny habit of showing up just in time to brew mischief on the most important days in her life. This morning his expression appeared innocent, but his eyes sparkled with mischief.

"Anything wrong?" he asked, seemingly amused at her discomfort.

"Certainly not," her father interjected quickly. "She is honored that you'll be there, as are all of us."

Bridget pursed her lips but said nothing. It was no secret that everyone in Salem, her parents and sister included, thought Benjamin was close to a saint.

When they were children, no one had ever believed that sweet, angelic Benjamin put spiders in her shoes and burrs in her undergarments, sheared off part of her hair with a carving knife, and stole her clothes when she was taking a forbidden dip in the ocean. It infuriated Bridget to no end that he could do whatever he wanted and no one would ever complain.

Of course, Bridget had perpetrated her share of tricks, too. She'd put rocks in his boots, ripped the seam in his pants, set fire to his favorite hat, and told Mary Hollingsworth that he liked her, when in truth he was sweet on Constance Wirth.

But Benjamin had always had the upper hand with her, and he'd known it. As the only son and heir to the shipping fortune of Charles Woodsworth Hawkes, his standing in the Salem community was impeccable. Bridget was simply the eldest daughter of the righteous Reverend Goodwell, who considered the patronage of the Hawkes family to the parsonage important enough to set aside proprieties and permit his daughter to become a playmate and close friend to the young boy. And important enough so that she'd been able to maintain the friendship long after they became adults.

But they were children no longer, and Bridget could not afford for anything to spoil her careful preparations for the wedding. The very last thing she needed was Benjamin Hawkes in Salem.

"It wasn't necessary to come back just for the ceremony," Bridget said, as if she somehow could convince him to leave again. "Peter and I would have been happy to see you upon your return to Salem."

He cocked his dark head to one side, studying her intently. "Nonsense. You and Peter are my two closest friends. I wouldn't dream of missing the most important day in your lives."

Bridget observed with annoyance that her mother was fluttering around the room like an excited bird, outrivaled only by Sarabeth, who hung on to his every word as if it were the Gospel.

Bridget supposed she couldn't blame them. Benjamin always had that effect on women. He had a ruggedness and vitality that attracted women of all ages to him. To make matters worse, he was so blasted handsome that Bridget was convinced that God himself had a hand in constructing his face.

In fact, Bridget had long thought Benjamin akin to a dark archangel from heaven. His bronzed skin stretched taut over high, classic cheekbones and a proud aquiline nose. His deep, gray eyes were both intense and intelligent, like smoldering ashes ready to ignite at the merest provocation. Thick, wild black hair fell in unruly waves to his collar, adding a touch of unspoken danger and passion to his appearance.

Yes, a dark archangel was an apt description of him, Bridget mused. Fallen, yet perhaps still redeemable. Exactly the quality that made him so irresistible to women.

"To think that you came back to Salem just to see our Bridget married," her father said, interrupting her thoughts.

"Oh, yes," Sarabeth gushed. "You are certain to be the most important guest."

"I'm certain I will be but one of many in Salem

wishing the new couple all the best in life," Benjamin said modestly.

Bridget rolled her eyes and Benjamin caught the gesture. Amusement touched his lips, and Bridget was more certain than ever that he had mischief on his mind.

"You've been a good friend to our family," the reverend boomed, slapping Benjamin heartily on the shoulder. "And a godly man as well. Your life has been a wonderful example of how best to serve our Creator. We are most thankful for your kindnesses to Bridget and the church. Heaven's fortune shall surely shine down upon you."

Bridget coughed loudly into her hands. Her father shot her a warning look while Benjamin quirked his eyebrows but said nothing.

Sarabeth took a chair near him, bubbling with innocent enthusiasm. "You haven't changed a bit since we've last seen you," she said scrutinizing his face. "Except your hair is a bit longer. And you seem different, too—more worldly, mayhap?"

He graced her with one of his mercurial smiles that could cause even the most hardened of women to melt. "Travel can do that to a man. But look at you, Sarabeth. Why, you're all grown-up now. When did you become such a beautiful woman? You are the talk of the town, you know."

Sarabeth blushed prettily. "I am?"

"Gentleman's honor," he said solemnly.

Sarabeth's flush deepened, and even Bridget realized it was difficult not to be charmed by his elegant and gracious manners. Besides, Sarabeth was right, travel and adventure did seem to suit him. He looked well and rested. Clad comfortably in a dazzling white shirt, open at the throat, and a pair of tan breeches, he seemed completely at ease in the humble parsonage parlor. She could see the well-toned muscles in his arms and shoulders ripple beneath his white shirt as he shifted slightly in the chair.

There was no question about it, Bridget thought with a twinge of envy; God had certainly been generous to Benjamin Hawkes. Suddenly aware of her own shortcomings in matters of appearance, she frowned.

"Bridget," her mother said suddenly, snapping her out of her thoughts. "Are you going to stand there all day and stare? Why don't you fetch some tea from the kitchen for our guest."

Bridget flushed, unaware that she had been staring so openly at Benjamin. "Of course, Mother," she said, hastily heading for the kitchen.

Benjamin quickly stood up. "I'm afraid that won't be necessary. I must go. I told my father I'd help him with the accounting today."

"Oh, no," Sarabeth cried, a distressed look crossing her face. "Can't you stay for a bit longer? We haven't had time to hear about your travels."

"There will be plenty of time for that later," he said, gently patting her hand. "I'm certain I'll see a lot more of you all before the wedding—that is, if you would be so kind as to allow me to visit again."

He bowed gallantly to press a chaste kiss on the top of Sarabeth's hand. He did the same for her mother and then heartily shook the reverend's hand.

Finally he turned to Bridget. Strolling over to where she stood, he reached out to take her hand. She stiffened at his touch, but he flashed her one of his dazzling grins and she felt her defenses melt away.

He stood with his back to the others and wrapped his fingers around hers, warm and strong. Her heart quickened in spite of herself, and she was surprised to feel her hand tremble. She waited for him to press a perfunctory kiss on her hand as he had with the others, but instead, he deftly flipped it over and kissed the sensitive palm, his tongue brushing against the skin.

A shocking and unexpected warmth flared through her. Stunned, Bridget took a quick, sharp breath and frantically snatched her hand from his grasp. At her sudden movement, Benjamin stumbled against her. Her parents, who had not been able to see what he had done, gaped at her apparently rude behavior. Benjamin quickly righted himself with a hand on her shoulder.

"Well, now, how utterly clumsy of me," he effused apologetically, but with a twinkle in his eyes that only she could see.

"What are you doing?" she whispered.

"Being clumsy around you, as usual," he whispered back. Then in a louder voice, he added, "Please, forgive me."

She stiffened as he flashed her a final grin and headed for the door. Bridget's father followed, mumbling something that sounded like an apology for his daughter's strange behavior.

"How could you act so impolitely?" her mother demanded as soon as Benjamin disappeared through the door. "Benjamin is an honored guest in this home."

Bridget knew it would be no use to explain Benjamin's behavior to her mother. She'd never believe it possible of him. "I know, Mother."

"Then why do you treat him with such disdain?"

"I didn't say anything impolite," she protested.

"It's not what you say, it's how you act. You appeared annoyed and upset that he had deigned to visit us. He is charming and kind, with impeccable manners and grace. Why, it's a wonder that he calls on us at all, the way you act toward him."

"Just because I don't sigh and flutter my eyelashes over his every word does not mean I'm being rude."

"Bridget, Mother is right," Sarabeth interjected. "You positively bristle every time he is near. You never act that way around anyone else. It's dreadful. Why, he's the most handsome, gracious man I've ever met."

"Just because he is handsome doesn't mean he is faultless," Bridget snapped.

Her mother frowned. "Now, you are simply being unkind."

Bridget sighed. "You're right. I apologize."

Her mother clucked her tongue. "As you should. It's a wonder he'll come to the wedding at all, the way you act toward him. Why, I've never seen such atrocious manners."

"I've already apologized, Mother."

"To me, but not to him," she continued, pursing her lips disapprovingly. "You will find time for that later. Remember that arrogance and rudeness are both sins. God is watching."

"I know," Bridget said wearily.

"I will not tolerate that behavior in my house again, especially since I intend to have him become a part of this family."

"What?" Bridget and Sarabeth exclaimed in shock.

Abigail raised an eyebrow and directed her words toward Bridget. "He's a perfect match for Sarabeth. Didn't you notice how taken he was with her?"

Bridget felt her mouth hanging open and closed it quickly. "I . . . I . . . Mother, he is like that with all women. He has this unusual ability to make each one of them feel . . . special."

"He doesn't do that with you."

Bridget felt a stab of pain that hurt more than her mother could know. "We're talking about Sarabeth."

"Of course we are. Sarabeth is able to maintain proper decorum around Benjamin."

Bridget opened her mouth to speak and then shut it abruptly. The image of Benjamin with Sarabeth in that way was so appalling, she was momentarily speechless.

"Sarabeth is just a child," Bridget finally managed to say. "She's too young to consider a suitor."

"She's nearly ten and four and already a woman," her mother countered. "Certainly old enough to began looking for a man who will provide her with a comfortable life. There is no need for her to wait until she is as old as you."

Bridget flushed hotly, but ignored the insult. "Mother, you can't be serious about trying to pair Sarabeth with him."

"Why not?" she replied, putting her hands on her hips defensively. "Benjamin Hawkes would be the perfect man for her. He comes from an honorable family, he has impeccable manners, and, of course, he comes from good money."

"But he's all wrong for Sarabeth," Bridget fumed. "He's a scoundrel, a rogue, and a womanizing cad. He leaves Salem at the drop of a hat to sail away to exotic ports. He's impulsive, reckless, temperamental, and has too high an opinion of himself. Is that what you want for Sarabeth?"

"He only needs the right woman to tame him," her mother countered. "Sarabeth would be the perfect influence on him—sweet, good-natured, nurturing, and protective. Can't you see what a wonderful match they would make?"

Bridget felt her temper rising. "No, I can't."

"Of course you can't. You're jealous that she might make a better match than you."

Bridget knew she should let the comment pass. But her temper was out of sorts this morning. She blamed it on Benjamin; his presence always seemed to stir up her emotions.

"I'm not jealous," she shot back. "I'm trying to be the voice of reason. It would be a sacrifice for Sarabeth."

"All marriages are sacrifices," her mother replied firmly. "Especially for women."

Sarabeth looked at Bridget with wide eyes. "Do you consider your match with Peter a sacrifice?"

Bridget flushed again. "I . . . I . . . of course not. I just want to spare you the pain of setting your cap for Benjamin. I sincerely doubt he'd ever consider such a match. Besides, you don't have a dowry and lack the social connections of other more prominent families. He'd only hurt you."

"You stop that right now, young lady," her mother interrupted angrily. "After all, if you were able to bewitch Peter Holton into holy matrimony given your ordinary appearance and sharp tongue, then a beautiful and godly young woman such as Sarabeth should certainly be able to meet the requirements of a gentleman like Benjamin Hawkes. Beauty and poise often can compensate for a lack of worldly goods."

Bridget stiffened. "Of course, Mother. Don't forget to remind me that I'm the social embarrassment of this family, redeemed only by my astonishing, and may I add, quite unexpected ability to make a catch like Peter Holton."

Sarabeth gasped. "Bridget, that isn't true."

"Isn't it?" she said, ignoring her sister and looking

steadily at her mother. "You never thought Peter would wed me, did you? You were shocked when he proposed. Why, Mother, haven't you ever had faith in me?"

"Bridget," Sarabeth whispered in horror. "Please, stop this at once."

Her mother frowned. "What I see in front of me now is a young woman possessed with the tongue and the temperament of the devil. I shall pray for your soul, child, and also that your husband may have the fortitude and strength to handle you."

Fighting back tears, Bridget rushed past her mother and dashed out the back door. Without having to think about it, she ran toward Rock's Point, the one place where she had always sought solitude and peace.

She was out of breath when she finally reached the spot. Two enormous white granite boulders stood guard over the harbor where the shore dropped steeply to the beach. Here she could look out over the sea and lose herself in the combination of sights, sounds, and smells.

She stepped between the boulders and sat down, reveling in the rich, salty aroma, listening to the seagulls cry out, and watching the golden sunlight glitter on the rippling water. She shut everything else out and let the wind sweep through her hair, allowing the ancient rhythm of the waves to lull her into calm. Eventually, she let herself enjoy the colorful array of sails and flags on the vessels in the harbor, the metallic ring of the caulking hammer and broadax, and the impatient whinny of horses ready to go wherever their masters would take them.

But her mind kept returning to the argument with her mother. Her mother was right—a sharp tongue and a fiery temper were two of her worst faults. But

Bridget knew it was more than that. All her life, she had never met her parents' approval no matter how hard she tried. She'd failed them as a daughter.

Bridget sniffled, rubbing her eyes with her knuckles just as something squirmed against her thigh. Squealing, she reached into her gown pocket and pulled out a tiny brown toad. She yelped in surprise as the toad slipped from her fingers to the ground, hopping madly between the boulders, seeking safety.

"Benjamin!" she fumed, wondering how long the poor creature had been wiggling about in her pocket without detection. She should have known that his stumble against her hadn't been innocent, and neither had the shocking kiss on her hand, certainly designed to draw her attention away from what he was slipping in her pocket.

She flushed, remembering the heat of his lips against her skin. His behavior was absolutely outrageous, and yet entirely predictable. Benjamin may be an adult now, but he still had the heart of a mischievous boy. What ludicrous behavior he displayed only weeks before her wedding!

Yet, so very Benjamin.

"Scoundrel," she muttered. "I knew you were up to something."

It had been a shock to see him this morning. His return to Salem had been unexpected, as well as his visit to the house. Although she had made peace with her feelings for him ages ago, she hadn't been prepared to see him. It dismayed her that she was not immune to his charm after all. Her heart still skipped in a funny way when she saw him. No matter how hard she tried, she couldn't seem to control that.

Bridget pulled her knees tighter against her chest, wrapping her arms around them and leaning her head against the cold surface of the boulder. The waves were crashing against the beach, riled by the wind, surging up the rocky slope.

She was going to marry Peter and be happy. He'd give her a safe home and a family to love, despite all her faults. Thinking of Benjamin only muddied the future. She should consider it a blessing that he had never returned her affections when they were younger. He was completely unsuited to the dreams she had of a stable home and secure family life. He was a rogue, a scoundrel, a trickster, and he was far too dangerous.

Dangerous because, of all her friends, Benjamin knew her the best. Other than her parents, only he had come close to uncovering her worst fault of all: her secret aberration. The horrible ability she discovered she had when she was but a child.

She shivered as the recollection of that day came back in a sweeping rush. . . .

Hidden behind an old barrel, six-year-old Bridget watched in awe as the men finished construction on the huge wooden cross for the new meeting house. It would be the crowning touch, and the good Reverend Goodwell had told anyone who would listen that he had spared no expense in purchasing the finest wood and materials to build it.

Hammers clanged and men laughed and talked as they put on the finishing touches. It would be tall enough to touch the ceiling, her father had told her. But Bridget thought it lofty enough to go right through the roof and reach up into the heavens to touch God.

Today, her father stood near one side of the meeting house, overseeing the work. Now that the cross was finally completed, the men began tying ropes around the wood in order to drag it into the building and raise it.

Bridget liked watching the men work and listening to them sing hymns in their deep voices. She was exhilarated that today was the final day of work on the cross. At last she would see the magnificent structure take its rightful place. She watched with mounting excitement as the men dragged their heavy load inside while shouting instructions to each other.

Bridget looked around carefully. She would not be permitted inside when they raised the cross, but she wanted desperately to see. Certain no one was watching, she darted inside the building, hiding behind one of the pews in the back. The men had already moved the cross into position and waited while Henry White and Daniel Mansfield climbed a wooden scaffold. A rope pulley had been set over the largest and steadiest crossbeam, ready to lift the cross into a standing position.

Bridget stayed hidden and peeked out only when she dared. She heard the men grunt with exertion as they pulled up the cross into the waiting arms of Henry and Daniel.

When the cross was upright, the rope went slack as Henry and Daniel steadied the huge piece of wood. Quickly they secured it with heavy twine to two smaller, sturdy columns of wood behind it. As the men released the pulley rope, a great hurrah erupted.

Bridget was so entranced by the sight that she barely heard Henry shout a warning. As she watched in horror, the heavy cross listed to the left, snapped its rope bindings, and began toppling over right toward the pew where she hid.

Everything seemed to move slowly after that. Bridget could hear men screaming and running. Too late, she realized that she'd stood up, revealing herself. For an instant, her eyes met those of her father's across the meeting house, and she heard him shout her name.

An enormous crash ensued, followed by a huge dust cloud and an eerie, deafening silence. Then the dust cleared and Bridget saw her father stepping toward her, his face pale as a sheet. He stopped several feet from her and just stared.

"Wh-what happened?" she croaked out when her father said nothing. She felt strangely hot and flushed.

She followed her father's gaze to where the cross had been, but now only a pile of ashes remained. Dazed and confused, Bridget smelled the acrid scent of smoke even though she had seen no fire.

" 'Tis a miracle," she heard Daniel whisper.

"Or the work of the devil," another muttered.

Her father reached out to take her arm. Crying out, he jerked his hand back as if he had been burned.

"You're scalding hot," he exclaimed.

"I . . . I am?" Bridget stammered and began to cry.

Her father studied the ashes for a long time and then turned his gaze back to her. "Did you do that?" he finally asked, his voice stern. "The cross . . . it has vanished to naught more than dust."

Bridget's whole body trembled. Her face felt tingly and warm. "I . . . I don't know," she whispered.

Without touching her, her father pointed to the door. "Go home, Bridget," he said sternly.

After the incident, her parents began to act oddly with her. They looked at her strangely, and her punishments for even the smallest transgressions came swiftly and more frequently. As time passed, they both grew more distant from her.

Bridget heard the gossip from town, that she was a

witch or the spawn of the devil, able to set things on fire simply by commanding it so. Curious, she tested their theory. To her shock, she discovered that with a little concentration, she could indeed conjure fire. At first, she experimented by setting little ones, and then she moved on to bigger things.

Even at six years of age, Bridget realized the danger in the power she possessed. Quietly and cautiously, she learned to control her ability. Occasionally, fires were lit by accident, especially when she lost her temper or became afraid. Because of her experimentation, she was exceedingly careful to keep her newfound ability as much a secret as possible.

She yearned for a logical explanation, but fear of her parents' response kept her silent. She'd heard her father thunder about evil and miscreants enough times from his pulpit, and she was terrified of what might happen if she confessed the extent of what she could do.

As she grew, sudden fires were quickly and secretly put out, and Bridget learned to adroitly explain away those incidents that caused damage.

Most of the time, she simply lived in peace with her unusual ability. Occasionally, it terrified her. Above all, she considered herself cursed.

Living in Salem as she did, she thought it only fitting to secretly name her deviation "the witch's curse."

Two

Benjamin sat on the steps of his family's waterfront mansion overlooking Salem's busiest wharves. He enjoyed watching the people go about their business, and this morning the sketchbook in his lap was ready to bring to life a ship or a scene that caught his fancy.

The wharves were already bustling, filled with a colorful variety of vessels: sloops heading out to fish, schooners bringing cod into the harbor for sale, and skiffs taking customs officials out to inspect anchored ships. He began to sketch, but then halted with a sigh. He was in a poor mood, and damned if he knew why.

By all accounts, he should be well satisfied with himself. His first foray into his father's business had been wildly successful. His father was delighted with the progress he'd made forging new shipping ties over the past nine months in Lisbon. He was the talk of Lisbon, his name favorably reviewed in the highest circles. And now, he was finally able to take a well-deserved rest from his busy schedule and return home to visit with his family. And, most important, attend the wedding of his two closest friends.

Then what was weighing so heavily on his mind?

Benjamin tapped his pencil absently against the sketchbook. Perhaps it had been the unexpected early-morning visit he had paid to the Goodwells yesterday. He still wasn't certain what had possessed him, just hours off the ship, to rush over there for a visit. He assured himself he was only concerned about Bridget's welfare, for he hadn't seen her for nearly a year. It was natural for him to worry about her, especially since they had been close friends since childhood.

Of course, that hadn't stopped him from slipping a toad into her gown pocket. He just couldn't seem to help himself around her. She always seemed able to bring out the mischievous, high-spirited boy who lived inside him.

He'd missed her, he realized with a jolt, and wistfully wondered if she'd missed him. She'd certainly been stunned to see him. Her lovely sea green eyes had widened with shock, her sweet, generous mouth opened in astonishment. It delighted him that she'd been caught unawares, unsuspecting. Had she really believed he would stay away from her wedding?

He rubbed his stubbled chin thoughtfully. Well, he supposed she might have thought that. After all, he'd been gone for most of the year in Lisbon, and before that had spent a good deal of time cultivating new shipping contracts in Barcelona and Bordeaux. In fact, now that he really considered it, he'd been in Salem very little since she and Peter had announced their engagement three years ago.

Yesterday she had looked contented, and rather pretty, in a Bridget sort of way. Her eyes sparkled, her color had been high. Her best feature, her wild mane of waist-length red hair, had been haphazardly pinned up beneath a lopsided white kerchief. She wore an old brown-and-yellow gown—one even he had seen before—and if he knew Bridget, she wore it for comfort rather than show.

Yet he had noticed something different in her manner and the way she held herself. She seemed more secure and at ease with herself. She was less of the girl who could best him in a race or catch a toad with her bare hands, and more of the woman with marriage and family on her mind. He imagined she had probably worked quite diligently at the new persona, and that she secretly hated every minute of it. He grinned at the image it brought to mind.

Her refinement and control were all a part of growing up, he supposed. But Bridget wasn't just any woman. She was an enigma. Protective, passionate, and prim, all rolled into one. Insecure, temperamental, and opinionated, yet far stronger than anyone he'd ever known. She'd been his best friend for years, and no one had ever angered, challenged, or delighted him as she had.

After seeing her, he had no doubt that she was a woman now. He suddenly realized that his best friend had grown into a lovely young woman right before his eyes and he'd been too damn busy to see it.

He exhaled deeply and remembered the look that had passed between Bridget and her mother when he had been at the house. There was little love lost there, he mused. A good part of that was his fault, he acknowledged with a twinge of guilt. Sometimes he got too carried away with his pranks, and Bridget was usually the one to pay for it, even if he confessed.

But there was something else at work between the two women: a deep-seated mistrust. It had existed for as long as Benjamin had known the family, and he was never quite sure what had so deeply disturbed the time-honored bond between mother and daughter. He'd heard the rumors about Bridget's being a witch, a devil's child, and other assorted hearsay about her burning a cross to ash, but he had never paid them any mind. He figured he knew Bridget better than anyone. She was the kindest, most honest person he'd ever met, despite her tendency toward being hotheaded and reckless—faults he shared with her.

Benjamin wondered if it were the damaged bond with her mother that caused her to long so fiercely for a home of her own, filled with children and laughter. He knew she must crave stability and happiness.

Now she would finally have what she wanted with Peter.

Benjamin stopped sketching and rubbed the back of his neck where the muscles were knotted and tense. Then why in God's name wasn't he deliriously happy? Both Peter and Bridget had been his friends for years. They would wed and Bridget would have her dream at last.

It would be the first time his two comrades would carry on without him. He'd always been the leader of the trio, getting them into one merry adventure after another. Bridget followed with enthusiasm except when she challenged his leadership, and Peter permitted himself to be led by the two of them.

Frankly, he'd never expected Bridget to fall for Peter. They seemed so different, so unsuited to each other in any way except friendship. He'd been outraged the first time he caught them in an embrace, kissing in the bushes behind the blacksmith's house when they were fourteen. He'd yanked Peter off of her, nearly beating him to a pulp before Bridget managed to bring him back to his senses by connecting her fist squarely with his jaw.

He rubbed it again now, recalling the memory. She didn't hit like a girl, and it hurt. She then proceeded to yell at him for five minutes, her cheeks flushed with anger, her red hair spilling about her shoulders in a fiery mass. She shouted that she'd initiated the kiss; that it had been her idea. Peter had simply stood by sheepishly until Benjamin had managed to clear his red haze of anger and apologize.

That was the first indication he'd had that something was happening between the two of them. Even then, he hadn't liked it much, but wasn't really sure why. Anyway, he'd been too busy exploring his own sexual urges to care much about it.

When Peter had proposed shortly before Bridget's eighteenth birthday, she'd been thrilled. But Peter, being the cautious person he'd always been, postponed the wedding until his legal studies were complete—a three-year wait. Bridget had been crestfallen, but accepted the delay gracefully. Benjamin had pursued his own interests, sailing to Lisbon and Bordeaux on his father's ships, exploring the world outside the confines of Salem. He had always been comforted by the fact that he could come home to his friends and family, and little if anything would have changed.

Things were about to change drastically now. Bridget and Peter were finally to be married, and Benjamin had the inexplicable feeling that he was about to lose something precious.

He sighed, his gaze wandering over to Peter's house, next door to his own. The Holton mansion was a large, hip-roofed brick-and-wood structure with a black iron gate and a pretty, tidy garden in front. How ironic that in just a few weeks Bridget would move in there with Peter. If Peter was still keeping to his ways, he had only just arisen, being one for late nights and even later awakenings. He wondered how Bridget, who usually loved to rise early, would adjust herself to Peter's habits.

He held up his hands, framing the Holton mansion within them, and then began to sketch.

Bridget would have to adjust to many things, he thought as he drew. But she had done well for herself. He never imagined that she could be so . . . womanly.

For so many years she'd been a spirited, tempestuous child, and permitted to behave as such, Benjamin suspected, largely because of her friendship with him. It had not escaped his notice how often the Reverend Goodwell called upon his father, praising the close friendship between their two children. Indeed, his parents were quite fond of Bridget and had responded by contributing generous and regular donations to the coffers.

Now, as an adult, Benjamin saw what it had cost her. Time spent with him meant less opportunity for nurturing friendships with other young women and training in the social and domestic arts. He knew that as Bridget had grown, other boys thought her odd, but he hadn't cared or realized the long-term impact it would have on her. Without any real social status, the promise of a hefty dowry, or stunning beauty, Bridget would never be much sought after by other men. Without realizing it, he had stood directly in the way of her dreams.

Thank God for Peter. He'd always seen Bridget differently. He'd been a bit afraid of her, yet fascinated, too. Benjamin could understand that fascination. Yet he wondered now, as he had wondered a thousand times before, what had really prompted him to propose to her. There was no question Peter was fond of her, but Benjamin always thought them fundamentally unsuited for each other. It puzzled him.

Peter was far too cautious a man to risk marriage to someone as unpredictable and passionate as

Bridget, despite her new, proper demeanor. And Bridget was far too full of life to be happy with someone as tedious as Peter. Then why would they agree to wed?

Benjamin sketched furiously, his mind racing. There had to be some logical reason for the match. Bridget chose Peter most likely because she had no one else—no one would be likely to propose to her at the ripe old age of twenty. At the same time, Peter was probably considering a run for some kind of political office in Salem. Reverend Goodwell had a large and vocal congregation. Bridget would certainly be an asset to him among God-fearing folk. Nonetheless, Peter had made her suffer through a long three-year engagement, using the excuse that he had to finish his studies.

That had been cruel, Benjamin thought. Peter had likely been waiting to see if Bridget could fashion herself into a social and practical asset—a good politician's wife. The more he thought about it, the angrier Benjamin became. He knew what the wait had cost her; he himself had heard the whispers about town that it was only a matter of time before Peter found someone younger or better. It surely had been an agonizing three-year period for her.

Exhaling an angry breath, Benjamin stilled his pencil and looked at his drawing. His mouth opened in surprise. He hadn't drawn the Holton mansion as he'd intended; instead, Bridget's face stared back at him, her lovely eyes flashing fire, her generous mouth parted slightly. He'd even caught the twinkle in her eye, the one she always had when she was about to play a trick on him.

"Hello, Benjamin!" he heard someone call out. He jerked his head up guiltily to see who it was.

Sarabeth Goodwell walked along the street in front of his mansion, waving gaily at him. Her mother and father accompanied her, but Bridget was nowhere in sight. Hastily Benjamin closed his sketchbook and left it on the porch, going out to greet them.

He presumed they were on their way to the market, and noted with some amusement that they had gone out of their way to pass by his house. Sarabeth's adoring gaze this morning had not been lost on him, and he knew both the elder Goodwells were probably encouraging her affection. Although Sarabeth had grown into one of the most stunning young women he'd ever seen, he knew he'd never be able to look at her as anything other than a child.

Sarabeth waved again, and Benjamin grinned, lifting his hand in a return greeting. He didn't want to encourage her attention, but neither did he want to hurt her. He'd have to manage this carefully.

He reached the gate and unfastened it, going out to greet the Goodwells.

"Good morning to you, Reverend," he said, shaking Ichabod's hand warmly. "Madam, Sarabeth," he added to the women, bowing his head slightly. "What brings you out this fine morning?"

"We're going to the market," Sarabeth said in a breathless rush before anyone else had a chance to answer. "Mother says I can buy a new ribbon for my hair. What color do you think would be best?"

Benjamin took a step back, thoughtfully looking her over. She looked remarkably pretty; her golden blond hair swept back off her face and neck, with little ringlets framing her cheeks. She wore a white gossamer dress with little blue flowers and a sky blue bonnet that perfectly set off her gorgeous blue eyes and long eyelashes. Her cheeks were flushed slightly, whether from the exertion of the walk or from meeting him, he wasn't sure.

He drew his brows together thoughtfully, as if he pondered a weighty question. In fact, he hadn't the slightest clue as to women's fashion, and really wasn't much inclined to care.

"Why, blue, I'd say," he finally answered.

Sarabeth's eyes lit up. "That's exactly what I thought. Mother, see how Benjamin and I think alike?"

Abigail smiled indulgently, patting her daughter gently on the shoulder. "Come, now, Sarabeth, we mustn't keep him from his duties."

Benjamin's mouth curved into a smile. "It's always a charming diversion to speak with you. In fact, you've only kept me from sitting on the porch and daydreaming." He looked casually over Sarabeth's shoulder. "Is Bridget already at the market?" he asked.

Abigail's smile faded. "No, she's at home, doing chores. At least, that's what I hope she's doing."

Benjamin nodded, immediately sensing the tension in the air. Something had likely happened between them after he left yesterday—something that most likely had to do with the toad he had slipped into her pocket.

"Yes, well, good day to you, then," he said, keeping his expression carefully neutral.

He watched them stroll off toward the market, feeling a sudden urge to talk to Bridget. She deserved an apology for his outrageous behavior, and he'd be damned if he'd wait another day to do it.

He waited until the Goodwells disappeared, and then strode determinedly toward the parsonage.

* * *

Bridget was in no mood to do chores. Instead, she wanted to take the rare opportunity of her solitude to dream about her wedding and the way her life would change once she was safely wed to Peter.

She had waited all her life for her wedding day, and she was bound and determined that it would be perfect. Even with Benjamin Hawkes back in town.

"Nothing is going to ruin it," she murmured as she knelt beside an old wooden chest that sat at the foot of her bed. "Not even you, Benjamin."

She unfastened the latch on the trunk and opened it, pulling out the ivory silk-and-lace nightgown that she would wear on her wedding night. It was the most beautiful thing she owned, and she would wear it when she was deflowered and at last became a woman.

She swallowed back a lump of fear that lodged in her throat at the thought of coupling with Peter. She loved him, but she was terrified she might not pleasure him properly. When he kissed her, she felt nothing but a warm pressure on her lips. The thought that she might be cold or unable to perform her wifely duties frightened her greatly.

Her anxiety grew. With only three weeks to go, she was still very much afraid the wedding would never take place. In truth, only a little of that fear came from her lack of physical response to Peter. The real fear came from within, and how Peter would react if he ever discovered her unusual talent with fire. She worried that if he discovered the truth now, he'd never wed her, and neither would anyone else in Salem. She'd be isolated, sentenced to a life of abject shame and loneliness.

Now, with Benjamin back in town, the danger her secret might be revealed increased tenfold. He, as no one else, could cause her to lose control of her emotions and perhaps accidentally expose her aberration. She'd have to be exceedingly careful around him.

Frowning, Bridget stood, holding up the beautiful nightgown and shaking it out gently. She must not dwell on such upsetting thoughts now. Instead, she would focus on what was good and right in her life.

"Mrs. Peter Holton," Bridget whispered softly to herself. It had a nice, prudent ring to it.

Her mood lightening, Bridget held the nightgown against her and lifted one hand to brush a coppery strand of hair from her forehead. "Would you like this dance, Mrs. Holton?" she asked the nightgown.

"Why, I'd be delighted," she replied with a small curtsy.

Humming, Bridget began to twirl about the room, still holding the gown against her. She was daydreaming, but alert in case her parents and Sarabeth returned home unexpectedly. So she was more than startled when she heard someone clear his throat.

Bridget shrieked in surprise, whirling around to see Benjamin standing in the doorway, leaning casually against the doorjamb, his arms crossed over his chest.

"Hello, Bri," he said, giving her a bone-melting smile.

"Are you mad?" she gasped when she could finally find her voice. "This is my bedchamber. How dare you wander in here without announcing yourself."

He had the audacity to chuckle. "Glad to see you, too. And I did announce myself—at least five or six times. You just didn't answer. After checking the garden and seeing you weren't there, I began to worry. I knew your parents were in town and had left you here alone. I thought it was best that someone look in on you. I didn't think they would mind."

He was right, of course. They wouldn't have minded

a bit. But she did mind, especially because he had caught her at a vulnerable moment. Bridget thrust the nightgown behind her with one hand and glared at him. He looked ruggedly handsome this morning, his black hair gleaming in the light, his expression one of casual self-confidence.

"I'd like you to leave this instant," she ordered, pointing at the door.

His smile faded. "Don't be angry with me, Bri. I just came by to say hello."

"You just can't march into my bedchamber," she said, still trembling from surprise and anger. "We're not children anymore, Benjamin."

"No, indeed we are not," he said agreeably. "All the same, I must admit it was charming to see you so unguarded for a moment and dancing with that delectable nightgown. It's for the wedding night, I presume."

Bridget flushed red to the roots of her hair. Marching over to the chest, she carefully folded the nightgown and closed the top with a thump. "It's none of your concern," she said haughtily.

He sighed. "No, I suppose it's not. But I do find it curious that I've known you all these years and didn't even know you could dance."

"You know that Father does not approve of dancing."

"Yes, I know, and yet you dance just the same. You never cease to surprise me." He bowed and held out a hand. "Would you allow me to show you the latest dance from Lisbon?"

"I would not," she snapped. "Have you completely lost your senses?"

"What's wrong with asking? Your father won't be watching."

"Because . . . it wouldn't be proper. Besides, need I remind you that we are in my bedchamber?"

Benjamin frowned. "Oh, and how could I forget? You are so proper now that you are about to be wed. It may be your last chance, Bri. We both know Peter doesn't dance."

"Why should he? I don't care."

"It didn't look that way to me just now."

She flushed again. " 'Twas foolishness. No one was supposed to be watching."

"There was nothing foolish about it. It was utterly enchanting. You are a fine dancer, Bri. Come and dance with me. Please."

She hesitated for a moment before common sense prevailed. "No," she said, her breath coming slightly faster. Why had she even dared to consider it?

"Coward," he uttered, and for the first time in her life, Bridget saw a spark of an unrecognizable emotion in his eyes. Disconcerted, she looked away.

"I'm not a coward," she said, although that was exactly how she felt.

"I wasn't talking about you."

Bridget flushed, uncertain of his meaning. A few minutes in his presence and he had completely unnerved her.

"Why did you really come back to Salem?" she asked directly.

He studied her face with his enigmatic gaze for a long moment. "I told you why. I came back for the wedding."

"Forgive me if I appear rather dubious. I thought for certain you'd be heading off to Amsterdam or some other godforsaken place on one of your father's ships after you tired of Lisbon."

He laughed. "Amsterdam is hardly godforsaken,

and I've not really tired of Lisbon yet. And, don't deny it—I can see the way your eyes light up when I talk about Europe and my travels. You're dying to hear about Paris, aren't you? It's a lovely city, Bri, full of bright lights, artists, and merriment. You'd love it."

"I sincerely doubt it."

His smile widened. "You don't need to pretend to be so sensible and staid with me. We both know you're as adventurous as I am."

"I am not."

"Are, too," he replied, chuckling. "And I assure you, Paris is full of spirited and remarkable women just like you."

She looked at him wryly. "So, that's the most fascinating aspect of Paris to you—its women? I see you are living up to your reputation as a rogue even abroad."

He raised an eyebrow in amusement. "Oh, please tell me you're jealous. I'd trade all the girls in Paris just for you."

"For one hour, perhaps," she snorted inelegantly. "But you're hardly the man to settle for just one woman."

The smile faded from his face, replaced by a touch of wistfulness. "There is no one in the world who knows me better than you. I'm going to miss you, Bri."

"I'm getting married, Benjamin. I'm not dying."

"I know. But time passes quickly, doesn't it?"

Memories of a simpler and happier time when they were children brought a smile to her lips. "Yes, I suppose you are right. It does seem like just yesterday I loosened the seam in your breeches."

His humor quickly returned. "That happened to be the last time I was in town. Do you know my pants split open right in front of Lilith Ward? She nearly swooned at the sight."

Bridget couldn't help but grin. "Lilith is always swooning. But pray tell, did it adversely affect your machinations with her?"

"It required a hasty retreat on my part, of course. Although, I assure you, giving her a glimpse of my undergarments only added to my mystique as a brazen rake."

"What mystique? You *are* a brazen rake."

He laughed again, his eyes sparkling with amusement. "I'd brazen my way a bit with you, if I thought it would get me anywhere."

"It wouldn't. Besides, you'd be amused for only an hour or so before you'd find another unsuspecting woman to ply with your charm. Which reminds me—what are your intentions toward my sister?"

"Sarabeth?" he repeated innocently, but Bridget's heart plummeted when she saw he wasn't much taken aback by her comment.

"She's not the woman for you, Benjamin."

He lifted a dark eyebrow. "She's not? Then, pray tell, just who *is* the woman for me?"

Bridget considered for a moment. "Well, with your tendency to dash off to foreign ports, walk into other people's houses without warning, and charm your way into the beds of unsuspecting women, I can't honestly think of a single person."

"There is nothing unsuspecting about the women I bed," he growled.

She wagged a finger at him. "Need I add discussing base and improper matters with ladies to the list?"

"You brought it up," he shot back, his gray eyes gleaming. "But I'll be the first to admit that Sarabeth is an incredibly beautiful young woman. A man would have to be a fool to refuse a chance to take a woman like that to bed."

Bridget's mouth dropped open in outrage. "How dare you talk like that about my sister! She's just a child."

"She's a woman, Bri. From the top of her pretty golden head to the bottom of her tiny, perfect feet."

"She's innocent. She doesn't understand men."

Benjamin raised a dark eyebrow. "And you do?"

"I understand you."

"Is that so?"

"Why, you're reckless, impatient, headstrong, and a dreamer. She needs someone more . . . sensible."

"What she needs is a man who can show her what life is really like outside the sheltered Goodwell household. A man like me."

"No!"

"Why not, Bri?" The amused glint suddenly left his eyes. "Why are you really so opposed to a potential union between Sarabeth and myself?"

She groped for a reasonable reply. "Because . . . because, I just know that you two aren't right for each other."

His gaze seemed to probe at her very soul before he shrugged. "You're right."

Her mouth dropped open in surprise. "I am?"

"You are," he said, inclining his head. "She'll always be just a child to me, Bri."

"But . . . but you said . . ."

"I said it just to rile your temper," he said with an insolent grin. "It was so easy, I just couldn't help myself."

She glared at him. "Why, you . . . you . . ." she fumed.

"Cad?" he offered helpfully.

She shot him a withering glare. "You will never grow up, will you? Still playing pranks on me as if we were children."

He sighed. "Ah, yes, there is the matter with the toad yesterday. But I owed you that for the debacle with Lilith Ward."

"Well, you're lucky that I wasn't still in the house when it hopped out of my pocket. I doubt my mother or Sarabeth would have been much amused."

"I daresay you are right. Anyway, I didn't come over to play any more pranks on you. I actually came to apologize for putting the toad in your gown pocket and for any other trouble I've caused you throughout our childhood. I won't say I didn't enjoy it, because they were the best times of my life. But I will say I'm sorry if it caused you any undue discomfort, especially with your family."

She was momentarily speechless. "You are apologizing?" she finally said. "To me?"

He shrugged matter-of-factly. "I just said so, didn't I?"

She narrowed her eyes suspiciously. "Why are you being so accommodating?"

"Because you're right. It's time for me to grow up."

"Why, Benjamin Hawkes, I think that is the most sensible thing I've ever heard you say."

"I'm wounded by your blatant disbelief," he said, wincing.

"But I genuinely mean it. And if we are cleansing our consciences, I suppose I should apologize for my pranks as well. Although none of them caused near as much harm as yours did."

His lips parted in a dazzling display of straight, white teeth. "Now that's the most preposterous thing I've ever heard. Your pranks were far more dangerous than mine, especially since the large majority of them involved burning something that belonged to me."

Bridget felt the first flutter of panic in her stomach. "That's not true."

"How about the time you set my breeches on fire in assembly when I was ten?"

"That was an accident. You backed into a candle."

"I did not."

"Did, too."

He took another step closer. "And the time my shoes mysteriously caught on fire when I was about to steal your clothes while you were engaged in a forbidden moonlight dip in the sea?"

She shook her head so furiously, the kerchief loosened, slipping down the back of her neck. "You can't blame me for that. I was in the water. You likely stepped on something."

"Then what about the inexplicable combustion of my favorite hat when I was on my way to the marketplace with Constance Wirth?"

She opened her mouth to say something but couldn't think of a single logical explanation. Apprehension coursed through her. He was closer to discovering her secret than she had ever suspected.

"Bri, you can't deny it," he continued. "I've had an inordinately large number of pranks against me by you involving fire. I swear, I think you can cause fires by simply having your temper riled."

"That's preposterous," she retorted, trying to steady her erratic and anxious pulse. Fear and anger knotted inside her. "Are you implying that I can conjure fire at will?"

A dark eyebrow shot up, his eyes regarding her frankly. "Can you? I do believe I can actually feel the heat emanating from you when you're angry. Your face gets flushed red, your hair seems to stand on end, and your eyes—well, they practically flash fire. Almost like now."

"Outlandish."

He chuckled. "Hardly. That strange red flush is starting to creep up your neck toward your cheeks this instant."

Bridget reached up to touch her cheeks. They did feel rather warm. "That's because you are riling my temper, Benjamin."

A thoughtful smile curved his mouth. "I am rather adept at that, aren't I?" he agreed, taking another step closer. She hadn't realized it before, but he had skillfully maneuvered her back against the wooden chest, giving her no room to move without touching him.

"I know you very well, Bri. And I must say, I've been fascinated by the way you've worked over the past few years to tame that infamous temper of yours and fashion yourself into a perfectly proper lady. If I didn't know you better, I'd say you'd be the perfect wife for someone like Peter. But the truth is that underneath that genteel decor is a passionate, tempestuous woman who is capable of living life to its fullest. You can't fool me."

Her stomach twisted sharply, the fears cutting deeper than ever. "I'm not trying to fool anyone," she said, hating that her voice wavered slightly.

He searched her face intently. "Bri, are you sure marriage to Peter is what you want? Truly?"

Her emotions careened wildly, taken by surprise at his abrupt change of subject and the close proximity of his body. Her pulse beat erratically; her mouth felt dry. She'd forgotten just how disturbing it was to be so near to him.

"Of course marriage to Peter is what I want," she said shakily. "He's everything I want in a man."

She thought she detected a flicker in his dark eyes. "Everything? Are you certain he'll be able to give you what you really need?"

Bridget's breath caught in her throat. He was so close she could feel the heat of his breath on her cheek. His nearness made her head spin, and she was extremely conscious of his virile appeal.

"I . . . I don't know what you mean," she said unsteadily. "Peter is decent, hard-working and thoughtful. Of course he can give me what I want."

"Did you say that to convince me or you?" he asked softly. He reached out and twirled a strand of her hair around his finger in a curiously tender gesture. Bridget trembled and hated herself for it.

"How thoughtful is he really, Bri?" he continued. "He's made you wait three years to be his wife. Three years! If it were me, once I'd decided to make you my wife, I'd do it without pause. I wouldn't make you wait a week—or a day, for that matter. You'd be mine as soon as it could be made legal."

"Well, thank God he's not you," Bridget retorted, her temper flaring. "Peter isn't reckless or impatient or headstrong. It was sensible to wait until he finished his studies and not rush headlong into something as important as marriage."

"Sensible, of course," he said mockingly, his voice granite-hard. "Peter the decent one. Peter the rational one. Forgive me, Bri, but I know Peter just as well as you do. Next to you, he's my best friend."

"And some friend you are proving to be," she said, her voice rising with emotion. "Coming here, disparaging him in front of the woman he is to wed." She suddenly had an irrational urge to weep, but swallowed hard instead. She'd rather die than have Benjamin witness another of her vulnerabilities.

"You'll hear me out, Bri," he ground out. "Peter's been my friend longer than you have. And my opinion of him in this particular matter has not changed. He's a cad for having made you wait so long, knowing what you'd have to go through. Do you think he hasn't heard or even fueled the gossip about you in town? The way you spend so much time with old witch Bayley, the way things just seem to catch fire when you are around. Let's be honest. Peter waited to see if you could fashion yourself into the kind of woman he wants to marry. He's fascinated and even attracted to you, but the truth is, he doesn't want the real you for a wife—at least, perhaps, not outside the bedchamber. And you know me well enough to realize I'd tell him that to his face."

Bridget gasped in mortification and then slapped him hard across the face, the force of it vibrating through her fingers. She seethed with both anger and humiliation, as furious as she had ever been with him.

"How dare you say that to me," she hissed, dangerously close to tears. "You, of all people, dare to speak of such things. You are a reckless, arrogant, womanizing cad. You don't have the slightest idea of what it's like to be in love, to really care about someone. Peter loves me, I know he does." In an attempt to wound him where it hurt, she added furiously, "I can tell by the way he kisses me."

Benjamin stiffened, clenching his jaw. His expression turned hard and dangerous, his gray eyes thundering.

"For God's sake, don't be so naive," he spat out contemptuously. "Any man can rouse a physical response from an inexperienced woman, Bri. But real passion . . . that, I promise you, is something you'll never get from Peter."

She reacted angrily to the challenge in his voice. "You know nothing of passion between two people who care deeply for each other. Besides, you don't have the slightest idea of what I want."

"Don't I?" he growled.

Before Bridget could retort, he pulled her roughly, almost violently to him. His mouth crashed down on hers, his kiss punishing and angry.

She slammed her fists into his chest, but it had no effect. Twisting in his embrace, she sought to free herself, but to no avail. His arms were like iron bands around her waist.

She could feel the frustration and anger of his kiss as he ravished her mouth with mindless ferocity. She gasped at his boldness as his tongue forced his way into her mouth, mixing and tangling with hers, exploring every secret recess. Blood pounded in her ears, and her pulse hammered dangerously. She shuddered as her blood pumped hot through her veins, drugging her with an intense, sensual awareness of him that set her entire body aflame.

Unbidden, a moan escaped her lips, and Benjamin abruptly shifted the pressure of his mouth. His lips, which moments before had been hard and demanding, were now suddenly soft and caressing. She tried to ignore the sensual command of his kiss, but her body refused to obey. Slowly, she succumbed to the dreamy intimacy, powerfully aware of his arms tightening around her, and yet feeling as if she were floating.

"Bri," he whispered raggedly against her cheek.

Bridget's anger melted as she heard him say her name, realizing that he no longer kissed her because he was furious, but because he wanted her. At the same time, she knew with complete certainty that she had wanted this kiss all her life. In a forbidden part of her heart, she had always wanted to taste him, to know him in this intimate way at least once before putting him out of her life forever.

As though his whisper released her, she flung her arms around his neck and kissed him back. She felt him start in surprise, before his mouth covered hers hungrily—tasting, exploring, and claiming. A flash of heat ripped through her while dizzying and wicked sensations exploded throughout her body.

Drunk with need, Bridget pressed against him, kissing with reckless abandon. A guttural sound came from deep within his throat as his mouth slanted across hers with a frantic urgency. Suddenly his hands were on her neck and in her hair, sending wooden hairpins scattering across the floor in every direction.

Dimly, Bridget realized she should stop the kiss, pull away and stop the embrace at once. Her behavior was immoral, disgraceful, and utterly reprehensible. After all, she would be married to another man in just three weeks. But her body would not heed the warnings in her head, and her heart would not listen to reason either.

Instead, she clung fiercely to him, the blood thundering in her head, her mouth burning. One hand slid down to his neck and shoulder, where she felt his muscles ripple and bunch beneath the fabric of his shirt. She dug her nails into the material as his hands seared a path down her back, touching and stroking her in ways that made her want to explode. When he groaned again, she realized with exhilarating clarity that she also wielded some power in this intimate embrace.

Boldly, she yanked the ribbon from his hair, tossing it into the air. Winding the thick strands of his gloriously dark hair around her fingers, she pulled his mouth even more firmly against hers. They stumbled a few steps and nearly fell, but Benjamin caught his balance and steadied them without ever letting his mouth leave hers.

Bridget's heart pounded an erratic rhythm, her lungs on fire and her nostrils filled with the heady smoke of desire and need. Her thoughts spun so madly, she could hold only a single coherent thought—that this must be true passion.

God help her, she thought in dismay, Benjamin had been right. She would never, *ever* know a passion like this with Peter. Their kiss had exposed the irrevocable truth. Benjamin had long ago conquered her heart, and now his mouth had branded every inch of her soul, spoiling her for another man forever.

She shuddered as his mouth left hers, grazing a hot trail from her chin to her earlobe. He then cupped her face in his hands and their eyes locked, their breathing coming in unison. She could see tenderness, desire, and regret mingle in his eyes. A hot ache grew in her throat as Benjamin slowly lowered his mouth to hers again. She closed her eyes, feeling the heady sensation of his tongue stroking the soft insides of her mouth. Kissing him made her feel as hot as the soldering heat the blacksmith used to join metal—glowing, melting, and powerful. She felt a flush of heat and then gasped as Benjamin abruptly shoved her backward.

Hard.

Startled, Bridget stumbled, tripped, and then fell to the floor on her bottom with a loud, unladylike thump.

Dazed and blinking, she looked over at Benjamin. He was doing some sort of crazed dance about the room, seemingly trying to undress himself.

"Hell's bells!" he shouted when he saw she was watching with wide eyes. "My shirt is on fire."

Horrified, Bridget realized he was right. She scrambled to her feet, just as he threw the burning cloth to the floor and trampled over it until the flames were out. For a shocked moment, they just stared at each other, until Bridget took a shaky step backward.

"Wh-what was that?" she whispered, her voice raspy and rough.

"That was my shirt on fire," he replied. "Good thing I got it off when I did. How in the blazes did that happen?"

Bridget looked over at him, his bare, muscular chest gleaming with sweat. He was breathing heavily, and she was fairly certain it wasn't just from the exertion of removing the flaming garment.

She swallowed hard. "N-no. I mean, why did you kiss me like . . . that?"

He pressed his hand to his forehead, looking rather dazed. Sweat trickled from his brow, his dark hair tousled about his shoulders. Bridget remembered with a horrible moment of clarity that it was she who had ripped the ribbon from his hair in wild abandon.

"I don't know, Bri," he said. "I don't know what came over me. I'm sorry. It just happened."

"How could you?" she whispered, her voice breaking. "How could you do this to me just a scant month before my wedding?"

"Bri—" he started, taking a step toward her.

She backed up hastily. "No, don't touch me. Don't ever touch me again. Get out."

"Bri, listen to me."

"No. Not a word of what happened between us ever goes outside this room. Ever. If you're any kind of a friend to me, then you will respect my wishes in this case."

"Bri, please—" he started, when she heard a noise from downstairs in the house.

"My parents," she exclaimed, throwing him a stricken look. "They're back from the market."

In a horrified instant, she realized that no amount of explaining, not even from Benjamin, would sufficiently explain why he stood half-clad in her bedroom, breathing heavily, his burned shirt on the floor. Nor did Bridget possibly see how he could explain her disheveled gown, wild hair, and flushed face.

Benjamin appeared to see the wisdom of a hasty and discreet exit as well.

Muffling a curse, he grabbed his charred shirt from the floor and raced to the window. He threw open the shutters and quickly slid out on the windowsill, wiggling to the edge until he was close enough to make a small leap to the sturdy branch of the ancient oak tree. He made the jump safely and began shinnying down the tree. He was so adept at the maneuver that Bridget wondered with no small amount of consternation how many times he had done this sort of thing before.

She moved quickly to the window to be sure he had left, when she heard his voice drift up to her. "This is not over," he warned.

"Oh yes, it is, Benjamin," she murmured under her breath. "It's over for good."

Three

Bridget swept the floor vigorously at the spot where Benjamin's charred shirt had been cast, trying to forget what had happened earlier in her bedroom. As soon as he left, she had quickly adjusted her gown, tucked her errant hair up under a fresh kerchief and run downstairs to meet her parents. They eyed her a bit oddly given her breathless and perhaps overly enthusiastic greeting, but said nothing. Sarabeth, bubbling with excitement over a new ribbon, didn't notice anything awry.

After a few minutes of unimportant chatter, Bridget returned to her room, where she now swept furiously, wishing the broom could whisk away the memory of Benjamin's mouth on hers. He had made her feel so . . . hot. Hot enough that she'd nearly set both him and the room on fire. This was definitely an unforeseen aspect of her ability, and one she'd better learn how to control before she wed.

She sighed, sweeping harder. She shouldn't be so surprised at what had happened. Benjamin's behavior, though completely unexpected, was not all that out of character. For as long as she could remember, he had always had an uncanny ability to catch her unawares and do the unexpected. What had shocked her was the hunger she sensed behind his kiss, coupled with moments of stunning tenderness—something she didn't think he had feigned. Yet even more disturbing was how quickly her heart and body had responded to what his kisses had offered.

Bridget flushed deeply, feeling sickened and horrified by her reaction to him. What in God's name had come over her? She had risked everything with that kiss and nearly thrown away her last chance at a marriage in the process. And for what? For the chance to know what a true moment of passion was like? Had it really been worth it?

Bridget paused, leaning against the broom. She didn't have to answer the last question, because her heart already knew the truth. It had been worth every moment, and the memory would last her a lifetime.

She shook her head sadly. Her mother was right. Her soul was in dire need of being saved from wickedness.

Yet she still couldn't make herself regret it. As reckless as her actions had been, for the first time in years, she had simply been herself. She'd abandoned the pretense of a proper and prim woman and had shown her true nature. It both embarrassed and infuriated her that Benjamin had seen that inner passion all along and coaxed it from her, somehow seeming to know her even better than she knew herself. It was difficult to admit, but whereas Benjamin often left her feeling disoriented and annoyed, he seemed also to be the only one able to touch the real woman who lived inside. Peter's most enthusiastic attempts at passion were nowhere near the sensual fervor Benjamin had so easily delivered with his heated embrace.

Bridget set the broom aside, picking up the dust rag and whisking it across the trunk at the foot of her bed.

She felt sickened and guilty that she was comparing the two men. If she were truly a godly and decent girl, it wouldn't matter that Peter's stiff embraces left her unfulfilled. Besides, mindless passion was not what she needed. She needed stability. She needed Peter.

Peter was honorable, intelligent, predictable, and had enough wealth to provide a comfortable life for both of them. Bridget knew that as a woman without means and the daughter of a reverend it would be fruitless to hope for more.

She held the dust rag aside and sneezed, rubbing her nose with the back of her hand in frustration. A moment of stolen passion was certainly not worth the lifetime of security that she would have with Peter. Benjamin promised nothing but tempestuous abandon and sin. That she would even continue to think about it was testament to her impiety.

She was going to marry Peter, regardless of what Benjamin said or did. It would be a practical union and one of the few things she had ever done in her life that would please her parents. Nothing would change her from that course.

She had worked so hard, preparing herself for marriage with all the meticulousness of a military general planning for battle. Making arrangements for the wedding had been exhausting, requiring scrupulous attention to an endless number of brain-numbing details, and far too many frivolous teas and parties. She'd been awkward and embarrassed at most of them. To make matters more difficult, she continually had to suffer the humiliation of having her efforts publicly scrutinized and criticized by well-intentioned members of her father's congregation.

Yet Bridget did not complain, primarily because she knew she was lucky. Lucky that Peter had proposed when no one else had, and even more fortunate because she was fond of him. Soon she would be the wife of a young, promising lawyer, and, God willing, would have a house full of adorable children. Perhaps then she could banish Benjamin Hawkes from her heart forever.

"I won't let you take my dream of a family and home away, Benjamin," she whispered fiercely. "No matter how persuasive you are."

She resumed dusting with renewed energy and was startled when Sarabeth ran into the room, tapping her excitedly on the shoulder.

"Peter's here," she said breathlessly, her eyes aglow. "He says he has something important to talk with you about."

Bridget dropped the rag and stood paralyzed with terror, certain he somehow knew every detail of her intimate encounter with Benjamin and had marched over to confront her about it.

"P-peter is here . . . now?" she stammered. "But he's not expected."

Sarabeth rushed over to the wardrobe, throwing open the doors. "Does it matter?" she asked, pulling out a fresh apron. "Put it on quickly, and I'll help brush out your hair."

Numbly, Bridget removed her old apron and tied on the fresh one. Her stomach rolled uneasily and she had difficulty swallowing.

Sarabeth yanked off Bridget's kerchief and brushed out her hair. She tied it back with a matching white-and-blue ribbon, letting the red tresses cascade down her back.

"There's no time to pin it up properly. It's not especially tidy, but it suits you," she observed.

Bridget stood up, her legs trembling. Sarabeth frowned and reached out a hand to steady her.

"Whatever is the matter, Bridget? You look pale as a sheet."

Bridget moistened her lips with her tongue. Her mouth had never felt so dry. "I . . . I suddenly feel rather unwell," she said weakly.

"Would you like me to tell Peter you are too ill to come down?"

Bridget shook her head. "No, I'm all right. Just give me a minute."

She took a deep breath and then straightened her shoulders. She only hoped that she'd be able to maintain her dignity and composure as Peter told her the wedding was off. Slowly she descended the stairs, walked into the parlor, and forced a smile to her lips as Peter stood to face her.

Bridget took in several things at once. He looked quite elegant this morning, dressed in a coat of honey-colored taffeta, a pair of light-amber breeches, and a white linen shirt with ruffles at the collar and sleeves. His golden blond hair had been neatly swept back to his neck and secured with a dark burgundy ribbon. Unbidden, the thought came to her that she had never really realized how he and Benjamin were in such contrast—Peter with an almost royal elegance and poise, and Benjamin, who projected a darker, wilder, and far more dangerous aura.

Peter smiled, but Bridget sensed no warmth behind the gesture. Nevertheless, she smiled back and held out her hand in greeting. Peter lifted it to his lips in a perfunctory manner and pressed a cool kiss on her knuckles. They both sat down without another word.

"Look who has come to visit us," Bridget heard her mother say. Abigail stood perched in the doorway between the parlor and the corridor to the kitchen, beaming at the two of them. "I'm preparing tea right now."

Peter turned his smile on her. "I do apologize for the unexpected visit. And I certainly appreciate the offer of tea, but I'd rather request your permission to take Bridget on a stroll into town to enjoy the beautiful summer weather. We need to speak about some matters related to the wedding. I shall return her within the hour."

His words were cool, his demeanor distant. Something was dreadfully amiss. Her mother noticed it, too, because she shot Bridget a reproachful glance. Bridget felt her stomach twist, fearful she might completely humiliate herself by heaving the remnants of her breakfast.

"Of course, permission is granted," her mother replied, returning her attention to Peter. "And no visit of yours is ever considered unexpected, Peter. Seeing that you will soon be a part of the family, you are always welcome in our home."

Peter bobbed his head graciously. Bridget nervously retrieved her bonnet and secured it under her chin as Peter took her by the elbow and steered her out of the house. They walked out the gate and began strolling toward the wharves before Peter spoke again. When he did, his words were frosty.

"There is something we need to talk about," he said, his words short and clipped. "Something you haven't discussed with me."

Bridget swallowed, a lump lodging in her throat. The sun felt unusually hot on her shoulders, and her stomach roiled queasily. "I'm . . . I'm sorry, Peter. I hadn't really had the opportunity yet to tell you myself, b-but I . . ." she let the sentence trail off, searching miserably for the best way to apologize for her inexcusable behavior with Benjamin.

Peter looked straight ahead, his shoulders ramrod stiff. "Well, you should be sorry. Esther Bellfree told me that the menu you submitted for the reception is completely unsuitable. Whatever were you thinking by suggesting such dishes as roasted sturgeon and Brunswick stew? Have you completely lost your senses? Do you want all of Salem to think we cannot afford better?"

Bridget stopped in shock and stared at him. "The menu? This is about the menu?"

"Of course it's about the menu. Unless you've decided to undertake some other wedding arrangements without consulting me first. What else could it be?"

She pressed a hand to her stomach to soothe her jitters. "Nothing," she lied, looking away. "Nothing at all." She felt the bile rise in her throat. It was her first lie to her future husband, and it frightened her just how easily it slipped off her lips. "I . . . I just thought since you liked Brunswick stew, it made sense to offer it at the wedding," she said weakly.

"Bridget, what I like has nothing to do with this wedding. It is a public event, our introduction into society. I may someday be an important political figure in this community, and it does not help my standing to have you announce to the world that I like something as common as Brunswick stew. I'd like you to prepare another menu. Cost is of no concern. But first you are to submit it to me for review. From now on, that goes for any future wedding arrangements."

"Peter, I . . ."

"I don't want to hear another word about it," he interrupted, taking her elbow firmly and pulling her along the sidewalk. "Sometimes I despair that you will ever quite come around to proper society."

She stopped abruptly, nearly causing him to stumble. "What exactly is that supposed to mean?"

"Exactly what I said. Bridget, dear, we both know you are not a natural at this sort of thing. But I do expect you to work hard at it."

"I have been working hard at it," she snapped. "What do you think I've been doing ceaselessly for these past three years?"

Perhaps sensing her growing anger, Peter sought to soothe. "Darling, please. There is no need to upset yourself. Overall, I'd say you've done a fine job of it. It's just that the wedding is an important event, and I'd like to ensure that every last detail is absolutely suitable. You do understand my position, don't you?"

He looked at her so beseechingly that Bridget felt herself relent. After all, in a way, he was right. Weddings weren't intended to be fun and frivolous, especially when they involved such an important Salem family as the Holtons. And as much as it vexed her, she supposed it was better to let him have the final say on proper decorum.

"I understand," she said a bit grudgingly. She took a deep breath to try and calm herself. Losing her temper would not help matters. Nor was it terribly ladylike.

"That's my girl," Peter said, tucking her hand in the crook of his arm as they started to walk.

He smiled at her, and for a moment, Bridget saw a glimpse of the young, lighthearted boy who had been her friend for years. A sense of nostalgia filled her, and she wished for a return to her childhood days, when matters of life were no more pressing than who would be first to climb to the top of the giant oak tree.

Peter began chatting idly about some debacle that had occurred earlier in town, oblivious to Bridget's wistful reminiscences. She listened to him with only half an ear, suddenly having the oddest sensation that she was being watched. As they turned onto Derby Street, Salem's main thoroughfare along the wharves, Bridget felt the hairs on the back of her neck rise. She couldn't explain it, but she somehow felt an ominous presence was near.

She looked over her shoulder anxiously but saw nothing unusual. The street was bustling with activity from the shipping-related businesses that crowded the area. In her immediate vicinity, an old man pushed a one-wheel cart of apples, a young mother sat on a shaded bench tending to two small children, and a distinguished-looking man rode past on a horse without a second glance at her and Peter. The sound of steady clanging came from just down the street at the anchor forge. She stole a sideways glance at Peter, but he chatted on, oblivious to the fact that she wasn't listening.

Bridget clutched his arm tighter, willing herself to calm down. The events of this morning had been overly stressful. First, the encounter with Benjamin, and now, the confrontation with Peter.

She was acting unbecomingly and irrationally. She had no right to be annoyed with Peter. After all, he was the injured party here. She and Benjamin, his two best friends, had engaged in a sinful and inexcusable activity behind his back. In fact, when she thought about the possessive way Benjamin's mouth had claimed hers and the enthusiastic way she had responded, a wave of shameful guilt engulfed her. What kind of person was she to have allowed such a thing to happen? Her parents had been more insightful than she had ever imagined—her soul must be naturally wicked. No wonder she felt as though someone was watching her; she probably wore her guilt like a sign around her neck.

"My parents are right," she whispered. "I am damned."

"What was that?" Peter asked, raising his voice to be heard over the clang of the anchor forge. They had just strolled toward the chandlery and now stood in front of the building.

Bridget mustered a smile for him. "Nothing. I just wondered if we might sit for a moment and have a rest."

Peter nodded, leading her a bit farther down the street to a wooden bench that sat in front of a warehouse that handled sail lofts. Bridget removed her bonnet and placed it in her lap, wiping her brow with her fingertips.

"It's so hot today," she commented, fanning herself with her hand. She leaned back on the bench and closed her eyes.

Peter agreed and removed his coat, draping it carefully over one arm before sitting beside her. "Did I tell you I ran into Benjamin this morning?" he said, causing Bridget to gasp in horror.

Peter looked at her curiously. "Whatever is the matter with you? You've been acting odd all morning."

Bridget fanned her face harder, her heart racing like a stallion at the mention of Benjamin. "Truthfully, I'm just feeling a little faint."

"It's probably just the sun," Peter commented. "I agree that it's unusually hot today."

"Yes, that must be it," she agreed. For mercy's sake,

LIGHT A SINGLE CANDLE 79

she had to be calm and stop acting so nervous when Benjamin's name was mentioned.

"Would you like me to take you home now?" Peter asked.

"Home?" she said quickly. "Why would I want to go home?"

"You said you were feeling unwell," he repeated in exasperation. "Bridget, you are positively somewhere else."

"I'm sorry. No, let's just sit for a bit."

He leaned back against the bench, lifting his face to the sun.

"So, how was Benjamin this morning when you ran into him?" she finally asked when he didn't say anything further about the encounter. She hoped her voice conveyed casual interest, even though her nerves were jangling unmercifully.

Peter shaded his eyes from the sun and looked over at her, chuckling. "Looked like our rogue was at it again. He strode down the street staggering as if half-sotted, his hair in complete disarray and his shirt burned and torn to tatters. I jokingly asked him whose husband he had offended, but he wasn't inclined to answer. He was in quite a dark mood, our boy."

"Perhaps he'd been just been working hard," Bridget offered weakly.

Peter laughed. "Oh, come now, Bridget. We both know Benjamin better than that. He's likely busy stirring up the ladies of Salem again and not really caring whom he dallies with."

Bridget felt another sweep of shame so deep that her hands began to tremble. Her bonnet slipped off her lap and rolled onto the sidewalk. As she stood up to get it, she heard an odd scraping noise behind her. She whirled around the instant a wooden crate toppled out of the second-story loft of the warehouse and slammed onto the bench exactly where she had been moments before. The bench collapsed into a heap of wood and splinters. Peter landed hard on the ground before toppling sideways and banging his head against the crate.

Horrified, Bridget glanced up at the warehouse just in time to see a figure disappear from the loft opening.

"Peter," she gasped, helping him come to his feet. "Are you all right?" He staggered a bit groggily and then looked at her in wonder.

"What happened?" he asked as people rushed over to help them. In moments they were surrounded, the excitement of what had just happened drawing a crowd of curious onlookers.

Bridget saw a tall young man pushing his way through the crowd. She recognized him as Spencer Reeves, a friend and a physician-in-training under the tutelage of his father. She raised an arm, waving wildly at him. When he finally got through, she took him gratefully by the arm.

"Spencer, thank God you are here," she said breathlessly. "There's been an accident. A crate fell from the loft and nearly hit Peter. He knocked his head against it. Can you take a look?"

Before Spencer could answer, a bald, burly man rushed out of the warehouse, apologizing profusely.

"I'm sorry, guv'nor," the man said to Peter in a heavy English accent, mopping his considerable forehead with a dirty rag. "This 'ere crate belongs to the warehouse. I 'ave no idea how it fell from the window. We just moved 'em up there this morning."

"I'm certain 'twas just an accident," Bridget said reassuringly. "I'm thankful that no one was seriously harmed."

"No one was harmed?" Peter snapped at the man, gingerly rubbing the bump on his forehead. "What do you call this? How dare you be so careless with your goods, man! Don't you know it's a threat to public safety to stack them so close to an open loft?"

Spencer smoothly stepped between the two men to examine Peter's forehead. "It's just a bump, Peter," he said after a moment. "My professional opinion is that you'll live. You didn't lose consciousness, did you?"

When Peter shook his head, Spencer patted him on the shoulder. "Well, then, be grateful it was nothing more."

Nonetheless, Peter continued to glare at the burly man over Spencer's shoulder. "You are fortunate that I find myself in a favorable mood today or I would see you fined for this," Peter said irritably.

"Come on, Peter," Bridget said, pulling on his arm, hoping to dissuade him from further berating the poor man. "My mother will be waiting for us, and you need to rest."

The crowd began to dissipate, sensing the excitement was over. Still glaring at the burly man, Peter let himself be led away.

"I think my coat is ruined," he said grumpily, brushing off his sleeves and examining the frock. "It was a new one, too."

"Well, I'm just relieved you weren't hurt."

"I could have been killed," he said emphatically, suddenly stopping and pulling her into the shade of a tree. She watched in astonishment as he glanced furtively over his shoulder and up the street before turning back to her.

"What—" she started to say when he abruptly pulled her into his arms and pressed a fervent kiss on her mouth.

His lips were cool and dry. Once she overcame her surprise at his actions, she relaxed, waiting for the same heady sensations she had felt with Benjamin. Instead, the longer he kept his mouth pressed against hers, the more she wished he would stop. In a desperate attempt to kindle some feeling, she threw her arms around his neck and kissed him back with enthusiasm. Still, she felt no heat, no desire.

After a moment, Peter pulled back and Bridget realized he'd gone stiff in her arms.

"What are you doing?" he said, looking at her with something akin to dismay and shock.

"Kissing you, of course," she said, a feeling of dread rising in her stomach. Had she done something wrong?

"When did you become so . . . schooled?"

Her cheeks burned so hot, she thought they might be on fire. "I don't know what you mean."

Peter rubbed his forehead where he had received the bump. "You seemed so eager, but I suppose you were only concerned for my safety. It was a bit forward of me to kiss you on a public street, but seeing how close I just came to death, I hope you will forgive me. I do care so much for you, darling."

Bridget suddenly felt like bursting into tears. "I'm the one who is sorry, Peter. I should not have acted so brazen."

"It's all right," he said, patting her hand. "I assure you, there will be plenty of time for such pleasures once we are in the privacy of our bedchamber. I'm certain you will be a most apt pupil." He rubbed his forehead again and then tucked her arm in the crook of his elbow.

They walked in silence a bit longer before Peter began talking about the wedding preparations. He nattered on about the music and guest list until Bridget no longer listened.

Instead, she tried to swallow the fear that rose in her throat, almost choking her. The kiss had just confirmed it—she had no feelings of passion whatsoever for Peter. In his arms, she felt wooden and cold, almost detached from his embrace.

There had to be something fundamentally wrong with her. How could she not be attracted to her future husband? Peter was good-hearted and kind. Perhaps she somehow wasn't fully appreciating his embrace in the proper manner. Or maybe Peter was simply holding himself back, as a true gentleman would before the wedding.

Yet Bridget knew deep in her heart that these were just excuses. Not one of Peter's kisses had ever held the excitement or promise that Benjamin's had. She had merely to think of Benjamin holding her and a rush of heat warmed her body. Horrified by her thoughts, she turned her head so Peter wouldn't see the guilty expression on her face.

Peter did notice and misunderstood. He chuckled. "My dear, passionate Bridget. Don't be ashamed of such wanton feelings. I hope it's not too ungentlemanly of me to admit I've been told once or twice that my kisses often produce such a response. But I assure you, I'll soon delight in teaching you all of life's lessons."

Bridget still couldn't bring herself to look at him. Passion was not important, she reminded herself. If a wife's duty was to please her husband in that way, then she'd learn how to do it and be glad for the opportunity.

Suddenly, she felt a sweep of anger at Benjamin. If

he hadn't kissed her, she never would have known what she was missing. Why had he done it?

"Is everything all right, Bridget?" Peter asked in concern, and she realized they had stopped and he was studying her face carefully.

"Of course," she answered, trying to smile. Peter patted her affectionately on the shoulder. "Soon these matters will not be so uncomfortable to talk about," he said reassuringly. "I promise you that."

If only she believed his words, Bridget thought miserably.

Once at the Goodwells', Bridget's mother made a big fuss over treating the bump on Peter's head, making him lie down and pressing a cool cloth to it. Bridget was banished to the kitchen to prepare tea and oatcakes and to boil pudding for him.

After Peter had rested and eaten, he finally departed. Bridget excused herself to her room, where she sat on the corner of her bed, holding back tears and wondering with a heavy heart just what her future held now.

At the same time, the Dark One sat in her house, brooding. Bridget Goodwell had been uncharacteristically lucky today. The little witch had a powerful aura about her, but it would not protect her for long. Trouble was brewing in Salem—trouble that hadn't been seen for a century.

For years, Bridget had been nothing more than a potential nuisance, a harmless, unknowing weakling. The Dark One had hardly paid her any heed. But there was a new danger now: the arrival in Salem of a force that threatened the delicate balance that had been maintained for nearly a hundred years.

Drastic measures would have to be taken to preserve things the way they were.

That meant removing the tools that could be used by the new force in town. Bridget Goodwell would have to be the first to go. Her special talent for conjuring fire made her particularly dangerous, regardless of whether or not she had somehow refined it. Although her power ran deep, the girl remained untried, unwitting, and untrained. That would make it easier to dispose of her.

The Dark One stood up. Today's mishap had been an aberration, a mistake borne of a hasty and rash attempt. The next accident to befall the girl would be less spontaneous—better planned, so as not to raise any undue suspicions.

There was little time left for failure.

If all went as planned, there would soon be one less witch in Salem and one less instrument to be used against her. The force would have no weapons with which to fight, and thus could be easily vanquished.

"Thou shalt never break the curse," she muttered. "I am not so easily challenged."

Cheered by such an agreeable thought, the Dark One rubbed her hands together. Triumph would be hers.

Four

Bridget did not sleep well that night and woke just as the sun rose over the horizon. Padding quietly across the floor so as not to wake Sarabeth, she slipped on her robe and perched by the open window.

In the distance, the early-morning mist was rising off the water, a dazzling display against the pinkish-gold tapestry of the Salem sky. Birds twittered happily, and the lulling sound of the incoming tide in the distance created a steady and soothing rhythm.

Bridget closed her eyes, inhaling deeply of the crisp air, taking in the mingled scents of salt, blossoms, and fresh grass. These sights and sounds never failed to calm her and give her courage to face the day.

Standing, she stretched and quickly dressed. If the glorious sunrise was any indication of the weather, Bridget intended to get her chores done early so she might have some time to enjoy the beautiful day.

She hastened into the kitchen, where she breathed life into the banked embers of the large hearth, adding kindling and finally some logs until a cheery fire blazed. Donning an apron, she deftly mixed the ingredients for bread pudding and poured the contents into a small fabric bag. She hooked the bag over the large kettle that hung in the hearth, letting the mixture steam.

She began to hum as she took out a bowl and added flour and water, preparing the crust for the afternoon's meal of battalia pie.

"You are up early," Bridget heard her mother say as she entered the kitchen. Abigail Goodwell put on an apron and stood next to her daughter at the small trundle table where Bridget had begun to work.

"Good morning, Mother," Bridget said as cheerfully as possible, determined to let all that had recently happened between them pass.

Abigail watched as Bridget cracked an egg and carefully separated the yolk from the white. "You seem in a good humor today."

Bridget tucked an errant strand of hair behind her ear. "God has given us a beautiful day. That's enough to make anyone thankful."

"Indeed it is," Abigail agreed, measuring a cup of milk and adding it to the mixture. "I wasn't certain your mood would be so tempered after yesterday's near-disastrous accident."

Bridget shrugged, carefully spooning out a dollop of butter. "God watched over us. Thankfully, no one was seriously harmed."

"Yes, blessed be His name. All the same, 'twas rather unusual of Peter to come by so unexpectedly."

Bridget stole a sideways glance at her mother. Her mother wished to know what had prompted Peter's visit.

Bridget stirred the mixture briskly with the wooden spoon. "We had some matters to discuss about the wedding."

"So timely they couldn't wait until a properly scheduled visit could be arranged? Why, the house wasn't adequately cleaned and I had nothing of substance in the house to offer him to drink or eat."

"I'm certain Peter didn't notice, Mother."

"Of course he noticed. He's just too polite to say anything." She pinched some salt between her fingers and added it to the bowl. "I presume the matter with the wedding was thus resolved."

"It was," Bridget replied, offering no further details.

Abigail frowned, clearly unsatisfied by the short answer. To her credit, she didn't press the matter and instead pulled out a loaf of sweetbread and began slicing it into several pieces.

"There is another matter your father and I need to discuss with you in regard to the wedding," she said.

Bridget stopped stirring and looked over at her mother. "What matter is that?"

"Your wedding gown. Due to some unforeseen expenses, your father and I are unable to meet Betty Corwin's final payment requests for it."

"What unforeseen expenses?" Bridget asked, the wooden spoon clattering in the bowl as she dropped it.

"Your father purchased a new cloth for the altar. As a result, we cannot afford to pay for the gown." Her mother calmly and artfully arranged the slices of sweetbread on a platter, as if she hadn't just made a momentous announcement.

Bridget stared at her mother with mouth open. "B-but how . . ." she stammered, not certain what to say next.

"Oh, Bridget, leave it to you to be so dramatic about the whole matter," her mother sighed in exasperation. "You will ask Peter for the coin, of course."

Bridget's mouth worked soundlessly before she

managed to gasp, "Peter? You want me to ask Peter for coin?"

"Of course. He can afford it."

"No," Bridget said instantly. "I won't ask him to pay for my gown."

Her mother stopped arranging the sweetbread and looked at Bridget in astonishment. "What did you say?"

Bridget took a calming breath. "I said I will not ask Peter to pay for my gown."

"And why ever not?"

"Because . . . because we are not yet wed. I can't just ask him for money."

Her mother snorted. "The wedding is only a formality. You are his betrothed. He'd gladly give it to you, and we both know he has coin to spare. Ask him for it."

"No," Bridget repeated emphatically, shocking herself by her adamant reaction. Peter did indeed have the money, but there was something else at stake here—pride. *Her* pride. She wouldn't go crawling to Peter before the wedding, asking for money.

"I didn't want such an extravagant gown in the first place. Peter insisted."

"All the more reason to have him pay for it."

"No, Mother. The gown is my responsibility."

"Pride is a sin, Bridget," her mother warned, wagging a finger. "You would be wise to free yourself of that transgression before joining with your husband."

"Perhaps, but I don't need to ask Peter for the money," she replied quietly. "I will earn the coin myself."

"You?" her mother laughed. "And how do you intend to earn it? The wedding is in less than three weeks."

"Helping Widow Bayley," Bridget said, surprised at how quickly her mind had formed a plan. "She's always trying to pay me for the chores I do around her cottage."

Her mother slammed the flat part of her hand against the table, shaking the bowl and cups. "Have you truly lost your mind? You spend too much time with that old witch as it is."

"She's not a witch. She's a kind old woman in need of assistance and company. Besides, she's one of Father's parishioners, and no one else has stepped forward to help her."

"She's a fright, an oddity. Living alone out there in that old cottage all by herself."

"She's a kind and fascinating woman. You aren't being fair."

"Don't take that tone with me, Bridget. Pride is at the root of all of this. What shame is there in asking your husband to pay for your wedding gown?"

Bridget held her tongue, trying to calm herself. For once, just once, she wanted to have a composed and rational discussion with her mother.

"Regardless of what you say, Peter is not my husband yet. And it's not just a matter of pride, Mother. It's just . . ." She hesitated, searching for the right words. "It's just that I want to enter this holy union having brought something of my own."

"You are tempting fate," her mother said quietly. "Peter is the one man in Salem who will take you. He'll be greatly displeased if the gown is not ready and paid for in a timely fashion."

"It will be ready," she said, praying she was right.

"It had better. I would not blame Peter for being furious at your impertinence."

Bridget felt the hot flush of her temper and fought

the urge to shout. "You may think of me as you wish, but I will *not* ask Peter for money to pay for my gown," she said, ripping off her apron and tossing it over the back of a nearby chair. "Even if that means I have to get married unclad."

Her mother gasped in horror. "You have gone mad."

"To the contrary, Mother. I feel more sane than I have in a long time. It's the first time during the entire engagement that I've done something I've wanted to do. In fact, I'm going to see Widow Bayley right now."

With those words, Bridget stormed out of the house and walked quickly down the street, keeping her head down so she wouldn't have to greet anyone. When she'd gone far enough away from the house, she ducked into an alley, her fists clenched so tightly at her sides that her fingernails bit into the soft flesh of her hands.

She took a quick glance around to be certain she was alone in the alley, and then let her anger out. She ignited a small pile of rubbish in a burst of heat so intense the refuse seemed simply to dissolve into black ash without even taking the time to burst into flames and burn.

Spent, Bridget leaned back against the cold stone wall and covered her face with her hands, shaking. What was wrong with her? How was it that she could never manage to have a single rational conversation with her own mother? Was she so wicked that she'd be denied this sacred relationship for the rest of her life?

For a moment, Bridget sincerely tried to imagine asking Peter for the coin to pay for the gown. But it felt so wrong, so humiliating, that she knew no matter how hard she might try to rationalize it, she'd never do it.

After allowing herself to wallow in self-pity for a few minutes longer, she finally stood, brushing off her skirts. Time was wasting and she had chores to do and money to earn. Better not to waste a moment more in useless and unproductive despair.

Bridget strode out of town and along the dusty road toward Widow Bayley's small cottage. It was about a ten-minute walk to the widow's place, and soon the warm rays of the morning sun were making themselves felt. So far, the weather had been unusually warm—not that she minded, it just seemed odd to jump from winter to summer with so little cool spring weather in between.

Presently the cottage came into view. Bridget loved the cozy dwelling and its seclusion from town. Close enough for convenience, yet far enough to provide what Bridget considered an enviable privacy.

Not that Widow Bayley had anything to hide. Unlike herself, the old woman certainly had no unusual propensities or supernatural talents. At least, none that Bridget had ever discerned, and she'd been visiting the woman for years. In fact, Bridget found all the gossip about town that the widow was a witch to be highly amusing. Despite being blind, the widow had the sharpest and most godly mind of anyone Bridget had ever known. In many ways, she had been more of a mother to her than Abigail.

Bridget opened the wooden gate and walked up to the front door. She rapped twice.

"Come in, Bridget," she heard the old woman call out.

As she opened the door, a white cat slipped out through the door and rubbed between Bridget's legs.

"Hello, Francesca," Bridget said, reaching down to scratch the cat's chin. "How are you this morning?"

The cat purred and allowed herself to be scratched a bit more before darting off into the yard in search of adventure.

Bridget stepped into the house, leaving the door ajar in case Francesca decided to return. The widow sat in her favorite chair facing the hearth, her back toward the door. Bridget could see the long flow of silver hair, tied back neatly at the nape of her neck.

"How did you know it was me?" Bridget asked.

Widow Bayley laughed gaily. "Who else visits me in this old place?"

Bridget walked over by the chair and patted the elderly woman's gnarled hand. "Mary Goodwin brings you bread three times a week, and I also understand Sarah Parsons has been by to help with some of your mending."

"Yes, that's true, largely thanks to your badgering. But none come as often as you, Bridget, bless your soul. I am thankful for your help, as well as for the company."

"The pleasure is mine," Bridget said, and she meant it sincerely.

Sometimes the cottage felt like home. It was the one place she could be herself, faults and all. She didn't have to be on her best behavior or act like a proper lady. She could engage in lively, intelligent conversation and not mindless chatter about seams and recipes.

Smiling, she looked around the room. The cottage had rough-hewn ceiling beams and walls of unpainted pinewood. Four small windows of leaded, diamond-shaped glass had been placed evenly along the walls, providing plenty of light and warmth.

A linen curtain hanging from the ceiling separated a small area where the widow slept on a small trundle bed. A square table and four chairs took up another corner of the room, and on the center of the table sat the most exquisite flower arrangement. Bridget knew the widow had arranged it herself, but how she had managed to do so without the benefit of sight was certainly a wonder.

The giant hearth provided heat and served as the widow's cooking fire. A black kettle now bubbled with a delicious-smelling concoction. After inhaling a deep breath, Bridget determined that the widow intended to have beef stew for a meal today.

"Come and sit for a moment," the widow urged, waving her to a nearby chair. "Tell me, how are the preparations for the wedding coming along?"

The sigh slipped out before Bridget could stop it. "Just fine."

The widow cocked her head and frowned. "It doesn't sound fine to me. What's wrong, dear?"

"Nothing, really."

"Yet you are troubled."

Bridget leaned back in the chair, studying the widow's face as she had done countless times before. The thin, frail face served little more than to frame a pair of round, remarkably blue eyes as bright as a summer sky. Although she could not physically see, Bridget often had the feeling that the widow observed more than anyone she'd ever known.

"I find it fascinating that you can sense things like that simply from the tone of someone's voice."

"We all make adjustments to overcome the difficulties God hands us. Wouldn't you agree?"

"I do."

"Come, now, won't you tell me what's troubling you?"

Bridget fiddled with her skirts. "I had a disagreement with my mother."

"I'm sorry to hear that. What about?"

"My parents do not have enough money to pay for my wedding gown, and I refused to ask Peter for the coin."

"Why?" the widow asked curiously.

"My mother says it's because I have too much pride."

"What do you say?"

Bridget looked down at her hands. "I suppose she is right."

"Are you certain that is all? Might you not be reconsidering your decision to wed Peter?"

Her pulse began to beat erratically. "Reconsidering? No, of course not. I simply wish to contribute something to this wedding."

"You would like to pay for the gown yourself, then."

She nodded. "I know it sounds foolish, but I want to enter this union with Peter without owing him anything."

"I understand."

"You do?" she said in surprise.

"I do. I hope you will let me help by paying you for the chores you do around here. It's the least I can do for all your help."

"I don't help you because I expect to be paid," Bridget protested.

"I know you don't. For years you've refused any coin I've offered. Nonetheless, this time I will insist."

Bridget felt the familiar tug in her chest, the one

that told her Widow Bayley was a part of her heart, if not her family.

"Truthfully, I hoped that you would say that," she said. "But now that you have, I don't think I can accept it. It doesn't feel right."

"Rubbish. Elias left me more coin than I can possibly spend. I don't have any children and I deeply appreciate your assistance with the things I can no longer do myself. But more than that, I enjoy your friendship and your kindness. You are a special young woman, Bridget, with a good and kind heart. I insist you take the coin."

"Only if you will consider it a loan. I promise to pay you back somehow."

"You have already earned it. There is no need to repay me."

"I must."

The widow fell silent for a moment and then nodded. "All right, as you wish. Now, let's have no more talk of money. Instead, shall we take a stroll in the garden and enjoy some of this remarkably beautiful weather?"

Bridget agreed and stood, picking up a basket on a nearby table and placing it over her elbow. Then, she offered the widow her arm, even though she didn't need it to find her way. They left the cottage, circling around back to the garden. Carrots, tomatoes, beans, and herbs grew in remarkable abundance as if cultivated in Eden.

Bridget led the widow to a wooden bench partially sheltered by a giant oak tree. The widow sat down carefully and closed her eyes, lifting her wrinkled face to the sun.

Bridget knelt on the ground, grabbing a handful of the thick black soil and letting it fall through her fingers. She marveled, as she always did, at how healthy and rich the soil felt here. Taking a breath of the air fragrant with blooming flowers, Bridget inspected the tomatoes on a nearby vine and picked a ripe one.

"I heard Benjamin is back in town," the widow suddenly said, nearly causing Bridget to drop it.

"Yes, he . . . ah, came by to say hello just the other day," she stammered, thankful the widow couldn't see the telltale flush of guilt that spread across her face at the mention of his name.

"He came back for the wedding, I presume."

"That's what he said."

The widow kept her face up toward the sun. "Benjamin is such a good boy—or should I say man? He's a handsome one, though, isn't he? I always hear the girls titter and giggle when he's around. Nonetheless, he always has a kind word for me when I'm in town. It must be very exciting for you to have the wedding just weeks away."

Bridget wondered at the odd way she had leaped between Benjamin and the wedding, and she stirred uneasily. "It is exciting, even though a good deal remains to be accomplished. Naturally, no detail is too small."

"Naturally." The widow paused for a moment and then turned her head toward Bridget. "You know, dear, in all the years you've been coming to see me, you've talked very little of Peter. Tell me what he's like."

Bridget sat back on her heels and rubbed her nose with the back of her hand. "Well, as you know, Peter is from a prominent family. After his exams, he'll be a practicing lawyer, and later, perhaps even a judge like his father."

"That's all very grand. But what is he really like?"

"He's a good man, hard-working, sensible, and stable. All fine qualities for a husband."

"Indeed."

"I'm very fortunate he will marry me."

"I see."

"After all, the daughter of a reverend doesn't have much to offer someone like Peter."

"I believe you have a lot to offer, Bridget," she said, a gentle reproof in her tone.

"I meant in terms of a dowry or even prestige."

"You would certainly be a political asset if his interest ever led him to politics."

Bridget looked at the widow, surprised by her intuition. "Yes, I suppose I would."

"And you and Peter have been friends for years."

She smiled wistfully. "Peter, Benjamin, and I were inseparable as children. It was Benjamin who usually led us into one merry adventure after another. Except that he never failed to charm his way out of trouble. Peter and I always seemed to take the blame. You see, Benjamin has this remarkable ability to talk his way out of anything." She laughed at the memory. "I learned a lot from him, but nonetheless, I couldn't match his ability to appear so innocent to everyone."

"You seem quite fond of him."

"Of course; he is my betrothed, after all."

"I meant Benjamin."

Bridget blushed hotly. "He is dear to me as well. I've known him for so long. But sometimes he can be so infuriating."

The widow fell silent and then returned her face to the sun. Bridget stood, brushed off her skirts, and sat down on the bench next to the widow.

"Do you mind if I ask you something?" Bridget asked.

"You may ask me anything, child."

"Did you love your husband? I mean, at first . . . before you wed him."

Widow Bayley's expression softened and Bridget realized how pretty she must have been when she was younger.

"I loved Elias from the moment I met him. Unquestionably."

"But how did you know it was love?"

"You just know, dear. Your heart beats a little faster every time you see him, and sometimes it feels as though your stomach has a thousand butterflies trying to get out when he's near. I missed him terribly when he was away, and I never ceased wanting him near me. When he kissed me, 'twas like nothing I'd ever experienced before. The world itself seemed to stop, and nothing else mattered but him and me."

Bridget thought of Benjamin's kiss and a small lump caught in her throat. "Did he ever make you . . . well, angry?"

The widow laughed. "More than once, I assure you. That's the nature of passion, Bridget. But he also treated me with respect and tenderness. He made me feel gloriously alive—more alive than I had ever felt with anyone else. No one knew me as well as Elias, and yet he loved me for who I was—faults and all."

"But how could you be certain this was love?"

The widow reached out and patted the top of Bridget's hand. "In order to understand love, you must listen to your heart. What does your heart say, Bridget?"

Bridget froze. "What do you mean?"

"What does your heart tell you about Peter?"

Bridget wiped her brow with her fingertips, suddenly feeling uncomfortably warm. "My heart beats faster when I see him. He's intelligent, kind, and witty, and I know he loves me. He'd never do anything to hurt me."

"And what of Benjamin?"

Bridget's eyes flew open. The question startled her deeply, as if the widow had been able to look into her soul and see the truth lying there. And if her feelings were so obvious that a blind woman could see them, then perhaps she was in more difficulty than she suspected.

"What about Benjamin?" she asked, trying to keep her voice calm.

"What does your heart say about him?"

"What an odd, not to mention scandalous, question."

The widow folded her fragile fingers and placed them in her lap. "Are you afraid of the question, child?"

"Why should I be afraid of a simple question?" Bridget said primly. But she was afraid. Terrified.

"Why, indeed?" the widow asked softly.

Bridget looked down at her hands. They were shaking uncontrollably. "I'm not afraid of the question," she said truthfully and then lowered her voice. "I'm afraid of the answer."

The widow sighed. "Why should you be afraid of what's in your heart?"

Bridget clasped her trembling hands together. "Because it frightens me. I love Peter and I'm going to marry him. It's the sensible thing to do. I have no time for foolish romantic dreams."

"There is no dream if love is not in your heart," the widow said quietly.

Bridget closed her eyes. "What happens if you don't listen to your heart?" she asked softly.

"I don't know," the widow answered. "For most people, I suppose that is their way of life."

Bridget opened her eyes, looking intently at the widow. "But for you?"

"I have always listened to my heart, child. There are some people who can do no less."

"Do you think I am one of those people?"

The widow lifted a silver eyebrow. "Are you?"

Bridget considered for a long moment. "I have neither the luxury nor the courage to follow my heart. Besides, what is the purpose if what is in your heart is unattainable?"

"There is peace," the widow answered quietly. "Contentment. A sense of being true to yourself. Some would say it is following your destiny."

"I know my destiny," Bridget replied firmly. "I'm going to wed Peter and have a home and family."

"If that is what you want, that is what you will get. We forge our own destinies, Bridget."

Bridget swallowed hard, looking down at the ground. "Perhaps, but at what cost?" she asked softly. "At what point does the heart command one's destiny?"

The widow shrugged. "That, child, is something only you can answer."

"I suppose that means I already have the answer."

"Perhaps you do," the widow said in a manner that caused Bridget to wonder if she truly did.

Five

Benjamin paused at the Holton doorstep, debating whether to knock or turn around and go home. Guilt and regret had formed a hard ball in his stomach. He felt it was only right that he confess to Peter about the kiss, or at least determine a way to make it right. He lifted his hand to knock but lowered it again. Exasperated with himself, he let out a loud sigh.

"Do it or go home, Hawkes," he said aloud. Yet he still did nothing.

Hell and damnation. He blamed this indecisiveness on Bridget. Only she could make him so daft and cause him to act like a complete imbecile.

As it was, he hadn't been back in Salem for a full day before he rushed over to see her, playing a prank on her as if they were still children. Then he'd fully intended to apologize for what he'd done, but instead had invaded her bedchamber, dragged her into his arms, and kissed her like an adolescent thirsting for his first sexual experience. Imbecile, indeed.

He rubbed his temples to calm the throbbing headache. He'd barely slept last night. He'd had the devil of a time falling asleep, tossing and turning, unable to put the kiss out of his mind. When he'd finally fallen into a restless slumber, he dreamed of her.

Dreamed that he'd held her in his arms and she'd been willing and pliant under his passionate ministrations. When he awoke, he was soaked in sweat, the bedsheets tangled about him.

He still didn't know what had possessed him to kiss her. One minute they were arguing as they had done a hundred times before, and the next, they were entwined in a heated tangle of mouths and limbs.

If he admitted the truth to himself, he'd felt something shift within him as soon as he'd entered her bedchamber and seen her dancing about with that exquisite nightgown. A subtle yet tangible tightening in his chest. Now when he thought about it, perhaps instinctively everything he'd done, everything he'd said to her from that moment on had been moving toward provoking a kiss, even if he hadn't been fully aware of it at the time. Then once he had her in his arms and had a taste of her, he'd surprised himself at how quickly he forgot everything except holding her and wanting her. When she'd responded with a passion and enthusiasm so typical of her, he'd lost any shred of control he might have had. It had been the most incredible kiss he'd ever had—astonishing, since he'd had innumerable.

So what in the devil was he to do now? He'd just kissed the hell out of his best friend's fiancée and now stood on his doorstep debating whether he should confess or just let matters lie. If he knew Peter, he'd be better off just forgetting about the entire incident. Peter would be rightfully furious, but Bridget would be the one to suffer. God knew, he didn't want to do anything more to hurt her. He'd done enough of that lately. But the thought of deceiving Peter left a bitter taste in his mouth. Honor in this particular case was a double-edged sword, because whichever way he decided, he'd hurt someone.

He scowled. How ironic that he'd gone to see Bridget yesterday with the intention of apologizing and had nearly ravished her instead. Now he needed to apologize for that as well, but he feared what he would do next given another moment alone with her. No, she'd be best served if he simply respected her wishes and just stayed away.

Today he'd simply chat with Peter and make certain the wedding preparations were moving along smoothly. It was a good time since Peter was alone. Earlier, while sitting on the porch and debating whether or not to approach his friend, he'd seen both Peter's parents leave. Now would be the perfect time for a casual visit. Benjamin could determine how Peter was faring and offer to lend a hand if it were needed. He'd see to it personally that Bridget had a perfect wedding day. It was the least he could do for her.

He raised his hand and knocked. In moments, a young maidservant with pale blond hair opened the door.

"Good morn to you, Mister Hawkes," she said, her face breaking into a wide smile.

"Good morning," he replied. "I've come to see the young master of the house. Is he awake yet?"

"I believe so, but he's yet to come down. Would you like to come in? I shall announce you," she said as Benjamin stepped inside.

"No need," he said, heading for the stairs. "I know the way."

He climbed the stairs two at a time and then froze when he reached the landing. Peter stood farther along the corridor, leaning against the wall to his bedchamber and nuzzling the neck of a buxom young maidservant. She giggled and Peter turned his head, kissing her long and hard on the mouth while another hand slipped beneath her bodice and brazenly fondled a breast.

For a moment, both were so preoccupied with the embrace that neither noticed Benjamin standing at the top of the stairs. Then the maidservant caught sight of him and quickly pulled away, adjusting her bodice and smoothing down her skirts. Peter looked over in alarm, then relaxed visibly when he saw it was Benjamin.

"Well, hello," he said, straightening. "It is an unexpected surprise to see you here so early."

Benjamin simply stared at Peter, a fierce, powerful rage rising inside him. He had a compelling urge to walk down the corridor and smack the smirk right off Peter's face.

Tightly reining in his anger, he instead turned his attention to the girl. She smiled at first, giving him a mildly flirtatious look, but retreated when she saw the fury in his eyes.

"If that will be all, sir," she said, glancing questioningly at Peter.

Peter nodded and she walked past Benjamin on the landing, careful to keep her eyes deferentially lowered to him. All the same, Benjamin caught the quick wink she threw Peter over her shoulder before she disappeared down the stairway.

Peter adjusted his shirt. "Well, it is quite an unexpected surprise to see you. Let's go down to the parlor."

Benjamin headed down first without a word, with Peter following. He refused to sit and waited until Peter sank onto the settee before speaking.

"What in the devil do you think you are doing?"

he finally said, his voice sounding remarkably calm, although he felt close to committing an act of serious violence.

Peter looked perplexed. "Pardon me?"

"The girl. What were you doing?"

Peter stared at Benjamin for a moment in surprise and then chuckled. "Need I really explain it to you?"

"You are to be wed in less than three weeks."

Peter lifted an eyebrow. "All the more reason to seek a little relief from the tension, wouldn't you agree? It was just a bit of harmless flirtation."

"I didn't see anything harmless in what you were doing."

Peter laughed. "What? A lesson in morality from Salem's most infamous rake? Are you jesting?"

Benjamin strode across the room, grabbing Peter by the front of the shirt and hauling him to his feet. "This is no jest, damn you. This is Bridget we are talking about."

Peter struggled in alarm, trying to free himself from Benjamin's grasp. "I know quite well to whom I'm betrothed. Now get your hands off me."

Benjamin shook him hard once and then let go, sending Peter stumbling backward into the settee, landing on his derriere with a hard thump.

"Do you have any idea how hurt she'd be if she discovered your little dalliance with the maidservant?" Benjamin ground out.

Peter shrugged, fingering his collar, but Benjamin noticed he was visibly shaken. His face had reddened and he breathed unsteadily. "She'll get used to it like every woman does."

"She's not every woman."

"No, she's not. She's a lusty woman in need of a vigorous man like myself to keep her satisfied. In fact,

I got a hint of her true passion when I kissed her just yesterday. I must say it surprised the hell out of me. It's almost like she'd been rehearsing for the wedding night."

Benjamin took a step back in stunned surprise, guilt rushing through him like an unleashed river. He opened his mouth to say something when an unexpected stab of jealousy ripped into his gut. Peter had held Bridget in his arms just hours after the two of them had shared the most incredible kiss of his life?

The image of Bridget in Peter's arms infuriated him. As much as he wanted to, he couldn't shake the irrational jealousy that clawed at his throat. Even worse, he worried about how devastated Bridget would be to learn of Peter's indiscretions with the maidservant.

"You saw Bridget yesterday? Why?" Benjamin asked, even as he realized the absurdity of the question.

"To discuss some wedding matters, of course. What the devil is the matter with everyone lately? First Bridget is unusually distracted and doesn't hear a word I'm saying. Next a crate falls out of the sky, nearly killing me, and then my best friend barges in on me, berating me for engaging in a bit of harmless fun. Has all of Salem gone mad?"

"A crate fell out of the sky?" Benjamin repeated in surprise.

"Yes, it was the damnedest thing. Bridget and I were resting on a bench after a pleasant stroll through town when the blasted thing simply fell out of a window and nearly crushed me."

"My God. Was Bridget harmed?"

"Fortunately, no. She'd just risen from the bench a moment before the crate landed. As it was, I was only slightly injured. Got a hard knock on the head, though."

"Thank goodness Bridget is safe."

Peter nodded thoughtfully. "Yes, and now I realize what this is all about. You are still trying to protect her, aren't you?"

Benjamin narrowed his eyes. "And if I were?"

"We are no longer children, Benjamin. Bridget will be my wife, not yours. She is no longer your concern."

Benjamin met the gaze with a challenge of his own. "She'll always be my concern," he said quietly. "And she trusts you. You will treat her accordingly."

"Of course I will. She'll be my wife, after all. Anyway, I assure you, in terms of any future dalliances, I will conduct them with the utmost discretion in order to spare her feelings. I think that is being more than accommodating."

Benjamin stared at him, wondering if, despite their many years of friendship, he really knew the man. Without saying a word, he walked over to the window, pulling the heavy velvet drape aside and staring out moodily.

"What's got into you anyway?" Peter said, rising from the settee but keeping a good distance away from Benjamin. "You've been in a foul mood ever since you set foot off that ship."

When Benjamin didn't answer, Peter sighed. "Look. I understand that you are fond of Bridget and that she's like a sister to you. But she's no angel, either. If you could only know what I've been through with her these past three years, working to fashion her into a proper woman. She's made progress, but nonetheless, she's still far too independent, temperamental, and opinionated for my taste. We both know I'm doing her a favor by wedding her. Try to see this from my point of view, old friend."

Benjamin stared out the window for a moment more before turning to face Peter. "I think I just have," he said simply.

After leaving Peter, Benjamin strode next door to his own house. He sat down on the porch steps and picked up his sketchbook.

"Well, that went damn well, Benjamin," he said aloud. "Jolly good of you to smooth things out for everyone."

He resisted the urge to hit his head against the porch post. For God's sake, he'd visited Peter with the sole intention of easing things for Bridget, and instead had nearly pummeled him. Was he able to do anything right lately?

Frowning, Benjamin began sketching, his pencil racing across the paper. He needed to put his thoughts into order. Somehow, he'd become too involved, too close to the impending nuptials of his friends.

Peter was right. They were no longer an inseparable trio. Marriage was a contract between two people, not three. Peter and Bridget were adults who had made a commitment to wed and spend the rest of their lives together. He had no right to interfere with that pact, no matter how much he cared about them.

The best thing Benjamin could do for his friends was to stand aside and simply be happy for them. The next time he saw Peter, he'd behave like a true friend—jovial and completely uninterested in the personal nature of his relationship with Bridget. Peter would come around quickly; he always had before.

The hard part would be mending his relationship with Bridget.

He desperately needed to apologize for kissing her the way he had. He didn't want to leave that matter hanging between them, tarnishing a friendship he still held dear. Regardless of what had transpired between them, she was still his best friend. He'd be damned if he'd let a stupid mistake on his part ruin something that meant so much to him.

Sighing, he looked down at his drawing. Somehow he was not surprised that he'd drawn Bridget's face again. This time, however, she wasn't smiling. Instead, he'd drawn her with a smoky, sensuous expression on her face, similar to the one he'd seen while kissing her.

He shook his head in wonder, remembering the way his shirt had seemed inexplicably to burst into flames simply by being near her. It had been the way his entire body felt, too. He couldn't ever remember feeling so powerfully aroused. Thankfully, the arrival of her parents had stopped them where they were. He knew without a doubt he would have taken their embrace further if they had not been interrupted.

He thought of Peter fondling the maidservant and swore under his breath. He really was no better than Peter, and perhaps worse. Peter had engaged in a dalliance with a maidservant, but he had nearly ravished—not to mention nearly ruined—an engaged woman. Bridget had done nothing to deserve his crude advance. He owed her a civilized apology, and then he'd step back for good. The sooner he set things straight with her, the better he'd feel.

Determined, he closed the sketchbook and stood. Walking out the gate and toward the Goodwells' house, he carefully rehearsed what he would say once he had her out of earshot of the others. He would be careful not to stand too close and certainly not to touch her. He'd keep his tone nonconfrontational and mature. He wanted only to make certain she understood how terribly sorry he was and how he'd never let it happen again. Then, he'd wish her well with Peter, and with a fond smile he'd leave, keeping his distance until after the wedding.

The more he thought about it, the more he liked it. Damn, it was a good plan, and he fully intended to stand by it.

Feeling increasingly more cheerful, he approached the Goodwell house and knocked on the door. Abigail answered, looking startled to see him. She fussed with her apron and kerchief a bit before opening the door and ushering him in.

Benjamin made up a story about Peter's asking him to consult with Bridget on a wedding matter.

"Bridget isn't here," Abigail told him.

Benjamin heard the tension in her voice, wondering if something had happened anew between the two of them. Then, for a horrified instant, it occurred to him that she might have learned of his advances on Bridget in her bedchamber. He looked at her in guilty shock, having no idea how he would extricate himself from such a dreadful situation, when he realized that Abigail looked at him in puzzlement, not judgment.

"I see Bridget is not home," he said, his words tumbling out in a relieved rush. "Do you know where she might be? It's rather important."

Abigail cocked her head, clearly bewildered by his odd behavior. "I'm afraid to admit it, but I fear she's likely gone out to Widow Bayley's cottage again. Shall I tell her that you came by?"

"That would be kind of you."

"Please do come in and sit for a while," she offered. "Sarabeth will be down in a moment."

Benjamin shook his head. "No, thank you," he said. "I couldn't possibly intrude again. Besides, I told my father I'd review some of the ship ledgers with him. I appreciate your generous offer of hospitality, though, and please give Sarabeth my kindest regards."

Abigail flushed with pleasure. True to his word, Benjamin stayed only a moment longer, fearing he might nonetheless be trapped into a longer visit if Sarabeth indeed came downstairs. Issuing a hasty farewell, he exited the Goodwell home.

Still thinking about Bridget, Benjamin headed in the direction of his house, when he suddenly realized that he would have the perfect opportunity to speak to Bridget alone if he could catch her on the way home from old Widow Bayley's place. Even if she still remained at the widow's cottage, surely he'd be able to manage a moment alone to speak to her privately.

Nonetheless, he hesitated in his tracks. He was not one for hearsay, but tales abounded about the old woman. She was considered an oddity in Salem, eccentric and witchlike. Benjamin didn't typically pay attention to such gossip, but then again, he had never considered going out to her cottage alone, either.

He shook his head in disgust. Bridget had been visiting the widow for years without any ill effect. How could an old, blind woman possibly be any threat? Widow Bayley was naught more than a lonely old woman, one Bridget had admirably befriended. It shamed him that he had never done the same.

Determinedly he switched directions and headed out of town toward the widow's cottage. The walk provided a pleasant respite, and Benjamin found it both calmed and focused him. The roadway was bordered with daisies and bright yellow buttercups, the breeze fresh and stiff. By the time he reached the gate of the small cottage, he felt positively relaxed. He paused to marvel at the lush array of colorful and lovely flowers that grew around the homestead, almost seeming to have been borne of magic. He chuckled in amusement as a spirited white cat chased around the meadow after a butterfly.

Benjamin opened the gate and strolled up to the door. As he knocked, he realized the door was ajar.

"Who's there?" he heard a female voice call out from inside.

He cleared his throat. "Benjamin Hawkes," he said loudly. "I apologize for the unexpected visit, but I am looking for Bridget Goodwell and heard that she might be out here visiting you."

"Come in," he heard the voice call out cheerfully. "I've been expecting you."

Puzzled, Benjamin pushed open the door and stepped into a comfortable and cozy room. A merry fire crackled in the large hearth, and a delicious smell rose from the black kettle hanging over the flames. A sturdy table of pine stood in one corner, atop which sat a cheery display of flowers.

The widow sat in an oversized chair, her back to him and her long silver hair loose and tumbling about her shoulders. A thick blanket had been draped over her lap and knees, her hands folded primly on top. She turned her head slightly toward him.

He took a step forward and she waved a gnarled hand in his direction. "Do come and sit a while," she said warmly. "I don't often get many visitors."

"I'm looking for Bridget," he answered politely. "I didn't intend to intrude."

"You aren't intruding. Please do sit down."

Benjamin finally complied, sitting stiffly in a chair directly across from her. "I presume Bridget is no longer here."

"You presume correctly. She left just a short while ago."

Benjamin frowned. "That's odd. I didn't pass her on the way to your cottage."

"She must not have gone directly home."

That indeed was typical of Bridget. "I suppose not."

The widow smiled and Benjamin realized she must have been quite a lovely woman in her prime. Her cheekbones were high and delicate, her nose straight and her mouth wide. Her remarkable blue eyes stared straight at him unblinking, but she cocked her head in his direction when he spoke, giving him the impression that she could see him.

"Bridget is a wonderful girl, you know," she said quietly. "You are lucky to have known her friendship, as am I."

"I will not disagree with you."

"I don't know what I would have done without her aid for the past few years."

"Aid?"

The widow looked surprised. "She didn't tell you she helps me with the chores I can no longer do? Merciful heavens, that girl must not have a boastful bone in her body."

Benjamin felt a curious stab of surprise and shame. He'd simply assumed Bridget had visited the old woman because she provided an interesting diversion from her troubled home life. Now he realized how important Bridget's visits were to the widow, not only because they provided much-needed company, but because the old woman was likely unable to handle many of the more physically demanding chores. He'd never given it any thought before, but how like Bridget that she had.

His eyes narrowing, he looked more carefully and thoroughly about the room. At once he saw several problems with the roof and walls that could use a man's hand. A decision was made.

"You are nearly out of wood and kindling," he said, standing. "Shall I bring some in from outside?"

The widow smiled. "That would be kind of you. There's a stack behind the house."

Benjamin left the cottage, and after stopping to scratch the white cat's ears, he carried in an armful of firewood, stacking it near the hearth.

"There isn't much left. Who chops it for you?"

The widow sighed. "Aaron Bickford aided me until he fell ill last month. Bridget has been trying to find someone else to help out, but so far without success."

"I'll do it," he offered. "I noticed several other things that need fixing that I can help with as well. If you would allow me to do so."

"That is kind of you, but certainly you are a busy young man with many more important things to do."

"Nonsense," he said firmly. "I really would like to help."

"I would be ever so grateful," she replied beaming.

"Splendid. Well, then it's settled. I'm not appropriately dressed for such work today, and I'll need to bring back some tools to work with. Would it be acceptable for me to come tomorrow morning?"

"That would be fine. Bless your good heart, Benjamin."

He stood and on impulse took her cold hand and pressed it to his lips. "It has been my pleasure," he said and sincerely meant it.

He walked to the door, pausing at the threshold.

"By the way, you said something odd upon my arrival," Benjamin remarked. "You said that you were expecting me. What did you mean by that?"

The widow turned in her chair and Benjamin saw a secretive smile cross her face. "Nothing, really. Just the fanciful conjecture of an old woman."

Benjamin shrugged at the mysterious reply and stepped out of the cottage, leaving the door ajar as he had found it. He unlatched the gate and walked out, carefully closing it behind him. However, instead of heading home, he turned in the opposite direction.

If he knew Bridget, he knew just where to find her.

Six

Bridget sat in her favorite spot between the two large boulders at Rock's Point, reflecting on her future. The wind had picked up and provided a nice breeze to counter the hot sun that beat down on her shoulders. As usual, she had left the house without her bonnet, which meant that in the morning she'd have a fresh sprinkle of freckles across the bridge of her nose and cheeks. That, in turn, meant another lecture from her mother. Sighing, she picked up a stone and tossed it down the cliff, listening to it tumble to the bottom.

She could hear the waves stroking the beach in a steady rhythm. Usually the sound calmed her, but today it only served to agitate. She had delayed going home from Widow Bayley's, knowing she'd most likely get into another quarrel with her mother about the wedding gown.

The small bag of coins Widow Bayley had given her felt heavy in the little bag tied around her waist, and Bridget felt a flush of dissatisfaction that her mother made her feel so wicked for wanting to pay for the gown herself. Peter had so far financed everything to do with the wedding and, as a result, had taken control of every aspect. The wedding gown was her sole contribution, and as insignificant as it seemed in the larger scheme of things, it was hers alone.

Bridget felt another surge of anger and directed it outward. A small tuft of dry grass near her foot burst into flames. Sighing, she stomped it out with her shoe without even bothering to get up.

"I thought I'd find you here."

Bridget gasped and twisted around, stunned to see Benjamin standing there. She had no idea whether he had just witnessed her little display with the fire.

"What are you doing here?" she asked.

"Looking for you."

She came to her feet and turned to face him, careful to stay within the safety of the two boulders. "Why are you looking for me?"

"I want to apologize."

"Like last time?"

A pained expression crossed his face. "Especially for last time."

Bridget felt the tension leave her neck and shoulders. "It's all right. It wasn't all your fault."

He leaned casually against one of the boulders, and Bridget noticed his sleeves had been rolled up to his elbows, exposing his muscular forearms. There was a faint coat of brown dust on his shirt, and she wondered what he'd been doing to get it soiled.

"Actually, it was. I shouldn't have walked into the privacy of your bedchamber uninvited, and I certainly shouldn't have pried into the personal nature of your relationship with Peter. You were right; it is none of my concern. I provoked you and caused emotions to run high. For that, I'm truly sorry."

She looked at him with skepticism. "You've apologized before."

"I know," he agreed easily, his loose black hair

brushing against the collar of his shirt as he nodded. "It seems I'm doing a lot of that lately with you. I assure you, I never wanted to do anything to hurt you, and I certainly didn't mean to disparage Peter. I'm certain you'll have a long and happy life together."

Bridget noticed a funny catch in his voice as he said the words. Although his expression looked remarkably sincere, it also seemed a bit melancholy.

"You're forgiven," she finally said. "Consider the entire matter forgotten."

She turned away from him so he wouldn't see the sadness in her own eyes. Her heart heavy, she sat back down between the boulders and stared out at the sea. The sun sparkled brightly on the blue water, making it look as though it were filled with shimmering diamonds.

"I haven't been out here for quite some time," Benjamin commented after a few minutes. "I'd forgotten what a lovely spot it is."

Bridget was surprised that he stayed. Since their kiss, she now felt awkward and anxious around him. Did he not feel the same? She stole a glance up at him over her shoulder and saw his gaze was calm and transfixed on the sea. Turning back around, she sighed. Seduction, kisses, and passion were as familiar to him as food. He would not be unsettled as she about what had happened between them.

"I still come here often for the quiet and respite," she said softly. "It's very peaceful here and allows me to think."

"Dream, you mean," he corrected and she heard the smile in his voice. "We are great dreamers, you and I."

"Perhaps once, when we were young and foolish. But I am not so carefree any longer."

He fell silent for a minute, his dark hair ruffling in the wind. "Don't you remember how we used to sit in this exact spot and envisage exotic ports of call?"

She smiled wistfully. "Of course I remember. And now, you have been to many of them."

"Yes. I wish you could have gone, too. You don't know how many times I thought of you while on those adventures, Bri. I tried to imagine your expression and wondered what you would think of the people, the food, and the magnificent architecture."

She picked at a piece of grass on her skirt. "I did see them, just through your eyes. I'm sorry I never thanked you for sharing all those memories with me. It really did mean a lot that you provided in great detail the wonder of your travels."

"I still intend to, you know," he said softly. "I'll certainly continue to visit you and Peter when I'm in Salem—that is, if you'll still have me after the idiot I've made of myself."

"Of course, we'll be thrilled to see you and hear about your adventures," Bridget said, but she couldn't keep a trace of regret from her voice. Peter had never shared their passion for travel, and she wondered if hearing about Benjamin's escapades with Peter present would somehow temper the tales.

Benjamin fell silent, perhaps thinking the same, so Bridget pulled her knees to her chest. An intense feeling of melancholy swept over her. So much had changed between them, yet so much remained the same.

"Did you have another argument with your mother today?" Benjamin suddenly asked, causing Bridget to start.

"Why do you ask?" she said stiffly.

"I went by your house to find you, presumably on

Peter's behalf to discuss a wedding matter," he said, keeping his gaze on the sea. "She sounded upset."

Bridget exhaled a deep breath. "She's always upset with me."

"I'm sorry. I hope it wasn't because of me."

"Everything isn't always about you, Benjamin," she replied wryly.

He winced. "Leave it to you to put me properly in my place."

"If I don't do it, who will?" she said with a trace of amusement.

"Indeed, who?" he replied, his voice serious. "I sometimes wonder about that."

Bridget laughed. "With all the young ladies in Salem eagerly lining up to have that opportunity, I wouldn't be overly concerned."

"Nonetheless, I remain quite concerned."

"Whatever for? Someday you'll meet your match, Benjamin. Then she'll remind you that occasionally others' needs come before your own."

He gazed at her with an odd burning in his gray eyes. Bridget suddenly felt flushed and uncomfortable.

"I didn't intend for that to be a criticism," she said. "Just an observation."

He nodded thoughtfully, crossing his arms against his chest. "You've always been one to go straight to the heart of the matter, Bri. And in this case, you happen to be right."

She narrowed her eyes at him suspiciously. "This isn't where you distract me by being so agreeable and then slip a spider down the back of my gown, is it?"

The burning light in his eyes abruptly disappeared, and instead an insolent, lazy grin spread across his face. "I vow that I'll conduct no more pranks before the wedding. You have my word."

"I think I should request that written in blood."

He laughed. "Speaking of blood, didn't we prick our fingers and mix the blood, swearing to be true and loyal friends forever?"

"We were ten, Benjamin."

"Nonetheless, a blood vow is a sacred, spiritual exchange. That should count for something."

"All right. I'll permit the blood vow to suffice."

"Excellent."

She smiled in spite of herself, resting her chin on her knees and staring back at the sea. "I will hold you to your word this time."

"Good, because I mean it, Bri," he said softly. "I'll not do anything to ruin your dream."

"What do you know of my dream?"

He shrugged. "I know how much you want your own family. I presume that hasn't changed. More than anything, you desire a home filled with love and children—a place where you can feel as if you belong. Am I right?"

She nodded, unable to say a word. It sounded so simple, so tedious when he said it aloud. Yet indeed, it was her dream, and he'd known it all along.

"I respect that dream, Bri," he said quietly. "In fact, in a way, I envy it. I'll not do anything to take that away from you."

Horrified, she felt the prick of tears at her eyes and blinked rapidly to force them back. "I . . . I thank you, then."

He held out a hand and Bridget looked slowly up into his face. She saw a curious mixture of tenderness and sadness.

"Come," he said. "I'll walk you home."

She hesitated to take his hand, to touch him. "It's not necessary. I know the way."

"I know. But just for a moment, I thought we could imagine ourselves as children again." He kept his hand outstretched. "Indulge me just this one time. I gave my word, Bri. I'll behave as the perfect gentleman."

Trusting him, she stretched out her hand. He took it, closing his warm, strong fingers around hers and giving them a squeeze.

"See," he said cheerfully as they began to walk. "Friends. Just like we used to be."

She mustered a smile, even as her heart shattered. Nothing could ever be as it once had. She, more than anyone, knew that to be the truth.

"I want you to know that I'll always look back fondly on those days," she said quietly. "Always."

"As will I."

He smiled down at her, a gentle, curiously tender expression on his face. Bridget felt her heart flutter and then settle in her chest with a heavy sadness, for those days would be no more.

Benjamin stood in the middle of his bedchamber, clad only in a pair of soft knee-length breeches. Restless, he paced back and forth in front of the hearth, muttering to himself. Frowning, he stopped at the small table to pick up a mug of hot spiced wine. He'd lost count how many times he'd filled the mug from the nearby kettle, but he was taking a damnably long time to feel any effects of the spirits.

He set the mug back down with a thump and resumed pacing. After a few minutes, he stopped in front of the hearth and stared into the roaring flames. The fire crackled and hissed, spitting out sparks in a heated shower. No candles were lit, so the room was dark, illuminated only by the flickering light of the fire.

That was good, because the darkness suited his mood. He'd been in an increasingly black temper since he'd left Bridget at her house this afternoon. He had no idea what had caused this downward spiral. His apology to her had been executed with the utmost assurance and grace. In fact, it was the first damn thing he'd done right since he got off the ship. But he couldn't shake the unpleasant, almost desperate feeling of wrongness that clung to him.

What the devil was the matter?

Irritated, he strode over to the table and took another gulp of the wine, wishing it could somehow wash away the disturbing knot in his stomach. Instead, it now tasted bitter on his tongue. It seemed he'd have no satisfaction with anything this evening.

The whole day had been one peculiar event after the next. First, the altercation with Peter, then a lengthy conversation with an old blind woman, and finally, a heartfelt talk with Bridget in which he offered a sincere apology.

Bridget.

It all kept coming back to Bridget.

He rubbed the aching muscles in the back of his neck. This afternoon when he'd seen her sitting at Rock's Point, a flood of memories swept over him. He remembered the first time they'd found the spot, and how they'd both been small enough to fit together in the sheltered space between the boulders.

Somehow, the spot had been just theirs. Peter, of course, knew of the hideaway but hadn't much liked it. Even at eight years of age, he'd been too much of a gentleman. He considered it too uncomfortable without the luxury of soft grass and shade. Instead, he preferred to sit a short distance away under the shelter of the trees and watch them.

Bridget, on the other hand, hadn't minded sitting on the pebbles, laughing and lifting her freckled face to the sun. How many hours had passed while they sat watching the ships on the harbor and dreaming of faraway lands? In a way, it was Bridget who had nurtured his desire one day to sail abroad on his father's ships, to explore exotic lands and experience for himself the world beyond the confines of Salem.

He sighed and shoved a hand through his hair. He hadn't lied when he told Bridget he'd thought of her often during those voyages. Of all the people in Salem, it was she for whom he saved the tales of his best adventures. Only she could fully appreciate what he'd seen and done, and only she understood the burning need within him to explore the world.

His time abroad had been exciting and thrilling, but this was partly because he could always come home to Salem, where life remained largely unchanged.

Now Bridget and Peter were getting married. Though they'd still be in Salem and would continue to be a part of his life, somehow he felt as though he was losing something irreplaceable. Something precious and rare.

Dissatisfaction burned in his stomach. Striding over to the window, he pulled aside the heavy drape and stared out at the moonlit sky. Golden light pooled on the grass in the front yard and reflected off the wrought-iron gate.

He had a feeling that some important revelation dangled just beyond his reach. A confounded mixture of exasperation, anger, and melancholy coursed through him. Yet he was unable to discern which was the most important of the feelings, or why in all hell and damnation he had any of them in the first place.

Blast it.

He'd royally mucked things up this time by kissing Bridget. As much as he tried to deny it, something had shifted in their relationship after the kiss. In the process, he'd unleashed something inexplicable and unexpected within him. Now he felt curiously restless, with a driving sense of urgency to undertake some nameless action. But what action and to what end?

"Curse it all to hell," he muttered, stripping off his breeches and going naked to his bed. He lay on top of the cool bedsheets, staring at the ceiling. He didn't feel like sleeping, but drinking hadn't helped and neither had the pacing.

He had no idea how long he lay there staring up at the ceiling. He prayed for a dreamless sleep. But when he finally succumbed to the welcome darkness, he dreamed of Bridget.

Seven

Bridget awoke early, dressed, and attended to her chores. Her mother greeted her politely, but thankfully did not bring up the matter of the wedding gown.

She decided to banish firmly from her mind any thoughts of what had happened between her and Benjamin. She had to think solely of her future with Peter and refrain from entertaining any thoughts that would further upset her or the wedding plans.

When she finished her chores, she left the parsonage and took the bag of coins Widow Bayley had given her to Betty Corwin's house. She chatted for a short time with the seamstress and inspected the gown, pleased with the progress she had made. Spirits rising, Bridget stopped by the bakery and picked up a long loaf of bread for the widow. Humming a merry tune under her breath, she set off for the cottage.

As she walked along the road, Bridget gazed up at the sky, marveling that it was yet another clear, warm day. Fortunately, today she remembered her bonnet. Though she enjoyed the sun, it had caused her freckles to become far too numerous, and the tip of her nose to redden and peel.

Nevertheless, the weather mirrored her cheery mood. Picking up the pace, she neared the cottage.

She opened the gate and waved gaily at the cat before knocking on the door. Bridget heard the widow call out for her to enter, so she crossed the threshold, holding out the crusted loaf of bread.

"I've brought you some—" she started and then stopped when she saw Benjamin lounging in the chair across from the widow.

"Hello, Bridget, dear," the widow said, looking remarkably cheerful. "I was just visiting with Benjamin here."

Benjamin rose from the chair slowly, crossing his arms against his chest. Appearing cool and handsome despite the heat, he was dressed casually in a pair of tan-colored breeches, a white linen shirt, and black boots. His hair was loose today, falling to his shoulders in a riot of black, untamed waves. He stood there, devilishly handsome, and her pulse quickened.

"Good morning, Bri."

"Benjamin?" she managed to say. "What are you doing here?"

"He stopped by yesterday looking for you," Widow Bayley interjected. "He was kind enough to stop and chat for a while. When he saw the state of disrepair the house is in, he generously offered to lend a hand."

Bridget's mouth fell open. "He did?"

"I didn't know you did chores here," he said, his voice light, but she saw an unusual glint in his eyes. "You could have asked for my help, Bri."

She snapped her mouth shut. "I never thought . . . I mean, it's not as if you've been around much to ask."

"Well, now I am." He turned to the widow. "In fact, I thank you for the tea, madame, but I believe I'll get back to chopping wood."

Benjamin passed by Bridget without a word. Still contemplating the reason behind his visit to the widow,

Bridget lay the bread on the table and removed her bonnet. She picked up an apron and tied it around her waist.

"He is a fine young man," the widow said lightly. "I can see why you've been friends for so long. But it seems as though something is bothering him."

"Me, no doubt," Bridget said wryly. "But why, I'm not so certain."

"Well, you've been friends for so long, surely you can resolve this."

"Perhaps."

"Why ever wouldn't you?"

Bridget sighed. "Because Benjamin and I often have a difficult time carrying on a civilized conversation. Usually one of us ends up shouting at the other, even if we don't know why."

"Well, you are passionate young people."

"It's more as if we have difficulty controlling our tempers. Benjamin seems able to rile mine effortlessly, and I seem to have the same effect on him." She picked up the broom and started sweeping vigorously.

"I swept the inside just this morning," the widow said calmly. "But the garden could surely use a bit more weeding, if you would be so inclined."

"Of course," Bridget said, setting the broom aside and taking off the apron. She picked up the wicker basket to bring in some herbs and vegetables and touched the widow gently on the shoulder.

"Are you coming?" she asked.

The widow shook her head. "If you don't mind, dear, I'll stay inside today. I'm feeling a bit tired."

"Certainly. I'll be back soon."

Bridget headed back outside, squinting in the bright sun. She could hear the rhythmic sound of an ax hitting wood coming from behind the cottage. Benjamin paused when he saw her, resting the ax on the ground and placing his booted leg on top of the tree stump.

Bridget set the basket down and crossed her arms against her chest. "I've upset you. Although I'm not certain how."

He raised a dark eyebrow. "How many years have you been coming out to the widow's cottage?"

She pondered the question. "About six or seven, I suppose. Why?"

"And in all that time, you never once mentioned that she could use a man's hand with some of the repairs and chores you do here."

She flushed. "There was no need. Aaron Bickford was kind enough to help me until he fell ill."

"Aaron Bickford is most likely the frailest man in all of Salem. He's a good fellow, but hardly with enough strength to raise an ax." He narrowed his eyes at her. "You asked him because he was besotted with you."

"It helped," she admitted. "But he still came even after he married Helen Fordy."

"Why didn't you ever ask me?"

Bridget put her hands on her hips, feeling ridiculously defensive. "Why should I?" She paused and then said more gently, "Frankly, I didn't think you'd want to come."

Benjamin's expression darkened as he lifted the ax above his shoulder. He brought it down with a hard swing. The metal cleaved into the wood so deeply, it caused Bridget to jump.

"Think so little of me, do you?"

"No, of course not. Don't be ridiculous."

"Perhaps you think that I am too wealthy, too well stationed, too preoccupied with other important social matters to be bothered with such a mundane request, right?"

He yanked out the ax and Bridget tried not to flinch. "No . . . yes. Well, you are busy. Besides, I wasn't certain you'd even want to come out here with everyone thinking she's a witch and such."

Thwack. The ax hit the wood again, this time halving it neatly.

"Now you are accusing me of being a coward?"

Bridget stepped back. "I don't think that. It's just I knew you'd have other matters to attend to. Besides, the way you breeze in and out of Salem these days, I hardly ever saw you to ask."

The muscles in his jaw tightened perceptively, but he said nothing. Instead, he used his boot to kick a piece of stray wood out of his way.

"You're not being completely truthful with me, Bri," he said, picking up a large chunk of wood and positioning it sideways. "Try again."

Her temper flared. "All right. The truth is, I was afraid you might think me odd for consorting so often with the widow. After all, we're judged by the company we keep, are we not? There, I said it. I didn't realize you'd be so offended."

He raised the ax above his shoulder again. "Well, I am. And when have I ever judged you? You, of all people, should know better."

Bridget flinched as the ax hit the wood again. His words rang true. He was hurt and rightly so.

She pushed back the hair from her forehead. "I'm sorry, Benjamin."

"You should be." He paused, resting the heel of the ax on his thigh. "What does Peter have to say about your visits here?"

She couldn't meet his eyes and instead fiddled with

an invisible thread on her skirt. "He's very preoccupied with his studies and the wedding, naturally."

"You haven't told him."

She sighed. "No. He doesn't approve of my friendship with Widow Bayley as it is."

"So you hide it from him?" He looked incredulous.

"I'm not hiding anything. He has yet to ask."

Benjamin scowled at her. "Bri—" he started warningly.

"I will tell him," she interrupted hastily. "I promise. Just not yet. Please, Benjamin, don't say anything to him yet."

"You know damn well he wouldn't approve. Yet you come anyway."

"She needs me. Who else would come?"

Benjamin grasped the handle and stopped. "I guess I will."

"You?"

"I can't simply abandon her because you can no longer come."

Bridget was taken aback. "What if people find out you're visiting her?"

Benjamin laughed. "When in God's name did you become concerned about my reputation?"

"I don't want you to suffer because of me."

He shook his head. "I intend to live my life the way I wish. I won't let gossipmongers dictate my course."

His voice was calm, self-assured. She'd always envied his confidence in himself.

"I thank you, then. But I want to keep coming for as long as I can. Besides, mayhap I can still turn Peter around. And there is always the matter of what to do when you're not in Salem."

"That shouldn't be an immediate problem. I intend to stay a while in Salem this time."

"You do?"

He nodded. "Travel is fascinating, but it can wear on a man. I've given my word I'll help the widow, and I intend to."

"That is kind of you, but it's not necessary to make such a rash decision. Besides, one call of the sea and you'll be out of Salem on the first vessel that can take you."

Benjamin set the ax aside and wiped his brow with the back of his hand. "I have listened to that call, Bri. I'll be the first to admit that the sea can be an irresistible siren. Of course, I intend to travel again, but not as often and not for such long periods of time. My home is here in Salem. Perhaps it's time that I started to build my life here."

This revelation surprised her. "Well, I must admit, I didn't expect you to say that. You can't blame me for being skeptical. Benjamin Hawkes, the most nefarious rake in Salem, is considering settling down?"

He pursed his lips wryly. "I'd hardly consider myself nefarious."

A smile touched her lips. "Benjamin, if this is true, I'm really proud of you."

"The way you say that is not exactly encouraging, Bri."

"I'm sincere in my words. It's wonderful. You'll find a nice woman to wed and have two or three children you can teach to sail and swim. I suppose you will continue to sail abroad for your father, but now you'll have so much more to look forward to when you return to Salem."

He rested his elbow on his thigh. "Now you alarm me. I've only just decided to think seriously about my future, and you've already got it planned out for me?"

She grinned. "Only promise me one thing—you

won't set your cap for Sarabeth. I fear even a reformed rake like you would be too much for her."

"Who said I'm going to be reformed?" he grumbled. When she pursed her lips at him, he added, "Besides, we've already talked about Sarabeth, and I told you how I feel about her."

"I know. But my parents can be very persistent."

"Never fear; I can manage my own future, Bri."

"I know," she said wistfully. "I'll be happy for you."

He smiled, but it didn't quite touch his eyes. "I'm happy for you and Peter, too. There, see what can be accomplished when we choose to talk to each other in a civilized manner?"

"I'm always civilized," Bridget protested.

"Except when you're being a hothead."

"Me?"

"Well, a good, charitable hothead," he amended. "By the way, I do like Widow Bayley."

"Really?"

He chuckled. "Really. She's a bit eccentric, but I can see why you come around so often. She has fascinating tales to tell of Salem. I was lucky enough to hear one before you arrived. I look forward to hearing more."

"She has hundreds of the most marvelous tales. She knows so much about the history of Salem. But I wouldn't consider her odd, just a bit unusual."

"In some ways, she reminds me of you."

"Me?"

"She's eccentric, fascinating, mysterious, yet practical and friendly."

"And that's how you think of me?"

"That, and a lot more."

"I presume you mean that in a complimentary manner, right?" she asked dubiously.

"Of course."

She narrowed her eyes. "That doesn't change the fact that I still consider you a nefarious rake."

"I'd prefer to be considered charming."

Bridget gave a harrumph. "You would. You know, some things never change."

"I suppose not," he said agreeably, lifting the ax.

Shaking her head, Bridget leaned over and picked up the basket. She moved over to the garden, where she knelt and began pulling weeds from the vegetables. For several minutes they worked in companionable silence until Benjamin spoke again.

"Do you usually come here so early?" he asked.

"No," she said over her shoulder. "It's just today I needed to finish up so I can go home and help mother and Sarabeth with the cooking for the church picnic tomorrow. Are you coming?"

He shrugged. "I'd forgotten all about it. I suppose I will."

"Alone?" she asked and then flushed. What business was it of hers?

He raised a dark eyebrow. "Now, I hadn't much thought about it. Perhaps I should, since I'm trying not to be so nefarious. However, it might be too late to find myself a willing young lady."

Bridget snorted. "You? Never."

"I'm surprised you have so much faith in me."

"False modesty doesn't suit you, Benjamin. Since when have you ever had trouble finding someone to accompany you to any event?"

"Perhaps since my breeches split wide open in front of Lilith Ward. There's no saying how many delicate sensibilities in Salem, including Miss Ward's, were offended that day."

"More likely all the girls were falling over themselves to see the rake of Salem exposed."

"Bri!" he said in mock horror, but she could see a glimmer of playfulness in his eyes. "Truthfully, I can't say I noticed, since I was too busy trying to politely extricate myself from the situation, all the while plotting madly what I would do to get even with you."

"A situation you eventually remedied with the toad," she pointed out wryly.

"Yes, I suppose I must count it as a fitting retribution, although it was not nearly as imaginative as yours."

They both laughed and returned to their work. Bridget weeded for some time, pausing only to wipe sweat from her brow. The steady thump of the ax kept her company until she finally sat back on her heels, removing her bonnet and pushing the damp hair off her forehead.

She glanced over at Benjamin and blinked when she realized he had removed his shirt, hanging it neatly over a nearby branch. He was bare from the waist up, the muscles in his arms rippling and bunching as he lifted the ax and brought it down. His skin was bronzed and a sheen of sweat glistened on his bare chest.

For a moment, Bridget simply stared in awe at him. She'd seen him a hundred times before without a shirt, but somehow today it was different. She had never seen him look so sinfully handsome, nor had she ever been so acutely aware of his broad chest and powerful shoulders. For a moment, she remembered the feel of those hard muscles bunched beneath her fingers as he held her tight in his embrace. Her heart thudded hard in her chest and she quickly looked away, her face flushing guiltily.

Peter. She had to think of Peter. She tried to summon

the image of his golden hair and elegant looks, but the image of Benjamin's bare chest was the only picture her mind would register.

"Are you all right, Bri?"

She nodded, hoping he attributed her scarlet cheeks to the heat. "Yes. I'm fine." She rose to her feet, trying to avoid looking directly at him. "I think it's time for me to go. Mother and Sarabeth will be waiting for me."

"I'll walk back with you," he said, striding over to the tree and pulling the shirt over his head. "I need to pick up a larger mallet to fix the roof anyway."

Bridget replaced her bonnet on her head, tying it firmly under her chin. "As you wish."

They entered the cottage together and found Widow Bayley resting in her chair, her hands folded lightly on her lap. Benjamin explained he'd be back in a short while, and Bridget bid the widow farewell.

Today Benjamin did not offer his arm. Instead, he remained quiet, seemingly lost in his own thoughts. Bridget kept a safe distance from him and tried valiantly to forget how magnificent he looked without his shirt. About halfway home, she realized that it was an image she would likely never forget no matter how hard she tried.

The widow listened as Bridget and Benjamin left the cottage, her heart heavy. Although she was blind, she didn't need sight to realize the two of them were in love. Yet sadly, neither of them trusted or listened to their hearts. Given what she knew, perhaps it was better that way.

Slowly she rose from the chair, ignoring the creak of her bones. She felt her way carefully along the back of the chair until she reached the table. Following the smell, she reached out until her fingers brushed the vase of flowers. She pulled it close, breathing in deeply the smell of freshly cut lilacs.

The scent reminded her of her friend Hannah. Hannah had loved lilacs and had them planted about her house.

"I wish you could see her, old friend," the widow said softly. "She's a beautiful young girl with a good heart. You would be proud."

The widow fumbled about for a chair and pulled it back from the table. She lowered herself into it, resting her elbows on the table.

It was a heavy burden for an old, blind woman to bear. She could only wait and listen to Bridget—unable to reveal what she knew, forbidden to guide the young woman to the choices that would shape her life and destiny. Bridget would have to chart this course alone, without the interference of an old woman, no matter how well intentioned she was.

As it stood, she was fortunate Bridget had been drawn to the cottage in the first place and had then found the courage to return. Now Benjamin Hawkes had come here, too. Did she dare nurture a glimmer of hope that all might be well?

Yet it was an intricate situation. She understood and deeply respected the power of destiny. Those from the MacInness clan had always been more closely tied to their fates, perhaps because destiny was often more capricious with her favorites.

Bridget Goodwell came from MacInness stock whether she knew it or not, and her destiny had been foretold for generations. There was naught an old woman could do except pray for a miracle.

Of course, it all came back to the curse. That black, wicked curse. How did destiny expect the MacInness clan to fight such a curse, if she would not permit them to listen to their own hearts? How many mistakes must be made? How many lives lost and ruined? Time was running out for the clan. With Bridget's own wedding just weeks away and the other vital members of the clan still missing, hope for any reprieve became dimmer and dimmer.

"Hannah, where are you?" the widow whispered aloud. "Time grows near."

The widow heard a small meow and knew Francesca had come into the room. She held out her hands and felt the cat jump onto her lap. Slowly she rubbed the cat's chin and felt the warm furry body circle and snuggle down. After a moment, there was no other sound in the room except for a steady purr.

"Bridget, it will have to begin with you," the widow murmured. "You must take control of your own destiny."

Francesca mewled in agreement and the widow sighed. Fighting off despair, she wished with all her heart that Bridget might learn of her heritage in time to change her grim future and protect those she loved most.

To think otherwise would be unbearable.

Benjamin strode beside Bridget down the dusty road, trying to remain aloof, but intensely aware of every step she took. He noted many things, such as how she kept a safe distance from him, and how she delicately lifted her skirts, careful not to expose an ankle. For a moment he felt a flash of annoyance, then remembered it was his own damn fault she was acting this way. After all, it had been he who hauled her into his arms and kissed her senseless. She had every right to be wary of him.

"There's been an appalling lack of rain," he finally commented, unable to stand the polite silence any longer.

He watched as she kicked at a stone on the road, raising a plume of dust. "I know," she said. "It seems as though we went straight from winter to summer. Nonetheless, the meadows still look lovely and it's wonderful to smell the fresh blooms."

Benjamin sniffed the air. He caught the scent of grass and flowers, of sunshine and lilacs, that always seemed to cling to Bridget. He stole a glance sideways at her and saw she had an unusually pensive look on her face.

"Bri, I'm not going to tell Peter about your visits to Widow Bayley," he said with a sigh. "So don't worry yourself needlessly."

She threw him a grateful look. "Thank you. I do intend to tell him, though. When I'm ready."

"I'm glad to hear that."

She gave him a tentative smile. "You know, I do believe Peter is quite pleased you've returned for the wedding."

Benjamin thought of the maidservant and their tense encounter and wondered about that. "And you?"

"Since you've given your word to refrain from any further mischief before the wedding, so am I."

He raised an eyebrow. "Truthfully?"

"Truthfully."

"You trust me that much?"

"Benjamin, you've been my friend for as long as I can remember. Do you still remember the time you taught me to swim?"

He did indeed remember that beautiful summer day.

They were eight and he'd taunted her from the water until she finally agreed to come in. She'd made her way hesitantly to the edge of the wharf, chewing her lower lip nervously. After some consideration, she'd finally cast him a look of sheer and utter trust and jumped into his arms. They'd both gone under hard and come up spluttering. Laughing, Benjamin dragged her back to the wharf. Her eyes had been bright and sparkling and it had taken her only a moment before she tried again. And again.

It had been the first time she'd trusted him. Just the memory of it flooded him with a sense of bittersweet nostalgia. Then, just as unexpectedly, he thought of their heated moment in the bedroom, her lips parted sweetly beneath his, her fingers tangled in his hair.

"Do you remember what you said to me before I jumped?" she asked, causing him to start.

He thought for a moment and a smile curved across his mouth. "I said a witch would float, whereas a true innocent would sink. You know that I only said that to provoke you into doing what I wanted."

She smiled back. "I know. But it worked and I floated. So much for true innocence."

"I floated, too," he pointed out.

Her expression softened. "I suppose I've trusted you since that moment."

He felt a strange clutch in his chest at her words. "Bri—" he started to say when out of nowhere an enormous black crow flew down over them, swooping by so closely, he could feel the swish of air from its wings.

"What the devil is that bird doing?" he said, watching in amazement as the huge bird circled oddly above them.

"I don't know," Bridget answered, looking up in the sky.

Again the crow swooped down, this time coming so close to Bridget that she took a step backward.

"What in God's name is it after?" Benjamin said, moving closer to Bridget. "Have you food hidden in the folds of your gown?"

Bridget shook her head and Benjamin was alarmed to see how pale her face had gone. "Don't worry," he said. "It's harmless enough. I'll get a stick and frighten it off."

He moved to the side of the road near the trees and searched around for a large stick. Finding one, he held it up and walked back to Bridget just as the bird dived again.

"Shoo," he shouted, waving the stick at the bird, but the crow seemed intent on Bridget's head. "Get out of here."

Benjamin caught the bird on the side with the stick and it screeched in anger before returning to the sky and circling ominously.

"It's after me," Bridget whispered.

Benjamin looked at her, frowning. "Likely, it's just hungry. Come on. Let's keep walking. It will probably give up and go away."

He took Bridget's elbow with one hand and kept the stick in the other, his gaze remaining on the sky where the damned bird followed.

"There's something evil about that bird," Bridget said softly. "Something is not quite right."

"I'll say," Benjamin agreed. "It's gone mad either with hunger or sickness. We'll have to be careful."

Just as he said the words, the bird descended upon them with such speed, Benjamin barely had time to step in front of Bridget and lift the stick. The bird slammed into him with such force, it knocked him back a step.

"What the devil is wrong with that creature?" he said, swearing, pushing Bridget behind him as it circled above, seemingly intent on another pass.

"It's seeking me," Bridget said softly.

Benjamin had no time to ponder her strange words as the bird swooped again and Bridget darted away from him. The crow changed its path and headed directly for her.

"Come back!" Benjamin shouted, running toward Bridget and throwing himself at her. He grabbed her around the waist, pulling her to the ground and rolling on top, shielding her with his body just as the bird alighted on his back, pecking furiously at his neck.

Uttering a curse, Benjamin rolled and batted it off with his elbow. The bird screeched and rose back into the air. A quick feel to the back of his neck told him the bird had drawn blood.

"We've got to get out of here," he said, rolling off Bridget and stretching out his hand. "That bird is utterly deranged."

She put her hand in his and screamed as the crow abruptly spiraled downward, claws extended. It slammed into Benjamin's back, causing him to release Bridget's hand and stumble forward. Off balance, he slid down a small ditch at the edge of the road. He staggered to his feet and then looked down in shock when he realized his ankle was caught in a tangled root.

"Benjamin!" Bridget screamed, as the bird fluttered up in the sky and turned back toward her.

"Blast it," he roared, kicking at the root. "I can't get free." No matter how hard he pulled and yanked, the root held his ankle securely.

He watched in horror as Bridget held her hands up to her face just as the bird made another pass, its claws fully extended. She ducked sideways, but not fast enough. The bird knocked the bonnet off her head and latched onto her upper arm, sinking its talons into the soft flesh.

"Bridget!" he shouted, tearing furiously at the root with his hands. It held him as tightly and mysteriously as if it were a giant hand.

Bridget shrieked, stumbling as the bird began to peck at her face, seeming to aim for her eyes.

"Get off her, damn you!" Benjamin shouted. Frantic, he looked about, his fingers closing around a stick. Picking it up, he hurled it at the bird. A corner of the stick hit the fowl on the back and it fell off Bridget's arm to the ground with a loud squawk.

He watched as Bridget staggered forward, gripping her arm where the bird had injured her. A dazed look had crossed her face and blood trickled out from between her fingers.

"Look out!" he shouted when he saw the bird fly up again. Slowly, methodically, it circled above her.

Benjamin tore at the root, still unable to free himself. He watched helplessly as Bridget hesitated, trying to focus. She seemed unusually confused, as if she walked in a fog.

"Damnation, Bri!" he shouted. "Run to the trees. Get out of its sight."

She blinked, and for a moment he saw the confusion lift. "Benjamin?" she whispered.

Just then the crow spiraled down at her with an unholy screech. A determined look on her face, Bridget spun around on her feet with amazing agility. Uttering a small cry, she thrust her hand out at the bird.

The crow screamed and burst into flames. It burned

for less than a heartbeat before a shower of gray ashes exploded into the air and floated slowly to the ground. Bridget sunk onto the road, her hands over her face, shaking.

Stunned, Benjamin kicked at the root, amazed that now it slid easily from his ankle.

"Bri, God in heaven, are you all right?" he said, stumbling up from the ditch. He knelt beside her, pulling her hands from her face to see if she was injured. When he saw she was crying, it shook him to his very core. He rarely saw her shed tears. In fact, in all the years he'd known her, he'd seen her do so only twice. That she would do so now unnerved him more than anything.

"Bri," he said, curving a finger under her chin and forcing her to look up at him. "Are you harmed?"

"My arm hurts a little."

Benjamin looked at the spot where the bird had torn a hole in her sleeve. Blood trickled out slowly from a few small and shallow scratches.

"You'll need to clean this. What about your face?"

She touched her cheeks gingerly. Benjamin saw the bird had pecked a tiny spot behind her right ear and jaw, but she was fortunate she hadn't been hurt worse. He fumbled for a handkerchief and dabbed it at her jaw.

"I'm all right, Benjamin," she said. "Just terribly shaken."

"Why did you run away from me?" he asked, his voice rough. When he saw the bird dive after her, murder in its eyes, his heart had constricted in a nameless terror. "You could have been seriously hurt."

"I didn't want you to get injured. It wasn't after you. It was after me."

"You didn't want me to get hurt?" he said incredulously. "Must you now add insult to injury? Hell's bells, Bri, as it is, this entire event just took me ten years closer to my grave."

"I'm sorry," she whispered. "I wasn't thinking properly."

Without thinking, he pulled her close, wrapping his arms around her. Now that the immediate danger had passed, he realized how close she had come to being grievously harmed or worse. He shuddered to think of what that damn bird might have done to her had he not been there.

I could have lost you, Bri.

The realization hit him like a fist in the gut. He slumped onto the road beside her, keeping her tight in his arms. A shudder racked her body as he pressed her head against his shoulder and brushed his lips across her hair.

"What in God's name just happened here?" he asked softly. "How did you destroy that bird?"

A sob caught in her throat. "Please," she whispered. "Please don't tell Peter."

He tightened his arm around her. "That's what you're worried about? Listen to me. An unbalanced crow just attacked you with the precision of a military general. In return, you burned it up like kindling. You could have been grievously injured or worse and all you can worry about is whether or not I'll tell Peter?"

"This is my life we are talking about."

"Damn right it is, and you could have very well lost it," he said with such feeling that she looked up at him, startled.

She must have seen the stricken expression on his face, because her voice softened. "I'm sorry, Benjamin," she said in a muffled voice, pressing her tear-stained face against his neck. "I didn't know what else to do."

He sighed and brushed a strand of red hair from her face. "Bri, tell me the truth. How did you do it?"

She avoided his gaze. "How can you be certain it was naught more than a natural phenomenon of some kind?"

"Don't lie to me," he said tightly. *"You* burned that crow to ash, not some damned phenomenon."

She sat up, dashing the tears from her eyes and raising her chin. "Do you know how ridiculous that sounds? How could I possibly burn up a crow?"

"I don't know. Why don't you tell me?"

She fell silent for a moment. "Are you very certain you want to hear the answer, Benjamin?" she replied, looking at him intently. "Do you really want to discover that I'm some kind of monstrosity?"

"I want the truth, Bri. No matter how strange it may be."

"No, you don't," she said bitterly. "Even I don't want to know the truth."

He seized her hands. "Yes, you do, and so do I. Tell me. I need to know. How did you do it?"

She looked at him fiercely for a moment, daring him to back down. When he didn't, she sighed.

"I don't know," she finally said, her voice weary. "I simply thought about it, commanded the fire to happen. And it did."

Benjamin thought he'd be more shocked to hear such a fantastic confession, but somehow he wasn't. Perhaps because in some part of his mind, he'd known all along. Nonetheless, the hairs on his arms and the back of his neck rose up.

"How long have you been able to do this?" he asked, surprised his voice sounded so calm.

"Since I was about six."

"The cross in the meeting house?"

"Yes, it all started then."

"Well, hell," he uttered, at a loss for anything more brilliant to say.

"I'm sorry," she said again, straightening and rubbing her eyes. "I'm sorry you know about me. I'm sorry you had to witness such an aberration."

He looked at her in surprise. "Is that what you think it is?"

"What else could it be?"

"Some might consider it a gift."

She was so startled that her mouth gaped open. "A gift?"

"Why not? You can do something that others can't do."

"Benjamin, I just made fire come out of air. I killed a living creature and burned it to ashes out of fear and anger. That's not a gift."

"Need I point out that this living creature just happened to be trying to kill you? It wasn't flying by for a cheerful look at us."

"The truth is, I'm cursed," she said quietly. "I'm a living peculiarity. There's a force within me that sets me apart from others."

He exhaled a deep breath. "This doesn't change anything. You are the same old Bri I've always known."

"Mayhap you don't know me at all."

"On the contrary," he said, looking her directly in the eyes. "I know you better than anyone."

She took his handkerchief and slowly cleaned the blood from her hands. "I'm dangerous, Benjamin."

"I'm not afraid. I may be amazed, curious, and unnerved, yes. But not afraid." He stroked her hair absently. "Does Widow Bayley know about this?"

"No," she replied. "No one knows anything, except perhaps my parents. I think they suspect something is different about me since the incident with the cross, although they've never talked to me openly about it."

Benjamin thought about the damaged mother-daughter bond and wondered if this might be the source of the problem. "So, you've kept this secret all your life?"

"What else could I do?"

"You could have told me."

"I feared losing your friendship," she said softly. "I don't think I could have borne that."

"Oh, Bri," he said with a sigh. "You should have trusted me."

When she didn't answer, he leaned his chin against her head, trying to look at this from her point of view. She must have suffered terribly, knowing she was different, yet afraid to reveal just how much. Certainly she would have been terrified of being exposed to her deeply religious parents, knowing how that would affect them. She'd even managed to hide this from him.

Silently he counted the ills and mischief he had caused her, and felt a rush of guilt and regret. How many times had he involved her in his misadventures, adding to her troubles? How much of her suffering was his responsibility?

Yet despite it all, she'd managed. Beautiful, brave, and steadfast Bridget. He tightened his arm around her with a strange surge of protectiveness. What should he do now?

Something as important as this shouldn't be kept a secret, especially not from Peter. The man had a right to know what he was getting into before he married

Bridget. If he were any kind of friend to Peter, he'd not keep such knowledge to himself. But should he tell?

Benjamin considered it for less than a moment before rejecting that action outright. He couldn't—*wouldn't*—betray Bridget's confidence.

She must have sensed what he was thinking because she raised her eyes to meet his. In an instant, something flashed between them, a question heavily weighted with regret. At that moment, Benjamin knew he'd keep her secret safe. He'd do so because he wanted with all his heart for her to be happy and because he wished for her dreams to come true. And yet there was something else lingering in his thoughts just out of reach.

I'll keep her secret because . . . I love her.

The realization jolted him with all the force of a knife being thrust through his chest. He gasped, and for a moment couldn't breath at all, couldn't move a single muscle. He simply sat in stunned and rigid shock, reeling from the epiphany.

I love Bridget.

This was not just the love of friends or the love between a brother and sister. He knew this with a heartrending certainty. What he felt for her was a fierce, possessive love that sprung from deep in his heart, as pure and real as anything he'd ever known.

I love her.

He drew in a painful breath, and his heart thundered wildly as he tried to collect his thoughts. For how long had he loved her? Since the first time he'd slipped a snake down her dress at assembly and watched as she squealed to get it out? Or since she'd punched him in the jaw so hard it had brought tears to his eyes?

Now he understood that it was Bridget who had encouraged him to follow his dreams, to become the man he'd always wanted to be. And because of her, he had always returned to Salem.

God forbid, how could I be so blind?

Now he understood why he had felt so irritable since returning to Salem, and why he had this nagging feeling that he was losing something precious.

Bridget is supposed to be mine.

For a desperate moment, he sought a way out of the revelation, but an odd sense of calm and peace had fallen over him.

This was right.

We are right.

Except for the fact that Bridget could somehow conjure fire, and that she was in love with his best friend and would be wed to him in a few weeks. How could he convince her his feelings were true and not just some rash disclosure on his part? Hell, at this point, he wasn't even certain it would be in her best interest for him to do so. Maybe she'd be better off with Peter anyway.

"Benjamin?" she asked and he looked down at her. Her freckled face was covered with dirt and streaked with tears. She'd lost her bonnet and her glorious red hair tumbled wildly about her shoulders with brambles and sticks poking out of it. To him, she was the most beautiful woman in the world.

Mine, he thought with a tightening in his chest.

"Bri," he started to say, but his voice clogged with emotion. He wanted nothing more than to hold her close and rain kisses across her delectable mouth and face. But he had to think, plan, and consider the consequences of his newfound feelings. This was no longer just about him. He had to consider what was in Bridget's heart, not to mention Peter's. If she loved

Peter, and Peter intended to fulfill her dreams by going through with the wedding, how could he stand in the way?

Still reeling from his thoughts, Benjamin stood, pulling Bridget up with him. He brushed off his shirt and breeches, watching her do the same with her gown. Gallantly he retrieved her bonnet and set it upon her head. She secured it under her chin, watching him with a mixture of wariness, sadness, and resignation.

"Benjamin," she started to say, but he shook his head to stop her.

"I'm not going to say anything, Bri. Not just yet. Give me time to sort out everything that has happened today. There are still many things I need to know, such as why you are certain that crow was after you and how that blasted root managed to conveniently secure my ankle for the entire duration of the attack. But we've got time for that. Now, I need to get you home before your mother becomes distraught waiting for you. Everything that transpired here today remains between us for the time being. All right?"

She nodded uneasily and Benjamin noticed her chin trembled. He longed to hold and reassure her, but he didn't trust himself to do just that.

"It's probably better that your parents don't see me, so I won't walk you all the way up to the door. Tell your mother you had a fall. I'm certain she'll understand."

"I suppose so," Bridget said doubtfully. "But what about you?"

"No one will give me a second glance." He cupped her cheek gently. "Everything will be fine. Your secret is safe with me. You'll just have to trust me."

For a moment, he thought she leaned into his hand

as if seeking comfort. Then he saw her green eyes flash and her chin lift determinedly.

"I do," she said quietly. "I know you'd never do anything that would ruin my wedding to Peter."

Benjamin swallowed hard and looked away. He loved Bridget, but if he had his way, he'd do exactly that.

Eight

A brooding silence lay heavy in the small room, broken only by the angry crackle of the fire in the hearth. Flames rose and died down, while sparks spit and dashed themselves against the stones in the fireplace. Shadows danced eerily on the walls like demented partners at an unnatural gathering.

The Dark One sat on a chair in front of the hearth, staring at the flames, chanting an invocation in a mixture of Scots Gaelic and Latin. Soon, she could feel the force begin to gather. A faint prickle raised the hairs on her arms and skittered across her back like a host of small insects. Her head pounded with the beat of a hundred throbbing drums.

In moments, the room filled with the tangible, pulsing beat of her fury. It pounded savagely against the walls as if trying to free itself, restrained only by the woman who had summoned it.

"I call upon thee, O Dark Power of the MacGow clan," the woman said, lifting her hands toward the fire. "Come hither and grant me your wisdom."

At once the pounding fury subsided, replaced by a cold, fierce breeze. Within moments, black tendrils of smoke began winding and slithering their way across the room. The slippery vapors curdled and writhed like poisonous sea serpents in search of prey. The fire shuddered and hissed as the smoke curled around the logs, but the flames burned hotter and higher as the smoke wound itself around the room and squeezed.

The woman felt the power gather in the air and smiled. The summoning was a rare occurrence, made only when times were desperate, and not more than once in a century.

"O worshipful Master," the woman called. "Your aid is gravely needed."

The smoke began to writhe and hiss. The woman felt a blast of cold air that whipped a long braid across her cheeks like the stinging snap of a whip. The draperies hanging at the window billowed violently as shadows on the walls spun and whirled in an eerie display.

Suddenly the Dark One felt a force slam into her so powerfully that she fell out of the chair and onto her knees. Moaning, she held her hands across her stomach, rocking and wheezing from the pain.

"Who dares summon me?" said a voice so chilling it frightened the woman out of her agony.

"It is I," she managed to gasp. "Keeper of the MacGow legacy, a humble servant. Lord of the Shadows, I beg of you to help me."

There was a cold pause. "For what purpose have I been summoned?"

The Dark One pushed herself up to her knees. "The young one, the MacInness, her power is stronger than I anticipated."

A sound whirled about her head, the hissing of a snake. "She is untried."

"Yes, but strong nonetheless. She appears to be protected in her sleep, and none of my spells seem able to penetrate her aura. She has escaped the numerous misfortunes I have caused to befall her. My efforts have regrettably become more . . . obvious. And now, I feel the presence of another MacInness in Salem."

"Have you consulted the Book of Spells?"

"Yes, O Wise One. I invoked such a spell today. It was powerful and I believe I would have succeeded, except she received aid from an unexpected source."

"A MacGow should always be prepared for the unexpected."

The words were harsh, and the Dark One gave a hoarse cry as her flesh seemed to ripple and burn. As suddenly as it began, the sensation fled and the woman shuddered.

"Her death must be soon. The time draws near."

"I know," she said, aware her voice sounded a bit too desperate. "But I fear the other MacInnesses are gathering. What shall I do?"

"Rely on the dark elements. But you must be careful. Her death must not raise the suspicions of the others."

There was a pause and then the wind began to pick up, sending tendrils of smoke whirling through the air once again. "I shall aid you."

Grateful, the Dark One lifted her hands and braced herself. She screamed only once as one of the tendrils wound itself around her head and slid into her throat, filling her with the blinding sensations of pain, darkness, and power.

"Good hunting, mistress," she heard the voice boom. "Fulfill your destiny and that of the MacGow clan. Be rid of the MacInness."

The Dark One whimpered once, crumpling to the floor unconscious.

* * *

Bridget lay still on her bed, looking up at the rough-hewn beams in the ceiling. Her fingers were linked behind the nape of her neck, cradling her head on the pillow. Shadows danced merrily on the walls, illuminated by the light of a single candle.

"Bridget, are you asleep?" she heard Sarabeth whisper.

Bridget turned her head to look at her sister. Sarabeth was snuggled under the covers, her pretty golden hair tucked up beneath a soft white nightcap.

"No. Is the candle bothering you? I intend to snuff it out soon."

Sarabeth shook her head. "I'm not sleepy, either. I wondered if mayhap you might tell me what is bothering you."

Bridget blinked. "Why do you think something is bothering me?"

"You've been so quiet lately. And I know the story you told Mother about falling down today was untrue. I've known you long enough to know that you are hiding something."

Bridget sighed. "I really did fall down."

"Was Benjamin with you?"

Bridget rolled over on her stomach, pushing up on her elbows. "Why would you think that?"

"Whenever you're in trouble, Benjamin is usually involved."

Bridget smiled wryly. "Sarabeth, you are far more perceptive than people realize. Yes, Benjamin was with me. He's helping Widow Bayley chop wood and do some repairs on her cottage. I would ask that you don't say anything about it to anyone."

Sarabeth laid her head on the pillow. "I wish I had the courage to defy Mother and Father and go out there to assist her."

"I'm not defying anyone. Mother and Father have not forbidden me to see her. After all, she is one of their parishioners. They just don't approve."

"Does Peter approve?"

"Not exactly," Bridget admitted. "As it is, he doesn't know how often I'm out there."

Sarabeth's eyes widened, soft and luminous in the candlelight. "Will you continue to see the widow after you become his wife, if it is against his wishes?"

Bridget looked down at her hands. "Of course not. But there is still hope that I might be able to convince him to let me visit."

"Mayhap Benjamin can help talk to him."

"No!" she said emphatically. "I don't need Benjamin to interfere anymore in this. Peter and I can suffice by ourselves."

Sarabeth fell silent and Bridget lay back down on her stomach, pressing her face into the pillow. She wondered if she would ever sleep. Tonight, for the first time in her life, she didn't want to face the dark. She was still deeply shaken by the encounter with the crow. She couldn't explain how, but instinctively she knew the bird had been a malevolent force. Somehow, she'd fallen under its power and had become dazed and disoriented. If Benjamin hadn't been there with her, there was no telling what might have happened. But why in God's name would someone want to hurt her?

Unable to get comfortable, she pounded the pillow with her fist. She felt vulnerable, exposed, now that Benjamin knew of her ability. He promised not to tell Peter, but would she really blame him if he did?

She wondered what he must think of her now—too weak, too cowardly, and too selfish to reveal her aberration to Peter before the wedding? Humiliation filled her. She'd been surprised that he had not recoiled in horror from her after the fiery display. She could only presume that he'd still been in shock from their bizarre encounter and hadn't been thinking clearly. Once he had time to fully comprehend what had happened, surely he'd be sickened and repulsed.

Then another possibility assailed her, something even worse; Benjamin pitied her. The mere thought of it sickened her. More than anything, she could not—*would not*—endure his pity. How much more shame could she bring on herself and her family?

"Bridget?" Sarabeth suddenly said softly. "May I speak to you forthrightly about something?"

Bridget lifted her head from the pillow. "Of course you may. You know you can always speak to me about anything."

Sarabeth inhaled a deep breath. "It's about Benjamin."

Bridget's insides coiled tightly and she willed herself to breathe slowly. "What would you like to ask about him?" she asked, surprised that her voice sounded so calm.

"You know that Mother and Father would like him to be a part of our family, and they are hoping that he will court me. You don't think I'm right for him, but I want to know why. I realize I'm not supposed to be thinking of such indelicate matters, but Jane Molloy told me that perhaps it's because Benjamin has a reputation around town as being quite . . . ah . . . worldly in certain matters."

"Sarabeth!" Bridget exclaimed, scandalized at her words.

"You said I could talk to you about anything," she protested stubbornly, jutting out her lower lip.

Bridget sat up on the bed, crossing her legs and

looking at her sister. "You're right, I did. I'm sorry. Please continue."

Sarabeth sat up as well, her blue eyes lovely and luminous in the candlelight. "Well, Jane told me that Benjamin has this particular skill for pleasuring women. Something he does with his hands." Her cheeks flushed pink, and Bridget could feel her own cheeks warm as well.

"Anyway," she plunged on bravely. "I decided that of all the people in Salem, you knew Benjamin the best, so you could tell me what this means, and if I am the type of woman who is suited to a man of such temperament."

For a moment, Bridget could only stare at her sister, at a loss for a single intelligent thing to say. "I—I," she stammered, desperately groping for the right words. "I'm not aware of the skill in question, but I think it's no secret in Salem that he is considered quite the rake. And I know it hasn't escaped your attention that he is most handsome and appealing to women in an irresistible and charming kind of way. I suppose it's possible that he might have . . . ah, refined a particular skill with women. I daresay, though, this experience would probably make the encounter all the more pleasurable for a woman."

She remembered how it felt being held so tightly, his expert mouth plundering hers, and those very capable hands burning a path along her spine. She considered for a moment just what kind of technique he had supposedly mastered, and her pulse quickened.

"Bridget?"

She flushed and reminded herself to pay attention to the matter at hand. "I'm sorry. You were saying?"

"You said Benjamin isn't right for me because he's

irresponsible, reckless, and a rake. But has he no endearing qualities at all?"

At first, Bridget could think only of the times he'd slipped spiders down her gown, rubbed burrs in her stockings, and put oatmeal in her bonnet.

Then she remembered how tenderly he'd bandaged her knee after she'd skinned it during a race, and saw his face streaked with dirt and laughing as he risked his neck to rescue a kitten from a tree. And finally she thought of how he'd thrown his body over hers to protect her from the crow.

Endearing qualities, all.

"Frankly, most of the time I don't know whether to hug or throttle him," Bridget said honestly. "But if the truth be known, he has a good heart. I'm certain that if you were ever to wed him, he'd never hurt you."

"It's not that I'm worried about; it's the lovemaking part. Jane said that Mary Pinehurst told her when Benjamin is with a woman, his eyes burn as hot as the devil's own jewels and the merest touch of his hand can give a lady mindless pleasure."

Bridget cheeks burned hotter. "Well, I . . . ah, I'm not certain I'd believe everything I hear, especially when it comes from Mary Pinehurst. But it doesn't matter. When a woman is together with a man that she loves, the pleasure becomes more than just two people touching. It's an emotional experience as well, a joining of mind and soul."

She remembered the drugging intimacy of Benjamin's kiss, the way his mouth seemed to brand her soul, and her blood pumping hot and furiously through her veins.

A slight noise sounded at the open window and Bridget turned her head, lifting her flushed cheeks to the cool breeze that had begun to rush in. She heard a faint clap of thunder in the distance, and suddenly it began to drizzle. The cool, sweet scent of rain floated in through the window, the breeze lifting a wisp of hair from her cheek. For that moment, Bridget permitted herself to envy deeply the woman Benjamin would eventually wed. He'd make her life an endless, crazy whirl, but oh, how gloriously passionate their nights would be.

Sarabeth sighed. "I suppose that is the way you feel about Peter. Tell me, does your heart go all aflutter when he kisses you?"

Bridget blinked and then looked at Sarabeth in mortification. Not once during the entire conversation had she thought of Peter.

"I . . . I . . ." she stammered as guilt and shame swept through her. "Peter kisses quite nicely," she finally managed.

Sarabeth sighed. "I know it's awful to admit it, but sometimes just looking at Benjamin makes me anxious. He's so handsome and self-assured. But I worry it's more fear than attraction. Fear that I might not like what he would do to me. To tell you the truth, I feel more comfortable around someone like Paul Higgins. I know he's not as handsome or adventurous as Benjamin, but he talks to me like a woman."

Bridget reached across the bed and took her sister's hand, squeezing it. "One day you'll find the right man. He'll treat you like a queen and make you happier than you ever imagined."

Sarabeth smiled. "It's my dream, you know. I rather like things quiet and staid. I'm not as clever or as passionate about things as you are, Bridget."

Bridget got out of bed and stood beside her sister. Leaning over, she pulled the covers up to Sarabeth's perfect chin, tucking her in as she had done so many times before.

"Be thankful for who you are, Sarabeth. You're a lovely young woman with a kind heart. I love you."

"I love you, too. You know, sometimes, I wonder why you didn't fall in love with Benjamin yourself. If there is any woman out there capable of living up to his reputation, it's you." She yawned and snuggled deeper under the covers. "Good night, Bridget."

For a moment, Bridget looked down at the face of her lovely sister, her heart swelling with affection and sadness. She leaned over and pressed a kiss gently on her brow.

"Sweet dreams, Sarabeth," she said, melancholy that her own dreams no longer seemed so bright and attainable.

As she snuffed out the candle with her finger and thumb, she heard Sarabeth say sleepily, "Do what is right, Bridget. Follow your heart."

Nine

Bridget walked alone down the road to the meeting house, two heavy baskets filled with food hooked over her elbows. Another glorious day had arrived; the little rain that had fallen in the night had disappeared and only a few puffy clouds dotted the sky. The air was warm and the sun shone brightly. Tender buds on the oak and beech trees burst to life and squirrels chattered happily and dashed across the road. Given the lovely day, Bridget felt certain the picnic was destined to be a success.

Nonetheless, she couldn't shake the feeling of gloom that had come over her. She'd lain awake most of the night, thrashing about, wondering whether she should reveal her secret to Peter. By the time the sun had started to peek over the horizon, she realized she had to be truthful with him now, before they wed. If he truly loved her, they would figure out how to manage this together.

Surprisingly, after making the decision she felt better. Peter was a rock of rational thought and sensibility. She trusted that he'd know what to do. All the same, the thought of the forthcoming discussion left her so filled with trepidation, she could hardly think of anything else.

After preparing several food baskets with her mother and Sarabeth, she'd ridden in the wagon with her father and twelve-year-old Timothy Ross as far as the Blue Shell Tavern, where they were to procure several trundle tables for the picnic. Upon arriving at the tavern, Bridget decided she needed some fresh air to clear her head. She'd told her father she'd walk the rest of the way to the meeting house, hoping to catch Peter on the grassy clearing behind the building where he and many of the young men were likely to be helping set up.

The plan was to entice Peter into a little stroll and then tell him honestly and forthrightly about her secret. Bridget prayed he would remain calm, understanding, and as concerned as she about how best to deal with this unfortunate matter. It was a leap of faith, but she trusted Peter and counted on his love. But why had her stomach begun to churn?

As she walked along the road, she tried to calm herself by admiring the meadow in its glory, cheerfully dotted with yellow and pink flowers. Daisies and buttercups grew in abundance near the roadway, and the fields and woods were carpeted with soft, green grass. Soon she began to feel herself relax.

She was nearly to the meeting house when a sound behind her on the road broke into her reverie. Puzzled, she stopped and turned around. In the distance, she saw a wagon rattling down the road, led by two large chestnut horses. It seemed to be coming at quite a fast clip. In fact, the closer it came, the more it looked like her father's wagon. Puzzled, she squinted, trying to distinguish who was driving.

As the wagon neared the meeting house, Bridget realized with some alarm that it was not slowing.

Hastily, she moved to one side of the road, waving an arm.

"Slow down," she shouted, still trying to make out the form huddled on the wagon seat. "You're going too fast."

From the corner of her eye, she saw someone run out from behind the meeting house to see what the ruckus was all about. At that moment, the wagon swerved and headed directly for her. Horrified, Bridget froze in place, the baskets sliding from her arms to the ground with a thud.

"Bridget!" she heard someone shout and saw that Benjamin stood across the road, running toward her and waving his arms frantically.

The wagon was so close now, she could hear the horses snort, and each frenzied clop of their hooves seemed to pound a death knell into her ears. Shocked, she realized the driver was not her father but a black-clad figure, the face hidden beneath the hood of a cloak. Dimly she realized that Benjamin was still too far away to reach her, but for some strange reason, she could not move her limbs.

As the wagon barreled nearer, Bridget felt someone grab her from behind and yank her backward. For an instant her feet seemed to lift off the ground, and she had the strangest sensation that she flew through the air. The wagon passed by so closely, she could smell the leather of the harness, hear the snort of the horses, and feel the wind rush past her.

Then she fell backward on the ground so hard her straw bonnet flew from her head and her teeth knocked together, taking her breath away. Dazed, she watched as the wagon careened wildly to one side and then tipped over. The horses whinnied in fear, dragging the wagon a bit farther before coming to a stop, snorting and prancing uneasily about.

Bridget tried to get up but found that she couldn't. Weak, she sank back to the ground, thankful when Benjamin skidded to a stop beside her in a cloud of dust, pulling her into the safety of his embrace.

"Benjamin," she uttered once before collapsing into his arms.

Benjamin tightened his arms around Bridget, so thankful she was alive that he could hardly breathe. When he had seen the wagon bearing down on her and realized he was too far away to help, his heart stopped beating entirely.

Then a miracle had happened. A passerby seemingly stepped out of nowhere, yanking Bridget to safety. He glanced around quickly, wanting to express his thanks, but Bridget stirred and he looked down at her.

"Bri," he whispered, tenderly lifting a strand of coppery hair from her cheek, not caring a whit that a small crowd had already gathered around them. "You're going to be all right."

"Get out of my way," he heard someone say and then saw Peter kneel beside him. "My God, Bridget," he exclaimed. "Are you all right?"

She nodded and held out her arms to him. Benjamin's heart tightened in his chest and he relinquished her to Peter. He ignored the surge of jealousy that clawed at his throat as Bridget wound her arms around Peter's neck and pressed her face into his throat.

"What happened?" Peter asked over the top of her head.

Benjamin stood, brushing the dirt off his breeches. "A wagon nearly ran her over. If it hadn't been for the quick thinking of an able woman, Bridget might not be here right now."

"A woman?" Peter exclaimed. "A woman saved Bridget? Good God, where is she?"

Benjamin frowned, looking around the crowd, searching for the woman in a yellow cotton gown and low-brimmed bonnet. She was nowhere to be found.

"I don't see her," Benjamin murmured. "That's odd. She was here just a moment ago."

Paul Higgins ran over, his young face red from exertion and excitement. "We can't find the driver of the wagon," he announced breathlessly. "It's as if he simply vanished."

"Do you know whose wagon it is?" Benjamin asked, striding over to the wreckage. Two men were unhitching the horses. Benjamin's frown deepened when he saw broken pieces of a long trundle table littering the road.

"It's mine," a commanding voice said, and Benjamin looked up as the Reverend Goodwell rode up beside him, sliding off a horse. "What has happened here?"

Benjamin looked over to where Bridget now stood, safely ensconced in the arms of her fiancé.

"The wagon almost hit Bridget," he said bluntly.

"Bridget?" the reverend gasped, looking over in horror at her. "Is she all right?"

"She's shaken, but alive. Peter is comforting her now. What happened?"

He reached in his pocket and pulled out a handkerchief, mopping his brow with it. Benjamin noticed his hand was shaking.

"Frankly, I'm not certain. The strangest things have happened to me this morning. Bridget rode with us as far as the Blue Shell Tavern, where we needed to stop to gather the tables for the picnic. She asked if she could walk the rest of the way to the meeting house and I granted her request. Then young Tim and I went into the tavern and brought out the first table and put it in the wagon. We were just about to go back in to retrieve another table when I ran into the young shipwright, Pierce Williams. He had a rather odd expression on his face when he told me I had an inconsistency in the bolt that attaches to the doubletree. I thought he had lost his senses, since I just checked the wagon this morning. But Pierce was insistent, so I looked again."

"What did you find?" Benjamin asked.

The reverend pressed the handkerchief to his upper lip, blotting the perspiration forming there. "I could barely believe my eyes, but he was right. I tightened the bolt and then thanked him, but he told me my thanks should be given to a young lady whom he'd just picked up from the wharf."

"A young lady?" Benjamin said, his eyebrow rising.

"She stood in the distance by his carriage, so I didn't have the opportunity to thank her myself. Pierce didn't seem inclined to introduce me, and instead seemed anxious to continue on home with his new charge, so I didn't detain him any longer. After that, Tim and I went into the tavern to secure the second table. When we came back out, we discovered the wagon was gone. Fortunately, I was able to borrow a horse from Edward Trask, who also happened to be at the tavern. I rode in this direction, hoping to find who might have taken the wagon and for what purpose."

Benjamin glanced over at the wreckage. "Whoever it was has long since disappeared."

"But why would anyone want to take the wagon?" he asked, a perplexed expression on his face.

Because someone is trying to seriously hurt your daughter, Benjamin thought grimly. *Someone might even want her dead.*

With another bewildered shake of his head, the reverend walked over to where Bridget stood with Peter. She threw herself into her father's arms, and he held her, patting her awkwardly on the back.

For a moment Benjamin simply watched them, his brow creasing into a scowl. What the devil was going on in this town? Too many peculiar things were happening, and at the center of all it seemed to be Bridget Goodwell. It seemed that someone was intent on harming her. But why?

And who was that woman who had appeared out of nowhere and managed so effortlessly to lift Bridget off her feet and out of range of the wagon? Even more troubling, why had she so quickly disappeared without even waiting to ensure that Bridget was all right?

Benjamin rubbed his chin, his scowl deepening. The only clue he had was what he noticed in the split second before the woman had pulled Bridget to safety. A slight shift of the mysterious woman's bonnet had revealed she had hair as flaming red and distinctive as Bridget's.

He searched his memory but could think of no one else in Salem with a hair color similar to Bridget's. He supposed the woman could be a stranger passing through town, but he just as quickly dismissed it.

"Too many coincidences, and too much of it having to do with Bridget," he murmured. "I don't like it."

He decided to pay a visit soon to Pierce Williams to learn more about this young woman he'd reportedly met at the wharf. Perhaps she was connected to all this. On the other hand, if she were with Pierce in the carriage on the way to the Williams estate, he didn't see how she could possibly be the one who had dragged Bridget to safety. But her timely discovery of the loose bolt might have contributed to saving Bridget's life. Had the wagon come unhitched and the horses bolted, even a passerby would not have been able to save Bridget.

After one last look at the wagon, Benjamin strode over to where Bridget stood with Peter and her father. Peter had his arm around her shoulders and tightened it as Benjamin approached.

"Did you find the woman who saved Bridget?" Peter asked.

Benjamin shook his head. "No. She seems to have vanished."

"What's this I hear about a strange woman saving my Bridget?" the reverend asked. "You seem to be the only one who saw it happen, Benjamin."

He lifted his hands. "I don't know who she was. Fortunately, she came along in time to pull Bridget to safety. She disappeared right after the accident. Perhaps we'll come across her again." But even as he said the words, he didn't believe them. Somehow, he knew this was not a chance encounter.

He noticed Bridget watching him intently, and he gave her a reassuring nod. "You were lucky, Bri."

"I know," she said softly.

"Well, I think we should abandon any thoughts of having the picnic," the reverend said firmly.

"Oh, no, Father," Bridget immediately protested. "People have worked so hard, and it's such a lovely day. I'm fine, really. Please, don't ruin the day for everyone just because of me."

Benjamin saw how pale her skin was beneath the dusting of freckles. "I think your father is right," he interjected. "It would best for you to rest."

She raised her chin stubbornly. "Why? I'm not injured in any way. It was just an accident. Please, Father, I beg you to let the picnic continue."

The Reverend Goodwell looked uncertainly at Peter. "If she says she's all right," he said with a quick lift of an eyebrow, "then I don't see why we couldn't continue with the picnic."

"Peter," Benjamin started to interrupt when he saw the cool look his friend threw him. The message was clear. Bridget's welfare was no longer his concern, and he'd be out of place to interfere. Biting back his words, Benjamin fell silent.

"Well, if you both are certain," the reverend said, lifting his hands, "I suppose we can have the wreckage cleaned up in time before most of the parishioners arrive."

"Thank you, Father," Bridget said.

Peter nodded in agreement and led Bridget toward the grassy area, his hand possessively on her elbow. Benjamin watched them go, his jaw tightening.

Officially, Bridget may not be his concern, but he'd be damned if he let anything happen to her. Something strange was afoot in Salem, and he intended to get to the bottom of it.

"I mean to find out what is going on here," he murmured determinedly. "Whoever you are out there trying to harm Bridget, you are going to have to go through me first."

At that moment, a cool wind rushed past the back of his neck, raising gooseflesh on his back and arms. Benjamin nodded grimly.

He had been forewarned.

LIGHT A SINGLE CANDLE

* * *

After nearly getting hit by the wagon, Bridget lost the courage to tell Peter her secret immediately, deciding to wait until later. Having postponed the moment of truth, she drew strength from his nearness, grateful for his calming pats on the back.

Despite her protests to the contrary, she'd been more shaken by the incident than she cared to admit. She knew only Benjamin had seen through her bravado. His gray eyes had narrowed when she insisted on going forth with the picnic, but he'd been powerless to stop her from getting her way. She wanted the picnic to continue for a selfish reason. She still intended to tell Peter of her secret, and she wanted to do it today before another day passed and she changed her mind.

Besides, she'd felt better after Peter took her home to change her gown and wash her hands and face. Mother and Sarabeth had been horrified to hear of Bridget's brush with the runaway wagon, but after repeatedly assuring them she was fine, they became too preoccupied with picnic matters to continue to worry.

Arriving back at the picnic, Bridget busied herself with the preparations, cleaning the benches and tables, then covering them with bright red-and-white gingham cloths. During her work, Bridget stole occasional glances at Benjamin. She sensed he was watching her.

As usual, he looked coolly handsome, despite the warm weather. His shirtsleeves were rolled up to his elbows, revealing muscular forearms, and his shirt was unfastened at the neck. He helped carry and set up benches across the grassy clearing, pausing only occasionally to wipe sweat from his forehead.

Bridget paused, lifting her arms and stretching them over her head to ease her aching back. With satisfaction she surveyed the picnic area. Everything looked wonderful. The weather remained warm and clear with only a faint breeze to stir the leaves. Food had been set on increasingly crowded tables as more and more parishioners arrived. Parishioners had strung hanging lanterns, as yet unlit, around the area on makeshift poles in the likely event the picnic would last well into the evening. People smiled and greeted each other happily as they arrived. After her father asked the blessing, they chatted while heaping food upon their plates.

Bridget lost sight of Benjamin for a while, but presently he returned, looking splendid in a fine shirt of snowy linen, dark breeches, and shiny black boots. His dark, curly hair was damp, and his eyes sparkled with mischief and humor. On his arm was the lovely Lydia Trask, daughter of the town moderator. Lydia looked petite and delicate next to Benjamin, and she clung on to his arm as if unable to walk without it. Several times she laughed and fluttered her eyelashes at him until Bridget couldn't bear to watch.

Nonetheless, it annoyed and shamed her that she felt so jealous. Benjamin was a handsome, wealthy, unattached young man, not to mention the fact that she herself had urged him to find someone to accompany him. She was simply surprised by his choice. Lydia made no secret of shamelessly pursuing every available man in Salem. She was shallow and vain. Bridget had never liked the girl much, and now found she liked her even less.

Nonetheless, Bridget, like many others, couldn't help but stare at them. They made a handsome couple, she admitted grudgingly, both strikingly attractive with thick black hair and flawless skin. As she watched, Benjamin whispered something to Lydia, who giggled and batted her eyes, causing Bridget to roll her eyes in disgust.

"I thought you'd know better than that," Bridget grumbled, absently tucking her own flyaway hair beneath her bonnet.

At that moment, she saw Benjamin look over and flash her one of his heart-stopping grins. She pursed her lips at him and marched off to find Peter.

Not surprisingly, she found him engaged in a heated discussion with Lydia's father, the most politically powerful man in Salem. Bridget knew Peter aspired to have Edward Trask's position as town moderator some day. So, with all the proper support a politician's wife would give, she beamed at Edward and slid up beside Peter. He smiled at her, taking her by the elbow and drawing her close as he argued the economic feasibility of constructing another anchor forge in Salem.

After a suitable amount of time had passed and a proper amount of support was given, Bridget excused herself and wound her way through the picnickers, making certain everyone had enough food and drink. She came across her sister, chatting gaily with a group of young men.

As usual, Sarabeth looked lovely. Clad in a stunning gown of white-and-red gossamer, she commanded attention on the grounds of sheer beauty alone. Her golden hair fell in ringlets around her shoulders beneath a straw bonnet tied with a bright-red ribbon. Her lovely blue eyes were wide and fringed with long lashes. Bridget was certain not a single man heard even a word she spoke, so awed were they by her appearance.

One young man stood a bit farther away than the others, and Bridget saw it was Paul Higgins. The poor boy's face was as red as a beet, but he looked at Sarabeth with such utter devotion that Bridget felt her heart go out to him.

She walked over, putting a hand gently on his shoulder. He practically jumped out of his skin.

"B-bridget," he stammered, his face turning a deeper shade of scarlet. "I didn't see you standing there."

"I'm not surprised," Bridget said wryly. "You know, Sarabeth has had a very busy day. Why don't you bring her something to drink. I'm certain she'd like that."

"She would?" Paul said, his eyes widening.

"Well, of course. Look at all these young men around her, and not a one of them thought to bring her something to drink. I'm sure she'd be very grateful."

Paul's gaze returned to Sarabeth's face, and then with a bolt, he dashed toward the table with the punchbowl. Bridget suppressed the urge to chuckle and walked toward the table where young physician Spencer Reeves, his father, and his fiancée, Phoebe Trask, sat eating and talking companionably. As she passed, Spencer waved her over, asking how Peter fared after his near brush with the crate.

"He's fine," Bridget said gratefully. "Thank you for your concern."

Spencer nodded, his golden-brown hair catching the light. Not for the first time she noticed how strikingly handsome he was.

"And how are you?" he asked kindly. "I heard about your accident with the wagon today. Seems you've been having quite a rash of bad luck."

Bridget swallowed hard. "Fortunately, someone was near enough to pull me from harm's way."

"Thank heavens for that!" Spencer's father interrupted with a wave of his hand. "You've gone your entire childhood without a single broken bone and not one illness, Bridget. I think you must be the healthiest citizen of Salem."

Bridget smiled at him with affection. Phineas Reeves had delivered both her and Sarabeth and carefully monitored their health over the years. He was tall and broad, with kind eyes, gentle hands, and a shock of white hair.

"I intend to keep things that way, thank you," she answered pleasantly.

"How frightening for you," Phoebe Trask interjected, artfully flipping her long dark braid over her shoulder. She was Lydia's older sister, but whereas Lydia was petite and had delicate features, Phoebe stood tall and voluptuous. Her skin was creamy white and her eyes were an almost-white light blue, with thick dark lashes.

"A wagon bearing down on you and a mysterious woman coming to your aid at the last moment," Phoebe continued. "Why, I can't even begin to imagine the terror you must have felt." She pressed her hand to her generous chest as if in shock, and Bridget felt a surprisingly strong ripple of dislike. The Trask sisters were not faring well in her book today.

"I appreciate your concern," Bridget said, feeling a distinct aversion to the woman. "And yes, I wish I knew who came to my rescue so I could thank her. Much to my dismay, she seemed to disappear after the accident."

"What a strange turn of events," Phineas said, breaking a piece of bread with his hands. "Are you certain you don't need me to take a look and see if you suffered any injuries?"

"That is kind of you, Doctor. But I assure you, I

feel fine. I'm just grateful events did not turn out worse."

Spencer reached up and touched her arm. "You know where to find me."

She smiled warmly at him. "I do, Spencer. Thank you for your concern."

Surprised, Bridget saw Phoebe's eyes flash with hostility and then followed her gaze down to where Spencer's hand rested on her forearm. Bridget almost laughed. Phoebe's jealousy was entirely misplaced. She'd known Spencer for years and had never once had any romantic interest in him, nor had he for her. Yet for some reason, it irritated Bridget that Phoebe would be so ferociously possessive of him, especially when Bridget was already a betrothed woman herself.

Purposely ignoring Phoebe's chilly gaze, Bridget thanked Spencer again. After encouraging everyone to eat more, she bade farewell to the Reeves and gracefully moved on to chat with other parishioners. As she walked among the crowd, she ran into her mother.

"How are you faring?" her mother asked politely.

"I'm fine, thank you. Is everything all right?"

"Of course it's not," Abigail replied, taking Bridget's arm and pulling her aside. "First, you are almost run over by your father's wagon, and then Benjamin brings that horrid Lydia Trask to the picnic. Whatever was he thinking, especially when Sarabeth would have been more than willing to accompany him?"

Bridget suppressed a sigh, preparing herself for her mother's tirade. "I can't possibly imagine."

"You haven't been trying to talk him out of courting Sarabeth, have you?" her mother asked, narrowing her eyes.

"I sincerely doubt that anything I say would affect

whom Benjamin decides to court, Mother," she said truthfully.

"Well, it's a pitiful state of affairs. Mercy, now look. Sarabeth is talking to that dreadful boy Paul Higgins."

Bridget glanced over to where Sarabeth chatted gaily with the young man. Paul's face had gone completely scarlet from her attention, but he looked so painfully happy, Bridget couldn't help but smile.

"There's nothing dreadful about Paul," she said. "He's sweet and completely besotted with Sarabeth."

"He'll never amount to much. Why, his father is a worker in the tannery. Benjamin is far more suitable a match for someone as lovely as Sarabeth. Why should her beauty be wasted on Paul?"

Bridget thought it highly unlikely that Sarabeth's beauty would be lost on Paul. But rather than quarrel with her mother, she mumbled something about being hungry and moved away to get something to eat. She was in such a rush to escape that she nearly walked right into Benjamin and Lydia.

"Whoa!" Benjamin said, putting his hand on her shoulder. "Wherever might you be going in such a hurry?"

"Oh, hello, Benjamin, Lydia," she said, noting with annoyance the way Lydia still clung to his arm. "I was just on my way to find a bit of food."

Benjamin's mouth curved into a smile. "Is that so? I should have known your haste had to do with food. Watch your step. I assure you, the food will not vanish before you are able to partake."

She flushed. "I'll endeavor to be more careful."

"That would be wise," Lydia chirped. "I mean, we wouldn't want you to walk your way into another accident, now, would we?"

Bridget suppressed her irritation and instead smiled

sweetly. "No, I guess I wouldn't want to do that." She turned her attention to Benjamin. "Have you seen Peter?"

For a moment, Bridget thought she saw his jaw tighten, but then he shrugged, pointing at the spit. "Last time I saw him, he was there, engaged in a heated discussion with Lydia's father. He's not there now, but I'm certain he's about somewhere."

"May I say that I think it's just delightful how you two are finally getting wed after all this time," Lydia said, trailing a finger down Benjamin's arm to his wrist. "Why, you two were engaged for so long, I wondered if the marriage would ever take place."

Bridget stiffened, drawing herself up so that she practically towered over Lydia. "In fact, I—" she started, when Benjamin intervened smoothly.

"Bridget is a discerning young lady," he said, his eyes glinting with a touch of amusement. "Why shouldn't she be careful about who she intends to wed?"

Lydia sniffed, clearly vexed. "Well, I still think you are fortunate to have found a man like Peter. My father says he might someday be a political force to reckon with in this town. Isn't that exciting?"

"It sounds more like your father may fear his job is in peril," Benjamin noted wryly.

"In peril? Whatever do you mean?" Lydia asked.

Bridget resisted the urge to snicker and instead, took the opportunity to move away. "Well, 'tis been lovely conversing with you two, but I must go and see to the other guests."

"Must you?" Benjamin asked, and Bridget was certain she heard a note of desperation in his voice.

She felt a twinge of pity for him. "Really, I must. Enjoy the picnic."

LIGHT A SINGLE CANDLE

"Be careful," she heard Benjamin call after her.

Resisting the urge to look back at him, Bridget sought out Peter and stayed close. She tried to listen and nod in all the appropriate places as he spoke, and held her tongue even when she knew more about the topic than he did. But more than anything, she tried valiantly to keep her eyes off Benjamin and Lydia as they strolled around the picnic, laughing and chatting with others.

More than once, Benjamin caught her eye, his gaze intense and thoughtful. As the afternoon wore on and dusk began to fall, Bridget felt increasingly uneasy. She knew Benjamin well enough to know when something weighed on his mind. She suspected he had more questions for her, about the crow, the accident with her father's wagon, and how her unusual propensity for fire fit into it all. The only problem was that she didn't have any answers. Instead, she had a sinking feeling in the pit of her stomach that even if she did, she wouldn't want to know them anyway.

Ten

Benjamin had never passed a more tedious afternoon than the one he had just spent with Lydia Trask. More than once he asked himself what he'd been thinking when he invited her to the picnic. If he were honest with himself, he invited her in order to try to banish the image of a betrothed red-haired temptress who presently dominated his thoughts.

He'd felt his mood deteriorate each time he witnessed Bridget walk up to Peter and laugh or speak in the soft whispers of people in love. His chest constricted painfully when Peter placed his hand possessively on her elbow or brushed his lips against her hair as he spoke something in her ear.

He had no right to feel this jealousy, but blast it all to hell, he did. He felt it deep in his gut, and it twisted and churned until he had to grind his teeth to keep from striding over to Peter and demanding he take his hands off Bridget.

To make matters worse, Lydia Trask chattered about the most inane matters in a giggly, singsong voice that made him want to wince. She flirted ceaselessly with him, leaning over to give him a look down the front of her bodice or pretending to innocently brush her breast against his arm. It couldn't have been any more

LIGHT A SINGLE CANDLE

obvious, inept, or unwelcome, Benjamin thought with a frown.

More than once, he considered putting himself out of his misery and simply disappearing from the picnic. But then he wouldn't be able to keep an eye on Bridget, and that was what he wanted to do until he understood more about the strange rash of accidents that had begun to befall her. Frankly, at this point, he didn't trust Peter to keep her safe. In fact, he didn't trust anyone.

". . . so, she had to cast a spell for Old Witch Bayley in order to earn the coin," Lydia was saying.

Upon hearing Widow Bayley's name, Benjamin snapped out of his reverie. "What did you say?" he asked, looking down at her.

"You know, Benjamin, I have this feeling that you aren't listening to a word I say," Lydia said, pouting. "I fear I must be boring you."

He gave her his most charming smile. "If anyone is the bore here, it's me. I apologize. Please, what were you saying about Widow Bayley?"

Seeing she had his full attention, Lydia leaned into him, standing up on tiptoe, presumably to whisper in his ear.

"I said Bridget Goodwell is thought to be doing spells for Old Witch Bayley in order to earn coin to pay for her wedding gown. Betty Corwin told Rachel Waldon that the Goodwells did not have enough coin to pay for the gown. But suddenly Bridget appeared with the money. When Betty asked if the coin came from Peter, Bridget fell silent and wouldn't say where she got it. But it just so happened that the coins were wrapped in a kerchief that Betty recognized as belonging to the old witch. Now, why would the woman give her money? So, either Bridget stole it or she was forced into casting spells that the old woman could no longer do."

Benjamin's jaw tightened, as did his hand on Lydia's elbow. She winced in shock, looking up at him with wide eyes.

"That's cruel and ugly hearsay," he said, his voice tightly controlled. "I would like to think that sort of talk was beneath you."

"I didn't say I believed it," Lydia protested. "I only said that's what I heard."

He released her and she took a step back, rubbing her elbow. "Then see it goes no further," he said.

Reining in his displeasure, he plastered what he hoped was a polite smile on his face and begged to be excused for a few minutes. Lydia agreed, going over to speak with her sister Phoebe and Spencer Reeves.

Benjamin strode past several young men who were lighting the hanging lanterns, and headed for the gentleman's table. It stood discreetly apart from the main picnic area and contained one large punchbowl. He carefully ladled out two cups of punch. But instead of returning to Lydia, he purposefully slipped into the trees, where he noticed Bridget had disappeared a few moments earlier.

He found her sitting underneath a tree, her skirt bunched up around her legs, tossing pebbles into the small creek. Her bonnet sat nearby, perched precariously upon a rock where he suspected she had tossed it.

"Bri?" he said quietly.

She looked up, startled. "Benjamin? What are you doing here?"

He sighed, sitting down beside her. "Most likely doing the same thing you are. Looking for a moment of peace. I rue the moment I decided to invite Lydia Trask to this picnic."

He saw she couldn't quite hide her amusement. "Hasty decisions often have consequences," she said.

"Hasty? You were the one who encouraged me to bring a young lady."

"Now you are blaming me for your poor choice of women?"

"I wish I could."

Her lips twitched. "Well, I'm sorry if you're not having a good time."

He scowled. "I'm not."

She laughed outright. "Oh, don't look so miserable. There are few men here who would consider having the lovely Lydia Trask on their arm a burden."

"I happen to be one of those men," he said morosely and handed her one of the pewter cups. "Here. I brought you something to drink. You've spent all day taking care of everyone else and you haven't had any time to see to yourself."

"Why, thank you." She took a sip and then grimaced. "Let me guess. This came from the secret gentlemen's table."

"It's not so secret if you know about it."

She pursed her lips. "Everyone knows about it. You do know that this has spirits in it."

"Really?" he replied in mock astonishment.

Sighing, Bridget raised the cup. "Frankly, it's just what I needed." She tipped her head back and drained the contents in one long drink.

Benjamin looked at her in amazement. "And I thought I was having a difficult day."

She gave a small burp and then looked at him in embarrassment. "Forgive me. I'm only trying to muster my courage to speak frankly with Peter."

"Where is he?"

Bridget lifted her shoulders. "The last time I saw him, he was engaged in a heated conversation with Spencer Reeves about the use of bloodletting before surgery. He probably hasn't even noticed I've gone missing."

He set his cup aside. "Well, he's no longer with Spencer. He's now talking with Lydia and Phoebe. I'm certain with those women present, their conversation is no longer as fascinating."

"You say that with such derision," Bridget observed. "Is Lydia not able company at all?"

"Actually, she is quite versed in the most sordid details of Salem's hearsay, if you like that kind of thing. Which reminds me, what is this nonsense I hear about you receiving coin from Widow Bayley to pay for your wedding gown?"

Bridget's mouth gaped open in astonishment. "Lydia told you that?"

He raised an eyebrow. "She did."

"Oh," Bridget said, dropping her gaze and curling her fingers around the cup. "Well, I don't know what she's talking about."

Benjamin leaned back on his elbows. "Supposedly Betty Corwin was paid by you in coins wrapped in a kerchief belonging to the widow. Bri, if you needed money, why didn't you just ask me?"

She raised her chin. "I'm not saying that it's true, but if it were, it would be for the same reason I wouldn't ask Peter. It's my concern, no one else's."

Benjamin shook his head. "Haven't we been through this before? We are friends. All you had to do was ask and I would have given the coin to you, no questions or explanations required. For that matter, so would have Peter."

"I'm not a child, Benjamin. I can take care of myself."

"Do you have any idea how damnably frustrating that way of thinking can be? Next time, consider relying on your friends and family first."

"Widow Bayley *is* my friend. And I don't need to rely on anyone. I took care of this matter by myself."

"Ah ha! So, Widow Bayley *did* give you the money. I knew it. Blast it, Bri, what were you thinking?"

Bridget flushed, setting the cup down with a thump. "It's only a loan. I promised to pay her back."

"And just what do you think Peter will do when he hears of this?"

"He won't," she said firmly. "Besides, would it have been any worse if he found out I asked you for the money?"

"He wouldn't have ever known about it. I, unlike Betty Corwin, know how to be discreet."

"Peter is *not* going to find out about this."

Benjamin raised an eyebrow. "Of course he will. I did."

"Only because you just spent an entire afternoon in the presence of the most able gossip in Salem. Peter doesn't associate with people like that."

Benjamin thought of Peter's amorous encounter with the maidservant and wasn't so certain.

"Oh, Bri, how can you be so incredibly hardheaded?" he murmured, brushing a hand across her hair. "And why do I find it so appealing?"

She froze and he realized he'd spoken aloud. Dropping his hand, he tried to act nonchalant.

"Speaking of Widow Bayley," he said, "I didn't see her today."

She looked down at her feet. "She told me yesterday that she didn't intend to come. I don't think she's been feeling well lately. I'll have to check on her tomorrow."

"So will I."

"I would appreciate that. I'm quite grateful for your assistance."

"Even though you didn't ask me for it?"

She sighed. "For how long do you intend to make me feel guilty about that?"

"I'm not certain yet. For as long as I need to, I suppose."

"Well, soon I'll be married and safely the responsibility of someone else. So you, Mother, Father, and everyone else in Salem can stop worrying and gossiping about me."

Benjamin picked up a rock and tossed it in the creek. "Yes, that's what we live for, isn't it? For God's sake, Bri, despite what you may think, the general consensus around town is that you've done well for yourself. Peter is a good man. In many ways, I envy him."

"You?" Bridget said in surprise. "I always thought it the other way around. Peter is endlessly comparing himself to you and believing himself coming up short."

"I can't believe that."

"Why not? Things come easy for you, Benjamin. Peter and I . . . well, we have to work hard at getting the things we want."

"And you think I don't?"

"Not in the same way that we do. It's a gift, Benjamin. You make people feel special, useful, and important. With just one kind word from you, people are willing to do almost anything. That's why you make a wonderful shipping agent for your father. It combines your love of travel and your skills with people."

He was quiet for a moment. "I do love to travel,

and the work for my father is quite satisfying, but do you know what I really dream about doing someday?"

"What?"

"Drawing. Being an architect, really. Designing structures and sketching plans for homes, buildings, and warehouses. This is what I'd truly like to do, Bri."

He dragged his hand through his hair, astonished to feel it shake slightly. Damn if he hadn't just revealed something he'd never told another soul. Then, just like that, he'd told her a dream he'd barely even dared to think about.

"That's wonderful," she said in astonishment, setting her cup down and reaching across to take his hand. "You're so talented. I've seen many of your sketches of buildings around Salem and they are astonishingly good. I had no idea you harbored a dream of someday making those sketches come to life. You'll be a fine architect."

His fingers tangled with hers, and he marveled at the warmth and softness of her hand. It felt so right to touch her, to be linked even if only through a meeting of hands.

"I'm glad to hear that," he said quietly. "Your opinion means a lot. For that matter, *you* mean a lot."

She gently withdrew her hand, and he felt cold without it. For a moment she stared pensively at the creek, hugging her legs to her chest.

"That's kind to say, but you don't have to lie to me, Benjamin," she finally said softly. "I know you think less of me because I intended to wed Peter without telling him about my aberration."

"It's not an aberration, and I do not think less of you. I understand you're frightened. Hell, I'm frightened."

"Which is exactly why I never told you. Why I never dared to tell Peter."

"Yet you have told me, and as fantastic and daunting as your ability may be, it hasn't really changed anything between us."

"How can you be so accepting?" she asked, and he could hear the wonder in her voice.

He shrugged. "Because you are still you, the girl I've always known. And I'm not going to turn away from the best friend I've ever had simply because she can do something no one else can."

She kept her gaze on the creek. "Have you not considered that I might be cursed—borne of an unnatural womb, a product of the devil? I could be dangerous, or even worse, evil."

"That's the most outlandish thing I've ever heard. When I look at you, Bri, I see a young woman who has an unusual gift. You have a good and kind heart. Not even the ability to summon fire can change that."

Benjamin saw her lower lip tremble. "Thank you," she said softly.

He moved a little closer. "Will you tell me how you do it? Will you show me how you make the fire appear?"

Bridget looked at him and then over her shoulder doubtfully. "I'm not certain that is a good idea."

"Please? Maybe if I can understand it better, it will help make things clearer."

"I've never shown anyone before. It's a bit disconcerting to reveal something so unusual about oneself."

"Would you dare to try? For me?"

"I suppose there wouldn't be any harm in it." She stared at a small clump of dry grass near his foot. After a moment, it burst into flames.

Benjamin leaped to his feet, shaking his head in wonder, and stomped the fire out with his boot. "Hell's bells, Bri! That's amazing. So that's how you set my hat on fire the day I tried to kiss Constance Wirth."

"Just be glad you didn't have it on," she said wryly.

"And when I was ten and beat you seven times in a row in that footrace? The seat of my pants started to smolder. That was no accident, right?"

"You made me run on marshy ground. I was angry."

He narrowed his eyes. "I suppose it was you as well when we kissed in your bedchamber and you set my shirt on fire."

Her cheeks burned in mortification. "Now, I'm genuinely sorry about that. It was completely unintentional. It's just that some aspects of my ability are apparently not yet refined. Sometimes I'm not able to control it. If I'm really angry or scared, or if my mind isn't working properly, then I lose my concentration and accidents happen."

He felt a surprising flush of pleasure that his kiss had caused her to lose concentration. "It makes a man wonder what other surprises you have in store for him in the privacy of the bedchamber."

Her blush deepened. "That is hardly an appropriate topic for an engaged woman to discuss," she said wryly.

"Speaking of your engagement there is something I want to tell you."

Desire and need swept through him so intensely, he felt the need to catch his breath. Somehow, he knew this was the time to tell her what he felt in his heart and what she meant to him—what she'd *always* meant to him. To hell with the consequences, he had to do this. To speak the truth of his heart.

He dropped to one knee beside her. "Bri, I—"

Bridget held up a hand, stopping him. "You don't

have to do this, Benjamin. I know what you want to say."

"You do?"

"You think I should tell Peter the truth about me—about my ability. That I should trust the man I'm going to marry. And you are absolutely right. In fact, I fully intended to tell him today at the picnic, but I lost my courage after the wagon accident. But talking with you has helped me regain that courage. I'm going to tell him right now. You made me see that I have to learn to trust those I'm the closest to. Peter loves me and I love him. There shouldn't be anything we can't share with each other. Thank you for being such a good friend."

She looked at him and smiled tremulously. Benjamin felt his heart sink to his toes.

"It's my pleasure," he said, forcing the words from his lips.

She rubbed her temples with her fingertips. "Well, while we're being completely honest with each other, I'll tell you something. I'm more worried about today's accident than I let show. I sensed an ominous presence behind the incident today, as I did yesterday when the crow attacked."

Benjamin frowned. "Do you think it has anything to do with your special ability?"

"Unfortunately, I do. Something came over me when the crow attacked, and again when my father's wagon was bearing down on me. I felt dazed, confused, frozen. Something strange happened to me."

Benjamin remembered the odd, vacant look in her eyes while the crow attacked. "Could it be that there is someone else in Salem with a similar type of ability?" he asked, a chill skittering up his spine.

"Perhaps," she agreed thoughtfully. "There is also

the matter of the crate that fell from the warehouse window. It would have crushed me had I not leaped up to retrieve my bonnet. I'm beginning to think these incidents are all related. But why would someone want to hurt me?"

He considered the possibilities for a moment. "It would mean someone other than the two of us is aware of your talent with fire. But who?"

"I don't know. But I had the distinct sensation that something very wicked was present during the incidents. I can't explain it."

Benjamin felt the hairs on his arms rise. "What does it mean, Bri?"

She shook her head. "I wish I knew. What can you tell me about the woman who pulled me to safety today?"

He rubbed the back of his neck where his muscles were corded tight. "Her face was mostly hidden beneath a bonnet. I couldn't even tell if she was young or old. But I did notice something interesting. Her hair color was red—quite similar, actually, to yours."

Bridget seemed to ponder that for a moment. "There was something about her . . . a feeling I got when she touched me. I felt as if I knew her, that somehow she was familiar to me."

Benjamin put his hand lightly on her shoulder. "Bri, I'm worried about you. Something is happening in Salem, and I think you should—"

"Spend more time with your betrothed?" A crack of someone stepping on a branch sounded behind them and Peter stepped into view.

"Peter!" Bridget exclaimed, leaping to her feet. "I was just coming to look for you."

"Really? You didn't seem to be making much haste." He glanced at Benjamin with a cool gaze. "I suppose I shouldn't be surprised to find you here, too."

Benjamin stood up, calmly brushing the dirt from his breeches. "Just keeping her company."

"You've been doing a lot of that lately," Peter said, and Benjamin heard an accusation in his voice.

Benjamin shrugged. "Why shouldn't I? She's my friend, too."

"Well, she's my *betrothed*," Peter replied firmly. "It is no longer proper for you to be in her presence so much of the time. Especially not alone."

"Oh, Peter, don't be ridiculous," Bridget interrupted. "This is Benjamin we are talking about."

"Which is exactly my point," Peter said, his voice cold. "He's done nothing but cause us trouble for as long as I can remember. And trouble is what I presume he is up to at this moment."

Benjamin stepped forward, crossing his arms against his chest. "Would you care to explain that?"

Peter walked past Bridget and kicked the pewter cup that sat on the ground. "This is what I mean. You've brought her spirits to drink." He turned, grabbing Bridget by the top of her arm.

"You drank it, didn't you?" he asked her coldly.

"Peter, it's not like that," Bridget started to explain. "You see, there's something I need to talk to you about and I was anxious about it, so Benjamin thought only to ease my concern when he brought it to me."

"Don't apologize to him," Benjamin said calmly. "I'm the one who gave it to you."

"*I* will be the one who decides when and if my wife is permitted to imbibe," Peter said rigidly. "Not you."

"She's not your wife yet."

"Soon enough. And I will not have her sipping spirits," Peter said between clenched teeth. "Ever. What would people think?"

"Of you?" Benjamin replied coldly. "This is not about you, Peter, and it's certainly not about your flawless reputation. This is about Bridget."

Peter dragged Bridget over to face Benjamin until they all three stood almost nose to nose. "Yes, it is. And Bridget is my concern now."

"Stop it, both of you," Bridget said, trying to yank her arm free. "Don't talk about me as if I'm not here."

"Let her go," Benjamin said, his voice dangerously low. "You're hurting her."

"What did you say?" Peter said incredulously.

"You heard what I said. Let go of her arm before I have to do something I might regret."

Bridget began to struggle in earnest now. "Peter, please. I really need to talk to you. Benjamin, would you mind leaving us alone now?" She jerked her head to the side, indicating he should leave. Benjamin ignored her, keeping his gaze steadily on Peter.

Peter suddenly released her and she stumbled a few steps away, rubbing her arm. "Peter, whatever has got into you?" she said worriedly. "You've given me spirits before."

"I'll tell you what's got into me. It's Benjamin. As usual, he swaggers back into town, meddling in affairs that are not his concern. Everything was going along fine until he came back. Now look at us. We're fighting, you're sipping spirits, and he stands there looking smug as ever."

"That's not fair," Bridget protested. "You can't blame this on Benjamin."

He laughed contemptuously. "Of course I can. Do you both think me dim-witted? I know what this is all about."

Bridget looked at him in shock. "You do?"

"I do. And I assure you, it's nothing like Benjamin told you."

"Told me?" Bridget repeated as Peter suddenly gripped her hands in his.

"It was nothing, darling, really. Just a harmless little flirtation to ease the pressure of the upcoming nuptials. She means absolutely nothing to me."

For a moment, Bridget simply stared at him in disbelief. Then she gasped and pulled her hands free, taking a step back.

"Flirtation?"

"You idiot," Benjamin snapped, stepping forward. "I told her nothing."

Peter's eyes widened and he quickly looked in alarm at Bridget. "You didn't know?"

She took a step back, shaking her head, and Peter moved toward her cautiously. "Darling, let me explain."

"How could you?" she whispered, but Benjamin saw that her gaze was no longer on Peter, but on him.

"You knew?" she said softly. "You knew and you didn't tell me?"

"Bridget," Benjamin said, taking a step forward. "I wanted to—"

"No," she said, shaking her head. "I thought you were my friend. Don't talk to me. Don't ever talk to me again."

"Bridget," Peter started, spreading his hands. "This is all a horrid misunderstanding. Please, we need to discuss this."

Benjamin saw she looked perilously close to tears, even though she held her composure. His heart ripped in two, and he flinched at the sound of betrayal and hurt in her voice.

"Yes, Peter, we do need to talk about a great many things," she said quietly. "But not now. I need time to think. I will let you know when I'm ready."

Whirling around, she lifted her skirts and fled back to the picnic, leaving the two men standing dumbstruck in her wake.

Finally Peter turned to Benjamin, his tone icy. "Well, old friend, there is exactly the trouble I was talking about. Nice of you to muck things up."

"I don't recall being the one having a dalliance with a maidservant," Benjamin said coolly.

"No, I suppose not, seeing as how you are the perfect gentleman. Stay out of my affairs, Benjamin. I'm giving you one last warning." Turning on his heel, Peter strode out of the trees.

Benjamin watched him go and then swore succinctly. Hell and damnation, he *had* mucked things up again. This time very badly, indeed.

Scowling, he bent down and retrieved his cup. He had to think, to consider his feelings for Bridget. But more than that, he had to determine what she wanted and needed. Of course, he had to first determine a way to get back into her good graces again.

His scowl deepening, he stared at the cup in his hand. All of that would have to be left for later. There was only one thing he wanted to do now, and it involved something considerably stronger than punch.

Eleven

A cool night breeze wafted in through the small open window of the cottage. Widow Bayley sat napping in her chair by the blazing fire, dreaming of a stroll through a lovely garden where she stopped to admire the flowers and breathe deeply of the fresh scent of lilacs.

It was the scent that awoke her, startling her into consciousness. Her eyes flew open and her hands gripped the edge of the chair as she fought to clear the last vestiges of sleep.

For a moment she sat perfectly still, letting her senses tell her what was happening. The scent of lilacs drifted in the air, real and fragrant, and she knew someone stood in the doorway, watching and waiting.

"Bridget? Is that you?" she finally called out. Her voice wavered and she felt ashamed of the fear in it.

She heard the soft rustle of skirts and a warm hand suddenly grasped hers.

"Do not be afraid. It's me."

"Hannah?" the widow whispered, stunned. "Is that really you? Or am I still dreaming?"

"I am real. I'm sorry if I startled you, Anne. It's been so long; I wanted only to look upon your face for a minute. You looked so peaceful, so happy. I've missed you dearly."

Hannah gave her a heartfelt hug. The widow squeezed back fiercely. It had been far too long since they had been together.

"I've missed you, too," the widow said as they broke the embrace. "I knew you would come. But it's been so long, I had begun to worry that something had happened to you."

Hannah sighed and sat down in a chair. "It's been a most arduous time. I had great difficulty locating the others."

"But have you?"

Hannah paused. "Only one."

"Only one? Oh, merciful heavens. What shall we do? The time draws near and the dark powers are gathering."

"I know, and there is more. Bridget is in grave danger."

"Bridget?" the widow exclaimed. "How do they know about her?"

"I'm not certain," Hannah said wearily. "They must be able to sense her. Her power is growing formidable, Anne."

The widow grew still. "Have you seen her?"

She heard the breath catch in Hannah's throat. "Yes. Oh, yes. She's a beautiful young woman."

"She's blessed with a good, kind heart, too. She's truly a lovely girl. We've become friends."

"I envy you that," Hannah replied and the widow could hear the regret and pain in her voice. "But I'm terribly concerned about her safety, especially after what I witnessed today."

"Today? What happened?"

"Bridget was nearly run over by a wagon near the

meeting house. A holding spell froze her in place. I arrived just in time to break the spell and pull her to safety. But the magic was very strong. Stronger than I had anticipated."

The widow looked worried. "They are becoming bolder and more dangerous."

"I'm afraid you are right."

"Did you speak to Bridget?"

"No. The time is not quite right for that yet. I wish I could."

"I'm sorry. What can I do to help?"

Hannah stood and began pacing. "I'm not certain. I cast another protection spell, a much stronger one, to shield Bridget from the magic. But I cannot protect her from physical harm. And I must leave Salem."

"So soon?" the widow exclaimed. "But you've only just returned. And Bridget is to wed in less than three weeks."

"So I've heard," Hannah said, her tone grim.

"She doesn't love him," the widow said softly. "He's not in her heart."

Hannah paused and then sighed. "I'm sorry to hear that."

"Why must you leave? Can you not remain here to watch over Bridget?"

The widow heard Hannah go to the window. "I want to, more than anything. I am finally home after all this time. But we have only five months to find the other girls, bring them to Salem, and train them. If I stay to protect Bridget, then I doom her and all who follow to a lifetime of pain and misery. And, as much as it distresses me, I must fulfill my destiny as well."

The widow nodded, a sense of foreboding filling her heart. "The girls will come to Salem, Hannah. It is foretold."

"I know. But I fear it will not be soon enough. Once they are here, I'll have to reveal myself to them. This will be difficult and the most dangerous part."

"They'll understand. They must."

"I pray it shall be so. Please, be as aware as you can of what is happening in town. Take notice of anyone new."

"I will. Bridget usually speaks of things like that, but she hasn't lately."

"Certainly with the wedding approaching, she's been preoccupied."

"That is so."

The widow could hear Hannah leave the window and return to her seat. "Anne, there is something else you should know. You may be in danger as well. If the Dark Ones suspect you are helping us, they will come after you."

The widow shrugged. "I've lived a long and full life. Why should I be frightened of them?"

"They would show no mercy or remorse in causing you pain . . . and perhaps worse." She paused and her voice caught. "I don't want anything to happen to you."

The widow held out a hand, waiting until Hannah grasped it. "If they are watching Bridget, then they already know that she comes to me often and has been doing so for many years. They either don't care or feel I am no threat to them."

"That, I hope, will work in our favor. I did not cast a protection spell on you because I feared they would sense it and try to harm you. But it worries me that you have no powers to protect yourself."

"I'm not afraid of what will happen to me," she said softly. "But we must protect the girls."

Hannah sighed. "I'm going to Boston, Anne. One of the girls is there."

"You are certain?"

"Yes."

"When will you return?"

"As soon as I can, and, I hope, with her. In the meantime, please, urge Bridget to be careful."

"I will."

Hannah leaned over and gave her another hug. The scent of fresh lilacs brought back bittersweet memories of happier days, and the widow felt a stinging pang of loss for her dear Elias.

"I'll be back as soon as I can with the others," Hannah whispered. "All will be well."

"Godspeed to you, friend."

The widow heard Hannah walk to the door and then pause at the threshold. "Anne, is there no one else you could trust to help watch over Bridget? Someone who loves her as much as we do?"

The widow considered for a moment and then nodded thoughtfully. "In fact, there is. Don't worry, Hannah, we'll take good care of her."

Benjamin felt like hell. His head pounded as if a sadistic gnome were hammering away from inside, his stomach felt queasy, and the morning sun shone so brightly he wished he could snuff it out with his fingers. Nonetheless, he strode toward the Goodwell house, keeping his head high and hoping he didn't look as bad as he felt.

When he got to the house, he lifted the heavy knocker and brought it down, wincing when the sound ricocheted through his head as well as the house.

"Blast this headache," he muttered just as Ichabod Goodwell opened the door.

"Good morning, Reverend," Benjamin said brightly, summoning a smile. "Sorry to come unannounced, but I wanted to inquire how Bridget is faring after yesterday's accident. And I brought this." He held out Bridget's bonnet.

The reverend sighed and took the bonnet. "I fear it is worse than I suspected. She's taken to her bed and refuses to see anyone. Peter was here earlier and she would not speak with him either, claiming fatigue and dizziness. She says she needs time to rest, so we are granting her that request. She so rarely falls ill that we are very concerned. She has no fever, yet she seems listless. I blame myself for letting the picnic continue against my better judgment."

"We both know how stubborn Bridget can be. I'm sorry to hear she's not well. Will you tell her I inquired after her health?"

"Of course. It was kind of you to come by."

Benjamin exchanged a few more words with the reverend, then left the house. He wondered what Bridget was thinking and if she would ever forgive him. He'd kept the confidence of one friend and betrayed the other. He was in a damnably tight spot.

Sighing, he shielded his eyes from the sun. He shouldn't have drunk so much, but the misery of his encounter with Bridget and Peter, coupled with the unpleasant task of enduring more time with Lydia Trask, had driven him to try to drown his sorrows both at the picnic and then later at home. The morning had come far too soon and with little relief from his wretchedness.

Now he had to decide what to do next. If Bridget remained secluded in her home, at least that meant she was safe from immediate harm. That gave him the opportunity to try to unravel the mystery of the strange woman who had pulled her out of the wagon's path. It would give him something to do to occupy his mind.

Determinedly he turned in the direction of the Williams estate. Although he'd been there several times for parties and gatherings in the past, he considered Pierce little more than a casual acquaintance. Nonetheless, his impression of the man was favorable, and he counted on that to help him in his quest for information.

When he reached the gate, Benjamin opened it, walked up to the door, and knocked. Soon the Williamses' housekeeper, a middle-aged woman with a friendly smile, opened the door.

"Mr. Benjamin Hawkes!" she exclaimed. "What a surprise. Please come in and tell me what brings ye round this morn?"

"I'm here to see Pierce, actually. Is he perchance at home?"

She shook her head. "I'm afraid not, sir, he's down at the shipyard. His new vessel must be ready to set sail by summer's end. We rarely see him these days."

"His ship is that far along already?"

"It is," she said proudly. "A fine lady she will be."

The throbbing in Benjamin's head renewed and he resisted the urge to wince. "Well, I look forward to seeing it, and I'm sorry to have bothered you. I'll find Pierce down at the shipyard."

"Would ye like a glass of lemonade first, sir?" the housekeeper asked kindly. "Ye look a wee bit flushed."

"That is very generous, but I must be on my way. Thank you for your offer, Mrs. Bisbey."

The woman blinked in surprise and then smiled as a faint blush touched her cheeks. "Why, sir, however did you remember my name?"

Benjamin managed a grin despite his pain. "I never forget the name of a pretty woman."

Mrs. Bisbey laughed in delight. "Always the charmer, aren't ye?" she said, shaking her finger at him good-naturedly. "Please come back any time."

Benjamin waved once more as he headed out the gate and then turned down the street in the direction of the wharves. He strode through the center of town and walked down to the beach area, where he remembered seeing Pierce's ship being built.

Turning the corner of a warehouse, he strode onto the beach and stopped to admire Pierce's ship. It looked magnificent. The gleaming copper hull sat cradled on a mold loft. Beneath it ran a long wooden ramp that would serve to launch the ship into the water when she was ready. Carpenters and caulkers milled about everywhere. Other workers stood on ladders, coating the hull with a mixture that Benjamin knew to contain resin, sulphur, and tallow to repel teredo worms and barnacles. Yet despite the bustling activity, he didn't see Pierce around anywhere.

Benjamin continued on down the beach, his boots sinking into the sand. As he got closer, he spotted Pierce standing to one side of the hull, holding up scraps of painted wood and presumably talking with the painter.

Pierce looked up and saw him, a puzzled look crossing his face. He said something to the painter and the man took the scraps of wood and walked away.

"Benjamin," Pierce called out, stepping forward to greet him. "To what do I owe the pleasure of this visit?"

"I'm sorry to interrupt your work," Benjamin said, holding out a hand. Pierce shook it, his handshake firm and friendly. "I wondered if I might have a moment of your time."

"Of course," Pierce said. Motioning with his hand, he lead Benjamin to a spot shaded by the hull and not occupied by any workers. "By the way, I heard your trip to Lisbon turned out to be quite a profitable run for your father. Congratulations."

Benjamin grinned. "Thank you. That means a lot coming from the competition. I must admit it was an exhilarating as well as exhausting journey. But none of that is what brings me here today."

"Then how can I assist you?"

"Frankly, I'm in search of information. The Reverend Goodwell mentioned an encounter with you yesterday near the Blue Shell Tavern. He said you observed a problem with the bolt holding the doubletree to the wagon tongue."

Pierce shifted uneasily on his feet. "Yes, but I wasn't the one who identified the problem. It was a passenger of mine, a young lady."

Benjamin raised an eyebrow. "A lady? How did she happen to notice it?"

Pierce shrugged. "While I was inside the tavern, she strolled by the wagon and saw the loose bolt."

"That's a bit of an odd observation."

"True, but you've never met Miss Gables. She's a particularly astute woman. Personally, I didn't give it too much thought."

He gazed out to the sea and Benjamin noted the disconcerted look in his eyes.

He's lying, Benjamin thought. *He's given it a lot of thought. He likely thinks something is odd here, too.*

But each of us is circling, not knowing quite how to talk about the strange occurrence.

"No, I haven't yet had the pleasure of an introduction to Miss Gables," Benjamin said casually. "But might I inquire as to what happened when you mentioned the loose bolt to the reverend?"

Pierce shrugged his shoulders. "He examined it and discovered she was right. He fixed it at once and then thanked me profusely. The team he had hitched were young and certainly would have bolted had the tongue come undone."

"Why didn't the young woman tell the reverend herself?"

"She is a stranger to this town, so she asked me to do it. I obliged her. The reverend was lucky she noticed it at all."

"So was his daughter."

"Sarabeth?" Pierce said, his brow creasing into a frown.

"No, the elder daughter, Bridget. The wagon was stolen shortly after your conversation with him. It nearly ran her over."

"My God, was she harmed?" The shocked look on Pierce's face told Benjamin that he had no prior knowledge of the incident.

"No. Thankfully, someone pulled her to safety in time."

Pierce combed his fingers through his hair. He, too, looked as though he hadn't slept much the night before.

"Would it be too forward of me to ask more about your new charge?" Benjamin asked.

"I don't see why it should. Miss Gables is the daughter of a friend of my father's in Boston. She's come to Salem for the summer to help my father catalogue and sketch a scientific collection for the Royal Society of London."

"Help your father?" Benjamin asked, surprised. "You mean she's educated?"

"Quite so, as far as I can tell. Her knowledge on many topics seems quite advanced."

"Then she is here for only a short time?"

"That is my understanding."

Benjamin paused and then spoke. "Pierce, after leaving the Blue Shell Tavern yesterday, did you happen to take an indirect route home?"

"Such as?"

"Such as past the meeting house?"

Pierce crossed his arms against his chest. "Is there something in particular you wish to know? Might I say your questions seem rather odd?"

Benjamin sighed. "A woman pulled Bridget to safety moments before the wagon would have struck her. I thought perhaps it might have been your passenger."

Pierce seemed genuinely taken aback at the suggestion. "I'm sure she would appreciate being credited with such a rescue, but it was not her. Miss Gables was quite tired from her journey. We proceeded immediately to the estate with no other stops."

Benjamin nodded. "I presumed as much. Well, thank you for your time. I'm sorry to have bothered you."

"It was no bother. Feel free to come by anytime. I'd be happy to give you a grand tour of the ship when the preparations are complete."

"I'd like that."

Benjamin watched Pierce walk away, feeling no closer to understanding what had happened to Bridget in front of the meeting house than before he came.

Rubbing the back of his neck, he trudged back into town, pondering the origins of the mysterious woman with red hair and wondering with a sinking heart if Bridget would ever speak to him again.

Bridget lay in bed, ignoring the sunshine beckoning from beyond the open window. She had a dull ache in the center of her stomach, which had naught to do with illness and everything to do with heartache. Her world was falling apart and she didn't know how to stop it.

She knew both Peter and Benjamin had come to see her, but she wasn't ready to face either one of them yet. The taste of Peter's betrayal was still bitter on her tongue, as was the guilt that assuaged her over the heated embrace she'd shared with Benjamin. How she would gather the shreds of her dignity still eluded her.

Hearing footsteps in the hallway, she rolled over on her stomach, pressing her face into the pillow. The footsteps came closer and someone entered the bedroom, closing the door.

"Bridget," she heard Sarabeth say softly. "I wish you would talk to me. I can't bear your silence anymore. I know this isn't just about the accident with Father's wagon. There is something else deeply troubling you. Peter and Benjamin are both clearly upset as well. Will you not talk to me? Please?"

Bridget didn't answer, and she heard the rustle of Sarabeth's skirts as she sat on the edge of the bed. The wood frame creaked with the extra weight and then settled.

"You've always comforted me, since we were children," Sarabeth continued. "Bridget, the strong one;

Bridget, the wise one. For once, I beg of you, let me be the sister to offer that solace."

Bridget remained still for a moment and then rolled over onto her back.

"I wish it were possible for your solace to ease my heart," she said miserably. "I don't think you can help me, Sarabeth. I can't even help myself."

Sarabeth reached out and touched Bridget's cheek gently. "Mayhap not. But I can listen. Sometimes that can be enough."

Touched by Sarabeth's concern, Bridget sat up, crossing her legs in front of her. The heat pasted her linen nightgown to her back, and her stomach churned.

"It is kind of you, but I fear in this matter, just listening will not be enough."

Sarabeth reached out to take Bridget's hand. "What troubles you, sister?" she asked softly.

"Everything," Bridget replied. "I've been dishonest with Peter; I've been dishonest with Benjamin; but most of all I've been dishonest with myself."

Sarabeth's delicate brow creased into a frown. "What do you mean?"

Bridget felt a soft breeze tousle her hair and she lifted her face to the open window, seeking relief from the heat. "I thought I loved Peter. Really loved him. Now, I'm not so certain. As the wedding approaches, I realize I haven't been very truthful with him about many things. And I discover he hasn't been truthful with me, either. What kind of love is this if we cannot talk to each other about the things that matter most?"

"It's not too late," Sarabeth said gently. "You still have time before the wedding."

"I want to, but I'm horribly ashamed of myself. I think I tried to make myself believe Peter was right for me because I wanted so much to be wed."

Sarabeth stared at her in dismay. "Surely you aren't reconsidering your decision to wed him?"

Bridget looked miserably at her sister. "I am."

Sarabeth paled dramatically. "Bridget, every bride is nervous. Surely matters cannot be that bad."

"I'm afraid they can."

"Whatever happened to provoke this? And how did Benjamin become involved?"

Bridget felt the sweat bead on her chest and trickle down between her breasts. "Can you keep a secret, Sarabeth?"

"Of course."

"An important secret. It can go absolutely no farther than this room."

"You can trust me, Bridget."

"I know. It's just that I don't know quite how to say this. It just seems that no matter what I do, Benjamin is destined to be inextricably involved in my life."

"In what way?"

"In every way. I had a feeling that from the moment I saw him in the parlor last week, something drastic would happen. Indeed, in just the few days since Benjamin has been back in town, my carefully stitched life has begun to completely unravel."

"Surely he didn't do anything hurtful."

"Not precisely. There was just this indefinable moment when everything changed between us."

"What kind of moment?" she asked hesitantly.

"A passionate one."

Sarabeth clasped her hand over her mouth in horror. "Oh, no, Bridget. He didn't."

Bridget nodded. "He did. I did. I don't know how it happened. It's just that one minute we are having one of our never-ending arguments, and the next, he's dragging me into his arms and kissing me like I've never been kissed before."

"He . . . he kissed you?"

Bridget nodded anxiously, winding a corner of the blanket around her finger. "It was naught more than an impulsive act, something both of us certainly regretted. I wanted to tell Peter, but I knew he'd be furious with Benjamin, and with me, too. But there is more than that. I wanted Benjamin to kiss me. I welcomed his embrace in my heart." Her cheeks flushed.

Sarabeth opened her mouth, closed it, and opened it again. "Oh," she uttered finally.

"I intended to avoid Benjamin before the wedding and simply forget the whole incident," she continued. "But it was impossible. Everywhere I went, Benjamin seemed to be there. Matters have definitely changed between us."

"I can see why. Did he apologize?"

"Profusely. He was embarrassed, I think. I was, too. But naught has been right since then. We both felt as though we had betrayed our friendship with Peter. During the picnic, Benjamin came to speak with me when I slipped into the forest for a few moments of quiet thought. I had just told him I intended to be honest with Peter about the kiss and many other things when Peter came upon us."

"Oh, my," Sarabeth breathed.

"He was furious to find us together alone and learn I'd had some punch from the gentleman's table. Benjamin had only brought me a cup to settle my nerves. Then, somehow in the middle of arguing about the impropriety of my partaking of the punch, I discovered Peter had engaged in a dalliance with another woman. I don't know the details; I didn't stay long enough to hear them."

Sarabeth shook her head in wonder. "You were drinking? Peter dallied with another woman? Oh, merciful heavens, Bridget. Nothing is ever simple with you. So Benjamin told you about Peter's dalliance?"

"No, and Peter confessed *after* he thought Benjamin had already told me. It's a wretched situation. Benjamin knew about Peter's indiscretion all along and didn't tell me; Peter betrayed me before we are even wed; and I permitted Benjamin to kiss me and didn't tell Peter. Everything is wrong."

Bridget walked to the window, lifting the hair from the back of her neck where it was slick with sweat. "I thought Peter was the man I wanted to spend the rest of my life with. Yet I hide secrets from him before we are even wed, and he looks to another for . . . well, for enjoyment. How can this be right?"

Bridget looked over to see Sarabeth's stricken expression. "You see, I shouldn't have told you," she said, looking back out the window. "I've upset you."

"No, Bridget, I'm honored you trusted me." She fell silent for a moment. "I don't know that much about the ways of men, but I have heard that sometimes they do occasionally seek out the company of other women. Mayhap Peter is no different in that respect."

Bridget pressed her lips together, feeling ridiculously close to tears. "I'm not naive, but I never thought that possible of Peter. I don't think I could bear the thought of him having indiscretions. I just couldn't."

Sarabeth stood, anxiously paced the room a few times, and sat back down on the bed. "What about Benjamin?" she asked. "Are you angry at him?"

"I feel betrayed. Hurt. Why didn't he tell me?"

"He's Peter's friend, too," Sarabeth said gently. "It

must have been very difficult for him to keep Peter's secret from you."

And now he held her secret as well. "I suppose," she conceded. "Nonetheless, 'tis something I wish he hadn't kept from me."

"He is very fond of you, Bridget. And you of him."

"Certainly. He's my best friend, of course. He's annoying, arrogant, and insufferable, but he's also kind, witty, and adventurous. He makes me feel so . . . alive."

"Mayhap his interest in you has changed into more than just friendship," she offered.

Bridget shook her head. "His kiss was not a show of interest. It was but an amusement to him, as such things are for men like Benjamin. He only did what he's already done with half the women in Salem."

Sarabeth pursed her lips. "Mayhap. But it doesn't change the fact he behaves differently with you, Bridget. In fact, he's always seemed to treat you differently, with genuine affection and respect. I've never seen him act that way with anyone else."

"Presumably because he never considered me in the same way as one of his conquests."

Sarabeth fell silent, thinking for a moment. "Are you in love with him?"

Bridget flushed, the denial on the tip of her tongue. Then she saw the earnest expression on Sarabeth's face and bit it back.

"I was once," she said quietly. "A long time ago."

"Why didn't you ever tell me?"

Bridget sighed, leaning her head against the wall by the window. "Because they were childish, foolish dreams. It doesn't matter now, anyway. I'm betrothed to another, and even thinking such things is a betrayal of what I should feel for Peter."

"Nevertheless, I wish you had told me. After all, I considered Benjamin a potential suitor." She pressed a hand to her breast. "Oh, heavens, Mother and Father still certainly think so."

"I would never have stood in your way if I thought Benjamin would be good for you," Bridget said honestly.

"I know," Sarabeth replied. "And I also know Benjamin isn't the right man for me. I think I've known that all along."

"I'm sorry."

"I'm not. I know the right man will come along. But this isn't about me. What will you do? You can't avoid Peter and Benjamin forever."

Bridget nodded. "I'm aware of that. But I'm afraid, Sarabeth. Afraid of being alone for the rest of my life. All I've ever wanted is my own family—a husband, a happy home, and children to love and nurture. We both know there will be no other suitor after Peter."

"You can't be certain of that," she replied quickly, but avoided Bridget's gaze.

"Yes, I can," Bridget said softly. "But if I marry Peter, will I betray my heart?"

"I don't know," Sarabeth whispered.

"Neither do I."

A tear trickled down Sarabeth's cheek. "Oh, Bridget. What will you do?"

Bridget closed her eyes. "The only thing I can. Marry Peter. If he'll still have me."

Twelve

Benjamin spent the better part of the day helping his father with the accounting books. As late afternoon arrived, he decided to look in on Widow Bayley.

When he knocked on the door, she called for him to enter. He first stopped in the doorway to scratch Francesca behind the ears. She purred and rubbed against his leg.

"You're a sweet girl, aren't you?" he murmured.

"I believe you've made a friend for life," he heard the widow say.

Straightening, he strode into the cottage. The room was dark except for a cheery fire that blazed in the hearth. He took her cold hand and pressed it to his lips.

"How are you feeling today?" he asked, studying her face. It worried him that she looked paler, drawn, and much more fragile than on his last visit.

She patted his hand before releasing it. "I'm fine now that I have some company. Do sit down. Would you like some tea?"

He sat in the chair across from her. "Please. Shall I pour?"

"That is kind of you, but there is no need."

He watched in amazement as she rose gracefully

from the chair and made her way to the table, where a teapot and two cups sat. He eyed the other teacup curiously.

"Were you expecting company?" he asked.

"Only you."

"You said that the last time I was here. How did you know I'd come?"

She lifted her shoulders delicately. "A fortunate guess, I suppose."

"You are quite a beguiling woman," he said in amusement.

"So my Elias used to tell me." Without pause, she lifted the pot and poured the tea, not spilling a drop.

Benjamin watched her, fascinated. "That's astonishing. How do you do it?"

"Many years of practice, I assure you."

"How many years have you been blind?" he inquired, then realized he might have offended her. "I apologize if that was too forward."

She sat the teapot back on the table. "It was not. I was born this way."

"I'm sorry."

"Why should you be sorry? We all have our burdens to bear."

"True, but would you not agree that some have more difficult ones than others?"

"Indeed, that is so. However, I consider myself among the fortunate. Until lately, there is little I could not do for myself. I will show you."

He observed with interest as she made her way over to a low wooden cabinet with drawers and picked up an odd device that sat on top of it. The object was no bigger than her hand and she held it carefully. Extending her other hand to guide her way, she walked back toward him until she felt the edge of the small table near his chair. While he watched with growing curiosity, she held the device near the unlit candlewick at his elbow and flicked her thumb a few times. To his utter astonishment, a spark suddenly leaped out, catching the wick and lighting it.

He blinked in astonishment. "What . . . how did you do that?"

She smiled proudly. "Elias made it for me. It's naught more than a means to help a blind woman strike a fire should her embers go out. It may also light a candle should a visitor come calling."

"It's magnificent," he breathed. "May I see it?"

"Of course." She handed him the object.

Benjamin took it carefully, holding the unusual device closer to the candlelight for inspection. "I'll be damned," he murmured.

Elias had taken a part of the mechanism of a flintlock pistol and made it into a contraption that produced a spark. All the necessary parts were there: the hammer that held the flint, the mainspring that powered the hammer, the frizzen—a piece of steel the flint would strike—and a small pan as big as his thumbnail, which contained a minuscule amount of gunpowder. The entire mechanism had been carved and set into a small piece of wood around which the widow could easily wrap her hand.

Simple yet practical. Functional and fantastic.

"It's utterly ingenious," he declared.

"I have only to replace the powder here," she said, reaching her hand across his and feeling with her finger until she found the small pan. "Truthfully, I use this only on rare occasions. Elias said it is a rather unstable and dangerous contraption. But no more dangerous, I suppose, than going without a fire in the dark of winter. I confess to using it now only to boast of Elias's intellect. I don't often have the proper company in which to do so, but I thought you might appreciate it. That, and I found myself missing Elias quite terribly this evening."

Benjamin handed it back to her and she replaced it on the wooden cabinet. "Well, I assure you, I'm suitably impressed," he said. "Do you have any other such fascinating devices around?"

She chuckled, and Benjamin watched as the years seemed to melt away from her face. "Many. Elias was quite an inventor. He liked to draw as well."

"Draw?" Benjamin's eyes lit up. "May I see some of his work?"

The widow returned to the wooden cabinet and opened a drawer. "Elias considered everything a subject," she said. "People, animals, nature. But he liked best to draw the magnificent buildings of Salem. He described each one in detail to me as he sketched. He was truly my eyes."

She handed Benjamin a curled parchment. With growing excitement he unrolled it, looking eagerly at a detailed sketch of a Georgian colonial house. The symmetry and detail of the sketch were breathtaking, the work of a master architect.

"It's exquisite," he murmured, shaking his head in disbelief. Who would have known that old Elias Bayley had so much talent? "He had no formal training and yet he's created a masterpiece."

Her smile widened. "I thought you might appreciate it. The first time I met you, I could hear in your voice the soul of an artist."

"Me?" he said, startled. "You are mistaken. I am nothing more than a shipping agent for my father."

"So, you do not draw, then?" She sounded disappointed.

He sighed, reluctantly handing her back the sketch. "I confess to doing a bit. But I am a novice compared to your husband."

" 'Twas but one of his many passions. I only wish he could have spent more time pursuing them. But we had to eat. Blessed are those who are fortunate enough to follow the dreams of their hearts."

With those thought-provoking words, she picked up the teacup and saucer and brought them to him without spilling a drop. She then carried her own to the chair and sat down, cradling the saucer carefully in her lap. For a moment they sat sipping in silence.

"Well, do tell me why you came by," she finally said.

He looked at her, momentarily at a loss for words. God help him, amid the fascinating conversation, he'd completely forgotten the real purpose for his visit.

The picnic. Bridget's accident.

"Actually, I came by to tell you about the picnic," he said.

"I'm sorry that I missed it."

"I am, too. There was quite a bit of excitement."

"Was there?"

He set his teacup on the table. "I don't wish to alarm you, but Bridget was involved in an accident."

"Oh, dear, is she all right?"

"Thankfully, she is well. But she was nearly run over by her father's wagon."

"Heavens! Did the reverend lose control?"

"No. He wasn't driving. It was stolen from the front of the Blue Shell Tavern."

She pressed her hand to her chest in horror. "Who would want to steal a wagon?"

Benjamin stared at her intently. Oddly, the tone of her voice did not match the concern he saw in her expression. "Who, indeed?" he answered, frowning. "Unfortunately, the perpetrator escaped. But what I would like to know is, why did he drive it straight at Bridget?"

The widow turned toward him, her expression innocent. "Are you saying you think this mishap was intentional?"

"The thought occurred to me."

"But why? Who would want to harm her?"

"I hoped perhaps you could tell me. Did she ever mention being troubled by anyone before?"

The widow thought for a moment. "No," she finally said. "But this worries me. It would certainly be prudent to keep close watch on her. Will you do it, Benjamin?"

He tilted his head, looking at her intently. The request seemed prompted by a genuine concern for Bridget, and yet, he had the distinct impression there was something else she wasn't telling him.

He sat back in the chair, stretching his legs out in front of him. "I'm afraid that is going to be rather difficult. At the moment, I'm not certain Bridget will see or talk to me."

"Why ever not?"

"We had a bit of a disagreement."

"Oh, dear again? Certainly she'll forgive you."

"Perhaps. But it is unlikely to be anytime soon. Nonetheless, I'm determined to do everything in my power to make things right for her."

He watched as her face clouded with uneasiness. "Is that for you to do?"

He shrugged. "Why shouldn't it be? I feel it is, at the very least, my responsibility to try."

She took a sip of tea, cocking her head in his direction. Her light-blue eyes stared vacantly, but he had the unsettling feeling that she could see him.

"Mayhap it is something Bridget needs to do on her own," she suggested quietly.

Benjamin waved a hand impatiently. "She's always had to do it on her own. But not anymore, and not when the trouble is partially my fault."

"She's a strong young woman."

"She is," he agreed. "However, this time she has more to lose."

The widow was silent for a moment and then set her cup back in the saucer. "You've been her friend for a long time."

"That's true. Bridget fascinated me from the moment I met her. Even at the tender age of six, she was stubborn, competitive, and temperamental. She stood up to me, dared me to better myself. But more than that, I admired her because she always did what she believed was right, even if it meant certain punishment."

The widow's expression became pensive, almost somber. "Integrity and courage are admirable traits. Yet there is a vulnerable side to Bridget as well. She mustn't be harmed, Benjamin."

"I agree," he said, leaning forward in the chair. "Is there something I should know in order to aid her?"

The widow's fingers tensed in her lap, a look of resignation crossing her face. "You know all you need to know."

"I'm afraid I don't believe that," he said, disappointed she did not appear willing to trust him. "If you have any idea who might have tried to harm her, I wish you would tell me."

"I assure you, if I knew, I would."

"I certainly hope so. Because when it comes to Bridget's safety, I don't intend to compromise."

"Neither do I," she said, nodding vigorously, and this time, he believed her. "We are on the same side, Benjamin."

He cocked an eyebrow. "And just what side might that be?"

"The side of righteousness."

He laughed, but the sound held no humor. "Must you continue to speak in riddles?" he asked, his jaw tightening. "Is all of this somehow intended to inspire my confidence?"

"Just your trust. Please, grant me a bit of humoring. I'm an old woman, entitled to be peculiar at times. It's just that Bridget's accident and the full moon tonight have quite unsettled me."

Frustrated, he rose and went to look out the window. Dusk had already fallen. The sun was just disappearing beyond the horizon, and streaks of pink and yellow crisscrossed the sky. Nonetheless, a full moon was already visible.

"How did you know about the moon?" he suddenly asked. "It is indeed full."

"A lack of sight does heighten the other senses. It's hard to explain, but the texture of the air and the sound of the insects change subtly during a full moon."

"That sounds positively mystical."

"In part, it is."

"You aren't going to start spouting rubbish about magic and witches now, are you?"

"Would that frighten you?" she asked softly.

He thought of Bridget and her odd propensity with fire and then shrugged. "No. I believe there are many things in the world that cannot be explained. It doesn't mean there is some otherworldly force at work."

The expression on the widow's face grew more serious. "You know, Benjamin, there was a time that many people did believe in such things. It was quite a serious matter. Exactly one hundred years ago in our very town, people were accused of witchcraft and sentenced to death."

Benjamin returned to his seat and leaned forward in the chair. "Hysteria and madness, none of it rooted in law. It was a shameful period of our history. Many innocent people died."

"Unfortunately, yes. My mother used to tell me stories about the trials. It was quite a frightening time for all of Salem." She paused a moment and then added, "Perhaps even more so because some had genuine cause to be afraid."

He frowned, sitting back in the chair and steepling his fingers together. "You aren't saying you actually believe some of them were truly witches, are you?"

"Who knows?" she replied, lifting her hands. "Legend says that a witch once lived in this very house."

"Here?"

"Yes. The woman's name was Priscilla Gardener. She was tried and convicted of practicing witchcraft, and sentenced to hang. Her husband, John, ultimately saved her by confessing that he dabbled in the occult."

He found himself morbidly interested. "What happened to them?"

"Priscilla was exonerated and John swung from the gallows. Priscilla was pregnant, you see, with their child. She gave birth about six months after his death."

"That's unconditional love," he murmured, "and it's also understandable why he confessed."

"He did indeed love her, even though many thought she was really a witch."

"How do you know all this? Are you a descendant of this Priscilla Gardener?"

"No. But I am a friend to one of her descendants.

In fact, years ago when she left Salem, she bequeathed this house to Elias and me."

"Bequeathed you this house?" he said in surprise. He'd always assumed Widow Bayley had lived here forever. "I didn't know that."

"Why should you? You were but a babe when Elias and I took up residence here."

He picked up his tea and took a sip. "I only thought that, as entertaining as this tale is, I would have heard it before."

She chuckled. "Have you not heard the cottage is presumably haunted? And surely you must know that even I am considered a witch by many of the townsfolk."

"I have," he admitted. "But I had no idea it came from the fact that this Priscilla Gardener and her husband once lived here."

"It is a rather disturbing tale. Many townsfolk believe this cottage is cursed, or at the very least, associated with witchcraft."

He shrugged dismissively. "I think little enthusiasm for the persecution of witches remains here in Salem, or in all of Massachusetts, for that matter. We learned our lesson one hundred years ago. Even back then, I'm not certain more than a handful of people believed in such nonsense."

"On the contrary," she said emphatically. "I think people then and now are still quite afraid of matters they do not understand."

"Such as?" he asked, lifting an eyebrow.

"Unnatural, supernatural events."

He snorted. "Nonsense. Much of that fear can be blamed on longtime superstitions and folklore, not witches, ghosts, or other assorted demons."

"Perhaps. But folklore and witches are in some

places intertwined. For example, in Scotland many legends speak of extraordinary people with special powers. People who are immortal, can move objects with their minds, foretell the future, heal with a single touch, and even conjure fire. All of this may seem fantastic, bizarre, and even astonishing, yet is not truth often rooted in legend?"

Benjamin narrowed his eyes at her mention of fire. He had no idea whether the widow knew or suspected Bridget had such a talent, but he wasn't about to betray a confidence.

"You talk of witches as if they were something that could actually exist," he said carefully. "But are they truly witches? Could they not be just ordinary people who might have, say, an unusual ability to do something others can't?"

"Yes, in many ways I would presume witches are just as ordinary as you and me," she agreed. "In fact, most of these people either use their power for good or suppress it out of fear. But with any kind of power, there are those who use it for darker purposes."

A flicker of apprehension shot through him. "Darker purposes?"

"Personal gain, revenge, betrayal, and more."

He considered her words for a moment. "How can you tell who those people are?"

"You can't," she said, lifting her hands. "But certainly they exist among us."

Restless, he got up from the chair and walked to the hearth. He stared at the fire, thinking of Bridget.

"Are you a witch?" he suddenly asked, turning to face her.

She started in surprise and then laughed. "No, I give you my word I am not."

"But there *is* something unnatural afoot in Salem,"

he insisted. "And Bridget is somehow involved. Am I right?"

The widow sighed. "I find you a perceptive young man, but I can tell you no more. It's for your own protection."

"My protection? Are you mad?" he said incredulously. "If Bridget is in some kind of danger, I need you to tell me how I can protect her."

"I have told you what I can," the widow said, helplessly lifting her hands. "You must have faith that what I do is in the best interests of Bridget."

He laughed harshly. "You ask for my faith, yet you offer me none of yours in return."

"Oh, but I do," she said softly. "More than you can possibly know or understand."

His voice was cool when he answered. "What I understand is that someone is trying to harm Bridget. Until I get to the bottom of this, I don't intend to trust anyone, and that includes you."

He strode to the door and then paused at the threshold. "I'd like to think you are a friend to both Bridget and me. But if you're not, consider yourself forewarned. I may not comprehend everything that is occurring in this town, but I damn well won't let anything happen to Bridget."

Without waiting for a reply, he left the cottage, not seeing the smile that slowly spread across the old woman's face or hearing her murmured words, "It is done."

Bridget held onto Peter's arm as they walked along Derby Street, watching the sun slip behind the horizon. They'd spoken of nothing substantial since he arrived at her house, and even that light chatter, which had brought them this far, faded minutes ago. Now they strode arm in arm in silence along the quiet streets of Salem, the tension almost palpable in the air. Nonetheless, Peter had been unfailingly polite, so she had responded in kind. Yet for the first time in all the years since she'd known him, she felt as though she walked with a stranger.

As her anxiety grew, Bridget stole a glance at him. She was impressed, as she had always been, by his cool, elegant looks and impeccable dress. Yet just as quickly, the image of Benjamin with his dark untamed hair, handsome face, and restless energy leaped to mind. How different these two men in her life were—a startling study of contrasts.

When they came to a bench, Peter invited her to sit, checking first to make certain they were not beneath any open windows. Bridget complied, fussing with her skirts to keep her hands from trembling nervously.

Finally, Peter leaned back on the bench and sighed. "Bridget, do you remember the day I asked you to wed me?"

She nodded, a wistful smile touching her lips. "It was the happiest day of my life."

"How long have we known each other?"

"Nearly all our lives."

"And when you know someone that long, it's only natural that you would come to know a person's strengths and faults. Wouldn't you agree?"

She stirred uneasily on the bench. "I suppose that's true."

He turned to look directly at her. "As much as it pains me to say it, neither of us has been honest with the other. These past few days, our faults have come to the forefront."

She felt an unwelcome blush creep into her cheeks.

"I know it has been difficult. But Peter, there is something I want to talk to you about."

He spread his hands impatiently. "I know you're upset about my little indiscretion. But I already told you that she meant nothing to me. Benjamin made it out to be more than it was."

She shook her head vigorously. "No, please don't blame this on Benjamin. He didn't tell me anything. But it's hardly fair of me to rebuke you when I am not without blame myself."

Peter looked at her incredulously. "You?"

Bridget put a hand on his arm. "Before you get upset, let me explain. . . ."

He looked at her and then recoiled as if she had slapped him. "My God!" he exclaimed. "This *is* about Benjamin. He touched you, didn't he?"

"No . . . yes, I mean, it wasn't like that."

"It wasn't like what?" he said, a sudden chill to his words.

She flinched at the tone of his voice. "It wasn't so unseemly. We were arguing when he suddenly kissed me, most likely to try to quiet me and . . ."

Peter leaped to his feet, his face reddening with anger. "I'll kill him!"

"No!" she cried, tugging on his arm. "You don't understand. I assure you, it won't happen again. He apologized and feels quite distraught about everything."

"Of course he does," Peter said, his voice icily disdainful. "Once he'd had a sample of what was mine. He wants you only because you belong to me."

Bridget felt the blood drain from her face. "That's not true. You're understandably angry, but if you would just calm down—"

"Calm down?" he spat out contemptuously. "Benjamin thinks he can return to Salem on a whim, claim something that is mine, and you want me to calm down?"

"He didn't claim anything."

"Didn't he?" he retorted, his lips forming a brief and bitter smile.

She hesitated a moment too long. "No, he didn't."

"The hell he didn't! Do you really expect me to believe you didn't enjoy being seduced by the rake of Salem."

"Peter!" Bridget exclaimed, totally unnerved by this side of him she'd never seen. "I told you this because marriage is a holy union and I want to start our lives together without any deception between us. I'm sorry for what happened."

"You believe that betraying me is an honest start?" he snapped.

"Now, that's calling the kettle black," she shot back, her own ire rising. "I never expected you to seek pleasure in another woman's arms."

He stiffened and then sat back down on the bench. "I worry about you, Bridget," he said, his voice icy and aloof.

His tone and demeanor pierced her heart, and she struggled to keep her emotions even. "Why is that, might I ask?"

He flicked a speck of dust from his coat. "Scandal follows you. Did it ever occur to you that if this incident with you and Benjamin gets out, it could ruin me? Were you even thinking of our future or me when you embraced him? There are plenty of powerful people in Salem who could use this as leverage against me."

"This is not just about me. What about your dalliance?" she asked quietly.

He sighed. "There is no shame in a man seeking a bit of harmless relief. But for you to engage in such wickedness—the daughter of a reverend and my future wife—well, it is utterly shameful. My opponents could use this to thoroughly destroy my reputation."

His words hurt, as did the remoteness of his tone. "But it's just gossip that can be easily dismissed," she argued.

He snorted inelegantly. "By whom? You? Benjamin? Who would believe it?"

"What does it matter as long as you believe it?" she protested. "Surely you do not think your position is so tenuous that it could not withstand a bit of hearsay."

His laughter raked her. "A bit? My dear Bridget, with you, it's never just a bit. Hearsay flocks to you like a moth to a flame. No, I won't see my life destroyed because of some ill-conceived tryst of yours."

She flinched as though he had struck her. "There was no tryst. I told you it was just a kiss."

He threw up his hands. "Disgraceful all the same. You've put me in an intolerable situation. For pity's sake, have you no care for how hard I've worked all my life? I have ambitions and plans that I don't want to see jeopardized."

"I see," she said, her own voice cool now. "And just what plans *do* you have for me?"

"I intended for you to aid me with my ambitions, not to serve as a burden."

She stiffened. "And since I'm the daughter of a well-respected reverend, I'll be able to add a measure of trustworthiness to your political aspirations. Is that it?"

He shrugged matter-of-factly. "I won't deny it. People trust you, Bridget. Ordinary people. And if they trust you, then they'll trust me. It's my intent to be considered a man of the people."

The sensible tone of his voice tore at her heart. Had he been like this all along? Had she been so blinded by her dreams that she'd refused to see it?

She took a deep breath. "Do you love me, Peter?" she asked, her voice wavering slightly.

He avoided her gaze, and she felt her stomach turn uncomfortably. "Love is untidy, unpredictable, and an inconvenient burden to bring to a marriage," he said carefully. "We've been friends for a long time, are comfortable with each other, and know each other's likes and dislikes. We are socially and politically compatible. I like you, Bridget. What more do we need?"

She bit her lip until it throbbed. For a moment, she felt detached, adrift, almost as if this were happening to another person. He saw her expression and his face softened.

"Don't look so wounded. I thought you understood the nature of our relationship."

A suffocating sensation tightened in her throat. Although she had experienced her own doubts about her love for Peter, she had nonetheless believed him to be the bedrock of their relationship. Now she realized how wrong she had been.

"I . . . I didn't," she managed to say.

He patted her shoulder, his voice courteous but slightly patronizing. "Don't worry, darling. Many people come into wedlock with far less."

She knew he was right and that his arguments were sound and practical. But then she thought of Widow Bayley and the glorious, all-consuming love she had shared with her husband, and knew with certainty that this was what she had always dreamed of.

"Some come with a lot more," she whispered. Her

eyes filled with tears and she blinked them back. "I want to know something, Peter, and I ask that you answer me honestly. Do you intend to continue your indiscretions after we are wed?"

He sighed, leaning back on the bench and crossing his legs. "This is not a matter with which you should be concerned."

"I shouldn't be concerned if my husband shares a bed with another woman?" she asked tersely.

"Darling, I give you my word that any such matters would be handled with utmost discretion. My conduct would be impeccable, respectable. I assure you, I'd never do anything to shame you."

"You already have," she whispered painfully.

Her heart shattered into little pieces. She'd been foolish and naive to expect more from him. Everything she'd ever dreamed of now lay in shards at her feet.

"Come now, Bridget, you're behaving childishly," Peter said, his voice carrying a trace of exasperation. "You can't really expect me or any other man to make such a promise. This will be a good arrangement. You'll never lack for funds. I'll give you children. You'll have the home and family you want."

"It sounds so . . . perfect," she agreed numbly.

"It is," he said, cheering a bit. "But I will insist on one matter."

"And what might that be?"

"You must stay away from Benjamin."

Her jaw tightened. "Why? Because you don't trust me?"

"I don't trust *him*. For God's sake, Bridget, this is nothing but a game to Benjamin. He used you to try to get at me. He knew you would tell me. Darling, it may be indelicate of me to say, but it's not the first time we've vied for the affections of a woman. It's been, dare I say, an amusement to us in the past. You must be wary of him. He'll do anything to try to spite me."

She thought of Benjamin's passionate embrace, and her cheeks burned in remembrance and mortification. "A . . . a game?"

"My dear, naive darling," Peter said with a sigh. "It was naught more than a diversion, a pleasurable pastime for him. We've both done it scores of times before."

A horrible heaviness centered in her chest, leaving her with an aching empty feeling. Tears gathered in her eyes, but she forced herself to meet his gaze evenly.

"I'm not going to wed you, Peter," she said. "I realize now that I can't live a life without love."

He blinked, an incredulous expression crossing his face. At that moment she realized he had never really considered that she might refuse him.

"What did you say?" he spluttered.

"I said I am not going to wed you," she repeated, this time more firmly.

"Have you completely lost your senses?" He looked at her in such utter disbelief that Bridget felt an urge to laugh wildly. "Of course you will wed me."

"I cannot."

"Think carefully of what I offer," he replied, his lips narrowing with anger. "I assure you such a union could work."

She nodded as a sensation of intense desolation swept over her. "Undoubtedly, that is so. We could live with each other and build a life. But it means we both would be living a lie. I thought I could do it,

Peter, but now I realize that I can't. I'm one of those people who must be true to my heart."

He spluttered, bristling with indignation. "True to your heart? What nonsense is that? Bridget, I urge you to think about what you are doing. Put aside these foolish romantic musings. We both know there will be no other suitor."

"No, there will not," she agreed.

"Yet you would rather live out your life alone, without the comfort of a family and home?"

"I don't expect you to understand," she said softly. "But I just can't do it."

Peter stood, frustrated. "I will give you a day to reconsider," he said. "I'm confident that a good night's rest and a talk with your parents will help you see how foolishly you are behaving."

She rose and took his offered arm, barely touching him. Her stomach lurched with the movement and she hoped she wouldn't be sick before she reached home.

"You'll feel better when you've had some time to think this through," he said confidently. "We've put too much time and effort into the wedding to simply abandon it."

"I wish you were right," she said trying to swallow the lump that lingered in her throat. "But I sincerely doubt that will happen. I'm sorry, Peter, but I'm afraid you're going to have to find yourself a new bride."

Thirteen

Benjamin left Widow Bayley's place in a black mood. His discussion with the woman had left him troubled and frustrated. Evidently, something increasingly strange was happening in Salem, and it involved Bridget. He had a disquieting feeling that it involved him, too, and he knew that somehow he'd just been tasked with keeping her safe. He'd intended to do it even if she hadn't asked, but the fact that she had unnerved him no small amount.

"Yet just how shall you keep her safe, if she won't even agree to see you?" he muttered aloud. Scowling, he stopped in his tracks and rubbed the back of his neck, where his muscles were knotted tight with tension.

His mood darkening further, he changed directions, deciding to walk along the shore and detour past Rock's Point before going home. There, at least, he could hope for some time alone to listen to the sea and clear his head.

Soon the shore appeared and he stopped for a moment to admire the moonlit water, listening to the calming rhythm of the waves. He breathed deeply, smelling the faint odor of fish and seaweed, and tasting the tang of salt on his tongue. The full moon shone brightly, reflecting off the water and causing it to shimmer like gold. He continued his stroll, wet sand sucking at his boots until he arrived at the Point and began the rocky ascent to the rise.

As he approached, he heard the soft sound of weeping. Guided by moonlight, he hastened his step, stunned to see a woman sitting between the boulders, shaking and crying into her hands. Her hair was unbound and cascaded down her back in a riot of gleaming curls.

"Bri?" he uttered in disbelief.

She jumped up, letting out a shriek. For a moment, he feared she had been hurt, and a spurt of anxiety rushed through him. "Good God! Have you been harmed?"

She pressed her hand to her chest. "No. You just frightened me. What are you doing here?"

Relief that she was unharmed quickly turned into irritation. "I might ask the same of you. What are you doing out here alone and at this hour? Have you completely lost your senses? Your parents will be beside themselves with worry."

"It's none of your concern what I'm doing here," she retorted. "You are not my keeper. Go away and leave me alone."

He crossed his arms against his chest, stung by her vehemence. "Oh, now there's a clever suggestion. I'll just leave you alone so that another deranged fowl or something worse can swoop out of the sky and attack you. Have you no concern for your own safety?"

She pressed her lips together, looking so miserable it made his throat tighten. "I don't care what happens to me," she said. "But I have no desire to be protected or coddled by you. Now go away."

His irritation faded and he came closer, standing

next to the boulder. "I care," he said gently. "Why are you crying?"

She swallowed hard, dashing the tears from her cheeks with the back of her hand. Her gown was wrinkled, the skirts awry, and it looked as though she'd been twisting the fabric in her hands.

"I have no desire to speak with you, Benjamin," she said quietly. "Leave me be."

When he didn't move, she stepped out of the shelter of the boulders, lifting her skirts to try to go around him. "Well then, if you have no intention of leaving, I will."

"I know you're still angry at me, but we will talk now."

"We will not," she said, her temper flaring.

He was relieved to see her anger. That he could handle; tears he could not. He blocked her exit, careful not to touch her. "I'm respectfully asking you to listen to me. You never gave me a chance to explain earlier."

"Explain what?" she snapped. "That you knew Peter didn't love me, or that he had taken pleasure in the arms of another woman?"

Benjamin felt as if she had slapped him, and took a step back. "I'm sorry. I didn't want to hurt you. Damn it, Bri, I was trying to protect you."

"Well, stop trying to protect me. And stop interfering in my life."

"Not until we discuss this properly. Your friendship means too much to me. I'm not going to lose that."

"You've already lost it. I don't want to speak to you ever again. I just want you out of my life."

"I'm afraid you cannot be rid of me so easily. We are friends, Bri."

Her voice caught on a sob. "I trusted you."

"You still can," he said, keeping his voice calm.

"Liar," she said, her anger practically jumping out at him. "Everything you've told me is a lie."

He narrowed his eyes. "What in the devil are you talking about? Blast it, talk to me."

She paused, still facing him warily. Her expression in the bright moonlight was one of such pain and wretchedness that Benjamin felt as though she'd twisted a knife in his gut.

"I'm not going to wed Peter," she said, throwing the words at him and leaving him stunned.

"You're not?" he said in disbelief.

"I'm not. There, does that please you?"

With those words, she tried to bolt past him. He cut her off, grabbing her roughly around the waist and yanking her against him with a thud.

"What do you mean, you're not marrying him?" he asked sharply.

"It's just as I said," she said, struggling against his hold. "There will be no wedding. Now, release me at once."

"No!" he ground out. His mind whirled at her sudden revelation and he tightened his hold around her, unsure what to do or say. Suddenly he was acutely aware of her breasts pressed against his chest. He could feel her frantic heartbeat as well as the warm puffs of breath against his neck. Strands of her unruly hair brushed against his cheeks and jaw, and as she moved, he inhaled deeply of her scent. She smelled like lilacs, fresh grass, and the sea. He found it earthy, astonishingly sensual, and uniquely Bridget.

"Please, Benjamin," she cried, wriggling furiously when he didn't release her. "Let me go."

Her body shifted against him and he gritted his teeth, locking one arm even more firmly about her waist. With the other hand, he nudged up her chin until she looked directly into his eyes.

"Don't try to run away from me. I won't let you. I'll release you only if you promise to sit down and let us talk about this like civilized people."

For a moment, she stared at him with rigid intent. He could see the fire burning in her eyes, the moonlight clearly reflecting her anger at him. Slowly she narrowed her eyes and tossed her hair over her shoulder, revealing the slender white column of her throat and sending a jolt of unexpected desire through him.

"No," she hissed, flinging out an unspoken challenge. "You are not my keeper."

Benjamin felt his own temper rise. "Hell and damnation, woman, I'm beginning to think I am. You will do as I say. Sit down."

"I will not."

He ground his teeth together. "Don't push me, Bri. You know I can make you do it."

Alarm flickered in her eyes. "You wouldn't dare!"

Dare. Dare. I dare you. How many times had she thrown that at him? At least a hundred times since childhood, a simple word that could spur him to reckless action regardless of the consequence.

Damn if she hadn't just called his bluff.

"Oh, yes I would," he snapped, trying to twist her to the ground.

But she was quicker. She jabbed him in the stomach with her elbow and then slipped out of his grasp, running toward the road. Benjamin swore, spinning around on one heel and racing after her. He tackled her from behind with a flying leap, knocking her to the grass. They rolled over twice, tangled in a jumble of limbs and skirts. Benjamin came out on top and yanked her over until she lay pinned faceup beneath his weight.

"Now, are you ready to tell me what the devil is going on?" he asked between clenched teeth.

"Never!" she retorted, swinging a fist and catching him solidly on the jaw.

"Ouch!" he roared, catching her wrist in a secure grip. "You little hellcat."

"It serves you right," she said, bucking him until he had to use the entire length of his body to hold her down.

"Be still, damn you," he said, his breathing harsh. "I don't want to hurt you. But if you keep fighting me, you'll get more than you bargained for."

She stilled then, her breath catching on a sob. He eased up a little, but still not trusting her, held his position. His eyes searched her face.

"Now, what in God's name happened today?"

To his dismay, she began to weep again. "Leave me alone. I hate you!"

Shocked by her outburst, Benjamin watched, stunned, as her body shook with sobs.

"Jesus, Bri," he said hoarsely and then let the sentence trail off. Her tears sliced into his heart, ripping it open and leaving him with a deep, searing wound. Whatever it was, he had caused her this pain, this suffering. Suddenly a list of every ill he had ever perpetrated ran through his head. Had it all been hastening to that one moment in time when he had dragged her into his arms for that infernal kiss, a kiss that had changed everything between them and left him so needy, so drunk with desire that he'd been oblivious to all else?

"I'm sorry," he whispered raggedly.

He wanted to atone for his grievances, to prove he'd

never meant to hurt her. And, God help him, he wanted to kiss away the pain until the suffering in her eyes disappeared.

He looked down at her now, her hair spread out behind her on the grass, shimmering in the moonlight like a red silken pillow. His gaze skimmed over her face, the high, proud cheekbones, wide eyes glistening with tears, a soft, generous mouth and stubborn chin. A face he knew so well. A face he thought he had loved forever.

His heart lurched in his chest as he reached up to brush a tear from her cheek. He was aware of the pounding of his heart and the blood rushing to his ears. His hips shifted ever so slightly against her and he felt his body stir with desire.

His mouth was now but a hair's breadth away from hers. Bridget stilled, her eyes wide and perhaps even a little frightened. He could hear his own breathing reduced to a shallow, uneven rasp. Without thinking about it, he lowered his head toward her.

"No!" she suddenly cried, twisting her head to the side. "No, Benjamin. Please, don't do this."

He exhaled a deep breath and rolled off her, sitting up. What the hell had he been thinking? He shoved his fingers through his hair and sat staring at the ground for a moment, disgusted with himself. When his heart stopped thundering, he extended a hand to her, his eyes offering a truce. She accepted and he pulled her up until she sat beside him.

"I'm sorry, Bri," he finally said. "I never meant to hurt you. Please, don't cry anymore. I can't bear to see your tears."

To his astonishment, she suddenly leaned against him, resting her head on his shoulder. "I'm sorry, too. I'm so weary of fighting my feelings. I don't care about the consequences. Please, I want you to kiss me," she whispered, her breath hot against his skin.

He blinked, not certain he had heard her correctly. "Kiss you? But I—"

She placed a finger on his lips, quieting him. "I don't care anymore. I don't want to think, nor do I desire reason. I only want the pain to go away."

She closed her eyes and lifted her mouth to his, innocent and trusting. It was what he wanted more than anything in the world, and yet as he looked at her, he felt paralyzed with indecision.

She must have sensed his hesitation, because she slipped her hands around his neck, pulling him toward her.

"Kiss me, please," she murmured.

Benjamin felt his control snap. He wanted her; God knew he *needed* her. Without another thought, he lowered his mouth to hers. He heard her gasp as their lips collided in a rush of heat, desire, pleasure, and need. He intensified the pressure, his tongue grazing and probing her mouth until she moaned and yielded to him.

Emboldened, his tongue plunged past her lips until he devoured the sweet softness of her inner mouth. She kissed him shyly at first, and then with bone-melting enthusiasm. He groaned as her hands moved up his neck and fisted in his hair. Off balance, they fell to the ground together, never breaking their kiss.

Dimly, Benjamin was aware of the fierce pulsing of his blood, and the heat that shot through his veins each time she shifted restlessly beneath him. As he coaxed and teased her into an erotic foreplay with his tongue, a distant part of his brain warned him to ease his onslaught. Yet he was so drunk on the taste of her, and too groggy with need to listen to his inner warnings.

All the same, the irony of the situation did not escape his notice. Only she could cause him to lose control—the temperamental, frustrating, passionate red-haired daughter of a reverend. God knew he'd bedded many more beautiful, exotic, and experienced women, but none made him feel so right.

He almost felt like laughing. The rake of Salem was in love with the Reverend Goodwell's daughter. A prankster extraordinaire. The girl who had set his hat on fire, loosened the seam of his pants, bested him in footraces, and dared him to swim in the ocean without a stitch of clothing. She infuriated him, challenged him, and made him complete.

She was his heart and soul.

He felt a rush of protectiveness as he lifted his mouth from hers and buried his face in her hair. For a moment, he simply held her tightly against his thundering heart. Then, with a supreme effort, he rolled off her for the second time, this time coming all the way to his feet.

Barely thinking about it, he walked a few feet away and absently stomped out a small fire that had started in a patch of dry grass. Sighing, he rubbed the back of his neck and tried to figure out how to adequately explain his feelings.

He watched as she sat up and adjusted her skirts around her. Her hair was full of grass and bramble, her mouth still swollen from their kiss. She rose, saying nothing, brushing the sand and dirt from her gown.

Benjamin stepped forward. "I won't say I'm sorry for doing that, because I'm not. But I didn't intend to ravage you. I wanted only to comfort you."

She raised her eyes to look at him. "You did," she said softly.

He rubbed his stubbled chin with his hand, asking

the question burning on the tip of his tongue. "Why aren't you marrying Peter?"

"Because I can't," she said softly.

His heart dared to leap with hope. "Why?"

Her lower lip trembled. "Which reason should I give you? Because Peter feared I would cause him scandal and ruin his grand ambitions to hold an important political post in Salem. Or because I . . . I couldn't bear the thought that he would continue to seek pleasure in the arms of other women after we were wed."

He could hear the misery in her voice, and his throat tightened with strain. "Oh, hell, Bri. I'm sorry."

She let out an anguished breath. "He knows about our kiss, Benjamin. I told him only because I felt it wasn't fair to rebuke him for his dalliance when I had my own to confess."

"You were innocent," Benjamin countered evenly. "I'll explain it to him. I forced myself on you."

She smiled sadly. "I may wish that were true, but it is not. I welcomed your embrace then, just as I did now."

"Of course you did. You are untried," he said, frustration edging his voice. "The fault is mine. I had no right."

"I should warn you that Peter was furious," she said. "He said you kissed me only to try to best him."

"What?" he said incredulously.

"He told me that you desired me only because . . . because I belonged to him."

A curse fell from his lips. "That's not true."

She shrugged. "It doesn't concern me anymore."

"Blast it, Bri, it concerns me. Just because you're not going to wed Peter, it doesn't mean I'll let you throw your dreams away. You will wed me."

Her mouth dropped open. "What?"

"I said you can wed me. If Peter won't have you, I will."

As soon as the words left his mouth, he knew they were wrong. What in God's name happened to the delicate declaration of love he intended to utter? Swearing under his breath, he took a step toward her. "No, I didn't mean it like that."

"Stay away from me," she warned, backing away from him.

"Bri, we should wed," he said, hating the desperation he heard in his voice. "It's the sensible thing to do."

He winced as soon as he saw the look on her face. How could he have blurted out something so idiotic at such an important time?

"What has gotten into you?" she asked, eyeing him as if he had sprouted horns. "Is this one of your bizarre plans to try to apologize again?"

He ground his teeth in frustration. "Why do you have to be so difficult? I simply want you to be my wife, damn it."

She raised her chin, her mouth forming a bitter smile. "Why? Because you feel guilt, pity, or even some misguided sense of responsibility?"

"No!" he snapped angrily. "Don't put words in my mouth. I want you, Bri, and I have for a very long time."

"There is no need to wed me for that," she said, her voice unnaturally aloof. "As you now know, drawing me into your embrace is not a difficult venture. I came willingly before and would likely do so again. Why bother with a wedding? The game is over, the victory yours."

He felt as though she had hit him in the stomach.

He caught his breath, taking a step back in shock. "What are you talking about?"

"Peter told me that you both enjoy vying for the attention of the same woman. He said it was a competition of sorts."

He could hear the humiliation in her voice, and his temper flared. "That's not true. It may have been so in the past, but never with you."

"Why not?" she asked, lifting her hands. "Don't I meet the standards of your other women?"

"You are not like other women," he snapped.

"No, I suppose I'm a bit more primitive, although I can hardly believe I'm the first engaged woman you have seduced."

"Hell's bells, Bri, don't twist my words. It wasn't like that with you."

"Wasn't it?" she retorted. "Think of the damage it will cause Peter when word gets out that his betrothed went willingly into the arms of the rake of Salem."

Benjamin felt a black anger come over him, so intense he could scarcely breathe. "He suggested this to you?"

Her hands clenched at her sides. "He didn't *suggest* it, Benjamin, he *said* it outright. For once in his life, Peter believed he had managed to attain something you hadn't. Imagine his disappointment when he realized his prize had been ruined, soiled." She spread her hands wide. "So, I commend you on your triumph. Once again, you have bested us all."

His breath burned so tightly in his throat, he could hardly speak. "He's lying to you, Bri," he said between clenched teeth. "It's not like that. Not between you and me."

He could see that she didn't believe him, and his frustration grew so bitter he could almost taste it.

She gave him a tight-lipped smile. "I want both you and Peter to understand that I am no longer participating in this amusing diversion. Now, I ask for nothing more than to be left in peace."

With those words, she turned and walked away from him, heading for her house. He didn't try to stop her this time, and didn't know what he could say to make her change her mind. He could only follow at a discreet distance, making certain she got inside safely. Once she disappeared into the house, he stalked toward town, his hands clenching into fists at his side.

He had only one purpose now—to find Peter.

The Dark One stood at the window, holding the drape aside and staring out at the night sky. The full moon shone bright and heavy, drawing long, eerie shadows across the darkened room.

She was worried. Events were not progressing as she had planned. Someone had cast a powerful protection spell on the girl. The discovery had first astonished, then offended, and finally angered her. After a careful but thorough probe of the spell, she realized the trouble she faced.

The woman felt a flicker of apprehension course through her. The spell was impressive, and she had no doubt a MacInness had cast it. But which MacInness, and how many had already come to Salem? She sincerely doubted that Bridget alone had the knowledge to manage such a feat.

A tiny spurt of panic shot through her. Every step she took, from this moment on, had to be faultless. If she failed, the blame would be hers alone to bear. She'd been too confident of her power, too certain that victory was just within her grasp. She had underestimated her opponents, and now the possibility of lurking danger filled her with a growing sense of dread.

A low warning rumble of thunder intruded on her thoughts, and she felt a disturbing quake in her senses. She knew she was being watched and evaluated. Tonight, even the angle of the moon seemed ominous, as if it also stood in judgment of her.

The Dark One looked up at the sky, aware of dark clouds thickening where there had been none just minutes before. To the east, the sky lit up as a jagged slash of lightning ripped toward the ground. The thunder boomed again, this time closer. She shivered in fear and anticipation, the hairs on her arms and the back of her neck rising. The storm's energy affected her even through the walls of her house.

For a moment, she drew on that energy, narrowing her eyes and strengthening her determination. Now was the time to focus, channel all her concentration into eliminating the girl. Neither magic nor physical violence had worked thus far. If Bridget could not be killed outright, another method would have to be devised to remove her altogether from Salem.

A cloud crossed the moon at the exact moment the woman envisioned a plan. It was an omen, and this time, a good one. She considered the plan from several angles and then smiled. Yes, the plan was sound.

The Dark One felt a familiar knot of excitement twist in her stomach. Mentally she catalogued a list of what she would need and how she would accomplish the task. The approach would be astonishingly simple. She had only to exploit Bridget's principal weakness—her softness for the ones she loved.

"Yes, it's time for the ill deed to occur," the Dark One whispered.

The rain started to fall, thick, fat drops splattering

against the windowpane. The wind rose, slamming the rain against the house and whipping it to a furious, slashing crescendo.

She smiled, slowly letting the heavy drape slide back into place. The room plunged into total darkness, not even illuminated by the light of fire or candle.

Aye, she would make her move soon. And why not? There was no better time for witches than during the cycle of the full moon.

Fourteen

Benjamin found Peter drinking ale at the Blue Shell Tavern, which was typical for most evenings. He sat at the same table where Benjamin and many of their other friends had sat a hundred times before. Tonight though, Peter was alone, his back to the door.

All the better, Benjamin thought grimly as he made his way past the other patrons and laid a heavy hand on Peter's shoulder.

"I need to talk to you," he said in a low voice.

Peter set down his tankard and turned around in his seat. "Well, well. If it isn't my dear friend Benjamin Hawkes. Come to share an ale with me, or have you set your sights on seducing yet another of Salem's innocent maidens?"

Benjamin's jaw tightened visibly. "Let's take this outside."

Peter shook his head, his eyes flat and cold. "I just arrived here and have no intention of leaving so soon. If you have something to say, you can say it to me here." Deliberately he turned his back and picked up the ale.

The other patrons in the tavern were starting to whisper and look at them with interest. Benjamin shrugged.

"If you want to cause a spectacle, that is your choice," he said. "But if you wish to keep your reputation unsullied, you may not want others to hear what I have to say."

Peter slammed his tankard down on the table and stood. "My reputation?" he said, his voice rising. "It's your reputation that will suffer."

Benjamin crossed his arms against his chest. "My reputation is far enough beyond repair that it no longer concerns me."

Peter swore under his breath, stalked past Benjamin, and headed to the door. After walking out into the night, he turned and faced Benjamin. Light from the open tavern door spilled across his face and onto the cobblestones. The scents of roasted pork and ale mingled with the aroma of the sea and the unpleasant smell drifting in from the tanneries.

"What could you possibly have to say to me that would be of any interest?" Peter snapped. He tugged at his neckcloth, loosening it. His shirt was rumpled, and for the first time in as long as Benjamin could remember, he looked anything but coolly elegant.

"I want to know what you told Bridget this afternoon," he said quietly.

A look of surprise crossed Peter's face and then quickly disappeared behind an angry facade. "Since when have the discussions of a young betrothed couple become any of your concern?"

"When such discussions involve me."

Peter shook his head in disbelief. "She came running to you, did she? Pour out her troubles to her sympathetic, caring lover?"

Benjamin's jaw tightened and he fought to keep his anger contained. "She was never my lover. I found her at Rock's Point in the middle of the night, weeping her eyes out. Have you any idea what you've done to her?"

"What I've done to her?" Peter said incredulously. "Did I seduce her, confuse her feelings, cause her to throw away her one chance at happiness?"

His words were like stinging barbs, all the more painful because they were so close to the truth. Benjamin felt frustration, anger, and guilt form a hard knot in his stomach. He wanted to lash out, hurt the man who had broken Bridget's heart and laid the pieces at her feet. But more than that, he wanted relief from the feelings of shame and pain that lingered in his own heart.

"You told her she was some kind of prize in a game we were playing," Benjamin said between gritted teeth. He heard a faint rumble of thunder and glanced up at the sky, where ominous dark clouds were gathering.

"Are you saying she isn't?" Peter said coldly. "It has always been that way between us. An inviting smile, a flutter of eyelashes, and the game is afoot. Now, just because Bridget is involved, you've suddenly acquired scruples?"

"Damn you, she was never involved in any of that."

"Wasn't she? Bridget belonged to me. She was *my* betrothed. You knew it, she knew it, and all of Salem knew it. You seduced her nonetheless."

Benjamin felt the heat of guilt burn on his face. "It wasn't like that. I never intended to—"

"Take what is mine?" His voice was so bitter that Benjamin flinched. "I don't believe it."

Benjamin steeled himself against the accusation. He could see the hate in Peter's eyes warring with the affection of a lifetime of friendship, and knew the same emotions were reflected in his own.

"Whatever you may think, none of this was a game to me. I apologize, Peter. You have every right to be angry with me, but it's not fair to punish Bridget for my mistake. She's innocent."

Peter laughed, but there was no humor in the sound. "No, you've taken that innocence from her as well. I wondered how she'd become so schooled in the art of kissing. She's an apt pupil, is she not?"

Benjamin felt his temper begin to unleash. "Say what you have to say, Peter, and do what you must. I've acted reprehensibly, and for that I'm sorry. But from this moment on, we are both to understand that Bridget is not to be held accountable for my actions. This is no longer about her."

Peter lifted his hands to the heavens. "You still don't understand, do you?" he roared. "This was *never* about her."

Another growl of thunder sounded, and a light rain began to fall. Benjamin ignored it and stood looking at Peter warily.

"What in the devil are you talking about?" he finally said.

Peter's mouth thinned with displeasure. "We are talking about you. Hell and damnation, man, think about it. Have you no idea of how much I detested constantly falling second to your wit and charm?"

Benjamin narrowed his eyes. "No, actually, I don't."

"No? Come, now. It's *always* been about you. You've been the toast of this town for years. Benjamin Hawkes can do no wrong. The rake of Salem, the consummate charmer. Women flocked to you in droves, practically falling over themselves to be near. Young, old, pretty, and reprehensible—they all wanted a part of the legendary rapscallion. You played the role with great relish, and yet, oh, how careful you were with each of their hearts. You became a damned legend. No one *ever* saw me beyond you."

Benjamin felt the breath go out of him in a rush, as if Peter had physically punched him in the gut. Pain, regret, and anger rolled into a hard ball in his stomach and lodged there uncomfortably.

"At a loss for words, are you?" Peter said, wiping a hand across his dripping face. "Or perhaps you're beginning to see things from my point of view. Year after year I had to endure the painful torment of being second best. The turmoil was agonizing. Somehow, I was honored to be counted among those in your inner circle, and yet I secretly loathed being the one perpetually in the shadows."

A jagged flash of lightning tore across the sky and a loud clap of thunder sounded. The rain fell harder, drenching them in a furious downpour.

"You had the world at your feet," Peter continued, raising his voice over the noise of the rain. "You've lived a charmed life. Whatever you wanted, you got. You were *never ever* denied."

Benjamin flung a lock of dripping hair back from his face. "You never really knew me, then," he said evenly.

Peter took an unsteady step closer until the two of them were nearly nose to nose. Water ran in rivulets down Peter's temples and dripped off his nose.

"I knew you better than anyone, except perhaps Bridget," he said angrily. "All my life, I looked for a vulnerability—a way that I might finally be able to best you. Then one day, fortune smiled upon me. I happened to catch a look you gave Bridget. And in that fleeting moment, I saw the affection, pride, and love you felt for her. Instantly I knew I'd finally found your greatest weakness."

Benjamin stilled, the pounding of his heart so loud it hurt his ears. Rain slashed against his face, but his feet felt wooden, almost paralyzed.

"You knew," he said softly. "Even when I didn't know, you did. You bastard. You knew I loved her."

Peter laughed coldly. "It took you long enough to realize it."

Benjamin felt his stomach turn over in disgust. "That's why you courted and even asked her to wed you? You did all that just to get at me?"

Peter's eyes glittered in the rain. "It was glorious, you know. For the first time in my life, I possessed something you wanted. The only problem was not having the satisfaction of you knowing it."

Benjamin felt as though a hand had closed around his throat, squeezing. "Did you ever intend to really wed her?" he managed to force out.

Peter shrugged. "At first, no. Christ, I gave you three years to come to your senses. But then I realized she wasn't such a bad choice after all. She was a little too temperamental and opinionated to suit my taste, but that sort of thing can often serve a man well in bed. And truthfully, I am fond of her. We spent a lot of time together; we know each other's likes and dislikes. Politically, she was an acceptable match, and over the past few years she became much more accommodating to my needs. Besides, I decided that if she were already wed to me by the time you finally realized what you felt for her . . . oh, then the pain you would suffer!"

Benjamin felt his anger become a scalding fury. He'd known Peter all his life, and yet it was as if he faced a stranger.

"Damn you, Peter! I thought we were friends."

"We were, in a way. I must admit, being your friend

did have its advantages. For a while, it was fun amusing myself with your castoffs. But soon I felt like a dog begging scraps."

"Whatever you felt toward me, you had no right to bring Bridget into this."

"On the contrary. Every person that came into your life was fair game."

Benjamin clenched his teeth. "And now, if she refuses to wed you? What then?"

"Take her," Peter said dismissively. "I got what I wanted. Now you will know what it is like to acquire one of my scraps. And all of Salem will know it."

Benjamin lunged then, slamming a fist into Peter's midriff. Peter roared in pain, the breath going out of him with a sickening explosion of air. When he recovered, he swung at Benjamin's face, snapping back his head and splitting his lip.

They circled each other, swinging fists with murderous intent, bones cracking and blood spilling. Benjamin's fury all but choked him as he slammed into Peter's stomach headfirst, grabbing him around the waist and hurling both of them to the wet cobblestones. Benjamin pummeled him with his fists, barely feeling Peter's knee jamming into his ribs. He rammed his elbow sideways and heard Peter's nose crack. Screaming in anger, Peter wedged a leg into Benjamin's chest, shoving him off. They rolled to their feet and squared off again, both breathing heavily.

Peter staggered a few steps backward, holding his nose. Benjamin wiped a hand across his mouth, tasting his own blood. Patrons from the tavern now crowded the doorway, watching the fight and cheering.

Peter charged this time, and Benjamin held his ground until Peter was almost upon him. At the last moment, he twisted to the left and forcibly kicked Peter's legs out from under him. Peter slid across the wet stones and fell hard to the ground. Benjamin watched as Peter struggled to get up, the blood running from his nose and mixing with the rain in a morbid display.

Abruptly Benjamin felt an intense sweep of disgust. Disgust with himself and with Peter. For a moment, he stood silently in the rain, staring at the man he had once called a friend. Without a word, he turned and began to walk away.

"No, damn you," Peter shouted from behind him, stumbling forward. A jagged flash of lightning bolted across the sky. "Let's finish this."

Benjamin whirled, catching Peter's fist in his own just as he raised it to strike another blow. "It's over," he said, his voice flat, dead. "The games, the friendship. Everything. You got what you wanted."

Peter yanked his hand free, hate blazing in his eyes. "Not yet. I still need to know one thing. Why Bridget? You could have had any woman in Salem, in all of Massachusetts, for that matter. Tell me, why her? For God's sake, she's nothing more than a simple reverend's daughter."

Benjamin stared at him with pity in his eyes, the rain obscuring his vision, the pain in his jaw throbbing. When he finally spoke, he did so softly.

"It's called love, Peter, and for as long as you live, you'll never understand what you cast aside. For that, I am forever in your debt."

With those words, Benjamin turned on his heel and stalked away. As he headed home, he lifted his face to the rain and prayed for the water to cleanse the guilt from his soul.

Fifteen

The Sabbath morning dawned bright and hot. Bridget walked along the street beside Sarabeth and behind her parents. Abigail's shoulders were rigid, and Bridget imagined her face still wore the dark scowl that had appeared when she informed her parents of the decision not to wed Peter.

Her father had been shocked into silence; her mother first pleaded and then begged her to change her mind. When that didn't work, anger prevailed and Abigail bitterly accused her of making a mockery of the family name. Bridget had tried to explain that there was no love to the match, but her parents dismissed her concerns and insisted, much as Peter had, that she forgo any such foolish romantic notions. Nevertheless, Bridget had stood steadfastly by her decision, as painful and humiliating as it had been.

Thank God for Sarabeth, Bridget thought, glancing gratefully at her sister. Quiet, meek, and ever-obedient Sarabeth had been her champion last night, standing up to her parents and siding openly with Bridget's decision to cancel the wedding. Then later, in the privacy of their room, Sarabeth had cried with her, alternating between being furious with Peter and Benjamin, and awash in tears over her lost dreams. Somehow, Bridget managed a tenuous hold on her resolve before falling into a troubled sleep.

Now, that resolve threatened to crumble as the family headed for the meeting house in strained silence. Sarabeth clutched her arm, her mouth set in a grim line, her eyes looking as red and puffy as Bridget's felt. The bell tolled loudly, calling the godly to assembly. Each ring seemed to pound against Bridget's skull.

She wished for more time to compose herself. But with each step, her dread grew at having to see Peter at assembly. She feared he might try to pressure her into going through with the wedding in front of her parents. Yet even that paled in comparison to the dismay she felt about having to face Benjamin in the light of day. After their passionate kiss and harsh words, she wasn't certain she could face him without her composure shattering to pieces. She had an overpowering urge to run home and hide in bed, pulling the covers up over her head. But the bell tolled steadily, seeming to call particularly to her. She would not be excused from prayer simply because she feared the shame and humiliation she would suffer once the news of the broken engagement came out.

"You brought it on yourself," she murmured aloud under her breath, and saw Sarabeth glance at her with a sad but knowing look.

Sarabeth squeezed her arm in support, and together they walked into the small clearing that fronted the meeting house. Bridget took a deep breath and looked anxiously around. Parishioners milled about the square, some leaning against the wooden stocks, others sitting on the grass beneath the shade of the giant oak trees. Children ran around the whipping post chasing butterflies. For a moment, Bridget thought it like any other Sabbath.

Then her parents went on into the meeting house, leaving Bridget and Sarabeth outside alone.

"I don't see Peter," Sarabeth whispered once their parents were out of sight. "Although I would be surprised if he dared show his face here after what he said to you," she added indignantly.

Bridget felt a small rush of relief. Mayhap she'd be granted a small respite from having to face him again so soon. Another quick survey of the square indicated that Benjamin wasn't present, either. Unless, of course, he was already inside. At least if that were the case, she'd be better able to avoid him.

"Look!" Sarabeth suddenly exclaimed, jabbing her in the ribs. Bridget felt her heart plummet when she saw Peter's parents enter the square. They'd never been overly friendly to her, but this morning, they both smiled politely and dipped their heads in greeting. Peter was noticeably absent.

Bridget felt the tension in her stomach ease slightly. Their lack of disapproval likely meant they didn't yet know about the broken engagement. It also meant that Peter still held out hope that she'd change her mind. For a moment, she was grateful to him, since it gave her a bit more time to gather the shreds of her badly shaken composure.

"Hello, Sarabeth," Bridget heard someone call out. She looked over her shoulder and saw Lydia Trask waving gaily from across the square. The young girl stood near her sister Phoebe and a few other young women, some of them whispering and giving Bridget pointed glances.

"They are acting suspiciously cheerful," Sarabeth hissed while gaily returning Lydia's wave. "I thought you said no one else knew about your broken engagement."

"No one except Benjamin," Bridget whispered back. "Mayhap he took it upon himself to make the announcement official."

"He wouldn't dare," she gasped, outraged.

Bridget felt her stomach churn uneasily. "I'm not certain of anything anymore, especially when it comes to him."

"Then let's go chat with Lydia," Sarabeth suggested, steering Bridget toward the girls. "Mayhap we'll discover what they are gossiping about."

"No," Bridget said, stopping in her tracks. "I can't. Please, I just can't do it this morning."

Sarabeth sighed. "All right. I'll go by myself. Will you wait for me here?"

Bridget pointed across the square. "There, under the tree." She walked over to the large oak tree and sat down in the shade. Trying to keep busy, she cleared away some grass and dry brush from a bunch of cheerful yellow buttercups. The bell still tolled unceasingly, and for the first time in her life, Bridget had evil thoughts about burning the rope that held the clapper. Thankfully, Sarabeth chose that moment to return and pulled Bridget to her feet hastily.

"Now I know why everyone is staring at you oddly this morning," she said breathlessly. "And it has nothing to do with a broken engagement."

"Then what is it?"

Some churchgoers wandered over to the shade, so Sarabeth steered Bridget away from the tree and toward an unoccupied part of the square. "Apparently Peter and Benjamin were engaged in some kind of brawl outside the Blue Shell Tavern last night."

"Brawl?" Bridget exclaimed. "Was anyone hurt?"

Sarabeth lifted her shoulders. "I don't know. Apparently, both were able to stagger away by themselves.

Peter's parents are here this morning without him, and I've yet to see Benjamin or his family. No one knows why they were fighting, but there is some speculation that you had something to do with their altercation."

"Me?" she uttered in horror. God forbid, just what had happened after she left Benjamin at Rock's Point last night? What had he done?

"It's time to go in," Sarabeth whispered urgently as the bell tolled a final time and fell silent. They quickly filed into the meeting house behind the others and took their spots on the pew. Bridget slid in next to her mother and tried to catch her eye. Her mother looked stiffly ahead without acknowledging her presence.

Bridget thought the service seemed to last far longer than the standard two hours. The hard edge of the bench bit into her bottom and she felt hot, then cold, restless, and nervous. She clasped her hands tightly in her lap and tried to concentrate on her father's sermon. But her thoughts kept straying to Peter and then Benjamin. She went over every bit of the conversation she'd had with Peter, and flushed with humiliation when she remembered his words about their relationship. By the time the first hour of the service had dragged past, she was emotionally drained from worrying, and physically exhausted from lack of sleep. She continually had to resist the urge to twist around in the pew and see if either Benjamin or Peter had shown up. Soon the heat in the crowded room began to wear on her. Several times she would have nodded off if not for a discreet elbow in the ribs from Sarabeth.

Finally the service was over and Bridget escaped outside for some much needed fresh air. Churchgoers spilled into the sunny square, shaking hands with her father and chatting with her mother. She looked about nervously but did not see either Benjamin or Peter. Removing her bonnet, she relaxed a little and began fanning herself with it.

A short distance away, she spotted the Trask sisters huddling and whispering with their friends. Bridget pursed her lips in annoyance as Lydia smiled at her and then whispered something, sending the women into a fit of giggles.

"Remind me why I tolerate the Trask sisters," Bridget hissed under her breath to Sarabeth.

"Bridget!" she chided gently. "This is the Sabbath, after all."

"I'm not feeling particularly charitable today," she replied irritably.

"I know, but you can't blame Lydia. I think she's still upset at the way Benjamin couldn't keep his eyes off you at the picnic."

Bridget rolled her eyes. "He was only concerned about my safety after the incident with Father's wagon."

"Mayhap. But nonetheless, I think she's jealous of you."

Bridget opened her mouth to reply when a strange flutter arose at the back of her neck. She reached up, but felt nothing. "Well, it's more than I can bear this morning. Come on. Let's go home and ready the midday meal. I'll need something to eat if I'm to endure another two hours of father's sermonizing."

They had taken a few steps off the square and onto the grass when Bridget suddenly heard a low humming sound behind her. Frowning, she turned around and realized it came from beneath the wooden platform of the stocks. The humming became louder, filling her ears with a buzz so intense she clapped her hands over her ears.

"Bridget," she heard Sarabeth cry as if from a long distance away. "Whatever is the matter?"

"Can't you hear it?" Bridget said, squeezing her eyes shut. The noise was nearly unbearable now, building to a strange crescendo in her head. She felt dizzy, disoriented, and sick to her stomach.

"Hear what?" Sarabeth said, looking around with a perplexed expression on her face.

Bridget opened her eyes, fixating on the stocks with a growing sense of dread. She had the most peculiar sensation that something evil lurked there, watching and assessing her. Then, as if recognizing her suspicions, the platform began to shake as if whatever contained inside was beating against the wood, trying to get out. The air seemed to thicken around her, the ground wobbled beneath her feet. She drew in a breath and held it until her lungs screamed for air.

Suddenly, one side of the wooden platform crashed open and a swarm of hornets flew out. The black mass swirled into the sky and seemed to hang suspended for a moment, blotting out the sun and shimmering like a shiny black curtain. Then the hornets seemed to gather in one breath and head straight for her.

Bridget heard the screams as everyone started to scatter. She pushed Sarabeth behind her, shouting at her to run, and stepped up to face the hornets alone. From the corner of her eye, she could see people running back and forth, shrieking and shouting in panic. Bridget held her ground, feeling a deadly calm come over her. An eerie wind roared in her ears, hot and fast, while her heart pounded furiously.

But to her surprise, the hornets did not attack, and instead shifted direction at the last possible moment. In horror, she realized the black cloud was headed directly for Sarabeth, who lay cowering and trembling on the grass behind her.

"No!" Bridget shouted, but it seemed only to drive the hornets into a frenzy. Panicked, she thrust out her hands and aimed at a patch of grass right in front of Sarabeth. The grass ignited into flames, sending a strange, dark smoke billowing into the air. The hornets buzzed in anger and scattered, temporarily confused and dazed.

"Sarabeth," Bridget yelled, ducking beneath the cloud of smoke to rescue her sister. She grabbed her by the upper arm, hauling her to her feet and half-carrying and half-dragging her toward the meeting house.

Somehow, Bridget got them both inside, slammed the door, and collapsed to the floor beside Sarabeth, coughing and trembling violently. When she finally looked up, she saw most of the congregation, including her mother, father, and Peter's parents, staring at her in open horror.

She opened her mouth to say something, but her throat was raw from the smoke, and her head pounded viciously. She couldn't seem to stop shaking.

At that moment, Phoebe Trask stepped forward. "Witch!" she screamed, pointing an accusing finger at Bridget.

Benjamin sat in his father's study, poring over the accounting ledgers, ignoring the steady throb of his jaw. The Sabbath was not a day to spend at work, but he was hardly in any condition to show up at assembly looking as he did. An ugly purple bruise extended from his cheekbone down across his jaw, and his lower lip was split and swollen. He hadn't slept except for a short, fitful doze sitting in the chair at the hearth. This morning his stomach churned with a mixture of anger, regret, and resignation. And not for a moment had he stopped thinking of Bridget.

He knew she'd be at the meeting house nice and proper this Sunday, sitting in the first pew as she always did with her mother and Sarabeth. He imagined her glorious red hair would be properly pinned beneath a kerchief, her shoulders straight and chin held high as if nothing of consequence had happened to her. Pride, if nothing else, would carry her through this. But his insides twisted just the same because he knew how she would be suffering beneath her brave facade.

He looked down and cursed when he saw the unsightly blot he'd just made on the ledger. Sighing, he set the pen aside and rubbed his temples wearily. He'd been looking at the same set of figures for close to an hour now and had made no progress.

Just then, he heard a noise at the study door and looked up as his father entered. He hastily picked up the pen and pretended to muse over the ledger.

"Would you care for a drink?" his father asked, going over to the wooden cabinet and pulling out a bottle of claret and two glasses.

Benjamin raised an eyebrow in surprise. It was the Sabbath and barely afternoon, but God knew he could use a drop. Apparently, his father knew as well. Without waiting for a reply, the elder Hawkes poured two glasses and brought one over to Benjamin. He sat down in a chair in front of the desk and lifted his lips to the glass.

"How's Mother?" Benjamin asked politely, although he knew she was fine and most certainly the instigator behind his father's sudden visit. When he'd run into her this morning, she'd taken one look at his face and had promptly pleaded too ill to go to services. Benjamin declared he would not go as well, and his father had insisted on staying home to take care of both of them. She'd retired to her bed while Benjamin had sought sanctuary in the study. Now it was clear that his father had been sent on a mission to discover just what had happened to cause the bruises on his face and heart.

His father took a drink and shifted uncomfortably in the chair. "So, how is the ledger balancing?" he asked brightly.

Benjamin took a sip of his claret and shrugged nonchalantly. His father was as good at discussing feelings as he was, and presently, Benjamin wasn't in a favorable disposition to talk about anything.

"As well as can be expected. I'll need some more time, of course."

"Of course," his father agreed and then took another sip. They sat in strained silence until his father spoke up again.

"Blast it, boy, you know why I'm here! Now tell me what I need to know, so we can end this charade."

Benjamin regarded his father over his glass, his own ire rising. Bradley Hawkes was a tall, handsome man with strikingly distinguished features and only the faintest trace of gray at his temples. He'd built his fortune through hard work and shrewd investments, as well as an uncanny knack for taking smart calculated risks. He treated all those who worked with him fairly and made certain everyone benefited. He'd been a damn good father, with an even hand and a warm heart. But he could be ill tempered when pushed in a direction he didn't want to go, and Benjamin sensed he was currently at that point.

Nonetheless, Benjamin's own mood was such that it didn't mean he was going to make this an easy task for his father.

"What exactly is it you want to know?" he said, taking a sip of his claret and leaning back in the chair.

His father scowled. "Why don't you start with why you've been in a foul mood since you set foot off the ship from Lisbon? After that, you can tell me with whom you brawled last night and for what purpose you're hiding in here with the ledgers instead of sitting at assembly. Although I must thank you for getting me out of that particular duty this morning."

Benjamin raised an eyebrow. "Did Mother send you?"

"What do you think?" he said, his scowl deepening.

"I think you're now wondering if you'd have been better off at services this morning."

His father grunted and tried to hide a smile behind his glass. "Just give me something to ease her sensibilities, boy, or I'll have no peace for the rest of the day."

Benjamin swirled the claret in his glass, thinking. "All right, then. You can tell Mother that she has a son who has been little more than a blind fool for most of his life."

Bradley appeared to consider that for a moment and then twisted his lips. "I find that hard to believe. You may be many things, son, but a fool is not among them."

"Well, believe it," Benjamin said sharply, pushing the chair away from the desk and standing. "How long must a man face the truth about himself before he finally admits to it?"

He saw a flicker of surprise in his father's eyes. "And just what might that truth be?"

Benjamin shoved his fingers through his hair. "That I've been narrow-minded and self-serving, and I've put the pursuit of my own gratification above the well-being of others. I won't apologize for going after what I want in life, but I didn't realize that the way I went about it deeply hurt people I cared about."

"You speak of Bridget," his father said quietly.

Benjamin threw up his hands. "Hell and damnation. How did you know?"

"I may be old, but I'm not an imbecile," his father said with a trace of exasperation. "Yet."

"Did everyone in this damned town know except me?" Benjamin said irritably.

His father shrugged. "It's one of life's most enduring lessons. There is only one thing in this world that can drive a man to such misery and madness, and it's a woman. It's just a hell of a time for you to come to your senses about her, son. Her wedding to Peter is fast approaching."

"There's not going to be any wedding," Benjamin said grimly.

His father raised an eyebrow in surprise. "There's not? Dare I ask if any of this is related to the unsightly condition of your face?"

Benjamin started to pace across the room, his boots beating a steady rhythm on the wood floor. "It all started when I . . . ah . . . compromised Bridget."

His father paled, clearly aghast. "You did what?" he gasped.

"No, it was nothing like that," Benjamin interjected hastily. "I just kissed her. But that was before I knew Peter didn't love her and was only marrying her to spite me."

Bradley opened his mouth to say something and then snapped it shut. After a minute, he opened it again. "Would you care to explain that further?" he finally asked.

Benjamin sank into the chair, picked up his glass, and drained it. His jaw still throbbed like hell, and the claret wasn't helping much. Nevertheless, his father walked over to the cabinet and brought back the bottle. He refilled both of their glasses, then left the bottle open where it stood.

"Peter never loved Bridget," Benjamin said wearily as his father sat back down in the chair. "He wanted her only because I did, but I was too blind to see it. Now Bridget isn't going to marry Peter, because she thinks this has been naught but a game to both of us; Peter thinks he's tossing Bridget to me like scraps to a dog; and I nearly beat the hell out of a man I've called friend for most of my life. Now Bridget won't have anything to do with either one of us, not that I blame her."

"You . . . you kissed Bridget?" his father repeated blankly.

Benjamin scowled at the memory. "She made me so blasted angry, Father. She yammered on about how perfect Peter was until I couldn't bear it a moment more. I kissed her mostly to shut her up, but then I realized for how long I'd wanted to do it. God help me, but it was extraordinary. She is extraordinary."

Benjamin blew out a frustrated breath and then took another swallow of the claret before continuing.

"I fully intended to end it at that, but every time I tried to apologize, I just seemed to make matters worse. I love her, Father. I wanted to tell her how I felt, but the words were like paste on my tongue. Whatever came out was laughable and woefully inadequate. Besides, deep inside, a part of me loathed ruining everything for her. Yet that's exactly what I did."

"And the bruises on your face?"

Benjamin sighed. "I called Peter out. He had told Bridget the two of us had been vying for her in some kind of competition. He played me brilliantly, I must admit. He's in an impeccable situation now. He's the one who has been wronged, betrayed by his betrothed and his best friend. If he somehow manages to convince Bridget to wed him after this, he looks like a champion. If she refuses to go through with it, he'll play on that sympathy to catapult himself into a stronger position to challenge Edward Trask for town moderator. Frankly I'm more than annoyed he used me to do that, but I'm damn well furious that Bridget will be the person to suffer no matter what happens."

His father took a drink and thought for a moment. "What do you intend to do about it, then?"

"What can I do? I think she still fancies herself in love with Peter, and for that I curse him to hell. I tried to convince her to wed me instead, but she looked at me as if I were the devil incarnate. She's not likely to see me in a favorable light, at least not in the foreseeable future. She's been publicly humiliated, disgraced, and must endure a broken engagement and gossip of a dalliance with me."

Benjamin finished his claret and picked up the bottle, pouring some more in his glass. He had yet to feel any effects of the liquor, but he needed to make the effort.

His father stared at his own wine intently, and Benjamin could almost see the thoughts running through his head. After a moment, his father set his glass down on the desk and stood.

"Then what is it you want, son? Retribution, revenge, satisfaction?"

Benjamin looked steadily at his father. "I want Bridget."

His father nodded, a look of approval on his face. "Then go after her, boy. Do exactly what you would do to get a desired contract. Persuade, negotiate, dominate, maneuver. Do what you must."

Benjamin lifted his hands in exasperation. "Bridget is hardly a shipping contract, Father."

"No, she's worth a hell of a lot more than that. How do you think I got your mother? Do you think it was easy? She made me sweat blood before she capitulated. It was the hardest thing I'd ever done. To this day, I'm still not certain how I did it, or that she hadn't been in control all along."

Benjamin looked at his father, flabbergasted. "Mother?"

"For God's sake, Benjamin, she's a woman. Bridget is a woman. Do you really think we have any idea what we are doing when it concerns them?"

"But I—"

His father waved his hand impatiently. "I'll give you a few words of advice. A man's actions speak louder than his words. Pursue and persevere. If you want her, then go after her with everything you have. Narrow your determination; fully intend to achieve your goal. Use everything at your disposal. I assure you, son, it will be the most important contract you ever secure, and if right, the most satisfying one."

With that, his father stood and replaced the near empty bottle of claret in the cabinet. "Just don't mention to your mother that we've been drinking on the Sabbath."

Benjamin felt the strangest urge to laugh. And yet,

he also felt as if the weight of the world had been somehow eased from his shoulders. As his father left the study, he had already begun to think—forming, planning, and developing an appropriate strategy.

In a few minutes he left the study, going into the parlor and summoning the housekeeper to bring his coat. He donned it and headed for the door, yanking it open.

To his shock, he saw Sarabeth Goodwell standing on the porch, her hand raised as if to reach for the knocker. In the split second before she spoke, he registered her disheveled appearance, the frantic look in her stunning blue eyes, and caught the puzzling but distinct scent of smoke.

He opened his mouth to speak when she suddenly raised a hand and slapped him hard against his sore jaw.

"That's for what you've done to Bridget," she said angrily.

Benjamin rubbed his jaw gingerly. "Blast it, Sarabeth. I won't say I didn't deserve that, but at least you could have said hello."

She sniffed. "You're a cad, Benjamin Hawkes," she said, raising her chin. "But I need your help."

Sixteen

"You can't do this," Reverend Goodwell shouted as he followed Constable Jeremiah Amerton and Bridget down Main Street toward the jailhouse. The constable held Bridget by the upper arm and walked so fast that they were practically running. A group of curious onlookers followed them, much to Bridget's dismay and mortification.

"She's my daughter and mine to punish if I see fit to do so," the reverend continued. "You can't lock her up for saving her sister's life."

Jeremiah sighed. "I don't want to do this, Ichabod. But she's been accused of creating a public spectacle. We both know 'tis an arrestable offense. Besides, I saw her do it with my own eyes. 'Twas the nearest thing to witchcraft I've ever seen, and on the Sabbath, no less. Let the committee decide what to do with her."

"There hasn't been a case of witchcraft in this town for nearly a century," the reverend protested heatedly. "You can't hold her on such ridiculous charges."

"I can if I think the safety of this town is endangered. Now leave me be and let me do my job."

Bridget listened numbly to the furious exchange, not even able to form a word of protest of her own. She stumbled and Jeremiah gripped her arm so tightly that she winced in pain.

"Look, Reverend," the constable said, his voice softening. "I'm doing this partly for her protection. You saw how those people looked at her. They was frightened out of their minds. She'll be safe in the jailhouse until we can decide what to do with her."

Still spluttering, her father followed them all the way to the jailhouse. He didn't cease his tirade until Jeremiah put her in one of the cold, dank cells and closed the door behind her. Bridget shuddered as the bolt slid across, locking her in with a frightful certainty. After a moment, her father peeked in through the small wooden slat at the top of the door and gave her a brave smile.

"Courage, child," he said softly. "God will protect you, and I will do everything in my power to have you released."

Bridget felt like crying, but she held her chin high. "I know, Father. I'll be all right."

After he left, Bridget resisted the urge to dissolve into tears and instead took stock of her surroundings. The small cell was devoid of furnishings except for a rickety wooden bench pushed back against one wall. A small barred window barely let in the light from the sun, making small stripes on the dirt floor. Gingerly she perched on the bench, putting her head in her hands. She shouldn't be surprised she was in here. It had been her nightmare for as long as she could remember. In a moment of fear, she'd let her guard down and showed the entire town her aberration. But when she thought of Sarabeth cowering on the ground in terror, and the way the hornets headed purposefully in her direction, she didn't regret for a moment what she'd done.

LIGHT A SINGLE CANDLE

The afternoon stretched on until she finally heard the bolt draw back and the door open. She sat up as the constable peeked in and then moved back. When Abigail walked inside, Bridget blinked in disbelief.

"Mother?" she whispered.

Abigail carried a blanket and a small covered plate. She set the food and the blanket on the bench.

"You have but a few minutes," Jeremiah warned as he closed the door and bolted it again. "If word of this gets out, I could lose me job."

Abigail perched on the bench beside her. "Are you all right?" she asked.

Bridget nodded, fighting back tears. "I'm fine. How is Sarabeth?"

"She's shaken and understandably distraught. But she's unharmed, thanks to you."

Bridget let out a breath of relief. "Oh, I'm so thankful."

"No, I am the one who is thankful." Her mother fell silent for a long moment and then, to Bridget's utter astonishment, put an arm around her, pulling her close.

"I'm so sorry, Bridget," she whispered, her voice breaking. "For everything I've done to you. Can you ever forgive me?"

Bridget gave a little sob, her eyes filling with tears. "Why are you sorry? This is all my fault."

Abigail shook her head, stroking Bridget's hair. "No, the blame is mine. I've wronged you. I've known all along that you were different. But that didn't stop me from trying to make you into someone you weren't. You've always been so strong, independent, and confident. It angered me, and in a way, I suppose, it frightened me. I thought only to protect you, but instead I pushed you away. You were my trial from

God and I have failed miserably. I hurt you deeply, and for that I beg your forgiveness."

Bridget felt the tears slide down her cheeks. For how many years had she longed to hear those words and to feel the comforting arms of her mother around her?

"I'm sorry I couldn't be who you wanted me to be, Mother."

"You've always been an important part of our family. God gave you to us for a reason. And now you selflessly risked your own life to save Sarabeth. I'm ashamed that it took something like this before I realized how selfish I've been and how much I love you."

Bridget's voice caught on a sob. "I love you, too, Mother."

For a moment they held each other, heart to heart, mother to daughter, until Abigail pulled away, brushing the tears from Bridget's cheeks.

"Are you going to be all right?" she asked, tucking a strand of red hair behind her ear.

"I don't know," Bridget replied honestly. "What will happen to me?"

Abigail rubbed her eyes wearily. "There will be an inquiry tomorrow at the courthouse. The magistrate and town selectmen will examine the charges against you."

"What charges?"

"Creating a public disturbance, unlawful use of a fire in a public setting, and endangering the safety of children." She paused for a moment and her lips trembled. "Unofficially, you are being accused of witchcraft."

Bridget gasped. "Witchcraft? Will anyone stand for me?"

"Your father, Sarabeth, and I, of course." Her mother flushed, a stain creeping across her cheeks. "Your father went to see Peter. He . . . he would not come, nor does he intend to speak for you. Bridget, you were right about him."

Bridget sat down on the bench next to her mother, her stomach turning. "I'm sorry."

"No, I'm sorry. I should have trusted your judgment. You always seem to have the ability to see into the hearts of people. I'll never doubt you again."

They both looked up as they heard the footsteps of the constable returning to the cell. Abigail hastily pressed a kiss to Bridget's cheek.

"Be brave, child. For all of us. You father and I will do what we can. It's in God's hands now."

After she left, Bridget felt more alone and bereft than she had ever been in her life. The day dragged on into evening more slowly than she ever thought possible. She wondered whether her father had canceled the afternoon service or had held it, pleading for God's assistance in this matter. When dusk fell, Bridget forced herself to eat some of the food her mother had brought, although her stomach felt queasy. She exercised her legs by walking briskly around the cell before she finally curled up on the bench, draped the blanket around her, and fell into a fitful sleep.

She awoke when the rusty bolt was being drawn back across the door. Quickly she stood, her muscles stiff and groaning in protest. Jeremiah stood at the door, a cup of water and a wooden trencher in his hands.

"Good morn to you, mistress," he said, shoving the trencher at her. "Eat some of this and I'll be back shortly to take you to the courthouse."

He slammed the door shut and Bridget looked at

the gruel in dismay. She set it on the bench untouched and instead drank a bit of water and tried to wipe away the dust and grime from her face and hands. When Jeremiah returned, she was as ready as she would ever be.

When she stepped out into the sunlight, she blinked and squinted, her eyes watering. Once again, Jeremiah secured his grip on her arm as if he thought she might try to whisk herself magically out of his careful charge.

The walk to the courthouse was a short one, but excruciating just the same. People lined the street, watching, whispering, and wondering. She realized with a heavy heart that the gossip about her would likely go on for years, if not for the rest of her natural life, however long that might prove to be.

She held her head high as they entered the courthouse, but was stunned at the sheer number of people present. All of the benches and chairs were jammed with spectators; those who couldn't find a seat stood pressed against the walls. A quick glance around told her that neither Benjamin nor his parents were present, but she saw Phoebe and Lydia Trask sitting near the front of the room with their mother. Directly behind them were Peter's parents. His father looked stiffly ahead, refusing to meet her gaze, while Peter's mother gave her a chilly and condemning look. Peter was conspicuously absent. For a moment, Bridget realized how absurd it seemed that just two days ago, she had intended to become a part of this family and spend the rest of her life with them.

She walked forward slowly and saw her mother sitting in the front row with an empty seat beside her. Abigail gave her a tremulous smile that bade her take courage, and Bridget returned the look with a reassuring tip of her head. She thought it likely the empty seat was for Sarabeth, and wondered if her sister had been too traumatized by the ordeal to attend today's inquiry.

In the front of the room stood a long wooden table, behind which sat several men. She immediately recognized the man in the center as Captain George Haft, the town magistrate. Edward Trask, the town moderator as well as Lydia and Phoebe's father, sat there amid various other selectmen, including her father. Ichabod's face was grim, but when he looked at her he gave her an imperceptible nod and a look that urged her to be calm.

The constable nudged her forward until she stood directly in front of the table. Bridget took a deep breath and raised her chin. A deathly silence fell over the chamber.

"State your name, please," Captain Haft said, not unkindly.

"Bridget Elizabeth Goodwell," she answered, surprised that her voice sounded so steady.

The captain motioned to a thin young man with a sallow complexion. "Clerk, please read the charges."

The man stood, nervously holding a document. Bridget could see his hands were shaking.

"Bridget Elizabeth Goodwell, you are hereby accused of consorting with the devil and, in doing so, exhibiting unnatural abilities that could threaten the public safety of this town. The committee has received numerous witness testimonies to the effect that you were able to summon fire without the aid of a flint and set aflame a patch of grass and flowers. In doing so, the well-being of those present, including young children, was directly threatened. And by creating this fire, you also risked causing damage to the meeting house as well as other nearby structures. What have you to say for yourself?"

Reverend Goodwell leaped to his feet. "She did not threaten children," he shouted, his face reddening. "These charges are outrageous. Her actions were in defense of herself and her sister, not to mention everyone else standing in that square, including myself. Now, let's end this mockery and go home."

The noise in the courtroom reached a dull roar until Captain Haft pounded the table with his gavel. "There will be quiet," he ordered until the room fell silent again.

"Your concerns are duly noted, Reverend," Captain Haft said calmly. "But the committee must finish its business. I respectfully ask that you return to your seat so we might continue the proceedings."

Bridget watched as her father reluctantly sat back down. Such a fierce love for him ran through her that she felt herself tremble with it.

Captain Haft looked at her and spoke almost gently. "Mistress Goodwell, the committee needs to know. Have you consorted with the devil?"

"No, sir."

"Did your actions hold the intent to cause injury to others?"

"No, sir. I meant only to help my sister."

"Did you or did you not summon fire?"

Bridget hesitated, drawing in a deep breath. "I . . ." she started when there was a commotion at the back of the room. She saw the magistrate look over her shoulder and frown in displeasure that the proceedings had been interrupted once again.

"Who is interrupting this inquiry?" he asked irritably.

Bridget turned around to see what was happening.

Stunned, she saw Sarabeth and Benjamin standing in the doorway, trying to make their way forward through the crowd. Benjamin stood tall above the spectators, and even though he had a horrid purple bruise stretching from his cheek to his jaw, she thought she had never seen a more welcome sight. Their eyes met across the room, and she could feel a rush of warmth and strength flow from him into her. His expression appeared serious and somber, but she saw a familiar sparkle of mischief in his eyes, and her apprehension increased tenfold.

"Begging your pardon, sir, and the pardon of the court," Benjamin's voice rang out. "But I have some important information that pertains directly to this case."

The room fell silent. Bridget stood stiffly, afraid to move a muscle. Captain Haft stared at him for several moments, most likely curious as to what had happened to cause such unsightly bruises on his face, but then motioned him forward.

"Mister Hawkes, do come here. This is not a convened court of law, but a simple inquiry. All information that pertains to this case is welcome. What have you to add to these proceedings?"

Benjamin strode into the hall and up to the table. "I'd like to ask the permission of this committee to share my information by conducting a demonstration outside, preferably in front of the meeting house where the incident with Mistress Goodwell and her sister occurred."

There was some tittering in the room and a swell of excited voices. Bridget thought wryly that there hadn't been this much excitement in Salem since Harriet Winford had caught her husband bedded down with another woman and shot them both.

"A demonstration would be highly irregular," the captain said, stroking his beard, but Bridget could see his curiosity was piqued. "Just what kind of demonstration are we talking about?"

Benjamin leaned over, putting his hands on the table. His expression was sincere, his eyes filled with concern. Bridget had seen him employ this charm nearly every day of her life. Only today, she prayed with all her heart, it would work to her advantage.

"I intend to duplicate Mistress Goodwell's fiery display, a feat which I believe will abruptly and rightly end these proceedings," he said dramatically.

A collective gasp came from the room, and Bridget looked at Benjamin in shocked amazement.

"No, he's in league with her!" a woman shouted, jumping to her feet.

Bridget turned and looked in puzzled shock at Margaret Trask. Her cheeks were red with anger, her eyes blazing. Sitting next to her were daughters Lydia and Phoebe, both of whom stared at Bridget with venomous hostility.

Captain Haft looked wryly at Margaret. "My dear woman," he said calmly, "Mister Hawkes has been in league with Mistress Goodwell for as long as I can remember." He turned his attention to Benjamin. "Are you telling me, young man, that this has been some kind of prank?"

Benjamin lifted his hands. "Certainly not the part about trying to protect her sister from the hornets. That, indeed, was an act of love. But how she accomplished the feat was part of a long-standing hoax we've played on each other since childhood. And I assure you, it requires no collaboration or conspiracy with the devil."

The captain began conferring in whispers with the

other selectmen. Bridget could hear a few dissenting murmurs, including a rather strident one from Edward Trask, but finally the magistrate looked up.

"It is the majority opinion of this committee that the evidence offered by Mister Hawkes bears further investigation before this inquiry continues. I urge you to proceed, sir."

Benjamin flashed Bridget a triumphant grin as he turned, and she wondered what in God's name he had up his sleeve this time.

It seemed that half the population of Salem filed out of the courthouse and toward her father's meeting house. The constable held her tightly, although it would have been nearly impossible for her to flee in such a crush of people. Benjamin strode up ahead, calm and confident. Bridget could see his dark head bobbing in the crowd. She managed to meet Sarabeth's glance once and saw a grim determination in her eyes. She felt a flutter of apprehension in her stomach. Just what had the two of them planned?

People milled into the square in front of the meeting house, giving Benjamin a wide berth. He stood near the grass, but in a different location from where she and Sarabeth had been standing when the hornets attacked. A quick glance in that direction showed the grass gone and only blackened dirt remaining. A faint scent of smoke still penetrated the air. The platform beneath the stocks remained broken, with shattered planks lying about, but there was no sight or sound of the hornets. Nonetheless, given her precarious situation, the stocks and whipping post held a much more ominous presence this morning.

Jeremiah dragged her near where Captain Haft and the other selectmen stood. Some watched Benjamin with open curiosity, others with wary suspicion.

Once the crowd had settled, Benjamin held up his hands and then slowly turned around in a circle. "As you can see, I am without means, just as Mistress Goodwell appeared to be. Now, imagine this with me. An angry swarm of hornets attacks without warning. Mistress Goodwell is afraid, but not for herself. She knows her sister becomes deathly ill if stung by even one of the insidious insects. So she employs a trick used by both of us on many occasions. Observe!"

He waved both hands in the air as if fighting off a swarm of flying insects, and then bent over. Magically a spark seemed to appear from his hand. The spark caught on a trail of dry brush that lay on the ground leading straight to the grass. The spark turned into flames that grew in strength as they moved, fueled by the stiff breeze and the dry condition of the grass. When the fire reached the grass, it ignited into larger flames, sending smoke whirling up into the air.

The crowd erupted into gasps and low murmurs. Bridget stood in shock, as flabbergasted as everyone else. Benjamin strode to the grass and stomped out the fire with his boots before it grew any larger. Smoke still lingered in the air.

Captain Haft stepped forward. "How did you do that, boy?" he asked, astonishment evident on his face.

Benjamin smiled and turned his hand over, palm up. "With this."

The crowd surged forward to see, and at once Bridget recognized the small, strange mechanism as the fire-lighting device from Widow Bayley's cottage.

Bridget held her breath as he pulled a small tin out of his pocket and carefully poured a small amount of powder into the device. Then he bent to the ground and picked up a large dry leaf. With everyone watching, he flicked his thumb against the device and a spark jumped out, igniting the powder to a flame and catching the leaf. It abruptly burst into flames as Benjamin dropped it and stepped on the embers with his boot. The crowd began to clap and roar.

"And that is the way it happened," Benjamin said calmly, raising his voice to be heard over the crowd. "There was no witchcraft or evil intent present."

Bridget was shocked when Peter's mother stepped forward. "She used no device to do it. I saw her with my own eyes. She summoned fire from air, and the smoke was thick, black, and unnatural."

"You just watched me do it, madame," Benjamin argued reasonably. "And until I actually showed you the device, you had no idea I even possessed it. In the midst of a frightening situation, with people running about in fear for their safety, just how certain could you be as to whether or not Mistress Goodwell had this in her possession? And as to the smoke, I just offered you a small demonstration. If I feared for my life or the life of someone I loved, you can be assured I would have employed the device to its full capability."

The constable, Jeremiah Amerton, spoke up, scratching his head. "She didn't have no device on her when I took her to the jailhouse."

"That's because she dropped it here," Benjamin said, pointing to a spot beneath the oak tree. "When I heard what had happened, I knew at once she must have been using this. I came here immediately and found it right where she must have dropped it after saving her sister from grievous harm."

The noise from the crowd was deafening now, and Captain Haft shouted at everyone to remain quiet. He stepped forward, asking to take a look at the device. Benjamin handed it to him.

"It uses the same mechanism you will find on a flintlock pistol," Benjamin explained. "It has a flint, a frizzen, a spring, and a small amount of gunpowder which ignites. It isn't always so stable, but never before have Bridget and I had to use it for so grave a purpose. I'm certain Bridget never imagined she would use it to save her sister's life."

"You constructed this?" the captain asked in wonder.

Benjamin shook his head. "No. It was a gift given to me by a friend."

"It's extraordinary," he replied, handing it off to another of the selectmen. After a moment, all the men had duly examined and marveled over the tiny invention.

The reverend stepped forward. "I call for this inquiry to be ended. It's clear that my daughter did not summon fire from air, nor did she employ the aid of Satan to conduct herself with evil intent. The fire harmed no structures, and the only repairs that need to be made are those to the stocks platform. I will do it myself."

"With my help, sir," Benjamin said, crossing his arms against his chest.

"And mine," added Abigail, stepping up to stand next to her daughter.

Captain Haft turned and gazed at Bridget. "Is all of this true, mistress? Did you or did you not consort with the devil to commit this act with evil or ill intent?"

"I did not, sir," Bridget answered truthfully.

"That's not true!" Lydia Trask shouted, pushing her way forward. Bridget was stunned by the fury in her eyes. Was Lydia really that jealous?

"The girl is afflicted, possessed!" Lydia continued.

"She's clearly cast a spell on Benjamin and is a danger to this community."

"Have you no shame, Lydia?" Benjamin said quietly, stepping between her and Bridget. "I assure you, I am under no coercion here. Do you really wish to return to the madness and hysteria of one hundred years ago? To our collective shame, our town condemned innocent people to death. Shall we revisit such a primitive and uncivilized state once again?"

Captain Haft looked slowly between Benjamin and Bridget and then shook his head. Walking over to the selectmen, he conferred with them for a moment and then returned to stand in front of her.

"By the power invested in me as town magistrate and with the consent of a majority of the selectmen present, I hereby dismiss the charges against you, Mistress Goodwell. You are free to go."

Bridget let out a huge breath of air as her father scooped her into his arms in a big hug. After a moment, her mother joined them and then Sarabeth came forward, weeping and laughing uncontrollably. Bridget held tight to her family, her relief so enormous that she could hardly breathe. When she finally untangled herself from her family, she was surrounded by a new crowd of well-wishers. She beamed and thanked them for their support and then eagerly searched the crowd for Benjamin.

But he was by that time gone, having disappeared into the crowd as mysteriously as he had appeared.

She felt a twinge of disappointment but then cheered. If she knew Benjamin—and she did—she knew just where to find him.

Seventeen

Benjamin sat near the boulders at Rock's Point, enjoying the strong breeze and watching the last rays of the morning sun dance across the waves. He'd been here for a good hour or so, thinking and preparing what he intended to say to Bridget. This time he would not permit the words to fail him. He had no intention of losing her again.

She came as the sun was at its highest point in the sky. Without a word, she sat down next to him, pulling her knees to her chest and looking out at the sea. She was without a bonnet, and her thick red hair hung loose in long, graceful curves over her shoulders and tumbled down her back. The wind whipped color into her cheeks, and an escaping curl fell over her forehead. They sat there for several minutes in silence before she spoke.

"You saved me," she said quietly. "And in doing so, you risked a lot. Why did you do it?"

"Why do you think I did?"

"Guilt? Anger? Pride?"

"Friendship," he answered firmly.

She tucked a strand of hair behind her ear. "You conspired with Sarabeth and Widow Bayley."

"Certainly. When Sarabeth told me what had happened, I was frantic to think of a way to extricate you from the situation. Then I remembered the device she'd showed me—the one Elias made to help her light fires. I thought I could replicate your feat using the device, and she kindly agreed to lend it to me. She was quite anxious about you and wanted to accompany me to the courthouse, but I didn't think her presence would help your case much."

A slight smile touched her lips. "No, I suppose it wouldn't have."

He swept a dark strand of hair from his eyes, the breeze was blowing harder now. "Of course, she was terribly relieved to hear you were absolved of the charges. And rather surprised to learn how I utilized Elias's amazing invention."

She looked at him now, her green eyes deceptively calm. "Did she not wonder how I started the fire in the first place?"

"It's most curious, but she didn't ask. I think she already knows, Bri. I'm not certain how, but there seems to be more to Widow Bayley than meets the eye."

She nodded, the hair snapping across her cheeks. "I think I've always felt that way. She's special to me, just as you are. My two guardian angels. How did you make her device work so exactly, Benjamin? Even I was astonished by your feat."

He grinned and then winced at the pain in his jaw. "It was simple, really. I went to the meeting house first and set up a trail of dry brush that led to the grass. I also made certain the device had fresh gunpowder. Then I concealed it in my sleeve. Using sleight of hand, I made it appear as if I'd conjured fire from the air. In all honesty, I wasn't certain it would work. I prayed a lot."

A smile touched her lips. "Of all the pranks you've ever played, this one is certainly the most spectacular, if not the most dangerous," she said.

He feigned a look of wounded dismay. "Did you doubt me?"

"Considerably," she said, "although I should have known better. You were magnificent, of course. I've never been so proud and so indebted to you."

He stroked his chin thoughtfully. "Ah yes, the matter of a debt. Well, I'm afraid I will have to collect on that."

"You will?"

"I must. You see, I require a favor that only you can provide."

"What kind of favor?"

"A simple one. I wish to return to your good graces."

She regarded him suspiciously. "That is all?"

"Yes."

"First tell me how you got that unsightly bruise on your jaw, and why you wince every time you move."

He narrowed his eyes. "That, I'm afraid, is none of your concern."

"It is if it involves me."

"I assure you, it's a matter that has been settled to my satisfaction. Now, back to the matter of your debt. Do you intend to honor it?"

She nodded. "I do. But there is something I still don't understand. How is it that you still desire my friendship? You know I possess something unearthly that sets me apart from others. Mayhap it is not inherently wicked, but it's still dangerous. Is there really that much of a difference between the two?"

He considered her words for a moment and then nodded. "Without question. I know in my heart that you would never use your power to harm others. I don't doubt there are such people who are malicious and might use power in the service of evil, but I'm convinced you are not among them."

He could see her blink back the tears. "I want to believe that, Benjamin; I desperately do. But I feel as though my life is falling to pieces and I'm unable to stop it."

"Perhaps it's not falling apart at all. Have you considered that maybe your life is falling into place, and that's what frightens you?"

The heavy lashes that shadowed her cheeks flew up. "I've just broken a three-year betrothal, condemned myself to an extended existence of loneliness, and been accused of witchcraft in front of the entire town. And you wish me not to be frightened that this is my destiny?"

Lightly he fingered a loose tendril of hair on her cheek. "What I'm trying to say is that sometimes life does not go according to our plans, no matter how carefully they are laid. Perhaps this has been God's plan for you all along."

"Why?" she asked, her voice tinged with bitterness. "Why did He make me like this? I don't understand why I am the way I am. I never asked to be different."

"We're all different, Bri, although I'll admit your ability is rather unique. But it doesn't change the essence of you, nor can you let it govern your future. Someone once told me that you need only to follow your heart and you'll find your destiny there."

She chewed uncertainly on her lower lip and then bit down on it. "Now you sound like Widow Bayley."

"I confess it was she who so advised me. She opened my eyes to a lot of things. In fact, after seeing Elias's sketches, I've decided I'm going to actively pursue my dream of being an architect. I'll still act occasionally as a shipping agent for my father, but I'm fortunate to have the means to pursue as many of my dreams as I wish. I fully intend to take advantage of that."

Her expression was earnest. "I'm glad for you, Benjamin. Truly. I always knew you'd accomplish all of your dreams."

He took her hand, squeezing it gently. The moment he'd been waiting for had arrived. Yet instead of feeling worried or anxious, a strange calm came over him. He took a deep breath and readied himself.

"You are a part of my dream, too, Bri. You always have been. I want you to wed me. Not because I feel guilty or because I have a misguided sense of responsibility for you, but because it is right. *We* are right."

He saw her lips tremble, but doubt still lingered in her eyes. He felt a wild urge to crush it, destroy it, and remove it from her heart forever. He needed her to know just how important she was to him.

"Why would you want to spend your life with an oddity?" she said, her voice wavering. "Marriage is not a practical solution for either one of us, especially not for you. You could have any woman in Salem— someone much wealthier, more beautiful, and better suited to your lifestyle than me."

He pressed her hand to his chest. "There is no one more suited to me than you. From the moment we met, you fascinated me. You were shockingly stubborn, delightfully outspoken, and the most remarkable person I'd ever come across. By all accounts you should have deferred to me. But you never did. Instead, you maintained an infuriating sense of self and dignity that I both envied and admired."

She shook her head. "We are no longer children,

LIGHT A SINGLE CANDLE

Benjamin. And this is a lifetime contract we are talking about. I know you're fond of me, but when will that not be enough?"

Benjamin frowned in frustration. Once again, things were not going as he'd planned. "Damn it, Bri. Can't you see what I'm trying to say? I'm not just fond of you. I love you. Peter knew, my parents knew, and probably most of Salem knew as well. I was simply blind to my own feelings until it was nearly too late. I swear upon the Bible that I'm not going to lose you again."

He saw the color drain from her face and she looked at him in shock. "You love . . . me?"

He laughed hoarsely. "With God as my witness. And I'm not going to capitulate on this one, Bri. I'll court you day after day until you're too weary to resist me anymore. I know you still love Peter, but if you'd just give me a chance, mayhap you'll find I'm not so disagreeable in that way."

"Disagreeable?" she uttered and then snapped her mouth shut. "Benjamin, there is something you should know. I don't love Peter. I'm not certain I ever did."

He stilled, his heart thudding hard in his chest. "You don't?"

"I thought I did. Heaven knows I tried, but I think I was more in love with a dream. We were both fond of each other, but I'm afraid love was absent. As the wedding approached and I took a more honest look at my feelings, I finally faced the truth: that my heart has always belonged elsewhere."

Benjamin felt a strange hitch in his throat. "And where might that be?"

"With you." She managed a smile. "You never knew, but I've loved you from afar since that first day in assembly when you slipped the snake down the back of my gown. Oh, how it infuriated me when the prettiest girls in town flocked to you, all vying for your attention. You were breathtakingly handsome, charming, and so utterly self-assured that you were irresistible to them—and to me. Sometimes I wished I would turn into a lovely princess so that you would notice me. But after a while I realized I had something much more precious than all the girls in Salem. I had your friendship and I shared your dreams. I learned to become content with that."

He gazed at her, hardly breathing. "Bri—" he started, but she held up a hand, stopping him.

"Please, Benjamin, I need to finish this awkward confession or I never will. All the things you are saying to me now . . . well, they were all a part of that dream. To hear you actually speak them aloud, it terrifies me. What happens if you wake up one day and realize what a horrid mistake you've made by wedding me? I don't think my heart could bear it if you became disappointed with me."

"Jesus, Bri," he said hoarsely, his voice catching in his throat. Turning, he pulled her into his arms, cupping her face with his hands. "I'll never be disappointed with you," he said quietly. "Angry, furious, annoyed, and irritated, perhaps, but never disappointed."

He looked at her, his gaze skimming over her high cheekbones, freckled cheeks, stubborn nose, and wide, generous mouth. The wind had brought color to her cheeks, and he saw both the delicacy and strength in her face. For the first time, he became intensely aware of an inherent beauty that made her look almost ethereal in the afternoon sunlight. His angel. His witch. Whichever one, she belonged to him.

"Do you know the pain I felt when I realized you were actually going to wed Peter?" he said softly. "I was desperate, wretched, and adrift. It was as though I had lost a piece of myself. I almost did. I'm not going to let it happen again. You won't slip away from me this time, Bri."

"I don't know what to say," she said, her eyes filling with tears.

"Say you'll wed me. Dare to live your dream. I need you. You are a part of me I don't want to live without. No one has ever challenged me, infuriated me, and made me feel more alive than you. I want to build us a house and fill it with children. We'll teach them to sail, climb trees, run races barefoot, and swim unclothed in the sea. I want you to hold my hand when I'm sick and sleep at my side at night. But more than anything, I want to grow old with you. Say you'll stay with me."

"I want to, Benjamin," she replied, her voice fragile. "But I fear you're not thinking properly. Have you any idea of the scandal this would cause?"

"When has scandal ever bothered me?"

"This will be different. People will talk about the broken engagement, about my advanced age, and about my complete unsuitability for Salem's most eligible bachelor. There are also your parents and mine to consider. How will they respond to this sort of painful discussion? And what if our children turn out to have some strange kind of ability like me?"

"It wouldn't matter a whit to me. I don't fear your gift, Bri. You do enough worrying about it for both of us. In regard to my parents, they wish for nothing more than my happiness. I assure you, they would be delighted to hear of our joining."

She groped about, looking for a plausible reason to end his foolish insistence. "But what of your future?"

"What of it?" he said irritably. "I have no intention

of changing course simply because a bunch of gossipmongers intend to speak of me. I mean to have you as my wife, Bri, and I'll do what I must to convince you of that."

As soon as he said the words, a fierce protectiveness surged through him. He'd never been so certain of anything in his life. He wanted her; he loved her. Pressing his lips to her throat, he splayed out his fingers against the small of her back. In fact, he'd damn well use all his powers of persuasion if that was what it took to convince her he was sincere.

"Say you'll have me," he murmured as he kissed her eyelids, temples, and cheeks. Slowly he lowered his mouth to hers, joining with her in a kiss of gentle reverence. He moved his lips from one side of her mouth to the other with excruciating tenderness. She trembled in his arms.

"I love you," he whispered. "We belong together."

A sob caught in her throat as she wound her arms around his neck and buried her face in his shoulder. "You don't know how long I've dreamed of hearing those words from you," she whispered. "If this is a dream, please don't ever wake me."

He smiled against her hair. "We're going to live our dream, Bri. You and me. I give you my word."

"I trust you." She lifted her head and gave him a tremulous smile. "I always have."

He kissed the tip of her nose. "Does that mean you'll wed me?"

Chewing her lower lip, she looked at him uncertainly. "Why do I feel as though I'm about to jump off the edge of a cliff?"

"We can jump together," he suggested.

"Leave it to you to propose the absurd."

"Leave it to you to dare me to do it. So, will you?"

"Jump off the cliff?"

"Wed me?"

"Are they not one and the same?" There was a trace of tender laughter in her voice as she gazed at him. "Yes, Benjamin," she said softly. "I will wed you."

He felt a rush of exhilaration, relief, and joy so intense he could hardly breathe. He gave a small whoop and hugged her tight.

"Ouch, you're hurting me," she protested, squirming in his arms.

"Only because I'm so blasted happy. I promise you, Bri, you won't regret it."

She smiled, pushing a strand of hair from his forehead. "Somehow, I know you're right. You always seem to be right. Do you know how maddening that can be?"

"I'll have a lifetime to find out," he teased gently.

She pursed her lips at him, and he thought she had never looked so beautiful.

"Well then, when shall we plan to do the deed?" she asked.

"Tonight," he answered without hesitation.

She gaped at him in horror. "Tonight? Surely you must be jesting."

"I told you once that if I intended to make you mine, I wouldn't wait one day to make it happen."

"I thought you meant that figuratively."

"I didn't." He stood, pulling her to her feet, talking rapidly so she couldn't protest. "We have much to do. I need to ask your father's permission to wed, and then I hope to persuade him to perform the ceremony this evening. I think we need no one else as witnesses except for our parents, Sarabeth, and Widow Bayley. You'll need to retrieve your gown from Betty Corwin.

I do hope it's finished and Betty has been properly compensated."

Bridget simply stared at him as if he had lost his mind. Maybe he had, but he was so deliriously happy, he didn't care.

"We'll stay tonight at my house, and then in the morning we'll head off for an extended honeymoon in Philadelphia," he continued, pulling her down the road toward her house. "That will give us time for the most heated gossip to die down. In any event, my uncle has been anxious to have me visit. He's a widower and loves company. A lovely lake adjoins his property. We can spend our days swimming, strolling, and exploring every inch of the city. The nights . . . well, I assure you, they will be reserved for more extraordinary pleasures."

She blushed, a slightly dazed expression on her face. "I . . . I don't know what to say."

He lowered his mouth and placed another long, lingering kiss on her mouth. "Just say you love me," he murmured.

She stood on tiptoe and softly kissed his cheeks, chin, and lips. "I always have," she whispered.

He smiled and pulled her closer. "Then that's all we really need."

Bridget stood in front of the looking glass, examining her reflection, amazed with what she saw. The woman who stared back at her looked truly lovely. She scarcely recognized herself.

Turning, she smoothed down the bodice of her wedding gown and studied it in the mirror. The garment had turned out more beautiful than she had ever imagined. Made of beautiful white silk and lace, the tight-fitting bodice molded to her body while a delicate frill of ecru net covered the skin just above the swell of her breasts. The sleeves were long and ended in narrow frills of lace; the silken skirts, which had been draped over a bell-shaped hoop, contained a short detachable train. White bridal gloves covered her hands and fingers, and a lovely set of pearls from Abigail rested at her throat.

Gently, almost reverently, she reached up to touch her hair. Tonight, Sarabeth had lovingly and expertly tamed her flyaway red tresses. Ringlets had been arranged around the sides of her head. In the back, her hair hung unbound and loose, cascading down in a tumble of curls. A small cap made of white silk and bound with a white ribbon trim sat pinned on her head. A veil of sheer white gauze hung down the back of her hair.

As Sarabeth hurried down the stairs to put the finishing touches on the flower arrangements, Abigail helped her apply a faint touch of powder to her face to hide her freckles. Still, her cheeks remained pink with excitement and her eyes aglow with love. It was everything she dreamed would happen on her wedding day, and it humbled her. Especially since she'd come so close to never knowing a life with Benjamin.

Abigail fussed over her train and stepped back to look at her in the candlelight. "You look lovely."

Bridget dipped in a small curtsy and then blushed. "Oh, Mother, I'm so happy. How can I thank you for all you have done?"

"I've done so little. We were fortunate that Benjamin's mother had already made a cake suitable enough for us to decorate and use for this evening. Widow Bayley kindly provided armfuls of fresh flowers for the arrangements, and Sarabeth helped clean and organize the parlor."

Bridget smiled. "But you were the one who somehow managed to talk Father into performing the ceremony tonight. That, above all, was the most important feat."

Abigail flushed with pleasure. "It wasn't that hard at all. We're very happy for both of you. I only wish I could have done more."

"No, everything is perfect. I never desired a big wedding; that was Peter's wish. A small, intimate wedding in the parsonage is much more suited to what I like. Benjamin knew it, bless his heart. I'm only sorry that the haste in which this has taken place will cause you scandal. Benjamin and I will be in Philadelphia, but you all must stay behind to face the gossip."

Abigail harrumphed. "I don't care about scandal. Not anymore. Your father and I couldn't be more proud of you if you were our own daughter."

Bridget stilled, her hand on the pearls at her throat. "What did you say?"

Abigail took a step back in horror, the color draining from her face. "Oh, Bridget. I'm sorry. I didn't mean to say that."

"What exactly did you mean?" Bridget asked, the blood chilling in her veins. And yet even as she asked, she knew the truth. She had never belonged.

Abigail let out a deep sigh, "I'm sorry. God forgive me, but I'm sorry. I should have told you."

Bridget shook her head in disbelief, stumbling back into the bed and sitting down with a thump. "Told me what? That I . . . that you're not my mother?"

Abigail raised her chin. "You are my daughter. That doesn't change just because I didn't bear you. I should have told you sooner, but I wanted to protect you."

"Protect me from what?" She felt dazed, hurt, and stunned by her mother's confession. She swallowed hard, trying to stop her body from trembling.

"From the truth about your past." Abigail sat on the bed next to Bridget, holding her head in her hands. "It's a rather complex affair. Your father and I, we tried for many years to have children. But God did not provide them. I was desolate, desperate, in despair. Then your father heard about three infant girls who needed homes."

"Three?" Bridget managed to utter. Her breath came in short, shallow gasps, and her chest suddenly felt as if it would burst.

"Triplets. You girls were just over a year old. Your parents originally lived on the other side of town. Your father was a sea captain and your mother died young. There was sordid talk that she'd had an affair and left your father for another man. Then she mysteriously disappeared. People said she had drowned. There was talk that she'd committed suicide, but her body was never found. Your father never remarried and died at sea about six months later. There were no other kin to take you girls. Ichabod and I, we saw you and fell in love with you. I wanted so much to make you mine."

Abigail's hands trembled and she clasped them in her lap. "From the start, you were difficult," she continued. "So headstrong and stubborn that I didn't know what to do. I was at my wit's end. Then God gave us Sarabeth. When I discovered I was pregnant with her, I turned all my attention to her and ignored my responsibility to you. Yet every time you defied or disobeyed me, it made me angrier and angrier until a horrid knot of bitterness wrapped around my heart.

I saw Sarabeth as our miracle, but I was wrong. It's been you all along."

Bridget closed her eyes, too stunned by her mother's confession to think coherently. "Why didn't you ever tell me?"

"The adoptions were kept secret," Abigail continued, taking Bridget's hand. "Everyone involved agreed to keep quiet to protect you girls from the shame and mystery surrounding your mother's death. No one wanted her tragedy to become your own."

"What happened to the other girls?"

"All of them were adopted. By whom, I do not know."

Bridget closed her eyes, trying to calm herself and sort out her emotions. She had two other sisters out there somewhere. Did they even know that she existed?

"Bridget, I didn't intend this to come out now on the most special day of your life," Abigail said. "Put all this aside for now, and I promise you later that both your father and I will answer any questions you may have."

She nodded numbly. "Does Sarabeth know?"

"No, not yet. But it won't matter to her, just as it matters naught to us."

"I'm aware of that. I just feel adrift, as if I suddenly don't know who I am."

Abigail knelt in front of her, taking her hands and squeezing them. "You are our daughter in every way. Ichabod, Sarabeth, and I love you with all our hearts. I have many sins to atone for, but I pray that you and God will give me a second chance. Mayhap it's not too late to become the mother you always wanted."

After a moment, Bridget reached out and embraced

her mother. "It's never too late. And perhaps I can be the daughter you once dreamed of."

Abigail touched her face tenderly. "You already are," she said as tears rolled down her cheeks. "You always have been."

Eighteen

Bridget stood on the threshold of the parlor, anxiously standing behind Sarabeth and trying to peer over her shoulder.

"Move aside," she whispered to Sarabeth. "I can't see anything."

"Good," Sarabeth retorted. "I don't want Benjamin to catch a glimpse of you before the ceremony. It's bad fortune."

"That's ridiculous. Besides, it's forbidden to believe in superstitions."

"I didn't say I believe in them," Sarabeth replied primly. "I simply have no intention of tempting fate."

Bridget rolled her eyes and stood on tiptoe. "Then at least tell me what is happening."

Sarabeth nodded. "Everyone is here. Benjamin's parents are seated to your right, while mother and Widow Bayley are on the left. Father is glancing through the prayer book—I think, preparing what he will say. Benjamin . . ." she said and then sighed dreamily, "Oh Bridget, he looks absolutely grand. It isn't fair that one man should be so handsome and self-assured."

"He always looks that way," Bridget said, her stomach twisting nervously. "He should at least have the decency to appear slightly apprehensive. It's his wedding, after all."

Sarabeth smiled. "I think he's quite certain of what he is doing. Aren't you?"

Bridget paused a moment. "I've hardly had time to consider it. But in all truth, I've never been more certain of anything in my life."

"Then it *is* right," Sarabeth said fiercely.

Bridget smiled, gazing at her sister with affection. She looked lovely this evening in her finest church gown, made of sky blue silk with narrow white stripes. Her hair had been pulled back and fastened at her neck with a matching ribbon. A halo of golden ringlets cascaded across her shoulders and down her back.

For the first time in her life, Bridget realized why she and Sarabeth had never remotely resembled each other. The thought saddened her, but she firmly pushed all thoughts of her adoption aside. She'd give it her full consideration later, when she had the luxury to think more carefully about it. Tonight she intended everything to be perfect. She wanted to etch every moment on her memory so that, no matter what she discovered, she could savor this night forever. And that meant giving her full concentration to the ceremony at hand.

"You look pale," Sarabeth said. "Are you really that anxious?"

"Mayhap a bit," Bridget said from behind her veil.

"About the ceremony or the wedding night?"

"Sarabeth!"

Her sister's pretty mouth formed a pout. "Well, it's only fair that I ask. Now that you will be the one fortunate enough to reap the rewards of Benjamin's legendary skill, you must promise to tell me everything." Her voice dropped to a hushed whisper. "Including information on that secret hand skill."

Bridget felt her face flush with heat. "I will not," she whispered back heatedly, but she and Sarabeth dissolved into soft giggles. The laughter faded abruptly when Ichabod called out.

"He's ready," Sarabeth murmured. "God be with you."

She gave Bridget an impulsive hug and then entered the room, strewing a few rose petals on the floor. She sat down between Abigail and Widow Bayley, and looked back at Bridget with an encouraging smile.

Bridget inhaled a deep breath and took a firm step through the doorway. She hardly recognized the chamber as the humble parsonage parlor. All the furniture except a handful of chairs had been removed. Flowers had been placed around the room in several beautiful arrangements. Since it was nighttime, dozens of candles glowed, casting a golden, almost holy light on the whitewashed clapboard walls.

Her father stood in the middle of the room, holding the family Bible in one hand and a leather prayer book in the other. His face held a mixture of pride, love, and relief as she appeared.

Yet ultimately it was Benjamin who caught and held her gaze. He looked so magnificent that her breath caught in her throat and lodged there. Dressed in his wedding finery, he looked as handsome as she had ever seen him. The dark blue coat he wore contrasted in sharp detail with the startling white linen shirt and neckcloth. His waistcoat was a softer blue, and his knee-length breeches were midnight black. He had swept his wild hair back and secured it at the nape of his neck with a leather thong, the black strands gleaming in the candlelight. His dreamy gray eyes locked onto hers in a smoldering and breathtakingly possessive gaze. She felt her stomach flutter wildly as she approached and took her place next to him. As was the custom, they did not touch, but she could feel his presence so strongly, it was as if he held her tight in his embrace.

Her father cleared his throat and Bridget bit her lower lip nervously. Everything was so perfect, she feared that at any moment someone would stand up and shout that this had all been a horrid mistake.

Instead, her father calmly opened the prayer book and read a psalm followed by a prayer. After the prayer, he asked them to join hands. Bridget slid her hand into Benjamin's, marveling at how warm and steady it was. He gave her a quick and encouraging squeeze, and she returned the gesture with a grateful smile.

As they stood hand in hand, her father gave a short sermon on the sanctity of married life and the responsibilities of the married couple to each other. When he finished, he looked at both of them with an odd mixture of affection and sternness, as if the reverend side warred with the father side.

"Love is the sugar to sweeten every condition of the marriage state," he said. "Bridget Elizabeth Goodwell and Benjamin Bradley Hawkes, tonight you shall become one in the eyes of God. Your vows are sacred. By honoring them and each other, you will honor God."

"I intend never to disappoint you, sir," Benjamin said firmly. "Or her."

Ichabod nodded approvingly. "Then it is time to exchange your vows."

Bridget felt her heart pound in her chest. She could

scarcely believe that in just moments, she'd be married to the man of her dreams.

Benjamin turned toward her and they held hands, gazing steadily at each other. As he recited his vows, Benjamin's expression was both tender and affectionate, and yet, even now, Bridget could see a mischievous twinkle in his eyes. When her turn came, her voice wavered and caught as tears of joy threatened to spill down her cheeks.

When she finished, Benjamin lifted her left hand and slid the bridal glove off in a surprisingly sensual move. She could feel a rush of heat burn all the way to her toes, and her cheeks flushed hot.

Benjamin's father stepped forward and handed him a simple gold band. Benjamin slid it onto her finger, his mouth curling into a possessive and amused smile.

"With this ring and God's favor, I shall prove worthy of you, my wife," he said, his voice resonating through the parlor. She marveled as the cool weight of the gold settled on her finger, and then it was done. She was married at last.

Slowly he lifted the veil and drew her toward him. His warm hands cupped her face as he pressed a long, full kiss on her mouth. Though it had not been spoken, Bridget recognized his promise of a lifetime of love, adventure, and something infinitely deeper. Her stomach fluttered as the pressure of his mouth deepened and held. Then he abruptly lifted his head, and the ceremony was concluded.

The parlor erupted into happy chatter and congratulations. Sarabeth rushed over to hug her and Abigail smiled broadly. Benjamin's parents enveloped her in a warm, welcoming embrace, and Widow Bayley kissed both of their cheeks in obvious delight. Through it all, Benjamin kept his arm around her waist, anchoring her firmly to his side.

After some time, the group retired to the dining room, where several servants borrowed from Benjamin's house had laid out a hastily prepared yet nonetheless sumptuous wedding feast. As everyone milled about, chatting and deciding where to sit, Bridget stole away from Benjamin and pulled Widow Bayley aside. The old woman beamed happily and gave Bridget another heartfelt hug.

"Well, child, how does it feel to listen to your heart?" she asked.

"Wonderful," Bridget answered honestly. "I have so much to thank you for, I'm not certain where to begin."

"You have naught to thank me for, Bridget. The decision was yours. 'Twas you who found the courage to do as your heart directed. 'Twas a great risk."

"Mayhap 'tis so. You were right about me. I could do no less than what my heart dictated."

"And Benjamin?"

She tilted her chin up. "I think he was the braver of the two of us. Once he understood what was in his heart, he went after it with relentless determination." She glanced down at the gold band on her finger. "You knew all along about us, didn't you?"

"Even an old blind woman could feel the passion between you two. When the heart speaks, it is quite loud. You have only to listen."

"I'm fortunate that I did." She paused a moment and then plunged on. "Yet there is something else I wish to ask, and I hope for naught more than honesty. Did you know I was adopted?"

Widow Bayley took a step back, visibly startled, the color draining from her face. Yet Bridget saw from her expression that it was not surprise, only dismay. So she *had* known.

Widow Bayley pressed a hand to her chest. "How . . . how did you find out?"

"My mother told me."

That seemed to surprise her, but she quickly regained her composure. "The timing of your discovery is rather unfortunate."

"Unfortunate?" Bridget exclaimed and then lowered her voice. "If you've known all this time, why didn't you tell me?"

"Because it wasn't my place. And because you would have learned the truth eventually."

"I don't understand. Do you know who bore me? Will you tell me more about my other parents?"

The widow nodded sadly. "Aye, child, I know. And when you return from your honeymoon in Philadelphia, I'll tell you all I know. It will be time. But tonight is your wedding night and belongs only to you and Benjamin. Revel in the beauty and wonder of your new love and put thoughts of your past aside. It is a rare thing for two people to find such a passionate, consummate love. Tomorrow will come soon enough."

Bridget looked at her with a mixture of exasperation and affection. She knew that none of the answers she sought would be forthcoming this evening. Resigned, she glanced over at Benjamin and caught the look he gave her. She felt a tug—the pull of a thread that had bound them together for so many years and had now knotted permanently. There was something else in his look—a promise that tonight would hold a special wonder for her. A flash of warmth shot through her, causing her to shiver in anticipation. The memory of his kiss and the way her body had so eagerly responded caused the blood to rush to her cheeks. She watched as his mouth curved into a slow smile, and she knew he understood exactly what she'd been thinking.

Instinctively she moved toward him. Mayhap her mother and Widow Bayley were right. Tonight the past didn't matter. Only the future. And in a short time, that meant she'd be living her dream, nestled in the arms of her husband.

Benjamin watched Bridget speaking earnestly with Widow Bayley, and grew curious when he saw the look of dismay on both women's faces. He wondered what the exchange had been about and whether it had caused the faint touch of sadness he now saw in Bridget's eyes. He made a note to talk to her about it just as soon as dinner was over and he could get her alone. He was firmly convinced that a wedding celebration and dinner had been designed with only one purpose in mind—to drive the bridegroom mad by delaying the long-awaited visit to the marriage bed.

Sighing inwardly, he sat at the table, making small talk and resisting the urge to grind his teeth in frustration. His mood improved only when Bridget joined him, the sadness gone from her eyes. She smiled at him and he felt a clutch in his heart.

My wife, he thought with fierce pride. *My beloved wife.*

The dinner progressed slowly, but eventually Bridget disappeared with her mother, presumably to change from her splendid wedding gown into something more practical. Earlier, one of his servants had carried her hastily packed valises to his house. They would spend the first night of their married life in his room and then leave at first light for his uncle's house in Philadelphia.

His father said something and Benjamin realized he hadn't heard a word. His thoughts were with his lovely bride, who was likely at this moment clad in naught more than a thin chemise. She was probably getting dressed in another fancy gown that he would only have to remove as soon as they reached the bedchamber. The thought of her beneath him in his bed sent an erotic message directly to his groin. Shifting uncomfortably on his chair, he wondered how long it took for two women to change one gown.

"Benjamin?"

He blinked, his father's face coming into focus. "Yes, sir?"

"I asked whether you wish to have any of the servants accompany you to Philadelphia." he repeated. "Your uncle has a few, but it may not be enough to provide for your entire stay."

"It will be enough," he replied. The last thing he wanted was a bunch of servants underfoot while he taught his new bride the more interesting aspects of married life. Especially when he wasn't certain what might burst into flames, including himself.

His father chatted on until Bridget finally reappeared, looking lovely in a soft green gown with a white velvet sash. He felt his heart race as she smiled shyly at him. How could he have taken so long to realize that she was his true soul mate?

He stood, laying his napkin aside, signaling that a sufficient time of celebrating had elapsed. He'd not wait a moment longer to have her as his own.

After they had thanked everyone, he fetched Bridget's shawl and draped it over her shoulders. As they stood at the threshold of the parsonage, he watched as she hugged her family and Widow Bayley once again. Abigail blinked back tears, but Sarabeth sobbed uncontrollably.

"We won't be gone long," Benjamin reassured them. "I assure you, we'll return by August's end."

Widow Bayley nodded, looking directly at him. "See you are no later than that, Benjamin," she ordered. "For there is much to speak of."

Benjamin felt Bridget stiffen beside him and wondered at the mysterious nature of her comment. Then he led her out into the night and forgot everything except the woman who stood beside him.

"My parents summoned a carriage," he said, gesturing toward the waiting vehicle.

She shook her head. "If you don't mind, I'd rather walk," she said. "It's so beautiful, and I could use a bit of fresh air."

He nodded and offered his arm. "As you wish."

Sending his parents on ahead, Benjamin strolled with her down the darkened streets of Salem. She held onto his arm and he caught the sweet scent of lilac.

"A penny for your thoughts," he said softly.

She stopped and looked at him. A pale ribbon of moonlight slanted across her face.

"What is it?" he asked, stroking her cheek with his fingertips.

"My mother told me something unsettling this evening," she began.

He held up a hand. "If this is about the wedding night, Bri, I promise you that I'll—"

She closed her hand over his. "No, I'm certain *that* will be perfect. It's something else. Benjamin, my mother . . . well, tonight she told me I'd been adopted."

His eyebrows shot up in surprise. Whatever subjects

he had thought she might bring up, this was not among them.

"Adopted?" he uttered.

"Apparently when I was but an infant."

He frowned, his brows drawing together. "I suppose that might explain a number of things, including the fractious relationship you've had with your mother. Do you know who your birth parents were?"

"Not yet. But Widow Bayley knows. She knew my parents. In fact, she's known all along and never told me."

He looked at her intently. "So, that is what you two were whispering about. Well, why should she tell you, Bri? It wasn't her place to do so."

"She could have trusted me."

"She could have. But would it really have changed anything?"

Bridget rubbed her temples. "I suppose not. But now I'm not certain who I am anymore."

He pulled her into his arms, resting his chin against the top of her head. "You are my wife. I love you, Bri. Frankly, I don't care one whit where you came from, only that you are here with me now. I've never been happier in my life."

She gazed up at him. "As am I. Without you, I would never have been whole."

He lowered his mouth and kissed her with tender, drugging intimacy. She parted her lips and raised herself to meet him, winding her arms around his neck. He deepened the kiss until she moaned and leaned into him. With great reluctance, he ended it, feeling his own breath coming faster.

"God help me, Bri, one taste of you and I'm nearly undone. I promise you I'll employ every resource I can to find out what you want to know about your adoption when we return from Philadelphia. However, I believe that Widow Bayley will be willing to answer your questions, as will your parents. But tonight let's not have anything else come between us."

She stood on tiptoe to kiss the tip of his nose. "Thank you," she said softly. "For believing in me."

He kissed her again and they walked in comfortable silence the rest of the way to his house. Together they climbed the stairs to his room. Thankfully, the servants had set a fire in the hearth and arranged two chairs comfortably in front of it. Candles had been lit in various locations about the room. A kettle of hot, spiced wine had been placed on a nearby table along with two pewter goblets. Her valises sat at the foot of the bed, the delectable nightgown he'd seen her dancing with had been unpacked and lay neatly on top.

The bed itself had been turned back, and Benjamin saw Bridget glance nervously in that direction. Despite her passion, he knew she was still afraid. As a result, he resisted the urge to strip her naked of her garments and take her on the bed. Instead he made a conscious if not reluctant decision to provide a slow, sensual introduction to the art of lovemaking.

He removed his coat and tugged off his neckcloth, draping both of them over the back of one of the chairs. Walking over to the wine, he picked up the flask and filled the goblets. He took a sip of his wine and handed a goblet to her. The flavor was sweet, thick, and tinged with spices. She stood awkwardly, clutching the goblet in front of her as if it were a weapon.

"Sit down, Bri," he said, swallowing a sigh of exasperation. "There is no need to fear me this night."

She accepted the goblet and sat stiffly in the chair. "I . . . I didn't think I'd be so nervous. But now that we're here alone, I suddenly feel inadequate. I . . . I don't know what to do," she blurted out.

He resisted the urge to smile and instead looked at her solemnly. "I know it may seem like a daunting task, but I'm certain we will muddle through. You'll just have to trust me."

"As I did that first time you taught me to swim?"

His mouth quirked with humor. "Something like that."

Her eyes brightened. "You will instruct me, then? A lesson of sorts?"

Heat shot though his body at the mere thought of it. "I will. Although I assure you, most of it will be instinctive."

She plucked nervously at her skirts. "Did any of the women you've . . . ah . . . instructed before ever fail to meet your expectations?"

He swore under his breath. "Blast it, Bri. I don't want to talk about other women."

She looked hurt at his tone. "I didn't mean to offend you. I only asked to try to understand. You can't blame me for being apprehensive. This is my first time, after all, whereas you've had many such encounters. I'm just worried that I won't be any good at this."

He resisted the urge to roll his eyes. "I assure you, you'll do fine."

"But what if I don't?"

He growled deep in his throat. "Bri, this is not some kind of footrace or competition. We must do this together. And if your kisses are any indication of what our lovemaking will be like, I'll be fortunate to survive this night intact."

There was a pensive shimmer in the shadow of her eyes. "I just wondered if you would tell me what it was like for you . . . you know, your first time."

He nearly choked on his wine. "What?"

"I'd like to know what it felt like for you the first time you did this."

"God help me. Only you would insist on making me relive such an event."

"Well, did it hurt?" she persisted.

He laughed in spite of himself. "Only my pride. If you must really know, it was over as soon as she dragged me behind the haystack and began unlacing my breeches. Bri, it's much different for a woman. I won't lie to you. The first time will hurt a little, but I'll try to make it as painless as possible."

She considered his words and then took a sip of her wine. "How? Do you have a master plan with all the steps memorized before you act? I have an excellent memory. You can just tell me what to do and in what order and I'll be certain to proceed accordingly."

This time he nearly spewed his wine. Firmly he set aside the goblet and stood.

"No more explanations, Bri. I prefer to show you. Let the lesson begin."

He pulled her to her feet, waiting until she set her goblet aside. "The first step is that we must remove any restrictive garments. In your case, I'm afraid that means everything."

"Everything?" she exclaimed, looking slightly alarmed.

He nodded, keeping a serious expression on his face. "Any garment that comes between you and me is too restrictive."

"But . . . but shouldn't I first get into my nightgown?"

"Why is it that women have an incessant need to change garments?" he growled impatiently. "I'll tell you a secret, Bri. Men prefer women without a stitch of clothing. I assure you that tonight the gown will not be necessary. Tomorrow, if you wish to wear it, I'll be happy to remove it from you at that time."

"Oh," she said in a small voice. "But what about the candles?"

"What about them?"

"Shouldn't we extinguish them . . . well, before we get started?" Her cheeks flushed hotly.

His mouth curved into a slow smile. "I do not intend to extinguish a single one of them. I have every intention of seeing you in all your glory. And just as important, I want you to see who will claim you this night. Now, let us continue."

Slowly he turned her so that her back was against his chest, nuzzling her neck as he untied the white velvet sash at her waist and dropped it to the floor. His lips nibbled a path to her neck and behind her ear, smiling when he heard a sharp intake of breath. His fingers began unlacing the stays at the back of her gown until they were loose enough to push it off her shoulders and to her waist. He moved a hand gently along her side to her stomach as he turned her toward him. His mouth slanted over hers as his palms skimmed along her rib cage. He could feel the heat of her skin through her chemise, and shivers of delight that followed his touch. Her lips clung to his, twisting hesitantly at first and then relaxing beneath the pressure of his mouth. He heard her moan as his tongue plunged inside to devour her softness.

His heart throbbed wildly as he moved his hands to her breasts, rubbing the taut nipples through the thin material of her chemise. She trembled in his arms, leaning into him and pressing her body against his in a gesture she didn't fully understand but which only heightened its erotic effect.

"Bri," he murmured, his need pulsing through him like a raging fire.

He pushed the gown down past her hips into a puddle on the floor, not caring when he heard the material rip slightly. She stepped out of it, her cheeks burning, clearly embarrassed to be clad in nothing more than her thin chemise, stockings, and shoes.

For a moment, he stood stunned by her natural beauty. The chemise hid little from his sight. One side had fallen off her shoulder, revealing the creamy skin of her neck and the top swell of her small breast. The thin material flowed over a flat stomach and clung to the gentle curve of her hips. The effect was both sensual and stunning. He drew in his breath and then held it, trying to control the wild thundering of his heart and the burning need to ravish her at once and be done with the seduction.

Misunderstanding his reaction, a fierce blush stained her cheeks. "I knew I would disappoint you," she said, kneeling and hastily trying to retrieve her gown from the floor. "I knew it would have been best to have done this without candlelight."

He took her arm, pulling her up. "No, Bri. You don't understand. You are astonishingly lovely. I simply had no idea how beautiful you really are until now."

Her blush deepened. "You don't have to say that. We both know I'm not beautiful."

He cupped her face in his hands. "You *are* beautiful, Bri. All the other women I've ever known couldn't hold a candle to you. In fact, I haven't slept worth a damn since I returned from Lisbon. Do you know why? Because I wanted to make you mine. I've been thinking of holding you like this, feeling your body next to mine and tasting your sweetness, until I nearly drove myself mad. The fact that you have no idea how lovely you are only heightens my desire."

Taking a step back, he removed his waistcoat and pulled his shirt over his head. He kicked off his boots and yanked the stockings off his feet until he stood clad in naught more than his knee-length breeches. He noted with amusement that she kept her gaze studiously averted.

Slowly he extended a hand and bowed at the waist. "Mrs. Hawkes," he said in a deep voice, "I beg for the pleasure of this dance."

She hesitantly raised her eyes, and then a small smile touched her lips. "Well, I would be delighted," she said, taking his hand.

He pulled her to his chest, suppressing a gasp as her breasts flattened against his bare skin. The utter softness of her body nearly was the undoing of him right there. Ignoring the searing ache in his loins, he began to hum as he twirled her about the room. She matched him step by step until eventually he felt the tension leave her body. They danced until they were breathless with both laughter and exertion, and then she accidentally stepped on his toe.

He feigned pain and hopped around the room holding his toe while she chased him, apologizing profusely. Laughing, he finally knelt in front of her, slipping her shoes off, and kissing her stockinged feet.

Smiling, he led her to a chair and insisted she sit while he filled her goblet with more wine. She accepted it gratefully and sipped it, chatting happily, all the while having no idea of the carnal thoughts racing through his head. He nearly spilled his wine when she leaned back in the chair and crossed her legs, revealing a long, slender thigh. He swallowed hard and shifted in his chair, but she didn't seem to notice his discomfort. Thankfully, her modesty seemed to have abated, as had her apprehension.

They sipped their wine in silence, watching the fire. Finally she spoke.

"I never thought I'd dance on my wedding night," she said softly. "You've already made so many of my dreams come true. I want to please you, Benjamin. I want to make you feel as wonderful as you have made me feel. Show me what to do."

She was a glowing image of fire, passion, and love. Not even the skillful promises of the most experienced women he'd ever known could have set him aflame more than her seductively simple words.

"Come to me, Bri," he whispered, watching as she rose from the chair, her hair spilling over her shoulders in a satiny red river. She knelt in front of him, her breasts brushing his knees, her hands resting lightly on his thighs. Her hands felt hot through the material of his breeches, and a trickle of sweat beaded at his temple.

Slowly he traced a fingertip across her lower lip. Bending his head, he pressed his lips to hers, the taste of her nearly shattering his calm. He reminded himself that he needed to pace this evening carefully, so he gently kissed her eyelids, cheeks, and throat.

"What's the next part of the lesson?" she asked, her voice deep and husky.

"Touch," he said hoarsely, snaking an arm around her waist and pulling her to him with a thud. As she gasped in surprise, he lifted her chemise and pulled it off over her head. He watched her gasp as the air rushed across her skin and he leisurely outlined the circle of her breast. She shuddered with need, and he felt the heat once again surge to his loins. Leaning over, he flicked his tongue against her nipple, her breasts jutting forward at the intimacy of his mouth. He took the bud into his mouth, teasing, pulling, and nipping until she squirmed. Closing her eyes, she threw back her head, revealing the slender white column of her neck. His tongue forged a searing path from her breasts up to the pulsing hollow of her neck and then to her mouth. As his mouth closed over hers once more, he slid his hand down her taut stomach to the swell of her hip. She was so damn hot, so perfectly suited to him.

Her magnificent green eyes opened and he swore he could see flames burning in them. Whether it was the reflection from the fire or something much deeper, he didn't know. He felt the sweat slide down his temples to match the scorching blood coursing through his veins.

"I want to touch you," she whispered softly. "Is that permitted under the rules of instruction?"

"In fact, it happens to be a requirement," he ground out. "Touch me, Bri. Anywhere you'd like. Just do it soon."

Bridget felt a thrill of unexpected power at his words. He needed her, wanted her, even desired her. No one had ever made her feel so beautiful and so cherished. Her heart swelled with a warm glow and all her doubts and fears drained away.

Now, a sense of urgency and curiosity drove her. She moved her hands slowly back and forth along his thighs and felt him stiffen. She glanced up curiously and saw that he sat perfectly still, his jaw clenched tight, a look of intense concentration on his face.

"What's wrong?" she asked in concern.

"Nothing," he ground out.

"But you look as if you are in pain."

"Jesus, Bri. Do you have to dissect everything?"

She sat back on her heels. "I'm obviously doing something wrong."

He sighed, frustrated. "It's perfect. You're perfect. It's simply so damn erotic, you are making me feel like it's my first time."

"Then you do like it," she said, thrilled.

"Bri!" he all but shouted. "Stop talking. But I beg of you . . . don't stop touching me."

Delighted with her success, she moved her hands up to his bare torso, marveling at the hard ridges along his ribs and his flat, granite-hard stomach. His muscular chest was covered with crisp black hair, and she lightly touched it, marveling at the sensual feel of it against her fingertips.

"You are so strikingly handsome," she breathed, leaning over to kiss his shoulder. "I tried never to look at you in that way. But now that I can, you utterly take my breath away."

The smoldering look he gave her both startled and excited her. She was intensely aware of his nearness and of the way he maintained such rigid control over his body. His fingers were hot and splayed out against her back as she continued her delicious exploration. She felt wildly reckless and uninhibited.

Slowly she stood, then sat straddled on his lap, stroking his shoulders and caressing the strong tendons in the back of his neck. He moaned and instinctively she rubbed against him, feeling his hips lift into her and press against the core of her.

"I do believe it's time for the next part of the lesson," he growled, seizing her around the waist. Abruptly he stood, cupping her buttocks and holding her tight to him. She gasped, wrapping her legs around his waist and winding her arms around his neck.

He carried her to the bed, tumbling them onto it in

a tangle of legs and arms. With one hand he tore off his breeches and tossed them across the room.

"What's this part of the lesson called?" she inquired innocently.

"Intimate contact," he said, his eyes dark and blazing. "Look at me, Bri."

Bridget caught her breath. She had never seen a more beautiful body. His skin was bronze across a broad chest, powerful shoulders, and down to the hard flat ridges of his stomach. His hips flared into strong, firm thighs. But her eyes stared in awe at the part of him that jutted up proudly, confirming his attraction to her. A burst of heat erupted within her at the thought of touching him.

Abruptly something on the chair began to smolder, and Bridget sat up, clasping a hand over her mouth in horror.

Benjamin followed her gaze, then rolled off the bed, walking over to a small table and picking up a jug. Seemingly unconcerned, he went over to the chair, picked something off, and poured water on it, dropping it to the floor and stomping on it with his bare feet.

"What was it?" she asked, mortified.

"My neckcloth," he said, shrugging. "I didn't like it anyway."

"I'm so sorry."

He returned to the bed, sitting beside her. "I'm not. And you should know, I'm prepared. There are six such pots filled with water should we perchance need them. Now, where were we?"

He bent his head, kissing one of her nipples and making her forget all about the smoldering neckcloth. He thrust his hands into her hair, releasing the wooden hairpins and scattering them across the bed. The ringlets that had been fastened to the side of her head spilled down and across his shoulders. She moaned as his hands skimmed down either side of her body to her thighs, pressing her back against the bed.

One hand caressed the skin of her thigh, and fire shot though her body. His fingers were burning a path along her body as they moved upward until he touched the small triangle of hair. Softly, he explored her there, unexpectedly brushing a thumb against a secret nub. She gasped in sweet agony, arching her body toward him. Passion pounded the blood through her heart, chest, and head. She gripped his shoulders so tightly, she feared she'd draw blood. His caresses became bolder now, and waves of hot ecstasy throbbed mercilessly in her loins.

She wondered if this magnificent torment was part of the legendary hand technique. If so, mere words were not enough to describe the white-hot rapture pouring through her veins.

"Wh-what exactly are you doing?" she gasped.

"Loving you," he replied with a mischievous smile, and then dipped his head down to touch his mouth to her there.

The pleasure was immediate and explosive. Her body seemed to shatter into a million pieces as gusts of desire shook her. When she finally stopped shaking, she looked at him in stunned wonder.

"That was . . . utterly remarkable," she managed, at a loss for a better way to describe pure and unadulterated pleasure. "I'd say you've most definitely improved since your first time behind the haystack."

"I'm relieved to hear that," he growled while pounding his foot at a part of the quilt that had started to smolder.

She started to giggle and he narrowed his eyes,

looking at her suspiciously. "What is so amusing?" he asked.

"I think I've been thoroughly ravished, and yet I'm still wearing my stockings."

"In fact, it has been a secret desire of mine for some time to ravish a reverend's daughter in naught more than her stockings. Shall I continue the lesson?"

She wound her arms around his neck as he lowered his mouth to hers. This time his kiss was hungry, devouring, and thoroughly possessive. Her mouth burned from his fiery onslaught, the pleasure radiating outward.

She curled into the curve of his body, flesh against flesh, man against woman. Then suddenly, she felt his manhood pressing against her entrance.

"God help me, Bri," he said, giving a tormented groan. "You are so wet and ready for me."

Bridget felt as if her body were half ice, half flame. The sweet, aching pressure was building again. She clutched his arms. "Please, Benjamin, show me what comes next."

"I don't want to hurt you," he said between gritted teeth. Nonetheless, he pressed against her and she dug her nails into his back, her body screaming for release.

"Now," she half moaned.

She heard him draw a breath and then plunge his hips forward. She felt a sharp burning pain, and he abruptly stilled, every muscle tense.

"Are you . . . all right?" he ground out, his jaw clenched tight.

The pain was still there, but something infinitely more interesting beckoned her. She began to squirm, urging him to move.

"I'm not certain. I think I need . . . more of the lesson," she said.

She watched as a bright flare of desire sprang in his eyes as he began to move with her in an erotic rhythm. She moaned aloud with pleasure, passion burning in her veins. She lost sight of all else except their seeking mouths, slick, straining bodies, and the complete joining of two hearts.

"I love you," she whispered. "You are my heart."

"I love you, too, Bri," he uttered, his eyes blazing fire, his mouth looking as sensual as the devil's. "I've loved you for so long, my wife."

Bridget felt as if she'd waited forever to hear those words. Perhaps she had.

She thrust her fingers though his gloriously dark hair, holding him close as she yielded to the burst of heated pleasure that flooded her, sweeping her away.

Benjamin pressed his face to her throat as he reached his release, his breath coming in long, shuddering moans. He collapsed on top of her, and Bridget couldn't breathe over the thundering of her heart. For some time they lay there, drowsy and satiated, still joined as one. A deep feeling of peace and contentment came over her as she finally understood what it meant to know what was in her heart.

She kissed his shoulder, feeling happier than she ever had in her entire life. He rolled to the side, flinging an arm over her waist and pulling her close.

"You were extraordinary," he said, a satisfied grin on his lips. "Who would have expected it from a reverend's daughter?"

She pushed up on her elbows, her red hair spilling over her shoulders and pooling onto his chest. "I do believe I had an excellent instructor."

He kissed the tip of her nose. "Can you get up?"

She groaned and fell back onto the bed, covering

her eyes with her arm. Her muscles were lax, and her body felt utterly boneless.

"Not yet, I'm afraid."

He sighed. "Neither can I. But if neither of us can move, then who will put out the blasted fire on the rug?"

Nineteen

Salem
August 1792

Bridget walked toward Widow Bayley's cottage, arm in arm with Benjamin. She felt secure, content, and at peace with herself. The sun shone brightly, warming her hair and shoulders. Tree leaves rustled softly in the breeze, and already some had begun the first change of color marking autumn's debut.

"Well, how does it feel to be home again, wife?" Benjamin asked, giving her a grin so charming that she nearly melted on the spot.

"Wonderful," she replied, lifting her face to the heat of the sun. She'd forgotten her hat again. "Not even the curious glances and hushed whispers can spoil our homecoming." She squeezed his arm happily. "Your parents are remarkable. They greeted us so warmly that I truly feel as if I am part of the family."

"You are part of the family," he said seriously. "You've always been. Remember the time we were seven and sneaked into the kitchen and ate seven hot crossed buns apiece? You got sick all over the floor, and it was Mother who cleaned you up, held your hand, and walked you back home. I think it was then that you wormed your way into her heart. Just as you did mine."

She looked at him wryly. "What about your father? Thankfully, I never retched on him."

"Oh, but you didn't hesitate to challenge him," Benjamin said, a glint of amusement in his eyes. "Remember when you dared him to recite the first three paragraphs of the Declaration of Independence? He failed miserably, but I am certain he was impressed when you could do it so easily."

She laughed. "They must have considered me a pest."

He shook his head. "No, they fell in love with you. Just as their hardheaded son did, and then took so blasted long to realize it."

He leaned over and pressed a kiss on her mouth. It was slow, thoughtful, and deliberate, and sent shivers of desire racing through her. When he lifted his mouth from hers, his eyes promised a thorough ravishing later, and she smiled.

"I'm not certain we'd should tarry here like this, Mr. Hawkes," she said primly. "Why, if someone were to witness such inappropriate public behavior, it might cause them to swoon."

"Let them swoon," he said lifting her off her feet, whirling her around, and kissing her again. "I intend to kiss my wife to my full satisfaction." When she was thoroughly disoriented, he set her down and straightened his shirt. "All right," he said. "Now I'm ready to continue."

Laughing, she fairly skipped along the road. Earlier this morning, they'd gone to see her family to tell them about their trip and ask them all they knew about her birth parents. Sarabeth had been told of her adoption in her absence, but as Abigail predicted, it hadn't mattered one whit.

From their conversation, Bridget had learned little new about her past—mostly because her parents didn't know much. A lawyer named Paul Wynn, deceased now for the past thirteen years, had handled the adoption. All the girls had been adopted shortly after their first birthday. Her biological father had been a ship captain who had died at sea about six months after her mother accidentally drowned. The only piece of new information she gleaned were the names of her natural parents: Phillip Joseph and Mary Hannah Bennett.

Bridget knew she should be able to glean more factual information about them in the records held at the courthouse. Eventually, she would pore over the old ledgers, but not today. Instead, on this beautiful August afternoon, she and Benjamin headed for Widow Bayley's cottage for what hopefully would prove to be more enlightening answers to their questions.

It didn't take long for them to reach the cottage. Francesca scampered across the yard, an eager bundle of white fur and claws, brushing up against Bridget's legs. Bridget reached down and scooped up the cat, scratching her under the chin until she purred happily.

"Hello, sweet girl," Bridget murmured. "Did you take good care of the widow for us while we were gone?"

Benjamin gave the cat a fond pat before knocking on the door—slightly ajar as usual.

"Come in," they heard Widow Bayley call out.

Bridget pushed open the door and they crossed the threshold.

The widow was not alone. Seated across from her was an older woman with graying red hair. An oval face with a square chin framed a generous mouth and startling green eyes that assessed her frankly.

Bridget felt a disturbing jolt of recognition even though she was certain she'd never met the woman before. In that instant, an odd though familiar connection shook Bridget to her toes. Apprehension swept through her. Instinctively, she reached for Benjamin's hand and clutched it so tightly she felt the blood flow from her fingers.

Slowly the widow and her guest stood, as Benjamin stepped forward protectively.

"We're sorry if we're intruding," he said. "We didn't realize you had company."

"You're not intruding," the widow said hastily. "I'm so glad you're here. I've missed your company. How was your journey?"

"Wonderful, thank you," Benjamin answered.

"I'm glad to hear that. Please, I'd like to introduce you to my friend Hannah Bennett."

Bridget gasped, taking a step back, the color draining from her face. "Hannah Bennett?" she said, her voice coming out as little more than a whisper. "Mary Hannah Bennett?"

Benjamin put an arm around her shoulders, and Bridget was once again grateful for the warmth and strength he provided.

"Is this some kind of jest?" he asked angrily.

Widow Bayley shook her head. "I presume the name has some significance for you."

"You known damn well that it does," Benjamin snapped. "What is this all about?"

The woman stepped forward. "I'm sorry you are dismayed. I know this may seem very difficult for both of you to accept. But this is by no means a jest. I am indeed your natural mother, Bridget."

LIGHT A SINGLE CANDLE

Bridget felt faint, grateful for Benjamin's steady arm at her elbow. The room spun dizzily and her pulse pounded in her head. For several moments no one spoke or moved. They simply stared at each other as if time itself stood still.

"That's not possible," Bridget finally said, her voice sounding distant, as if someone else spoke. "My parents told me she died years ago."

"So everyone was intended to think," Hannah replied. "I assure you, however, I am alive. And I am here to offer you an explanation."

"It had better be a good one," Benjamin said grimly.

Widow Bayley stepped forward. "Please, I know that you both must have dozens of questions. But let us not do this in the doorway. Do come in and sit down. Benjamin, I would ask you to pull two chairs from the table to the hearth. I shall first pour us some tea and then we will talk."

Bridget nodded slowly when Benjamin threw her a questioning glance. He complied, but Bridget could see the tight clench of his jaw and the concern in his eyes. When all the chairs were arranged and the tea poured, Hannah began to speak again.

"I know that meeting me and learning who I am after all these years seems inconceivable. Even now, I see the doubt in your eyes, Bridget."

"Why shouldn't she doubt you?" Benjamin said angrily. "If I were her, I wouldn't want to believe that you are my mother. What kind of woman abandons her children?"

Hannah flinched at his words, and Bridget put a hand on his arm. "It's all right. Let her speak, Benjamin."

Hannah took a deep breath, settling back in her chair. "I wish there were another way we could do this. But perhaps it will be best to start at the beginning. You come from a proud and respected lineage, Bridget. You are a MacInness."

"MacInness?" Bridget repeated in puzzlement.

"Yes, the MacInnesses were once a powerful clan in Scotland, many of whom possessed a number of extraordinary talents. Some had 'sight' or the ability to see into the future, while others could move objects with their minds, speak with animals, heal with a touch, and hear others' unspoken thoughts. Some even had the ability to summon fire from air."

Bridget pressed her lips together tightly. It was one thing to admit her secret to Benjamin, but to reveal it to others, and one a complete stranger, was unthinkable.

"That's fascinating," she said stiffly.

Hannah cupped her hands around her teacup, looking down into the liquid. "I'm sorry you had to spend your life hiding your talent, Bridget. Wondering why you were different, afraid of finding out why. At least I had my mother to explain it to me. You have no need to hide it from me. I know of your ability with fire. Your sisters also have unique abilities."

Bridget opened her mouth to deny it vigorously, but after another glance at Hannah's face, only sighed instead.

"Have you a talent as well?" she asked, resigned.

"I am both blessed and cursed, for I have a little of many talents. It makes me both weak and strong. Those of you who have a single talent are typically the strongest."

Hannah lifted her cup and took a sip of tea. Bridget watched her, torn with conflicting emotions. A part of her wanted to reject everything she said, yet somehow she knew with increased certainty that Hannah spoke the truth. A hard knot twisted in her stomach, causing her to shift uncomfortably on her chair.

"Why did you leave us?" Bridget suddenly blurted out, unaware of how badly she had wanted to ask the question, and of how terrified she was to hear the answer.

Hannah's eyes filled with tears; her expression was marked with deep-seated grief and sorrow.

"I think it will help you to understand if I tell you first of a woman named Priscilla MacInness, who was among the first of the MacInnesses to emigrate to the New World. She was a beautiful young woman who fell deeply in love with a man by the name of John Gardener. He was a carpenter, a simple man, but handsome and good-hearted. They married and moved to Salem Village. Priscilla had a special talent as well, although which one, I do not know. She did not practice her craft, as her mother had not before her, and I'm not certain her husband ever knew of her secret. But when the witch hunts in Salem began, Priscilla fell victim to the hysteria."

"She was hanged?" Bridget asked, taken aback.

"Accused and found guilty. She was eventually exonerated when her husband confessed to witchcraft in order to save her and their unborn child."

"What happened to him?"

"He swung from the gallows."

Bridget swallowed hard. "How dreadful!"

"Priscilla Gardener," Benjamin mused aloud. "Widow Bayley, didn't you tell me this cottage once belonged to her?"

"Yes," Widow Bayley said. "It did."

"What does any of this have to do with me . . . and with you?" Bridget asked.

Hannah tucked a strand of red hair behind her ear

in a gesture that Bridget thought eerily reminiscent of herself. "There was another ancient clan by the name of MacGow who emigrated as well to Massachusetts. The MacGows also possessed unusual abilities, but they used their talents for darker purposes."

"Such as?" Bridget asked.

"Greed, revenge, and power. Seldom for good. As it happened, a woman of the MacGow clan accused Priscilla of witchcraft. She had long been in love with John and was furious when he chose to marry Priscilla. She hoped that after Priscilla was hanged, John would turn to her for comfort. But when her accusations resulted in John's death instead of Priscilla's, she became enraged and cast a black curse on the MacInness clan."

She took a steadying breath and continued. "According to the curse, each female in Priscilla's line would be destined to live a lonely life, for the men they chose to wed would die at age twenty-six, the same age John had been when he was hanged."

"That's ridiculous," Benjamin said. "You can't curse someone to death."

"I'm afraid you can," Widow Bayley said sadly. "This type of curse is extremely rare, but if one is skilled enough, it can be done."

Hannah nodded in agreement. "If you check the records of the descendants of Priscilla Gardener's line, you'll discover the curse has indeed worked for nearly a century," she paused, her voice catching. "It killed my own husband—Bridget's father—in his twenty-sixth year."

Bridget leaped to her feet as something occurred to her, a cold chill clawing at her heart and throat. "What are you saying? That I've just condemned Benjamin to death by wedding him?"

"Not if we can break the curse," Hannah said firmly.

Anger boiled in Bridget's blood, threatening to spill over. The fire in the hearth flared up, nearly leaping out to singe Widow Bayley, who sat the closest.

"How *dare* you!" Bridget exclaimed, a thin chill hanging on the edge of her words. "If any of this is true, how could you let me wed Benjamin knowing all this?"

"Because it is your destiny," Hannah replied calmly.

Bridget clenched her teeth, so furious she could barely speak. "That is rubbish. You wish only to use me and my ability to help yourself."

"That's not true," Hannah protested.

"Sit down, Bridget," Benjamin said firmly, standing and taking her by the arm. The fire flared dangerously now; another inch and Widow Bayley's gown would catch.

"I don't give a damn about some ancient curse," he said softly. "I would have wed you regardless."

Bridget looked at him, saw the love and strength in his gaze, and sat. The fire died down, but she was still shaking with fury.

"You could have told me," she said, her voice tight with strain. "You could have come forward years ago, if you knew who I was. Certainly long before I decided to marry."

"Your anger is justified," Hannah agreed softly. "Indeed, I would have told you sooner, but I had already foreseen that you would not wed Peter. What I did not foresee was that you would unexpectedly elope with Benjamin. At that point, I realized that even I could not control your destiny."

They all considered her words in silence before Benjamin spoke.

"So, where does that leave us?" he said, and Bridget marveled at how calm he sounded. As if it weren't his life that hung in the balance. "You said there is still a way to break the curse."

Hannah nodded. "There is. While Priscilla's powers were too weak to prevent the curse from being set, she still managed to issue a counter curse. She gave her descendants one century's time to break it. If we are successful, the curse will be reflected back upon the MacGow clan."

"One hundred years?" Benjamin said. "But the witch trials took place exactly a century ago this year."

" 'Tis so," Widow Bayley said. "But the curse was set on All Hallows' Eve, when our power is at its strongest. We have until then to break it."

"That's but two month's away," Bridget exclaimed and then narrowed her eyes. "If I decide to believe any of this."

"You will," Hannah said quietly. "Because you love him, and because you will do anything to protect him."

"No, damn you," Benjamin said between gritted teeth, his own temper flaring. "I will not let you use me to try to get her to do something you want."

"It is not for you to decide," Hannah said quietly.

Bridget stood up and walked to the window, looking out. Silence lay heavily in the room. Finally she spoke.

"Widow Bayley, for most of my life I felt as if you were my mother, the one person I could trust, someone who understood me and cared about me when no one else did," she said softly. "The taste of betrayal is especially bitter now that you're involved."

"In this instance, silence is not a betrayal, child," she answered just as softly.

"It is! You could have trusted me."

"When you didn't trust me?" the widow said sadly. "Not once did you speak to me of your ability."

"I spoke to *no one* about it!" Bridget exclaimed, anger lighting her eyes. "How could I? I thought I was an aberration, a monstrosity. Yet you knew all along about me, about my past, but you didn't tell me. It could have helped me, shaped me."

Widow Bayley gave a deep, sorrowful sigh. "I had no authority to do so. I am but a Guardian."

"A guardian?"

The widow nodded. "Centuries ago my clan served the MacInnesses. The MacInnesses were powerful, but their talents left them vulnerable, hunted, and naturally, much desired as captives. Imagine how useful it could be to have a seer or a healer at your disposal. The MacInness clan was good to us, and in exchange, we dedicated our lives to keeping them safe. There is a special bond between us, forged of trust and magic. It is this bond that drew you to me in the first place, and it is this bond that gave you comfort and peace when you needed it most."

Bridget felt her eyes fill with tears. "You lied to me."

"Never," the widow said firmly. "But Guardians cannot interfere. I spoke the truth when I said it was not my place to tell you about your past . . . or your future."

"And as fascinating as all this is," Benjamin interrupted, his voice cool, "we still don't know why you abandoned Bridget and her sisters in the first place."

Hannah rubbed her temples wearily. "As was typical in our family, I didn't discover the curse until after I'd wed Phillip. I know it sounds cruel, but there was no other way to assure our line would continue."

"You mean there were no male descendants?" Benjamin asked.

"None," Hannah replied.

"Then what did you do?" he inquired.

"Everything I could," she said, her voice catching. "I loved Phillip dearly. He was everything to me: my heart, my soul, my life. He was an honorable man, so handsome and kind. After I learned of the curse, I decided to do whatever I could to save him, no matter how drastic."

Her anger fading, Bridget returned to the chair. Hannah had been right. There was one thing she knew for certain. She would do whatever it took to save Benjamin.

"What did you do to save him?" she asked quietly.

Hannah paused for a moment, misery evident on her face. "I divorced him."

Bridget and Benjamin gasped at the same time.

"That's impossible!" Benjamin exclaimed. "Divorce is rarely ever granted in Massachusetts. And I assure you, if you had succeeded, all of Salem would have known about it to this day."

Hannah nodded. "I know. That's why I sought the divorce in Connecticut. Phillip begged me not to do it, but I insisted. I wouldn't risk his life."

Bridget was fascinated in spite of herself. "Was the divorce ever legalized?"

"It was. But later an aunt told me the divorce would not be enough to save Phillip. In order to save him, I also had to remove his love for me from his heart. I knew then that I had to make him believe I had perished. The decision meant I would have to give up my children and Phillip. But I could not stand by and let him die because of me. You see, just weeks earlier, we had celebrated his twenty-sixth birthday. His life was in immediate peril. Besides, I knew in my heart that he'd take good care of you girls, be an able provider and a loving presence in my absence."

Hannah's hands trembled as she lifted the teacup to her lips.

"So one day when the waves were stormy, I took the necessary actions to make it seem as though I had drowned," Hannah continued. "Everyone in Salem believed me dead—everyone except Anne and Elias Bayley. They were my Guardians and I trusted them with my ploy. After that I simply prayed that Phillip would find another to love. To my great dismay, he did not. He died at sea about six months after my supposed death. I did not reside near Salem at the time of his death, as I could not chance his seeing me. By the time I learned of his death and tried to find you girls, the adoption records were sealed."

Bridget wondered how many times in her life Hannah had replayed those horrid events in her mind. Widow Bayley cleared her throat, and Bridget felt her heart twist painfully when she saw the look of sorrow and regret on the blind woman's face.

"Elias and I tried to adopt you and your sisters. But we were considered too isolated and eccentric. Besides, there was no shortage of people willing to adopt such adorable girls. The adoptions took place in great secrecy. I could do nothing but watch around town to see who might appear with a new daughter. I found only you, Bridget. You became the daughter of the Reverend Ichabod Goodwell and his wife, Abigail."

Hannah broke in. "After Anne had managed to inform me of Phillip's death, I revealed myself to Mr. Wynn to beg him for assistance in getting you girls back. Instead, he threatened to disclose the divorce decree if I tried to take you from the Goodwells. He assured me no judge would return a child to my care. I had no choice but to believe him. In any case, I didn't know where my other girls were."

Hannah's face was bleak with unhappiness as she continued. "Despondent and in despair, I did the only thing I could. I honed my craft in secret and spent years looking for your sisters. I'm determined not to let you girls or your descendants suffer this curse. I refuse to let Phillip's death, and those who came before him, be in vain."

A war of disquieting emotions raged within Bridget: pain, confusion, anger, and regret. Yet another feeling had begun to surface as well: resolution. Whether or not she fully believed this curse to be true, she'd not risk Benjamin's life by ignoring it. She'd do whatever Hannah wanted her to do.

"What must we do to destroy this curse?" she said quietly, and she felt Benjamin's questioning gaze on her.

Hannah looked at Bridget steadily, unable to hide the relief in her eyes. "The MacInness sisters must unite. I have foreseen all of you here in Salem together before All Hallows' Eve, but I do not know if it will be in time to break the curse."

"Once we are all together, then what?"

"We will perform the reversing ceremony. The four of us must share our talents and power to reverse the energy of the spell. It must be done on All Hallows' Eve, the same day the curse was set, and the night at which our power is at its strongest. It will not be an easy task. Dark spells are extremely dangerous and volatile. There are also the physical threats. They will intensify as the time grows near. And yes, I know of the attacks on your life, Bridget."

Somehow, Bridget wasn't surprised to hear this.

Hannah seemed to know a great deal. "I suspected there was an unearthly force at work."

"Who is behind it?" Benjamin asked, his voice rigid with anger.

"The MacGow descendants. They are still in town and will use any means to see that the curse remains in place."

"Including murder?" Benjamin said, his voice tightening.

"Yes," Hannah said honestly. "I've had a protection spell on Bridget for some time, but their powers are strong. Fortunately, I think they only recently discovered her true heritage."

"Who are they?" Benjamin asked coldly, and Bridget could see the threat of violence in his eyes.

"I am not certain," Hannah replied, avoiding his gaze.

Bridget realized that she knew but would not say. In this case, if Hannah held her tongue, it was wise. Bridget had no doubt that Benjamin would go after them, do what he could to protect her. But sheer physical strength would not be enough to vanquish this dark force, and both she and Hannah knew it.

"How do we go about finding my other sisters?" she asked, breaking the silence.

"I have found one already. She is here in Salem."

Bridget looked at her in stunned amazement. "She's here? Now? Does she know any of this?"

Hannah shook her head wearily. "Not yet. You are the first to know. But I have met her and spoken with her in a casual manner. I needed to be certain she was indeed the one I sought, and that her power was intact. I am convinced she is one of my daughters."

Bridget's mouth felt dry. "Wh-what is her name?"

"Before I tell you any more, you must know that

she is in great danger, as are you. I've told her naught substantial because I've awaited your return from Philadelphia, so that we may go together to tell her. The two of us will be more persuasive than one, and time has become of the essence. But events are such with her that I can wait no more than one day before I must reveal all to her, with or without you."

"One day?" Bridget said incredulously. "You expect me to convince another of all of this within one day's time when I'm not certain I believe it myself?"

Benjamin abruptly stood, taking her firmly by the elbow and causing her to rise from her seat.

"We need to think about what was said here and speak privately," he said firmly. "When our decision is made, we will inform you."

"I understand," Hannah said quietly. "I am staying here with Anne. I shall await your decision."

Bridget looked between Widow Bayley and Hannah, a whirl of thoughts and emotions assailing her. Then she turned to Benjamin, the love of her life, and knew in her heart that her decision had already been made.

She let him lead her to the door, and as they left, she heard the widow speak softly behind her.

"She will help, Hannah, for she knows the truth in her heart. All that is left is to find the last girl."

Hannah sighed. "Aye, old friend, and we have just two months to find her."

Bridget walked quietly alongside Benjamin, the peace that had been in her heart before the visit to the cottage now replaced with agonizing concern for the man she loved more than anything in the world.

Without her realizing it, Benjamin had steered them toward Rock's Point. They found their usual spots by the two large boulders and sat shoulder to shoulder, staring out at the sea silently. Several ships passed, and she could hear the bell of one of them calling out a warning.

After a few minutes, Benjamin put his arm around her, pulling her close and pressing a kiss on the top of her head.

"How much of that do you believe?" he asked quietly.

She closed her eyes, leaning against him. "All of it. I can't explain it, Benjamin, but I do believe Hannah is my natural mother. I felt an odd but familiar connection between the two of us."

"I think she is the woman who pulled you to safety from the wagon's path," he said. "And I don't think she employed just strength to do it."

Bridget opened her eyes and looked at him in surprise. "Then you think she might have an unusual talent as I do?"

He shrugged, a lock of dark hair falling over one eye. "I don't know. Perhaps. Do you believe in the curse?"

Bridget sighed in frustration and worry. "It seems so fantastic and inconceivable. But it makes sense, in an unfortunate sort of way."

He nudged her chin up until she looked at him. "You do understand that it would have taken a lot more than a hundred-year-old curse to keep me away from you," he said gently.

"I don't care," she replied fiercely. "I'm not going to let anything happen to you. If it is true, I refuse to live my life as Hannah's, with naught more than regret and loneliness. Both she and Widow Bayley believe we can vanquish this curse. I have to help them try."

He shook his head. "No you don't, Bri," he said,

his gray eyes flashing. "Not for me. I have no intention of letting you put yourself in harm's way for me. People have already tried to discredit and even kill you. God only knows what they might try next."

"It's the only way."

He seized her hands. "It's not. Let's move away from Salem, away from these disturbed individuals. We'll go to Lisbon, Paris, or London. As long as we are together, it doesn't matter where."

"But it does matter, Benjamin," she argued. "If the curse is real, it is likely to respect no boundaries."

"You don't know that."

"I do," she said sadly. "It's hard to describe, but everything Hannah and Widow Bayley said . . . it resonated deep within me, as if I already knew what they would say. I resisted because I didn't want to believe it. But Benjamin, you are already three and twenty. If we choose to do naught and the curse is real, then you have but three years to live. I will not let that happen."

"Blast it, Bri, this is not about me. This is about you. Both Hannah and Widow Bayley admitted that this is a very perilous undertaking. I would rather risk my life with this wretched curse than have you risk yours trying to break it."

"I have to do it, Benjamin," she said firmly. "I have to try. I could never live with myself if anything happened to you. Please try to understand."

His eyes darkened. "What I understand is that you're being maneuvered into something we know little about."

"Magica tua anima tua est," she whispered.

"What did you say?"

"Thy magic is thy will. It's a phrase that has haunted me for years in my dreams. I think I understand it now. If my talent is some form of magic, then I must will it to work for me. To protect those that I love."

He gazed at her, his expression inscrutable. "Then you've made up your mind."

She nodded worriedly, her hair coming loose from her pins and falling onto her shoulders. "I'm sorry, Benjamin. I can do no less. I love you too much."

He kissed her again and she felt tears fill her eyes. "I understand," he finally said. "I may not agree, but I understand. Is there nothing I can say to change your mind?"

"Nothing," she whispered.

He fell silent for some time before he spoke again. "Then, if you intend to go through with this, you will not be alone. We proceed together or not at all. Is that understood?"

"But you just acknowledged this is a dangerous matter," she protested.

"Hell and damnation, woman! Will you now insult me by insisting I cannot aid you in a dangerous undertaking?"

The corners of her mouth twitched. "Of course not, sir. I dare not insult you, for who knows what the punishment might be?"

He growled deep in his throat, easing her down to the grass. His hand slid across the bodice of her gown toward her breasts as he bent his head to kiss her. After he'd teased her with several hot, tantalizing kisses, his mouth grazed her earlobe.

"Whatever happens, Bri, we stay together," he whispered. "You and me. I intend to live in that dream of yours."

She felt her heart brim with happiness. He would stand beside her no matter what happened, and with him at her side, she was certain she would not fail.

"I love you, Benjamin Hawkes," she said, squeezing him tightly. "You are my heart."

He lowered his mouth to hers again, the gentle caress of his lips setting her aflame. Her body melted against his, and the world was filled with him.

At that moment she sensed the future's bright promise. For she understood that the magic of love was infinitely more powerful than any other form of enchantment.

And now, she had both.

COMING IN APRIL 2002 FROM
ZEBRA BALLAD ROMANCES

__WITH THIS RING: The Brides of Bath__
by Cheryl Bolen   0-8217-7248-1 $5.99US/$7.99CAN
Glee Pembroke had always been secretly in love with her brother's best friend, Gregory Bankenship. So when she learned that he must marry by his twenty-fifth birthday or lose his inheritance, she boldly proposed a marriage of convenience, while planning to win his love.

__THE NEXT BEST BRIDE: Once Upon a Wedding__
by Kelly McClymer   0-8217-7252-X $5.99US/$7.99CAN
To Helena Fenster, the only thing worse than her twin sister marrying the man she loves, is having to tell him that his fiancée has jilted him. Rand Mallon's reaction is quite surprising—he's prepared to marry Helena in her sister's place. Yet how can she marry the man she adores when it's obvious that, for him at least, one woman is as good as another?

__NIGHT AFTER NIGHT: The Happily Ever After Co.__
by Kate Donovan   0-8217-7273-2 $5.99US/$7.99CAN
Maggie Gleason never wants to marry. So when she hires a matchmaker, it's to find a teaching job, not a husband. Scenic Shasta Falls, California turns out to be the perfect match for an independent woman determined to start a whole new life. The boarding house where she lives even has a magnificent library . . . if she can get past the mysterious recluse in the room next door.

__LOVER'S KNOT: Dublin Dreams__
by Cindy Harris   0-8217-7072-1 $5.99US/$7.99CAN
Dolly Baltmore, Millicent Hyde and Rose Sinclair had conquered their past heartaches to discover that love was more than possible—it was irresistible. Lady Claire Killgarren isn't so sure, but with help from her newly happy friends, and a very special man, she's about to find that she'll give anything to be caught in a lover's knot . . . for all time.

Call toll free **1-888-345-BOOK** to order by phone or use this coupon to order by mail. *ALL BOOKS AVAILABLE APRIL 01, 2002.*

Name _____
Address _____
City _____ State_____ Zip_____
Please send me the books that I checked above.
I am enclosing $_____
Plus postage and handling* $_____
Sales tax (in NY, TN, and DC) $_____
Total amount enclosed $_____
*Add $2.50 for the first book and $.50 for each additional book.
Send check or money order (no cash or CODs) to: **Kensington Publishing Corp., Dept. C.O., 850 Third Avenue, New York, NY 10022.**
Prices and numbers subject to change without notice. Valid only in the U.S. All orders subject to availability. **NO ADVANCE ORDERS.**
Visit our website at www.kensingtonbooks.com.

BOOK YOUR PLACE ON OUR WEBSITE AND MAKE THE READING CONNECTION!

We've created a customized website just for our very special readers, where you can get the inside scoop on everything that's going on with Zebra, Pinnacle and Kensington books.

When you come online, you'll have the exciting opportunity to:

- View covers of upcoming books
- Read sample chapters
- Learn about our future publishing schedule (listed by publication month *and author*)
- Find out when your favorite authors will be visiting a city near you
- Search for and order backlist books from our online catalog
- Check out author bios and background information
- Send e-mail to your favorite authors
- Meet the Kensington staff online
- Join us in weekly chats with authors, readers and other guests
- Get writing guidelines
- AND MUCH MORE!

Visit our website at
http://www.kensingtonbooks.com